MURDER IN FIVE MOVEMENTS

An Inspector May Murder Mystery

David Baker

authorHOUSE®

AuthorHouse™ UK
1663 Liberty Drive
Bloomington, IN 47403 USA
www.authorhouse.co.uk
Phone: UK TFN: 0800 0148641 (Toll Free inside the UK)
  UK Local: (02) 0369 56322 (+44 20 3695 6322 from outside the UK)

© 2024 David Baker. All rights reserved.

No part of this book may be reproduced, stored in a retrieval system, or transmitted by any means without the written permission of the author.

This is a work of fiction. All of the characters, names, organizations, and dialogue in this novel are either the products of the author's imagination or are used fictitiously.

Published by AuthorHouse 01/11/2024

ISBN: 979-8-8230-8600-4 (sc)
ISBN: 979-8-8230-8601-1 (hc)
ISBN: 979-8-8230-8599-1 (e)

Print information available on the last page.

Any people depicted in stock imagery provided by Getty Images are models, and such images are being used for illustrative purposes only.
Certain stock imagery © Getty Images.

This book is printed on acid-free paper.

Because of the dynamic nature of the Internet, any web addresses or links contained in this book may have changed since publication and may no longer be valid. The views expressed in this work are solely those of the author and do not necessarily reflect the views of the publisher, and the publisher hereby disclaims any responsibility for them.

List Of Main Characters

ORDER OF ST SAVIOUR

Father William
Brother Bernard
Brother Germain
Brother Jeffery
Brother Lawrence
Brother Simon

BOARD OF GOVERNORS, TEMPLETON TOWERS

Professor Andreas Day, Chair
Commander Janos Szabo, RN, Principal
Barbara ('Babs') Halliday, property developer
Melody Grimshaw, ex supermodel
Pauline Philbey, local archivist
Clement Rankin, Deputy Lieutenant (DL) of Hartleydale
Harry ('Hal') Riddles, ex-owner, Riddles' Mills
Lisa Watson, Clerk to the Board, and Personal Assistant to Janos Szabo

STAFF OF TEMPLETON TOWERS

Dr Diana Foster, Educational Psychologist
Dr John Sebastian ('Quick Draw') McGraw, Director of Music

HARTLEYDALE CID

Assistant Chief Constable Jean Samson
Detective Chief Inspector Donald ('Don') May
Detective Sergeant Charlie Riggs
Detective Constable Georgiana ('Georgie') Ellis
Dr Felicity ('Fizz') Harbord, Chief Medical Examiner

OTHER CHARACTERS

Freddie May, Donald May's son
Catherine ('Caz') May, wife of Donald May and mother of Freddie
Camilla and Vanessa, two students at Templeton Towers
Victoria ('Vicky') Perry, crime reporter, *Hartley Gazette and Argus*
Tiggy, Georgie Ellis's elder sister
Aethelred ('Aethel') and Throthgar ('Throth'), Tiggy's children and Georgie's nephews
Lucian, Tiggy's (ex-) husband
Tristan Bishop, Georgie and Tiggy's former music teacher
Jo Bishop, Tristan's younger sister
Reverend Paul Gordon, deceased priest, former incumbent of St David's Church, Hartleydale
Nicholas LeGrand, former student at Templeton Towers
Boris, Pauline Philbey's cat

Movement I

Allegro, Ma Non Troppo

1

Forgive Them That Trespass Against Us

ONCE ALL THE CANDLES WERE ALIGHT, FATHER WILLIAM CLAIR TOLD his fellow monk to leave the chapel.

'Thank you, my brother in Christ. I need to meditate alone this evening.'

The hooded figure extinguished his taper and left.

It had been a long day. The Head of the Order of St Saviour tried to pray, but the words would not come. The events of the last seven days went round and round in his mind: Szabo, Principal; Foster, Educational Psychologist; Day, Chair of the Board. Each and every one of those three had a lot to answer for.

Clair pushed himself up to a standing position. Every bone in his body ached. He shuffled to the high altar. There was a sound in the organ loft at the West End of the chapel. Or so he thought, but nothing could be seen when he turned to face the grandiose instrument.

If only our founder were still with us! Templeton Taylor would never have let us run out of money!

Clair looked up and around the ceiling of the grand, mock-perpendicular chapel. Between the gold stars, backed by a Cambridge-blue sky, the letters 'TT' intertwined around every apostle, all the angels and archangels and even, if one knew where to look, the Lord God Almighty himself were depicted there. Rumour had it that one of the greater saints was based on a portrait of Taylor himself! What vanity and arrogance! Was this chapel a holy place or a monument to the works of Sir Templeton Taylor?

There was a creak, as if someone were tiptoeing round the West Gallery. Once more, the Head of the Order of St Saviour turned round.

'Who is there? Show yourself!'

Clair thought about turning on the electric lighting, then remembered that the power had yet to be restored. The back-up generator was proving difficult to start, despite its being hydraulically powered. Clair pondered on how TT had been ahead of his time: a green Victorian! Despite all the smoke from his factory chimneys down in the valley and across Hartleydale.

'I say again – who is there? Show yourself?'

The candle flickered. Perhaps a door was slightly ajar: the acolyte may not have shut it properly as he left; or could an unknown visitor be joining the evening prayers? Or was someone wanting to have their confession heard?

That would be something of a surprise, given the numbers we now have within the school who profess any kind of faith, let alone the Anglo-Catholic variety. I am just tired; stressed; overwrought. This business about the future of the school will not go away. Szabo is making it worse; wanting to sell all that land for housing; and Diana Foster's grand ideas about how to educate high-functioning autistic children are pure academic balderdash! We have been doing it for nearly 100 years without any interference from educational psychologists! I wouldn't have employed that woman if it hadn't been for Szabo and Day!

Father William determined to pray, and in earnest. If he brought all his problems to God, then God would take away the worry and the pain and show the way forward, both for the Order of St Saviour and its Head. He bowed in prayer once more; still the words would not come; there was too much going around inside his mind – his soul, even - to wash away the anguish and the anger of what was happening to his beloved school and the OSS. Was there no future for men like him in this modern, target-setting, objective-bound, profit-dominated world?

Clair decided that there was nothing for it but to recite the Lord's Prayer. He had got as far as the words 'And forgive them that trespass against us' when he was murdered.

Frederick Dawson May was pleased with himself. He had not gone home but stayed at Templeton Towers for the weekend and, with great satisfaction, was coping rather well. Not only that, but he had got himself a girlfriend; two, in fact. It could have been just the one, but here was a package deal! Freddie had encountered Camilla at the introductory week. She shared his interest in criminology and was super-impressed when he told her who his father was.

'Detective Chief Inspector Donald May, Head of Hartley CID; the man who solved the Holme Hill Murders?' she had said.

'Yes', Freddie had replied, 'with my help, that is!'

'I saw that programme on television about it all. What was it called?'

'I think you mean *Murdertown*. It made my father a celebrity, sort of.'

'How do you mean?'

'Well, there were all kinds of reminiscences and serialisations in the tabloids. A woman called Pauline Philbey sold her story to the *Daily Mail*. "I was serial murderer's secret lover", I think it was called. My father was very angry at the time.'

'Gosh! But it must be so ace! All that detective stuff to talk about when your Dad gets home from work!'

'You talk like something out of a 1950s adventure story for boys and girls, Camilla!'

So do you, Commander Frederick May of the Yard!'

'How do you know I call myself that?'

'I have my ways of finding things out.'

Freddie was cross; his secret was out. But this girl intrigued him. He had never met anyone like her. She could be so changeable, both in temperament and appearance. Then it had dawned on him.

'You aren't Camilla, are you? You are sometimes, but not now.'

'I don't know what you are talking about, you silly boy!'

'It took me a while to work it out, but I did eventually. How you could sort of forget things that we had talked about only the previous day and then seemingly remember them clearly the next. That's when I started to become suspicious. Then I noticed that sometimes you wrote with your right hand; then at other times you used your left.'

'So what? I am ambidextrous, that's all.'

'Well, you might be, but that was not the piece of evidence that gave the game away.'

'No? What was it then?'

'Camilla – if that is her name – has a slight nervous tick in her left eye. You do not.'

The girl smiled at Freddie.

'Very well, Commander May, of the Yard. If I let you into my secret, will you keep it absolutely to yourself and not tell anybody? Not even your father?'

Freddie May nodded, at which point the girl took him by the hand, pulled him up the staircase and into the wing containing the student bedrooms. Freddie's hand grew sweaty with nerves, anxiety, and the exertion of running along the corridor, as well as the first experience of touching a girl. He was excited; male student access was forbidden in this part of the dormitory. Without knocking, the girl pushed open the door of the room at the far end of the student wing.

'You are right. I am not Camilla. This is Camilla, my sister. I am Vanessa.'

Freddie May looked from one to the other, then back again. He had never seen twins before – at least not identical ones – so close up. He could not stop looking.

'Stop gawping!' Vanessa giggled.

'I cannot help it. But why? And how?'

Camilla and Vanessa smiled at each other and told Freddie to sit down on the chair by the study table. They then sat on the bed. The girls spoke in unison.

'Money, that's why, Fred.'

'I prefer to be called Freddie or Frederick, thank you.'

'He does, Vanessa. I forgot to tell you that.'

'What do you mean "money"?'

'Well Fred – Freddie – our Mum so wanted to send us to Templeton Towers, but, as I imagine your Dad has told you, it is very expensive here. So why not make the most of the fact that we are identical?'

'You mean…'

'Yes, we do, Freddie', Camilla nodded. 'Two for the price of one!'

'We take it in turns to go to lessons, and stuff', Vanessa added.

'And what about accommodation?'

'Easy, Fred – Freddie – basically, there are lots of spare rooms, and we are very good at picking locks and things like that. Don't be so shocked. I bet you know how to do it, thanks to that Dad of yours!'

Freddie May blushed. 'Well, I do actually.' He paused for a moment, then continued. 'What are we going to do now?'

'What should we do? What do we need to do?' Camilla and Vanessa spoke in turn.

'I don't know. Nothing, I suppose.'

'Good. That was the right answer, Commander Frederick Dawson May. We have a little case that we need your help with.'

Freddie scratched his hand.

'Don't worry; we won't bite. It will be fun. We can all play detective!'

'OK. What is the case, then?'

'Well, this room looks out onto the School Chapel. And we have seen some strange goings on over the last few days. We want you to help us find out if the chapel really is haunted.'

'Haunted?'

'Yes, Freddie. We keep seeing a ghost.'

János Szabo was beginning to wish he was back in the Royal Navy. The post of Principal at Templeton Towers had seemed so attractive: what better way to continue his career than by going into teaching? After all, he had been rated as one of the Senior Service's top trainers; teaching was in his blood and the opportunity to develop genius children – despite all the challenges that some of their behaviour might bring – was one that the former Commander had to take.

The job had started well enough, and Szabo was welcomed both at Templeton and within the local community, despite the school's remoteness, perched as it was on top of the hills overlooking the Hartley Valley. Szabo looked out of his study window. He smiled in satisfaction at the links he had already made with the villages down below, and especially Holme Hill, the nearest place of human habitation.

But Templeton Towers was not what it seemed. Though espousing the need for change, Father William had so far resisted every attempt Szabo had made to improve the school's finances. The proposal to sell off two-thirds of the grounds to a property developer met with outright refusal to co-operate, despite the Chair of the Board's strong support. At least Andreas Day was enough of a realist to accept what needed to be done to keep the school solvent. Szabo was about to send an email to Clair asking for an urgent meeting in the morning to see if a compromise could be reached, when there was a knock at his office door. It opened as soon as he uttered the words 'come in.'

'Diana! I didn't expect to see you this evening. You should be enjoying your weekend.'

Foster looked flustered; she was breathing heavily, and her face was red.

'Are you OK?'

'Why do you ask?'

'Your appearance.'

'I've been out running. I'm training for the local triathlon. I find that exercise de-stresses me.'

'Perhaps I should join you. I could do with less stress.'

'Tomorrow's Board meeting preying on your mind, Jan?'

'Just a bit.'

'You'll get what you want, I know it.'

'Perhaps; perhaps not. What was it you wanted to see me about?'

Foster took out a plain brown envelope and handed it to Szabo.

'What do you make of that? I've never had a death threat before, but I suppose there is always a first time.'

Detective Constable Georgie Ellis was feeling smug. She was pleased enough to open a second bar of Old Jamaica chocolate, a treat reserved for the most special of occasions. This was one such: her appointment had finally been confirmed. There had been times when she thought the transfer from uniform would never happen, especially in the light of her going off grid during the Holme Hill murders. She might have disobeyed orders, but a certain PC Ellis had been a major player in catching the criminals. This had stood her in good stead when it came to the inevitable disciplinary hearing, along with Donald May's arguing strongly that she was an asset to the police and should be treated as such. As she savoured every bite of the chocolate, Ellis relived the meeting with her DCI.

'I want you to be my first DC, Georgie, now that Charlie has been promoted to DS. You showed both initiative and determination in that hostage situation, and you deserve a chance to develop your career, with grit like that.'

May had started to form the word 'balls', then must have thought better of it, changing the compliment to 'grit'. Now she was plain clothes; DCI Ellis one day! It was as if the telephone had read her mind, the ringing cutting through the daydream like a knife through a Cornish pasty. It would be Tiggy, blissfully ignorant of the fact that ordinary working people had to get up to go to their jobs on a Monday morning. It was not her elder sister, but the boss. She was to be involved in a murder investigation; her first, but not her last, as a DC.

Catherine May was convinced her husband was putting on weight, despite his protests to the contrary. It was the way he struggled to do up the button on his trousers, grunting as he closed the clasp. The joke about how his dinner jacket was shrinking every time he wore it had grown as thin as it was predictable. After much nagging, Donald May had been persuaded to buy a new suit for the dinner where he and Ellis would be presented with awards for bravery in the Holme Hill murders.

The obvious reason for May's gradual 'ballooning' was lack of exercise. Freddie was now a teenager, and, despite his neurodiversity, the hormones had kicked in and time out with Dad was decidedly 'uncool'. The boys' days out on bikes were the first activity to go; then the weekends working on the garden railway. Frederick Dawson May was still 'of the Yard' but being reminded of his obsession with detection had become embarrassing for May junior; banter and bonhomie between father and son had dried up. Just occasionally there was a glimpse of the old boyish Freddie, usually when his father talked about a case and, in all seriousness, asked his son's advice, which was still freely, and enthusiastically, given.

Catherine May knew deep down that there was another cause of her husband's weight-gain: Vivienne Trubshaw. She had never challenged Don about his affair with the former Detective Sergeant and on the single occasion he had tried to bring up the subject, she had stopped him. In any case, she was aware of what had been going on ever since Trubshaw had joined Hartley CID. Who was it that said, 'when a middle-aged man loses weight, there's usually a woman involved?' DCI May had certainly done that; within six months of the DS starting work in his department, he was two stone lighter. He had even taken up running, and there were as many long cycle rides without Freddie as there were with him. Trubshaw had been gone from Hartley CID for over 12 months. Her move to Lancashire had been delayed while she helped May finish off the case of the Holme Hill Murders: not an easy task, but one that needed doing, especially given the impending arrival of a new ACC.

It was with sadness rather than relief that Catherine and Donald May had enrolled Freddie at Templeton Towers. There were so many advantages. May junior himself had said it was 'a no brainer', having completed a detailed SWOT analysis, listing, and commenting on, the advantages and disadvantages of being educated for the next three years at Templeton. Among the many strengths of the proposal were: the outstanding reputation that the school had for educating high-functioning children on the autism spectrum; its focus on music and the creative arts, areas in which May junior had developed a real talent – singing, playing the piano, acting – over the previous two years; its pastoral care, second to none, according to its latest Ofsted; the fact that it was only ten miles from home and weekly boarding with the possibility of weekends at home (or not, depending upon the student's choice). Donald and Catherine May had quietly noted to each other that their son had not put 'time away from home' as a strength or a weakness; neither an opportunity, nor a threat.

Off he had gone at the beginning of September, without a backward glance. Freddie said little to his mother and father about Templeton

Towers. Now he seized the chance to stay for weekends whenever he could. He had even started to make friends, according to the resident educational psychologist. 'That's a first!' they had said in unison. His schoolwork was better than ever. The Mays had joked that the next thing would be a girlfriend. 'Think of it, Caz: our Freddie in love!' Donald May had laughed.

The new stability was about to be threatened. Donald May had just walked through the front door, taken his overcoat off, loosened his tie and poured himself a non-alcoholic beer, when the telephone rang. On hearing the news about a fatality in suspicious circumstances at Templeton Towers, he had told Georgie Ellis to pick him and DS Riggs up and drive them to the school.

'Don't worry Caz. I am sure Freddie will be fine. The incident appears to have been in the chapel and not the school or the student quarters. Szabo will have everything in hand; he seems very efficient – someone after my own heart, in fact!'

The attempt at humour fell flat.

'Please don't let anything happen to our Freddie. I couldn't bear it! I just could not bear it.'

May felt her tears on his face.

'It will be fine, Caz. I promise.'

She continued to hold him tightly, despite his efforts to move away. The doorbell rang.

'I must go, Caz. That will be George.'

The doorbell rang again.

'I *must* go now!'

Catherine May went down the hall and opened the front door.

'Hello Mrs May. I am so sorry to disturb you on a Sunday evening like this. It's a while since we met. I'm DC Ellis, but everybody calls me George, or Georgie. I prefer Georgie!'

Catherine May watched her husband and his DC get into her BMW Z4 and drive off at speed. She stayed at the door long enough to shiver in the cold of the autumn evening.

2

May He Rest In Peace And Rise In Glory

Georgie Ellis loved driving. The Z4 was her baby. Nobody else – not even her father – was allowed to touch that car. Just because Daddy had bought it for her did not give him rights to the wheel.

'Great car George! Just needs more room in the back!' Riggs attempted every which way to get comfortable, not realizing it was only a two-seater.

'Whoever thought to build a place up here?' Riggs was beginning to get pins and needles as Ellis struggled to negotiate the narrow road.

'A local lad made good, Charlie. Sir Templeton Taylor. Working class boy from Hartley, turned mill owner, turned landed gentry. He ended up in the House of Lords!'

'Textiles, wasn't it, sir?'

'That's right Georgie. Then when he had made his money, he built this place, got himself knighted and then ennobled by crossing important palms with silver, no doubt, then lived the life of a country squire-cum-medieval baron, paid for by the hard labour of his mill workers. Taylor had the Towers constructed on this hill so he could look over the whole valley and see what everybody else was up to. He decided he was descended from the Knights Templar and discovered irrefutable "evidence" that the old chapel up here was where the order met.'

'Some say they still meet.'

'How do you mean Georgie?'

'I remember reading a feature about this place in *Homes and Gardens* a while back. There was a story about the place being haunted by the spirits of dead Templars bemoaning the loss of their treasure.'

Riggs guffawed and May snorted.

'You'll be telling us next that the Holy Grail is buried in the grounds!' May began to laugh. 'I think the Addams Family might have something to say about that!'

'Sir?'

'Just look ahead Charlie. What does that remind you of?'

The Z4 purred past a gate house and up a sweeping drive.

'Blimey, what's this place? Has it ever featured in a horror film?'

May and Ellis laughed.

'I know what you mean, Charlie. It has bits of every well-known castle and keep in the country. Here's the Tower of London; Caernarfon over there; and a bit of Glamis over the portico? Goodness – I sound like Pevsner!'

'Who's Pevsner, sir?'

'Never mind, Charlie. If you are not into architecture, there's no reason why you should have heard of Sir Nikolaus.'

'I have all his guides, sir.'

'I thought you might, Georgie. Perhaps you could lend DS Riggs the volume on Hartleydale.'

The three sighed inwardly as the Z4 drew up outside the main entrance. Each of them knew there was difficult work to be done and they had to focus. May greeted the senior uniformed officer, then entered the building, followed by his two officers.

'It looks like Downton Abbey, sir!'

'It does a bit, Charlie. It might even have been a contender, I suppose. They pay well, these TV companies, and I suspect the money would have helped with the capital refurbishment they need to make. Look around; the place has seen better days, hasn't it?'

Riggs and Ellis nodded, still taking in the vastness of the entrance hall, complete with minstrels' gallery and gargantuan pipe organ.

'Where are all the children, sir?'

'Students, George. They are too old to be called "children". I should know, my son is a "student" here. I thought you both should know that. He started six weeks ago. He loves – loved – it at Templeton. We thought it was the perfect solution for him. Everything is up in the air again now, though, I suppose.'

'What is going to happen to the school while we carry out our investigations?'

'I will determine that once we have finished our initial inspection. The modern buildings where the teaching takes place are quite separate from the original hall – or castle – or whatever we should call this place. Maybe they can continue in some way. The original student rooms are a different matter; they are on the other side of this quadrangle, opposite the chapel. It might be difficult for them to remain occupied. We'll see.'

May, Riggs, and Ellis reached the large quadrangle at the back of the main house. Two uniformed officers stood guard at the entrance to the chapel. Above the huge, pointed arch were the words *In hoc signo vinces*. Before Riggs could ask the meaning of the motto, Ellis explained.

'It means "conquer in that sign", Charlie. That's right, isn't it, sir?'

'Yes, the motto of the Knights Templar, would you believe?'

May saw Ellis was listening to his every word; Riggs was impatient to get on with the investigation. They donned their protective overclothes and entered the chapel.

Despite the ceaseless hum of activity brought about by a suspicious death, the chapel remained a haven of peace. May looked towards the high altar and then the stalls on either side of it. The body was where Szabo had found it. Clair looked peaceful, lopsidedly kneeling over one side of his priest's chair. May had met him once, at a 'Churches Together' meeting in Hartley. He had been impressed, both by the man's intellect and his striking appearance. Even in what must then have been his late sixties, the Head of the Order of Saint Saviour was a handsome man: tall, slim, athletic (reputedly a double Cambridge blue in his Varsity days), with a face that looked like the Jesus of a Burne Jones window: long flowing hair, beard, aquiline nose, piercing blue eyes. Yes, Clair had it all. Despite their widely differing views on theology, May and Clair had 'hit it off'. They had never met again, despite Freddie now attending the Order's School. Szabo oversaw the educational side of things. May made a mental note to interview the new Principal, at least briefly, before the evening was out.

As he walked towards Clair's body, May was aware of a strong, sweet, almost overpowering, odour. It smelt like lilac and lime and a sugary tobacco, all at the same time. It must be the infernal incense that was regularly burned at the high masses Freddie had described in lurid detail on his last weekend home. What did his son make of religion? He had rejected the Methodist way, but since starting at the school here, Frederick Dawson May had taken a keen interest in the Christian faith, and, somewhat to Donald May's concern, the Anglo-Catholic variety.

Felicity Harbord was busy inspecting the body. Kneeling alongside the penitent corpse, the medical examiner was looking closely at Father Clair's neck. May was standing right next to her before she noticed his presence.

'Oh you! Where have you been? I expected you an hour ago!'

'Sorry Fizz, it took us some time to round up the troops.'

Harbord looked to the back of the chapel where Riggs and Ellis were chatting with the uniformed officers guarding the entrance.

'How's she shaping up then?'

'Who?'

'You know who, Don. She's no Trubshaw, is she?'

May laughed briefly, trying not to think about his former Detective Sergeant – and, briefly, his lover. 'Ellis is not meant to be, Fizz. She's just – well – she's just Georgie. She will make a great detective one day'.

'DC Ellis is very lucky. I thought she was going to be drummed out of the force after her escapades at Holme Hill back in 2019'.

May smiled. 'She deserved a second chance'.

'If you say so, Don. Unlike Father Clair here'. Harbord pointed to the victim.

'How do you mean, Fizz?'

'Look at his neck, Don. At first, I thought that he had been strangled. But the marks don't make sense.'

'What?'

'Clair was already dead when the hands were placed around his neck as if to strangle him. I won't really know what killed him until after the postmortem.'

May rubbed his hand through his hair and wondered. There had been another murder like that round here; a long time ago. And it had never been solved.

János Szabo looked out of his office window. It was difficult to make out the comings and goings of the many police now on site, though he recognised Donald May. They had met at a Rotary Club lunch only a few weeks before. Szabo had taken to May straightaway. The two men were to meet up for coffee as Szabo sought to expand his network of key movers and shakers within the region. Clair's overbearing attitude had to be countered if the fund-raising campaign was to be successful. Diana Foster had not been working at Templeton Towers for long, but she was already taking out a grievance against the old boy. Szabo had tried to persuade her to stay calm and leave well alone, but despite being a pre-eminent member of her profession, she could also be a hothead.

Szabo took one last look at the enormous, Gothick-Perpendicular monstrosity that was the School Chapel, its ugly pinnacles prodding the clear night sky, then pulled the curtains and sat down at his large desk, said to have been Sir Templeton's own. Having poured himself a large whisky, he unlocked and opened the drawer where he kept his confidential documents.

He fanned the Board papers: over 200 pages. Micro-management of the highest order; all Clair's doing, spending more time on hoovers and paper clips than tackling the real problems facing the school! And to add insult to injury, the Strategic Plan was item 20 on the agenda! Clair had made sure of it.

Just as Szabo was contemplating how Clair's death would affect the school, his own position, and the growth plans, the phone rang.

'Thanks for calling back, Andreas. I have some terrible news. Father William is dead. The police are here. There is a suggestion that he has been murdered.'

After a pause, Day replied.

'My God, how did it happen?'

'I don't know. Clair was found in the chapel. I was alerted by one of the Order and went to see for myself. At first, I thought it was a heart attack – he is 80 after all – but then I realised something was wrong. He looked as though he was praying, though when I tried to rouse him, there was no answer, and as I touched him, he fell onto his side.'

'So why not a heart attack, János?'

'When I looked more closely, there were marks around his neck, as if he had been hanged.'

'Bloody hell, Szabo! What do we do about the meeting tomorrow?'

'You're the Chair, Andreas. What do you think?'

'I propose we go ahead. That land deal won't wait, and we have an opportunity now Clair has gone, unfortunate and frightening though that might be.'

Szabo smiled. Day was ever the mercenary Yorkshireman; 'brass above all' should have been the man's motto.

'You're the boss. It all depends on what the police say, though, as to whether we can proceed. It looks as though May will oversee the investigation.'

'A good man. Knew his father. Anyway, I'd better go. My son is calling; time for supper, or something. I'll call you in the morning.'

Szabo wondered what the 'something' might be at this time of night, then determined not to think about the possibilities. He slammed the papers down hard on the desk, unbound the pack, and took out all but the agenda, the minutes, the accounts, and the Strategic Plan. The rest were thrown unceremoniously in the bin. What was left was then put back in the drawer. As he closed it, he noticed a photograph of his old Royal Navy training college. There he sat as Principal, in the middle of the front row, surrounded by smiling, uniformed officers.

'Those were the days. I begin to wish I were back there. Did I have to retire when I did? I could have stayed on...'

Szabo's inner smile turned to a frown as he noticed who was standing right behind him in the photograph. He quickly turned it face down and put it back in the drawer. As he did so, he took out his revolver and checked to make sure it was loaded.

Pauline Philbey was fed up. There was a limit to the amount of time she was prepared to spend being an archivist; and after twelve hours with yet more dusty files, she had reached it. At least she had been able to take this latest batch home, unlike the more fragile files.

'Time for a gin, Boris. A very large one!'

Boris looked up and meowed.

'And you will get fed too, my lovely!'

The cat jumped up onto his owner's lap, circled a few times and then, having found the most comfortable position, settled down, curled up and promptly fell asleep. Philbey did not have the heart to disturb Boris, despite her urgent need for alcohol. The bottle leered at her from the sideboard on the other side of the room. Perhaps she could carry her cat over to the gin bottle, pour herself a drink, then return to the armchair without any harm being done.

It was not to be. Boris, realising what was about to happen, dug his claws deep into Philbey's legs in sharp protest.

'Ow!'

The cat meowed unapologetically. As she stroked her beloved cat, Philbey thought back to the day's work. The triumph of finally gaining access to the archives of Templeton Towers had been tempered by the daunting task of sorting, indexing, and then digitising the thousands of pages of documents: letters, photographs, maps, and much more. As she dozed off, Philbey began to dream of the Templar legends she had learned as a child. Were any of them true? The castle on the hill certainly had its secrets …

Diana Foster wondered whether to stay up or turn in for the night. On the one hand, the students were all settled back in their bedrooms, and she was only at the far end of the dormitory corridor if any of her charges woke in the night; on the other, the police were still on site and might need to talk to her further.

Foster went over the brief statement she had given earlier to the uniformed officer. Where had she been at the likely time of Clair's death and later discovery? *In her office going over the report to the Board of*

Governors' meeting the following morning. Could anyone vouch for that? *No, other than a phone call from Janos Szabo halfway through the evening.* What time had that been? *About 8.45 pm, on the school's internal system.* What had the conversation been about? *Just some school business – whether the archaeological project could be afforded any longer.* Archaeology? *The gardens and woods behind Templeton Towers were of great historical interest: people had lived on the site since the Iron Age. Father Clair had long organised a dig for past, present, and future students at the school during the summer holidays and some work continued throughout the academic year. It was a good way of creating and reaffirming the community that was the Order of St Saviour. And there was so much that could be learned in a practical way from being involved in archaeology, right through from history to geophysics to virtual reality to team building and collective effort.*

Diana Foster paused as she remembered the police constable's boredom at her description of the dig. She needn't have said so much, but it was a remarkable project and one that the children enthused about almost every day.

And could you think of anyone who might want to harm Father William? To murder him, even? *No, I could not. Not at all. He was a saintly man. How could anyone do such a thing?*

Diana Foster wondered if the young PC had seen her blush. She had felt her cheeks reddened as she had answered this last question. Could he have had any inkling that she was not telling the truth, the whole truth, and nothing but the truth? Not that she believed in God anyway, so there was no need for help from that quarter …

3

Secrets And Suspects

Georgie Ellis smiled as a WPC brought the regulation morning mugs of coffee and accompanying biscuits into May's office. Twelve months ago, she had been the waitress, the factotum, the dogsbody. Now she was part of the inner cabinet, ready to take on the case of William Clair's murder.

'Are we sure he was killed, sir?'

'Well, there was certainly foul play, Georgie. Though it's odd someone should try to strangle the victim *after* death. Fizz – Dr Harbord – will not know for certain what the cause was until she can do the postmortem.'

Ellis looked at May and then at DS Riggs.

'So, Clair *could* have died of natural causes?'

Riggs shrugged; May nodded gently.

'Could it have been someone wishing they had murdered Clair, but the Grim Reaper got there first? Possible. But for now, we treat this as a death in suspicious circumstances.'

'Noted, sir.' Ellis smiled. 'Shall I give you both a summary of what we know so far, after last night's interviews?'

'Yes please, Georgie.'

Ellis opened her laptop to begin the presentation. The first slide appeared on the murder wall.

'This is a summary of the key findings from the interviews carried out yesterday at Templeton Towers.'

'Very impressive, Detective Constable; very impressive'. May and Riggs nodded in tandem.

Ellis reddened slightly. May sipped his coffee and bit on a biscuit.

'Well, sir, it seems that Clair was not well liked. There was antagonism between him and Szabo from the start.'

'Say more.'

'Differences of opinion as to how the school should be run; education versus business, in a nutshell!'

'That's the norm these days, Georgie, though I thought St Saviour's was different.'

'What does that mean?' Riggs finished off a Digestive as he spoke.

'Sir Templeton Taylor endowed the school. It was in memory of his son David – you know, one of those Victorian child deaths of something awful from which the father never recovers – and, by all accounts, he endowed the school very handsomely.'

'But the school was in financial trouble, sir'.

'Really?'

'If you look at this slide – I will just fast forward to it – you will see that it is touch-and-go as to whether the place is still a going concern.'

'How the hell do you know all this?'

'I got up early this morning and did some background research. I thought it might come in handy for our briefing.'

Riggs made no further response.

'We are interrupting your presentation, Georgie. Proceed.'

'Thank you, sir. Well, the school was haemorrhaging money, and the endowment funds were almost exhausted.'

'I suppose there comes a point when the money runs out. We need to investigate further. Another appointment with Szabo for later today, I think. And what about the Chair of Governors?'

'Noted, sir. Andreas Day used to be Vice-Chancellor at the University of Hartley. Turned it from a polytechnic into a university. It does very well in the NSS now.'

'NSS?'

'National Student Satisfaction Survey, Charlie. Students rate how good they think the place is under a series of headings. They came top for student support last year.'

'Too many universities if you ask me. All those mickey mouse degrees.'

'Enough Charlie. Keep going, Georgie. Do you know how long Day has been on the Board?'

'He joined two years ago; became Chair straight away.'

'Unusual to do that immediately after becoming a member; and when Szabo was appointed Principal. Let's get him on the interview list. What else do we need to know, Georgie? How many more slides have you got?'

'Just a few, sir. It's more about the history of the school and the present arrangements.'

'Proceed, then, Detective Constable!'

'What do you make of it then, Vanilla 1 and Vanilla 2?'

'Stop calling us that! We have separate names! We are two different people.'

'But you are one person really, aren't you?'

'No, we are not! And we won't have you as our friend if you don't behave. No more of this silliness, Freddie!'

Freddie May sulked for a moment and then thought better of it. They were his friends and he wanted to keep it that way, especially now Dr Foster had told them that school would continue, despite Father Clair's death.

'Very well, I am sorry, Vanessa and Camilla. I will stop calling you Vanilla 1 and Vanilla 2, even though I think it is rather clever of me to think that term up. You know, a cross between Vanessa and Camilla gives you Vanilla, and the term "vanilla" means "having no special or extra features; ordinary or standard".'

'But Camilla and I are NOT ordinary; we are very, very, special. That is why we are here! How can you say we "have no special or extra features", you silly boy?'

'I – well, I just meant that nobody could tell you apart – there are no defining or differentiating features between you.'

Vanessa and Camilla fell into silence; they looked at each other and then at Freddie May. He decided it was time to move on.

'No, you are right; both of you. We have a murder to solve!'

'How do you know Father William was murdered, Freddie?'

'Because I heard Mr Szabo and Dr Diana talking the other night. Mr Szabo said he wanted to kill Clair. Those were his exact words: "kill Clair".'

Vanessa and Camilla laughed. 'That is just a figure of speech, Freddie. I am sure Mr Szabo didn't really mean that he was going to kill Father William.'

Freddie May stamped his foot. 'I know what a figure of speech is! But he meant it!'

'How do you know he meant it, Freddie?'

'Because he said, "it has to be sorted before the Board meeting". I heard him when I was waiting outside his office for my regular 1-2-1, as he calls it.'

The twins looked at each other once more. 'We don't have a "1-2-1" with Mr Szabo.'

'My father insisted, at least for the first term, until I got used to the place.'

'And are you, Freddie?'

'I thought I was, until you two started having a go at me.'

Vanessa and Camilla got off their bed, walked over to Freddie and kissed him, one set of lips on each of the boy's cheeks.

Commander Frederick Dawson May of the Yard blushed like he had never blushed.

Andreas Day took out a Gurkha and lit it. He drew and then puffed on the cigar as the match flame transferred its energy to the rolled bundle of dried and fermented tobacco leaves. How many times had his doctor told him to give up? How many times had he tried and failed to stop smoking? But then Andreas Day never did anything by halves; everything to excess – food, drink, women - that was what his wife had said. He looked across at the photograph on the grand piano. There they were, the two of them; on their wedding day – a happy event now forever tinged with the sadness of loss.

Day walked over to the piano and held the picture in his hands for a moment, then put it back down. He went to the cocktail cabinet and poured himself a large brandy. He swirled the drink around in its glass, remembering his time at Stellenbosch and his regular visits to the local distillery there. What a different world that was!

Leaning over the Steinway's tail, he looked across the valley. Templeton Towers was clearly visible, despite the heavy rain. The police were coming and going; an ambulance drew up. That must be Clair's body, Day thought. Good riddance! At least we can get on with our plans. That stupid Order of St Saviour's. What a lot of mumbo jumbo that man talked! How could anyone believe in any of it? Pure superstition! We will have our way before the year is out!

Day laughed out loud as his mobile phone began to vibrate. He looked at the screen: an unknown number, though it did not register as a possible scam. He answered it.

'Who is this?'

'A friend.'

'Who are you?'

'You do not need to know who I am.'

'I am going to ring off.'

'I wouldn't do that if I were you, Professor Day, not if you want to find out about William Clair's secret.'

'Very well. You have five minutes before I leave for my Board meeting.'

Day sat down in his favourite leather armchair and listened.

Janos Szabo hated Board meetings; and loathed the paperwork that went with them even more. At least now Clair was out of the way there was a chance the school could get on and *do* something; anything was better than the endless going round and round in ever decreasing circles without a decision: anything would be better than the continuing impasse. Szabo felt his blood pressure rising as he thought back to

Clair's filibustering. The man was a master! Could the old duffer not see Templeton Taylor's foundation was going bankrupt?

Szabo looked up at the Tompion longcase clock as it chimed the hour: another fifteen minutes to the start of the Board. Any minute now, Lisa would usher Andreas Day into the office. Day would then sprawl in the armchair on the other side of Szabo's desk and say: 'what do I need to know, then, Jan?'

Except today was different. Szabo's mobile phone beeped. It was a message from Day: 'meet me in the cloisters in two minutes; walls have ears.'

Szabo stood up abruptly and walked over to the door, returning hurriedly to pick up his papers on the assumption he and Day would go straight to the Board Room after their *tête á tête*. To Lisa's surprise, Szabo walked out of the office without saying a word. Donning his gown, he ran down the corridor to where the administrative suite joined the vast cloisters of the chapel.

Day was waiting for Szabo, a half-smoked cigar in his mouth.

'What is it, Andreas?'

'Somebody knows about Clair's secret.'

'Nonsense. Nobody could know. It's more closely guarded than the crown jewels.'

'Well, then, the jewels are under serious threat. I tell you; someone knows about Clair's secret. What's more, they have a better idea than we do about it all.'

'What makes you say that?' Szabo looked at Day, wondering if he could trust the Chair.

'I had a phone call earlier.'

'Who rang you?'

'I don't know; they didn't say, and I couldn't recognise the voice.'

Szabo laughed. 'You mean they were using one of those distortion machines.'

Day shook his head. 'Don't be daft! No of course not. I just didn't recognise the voice.'

'Male or female?'

'Female, I think.'

'Educated or uneducated?'

'Well, their grammar was correct – more or less.'

'What do you mean?'

'Just something about how they spoke – made me think that English was not their first language.'

'So, a foreign accent?'

'If you count somebody who sounds as if they are from Leeds as being foreign.'

The two men laughed, breaking the tension briefly. Day put his hand on Szabo's shoulder.

'We'll get through this, Jan. It is all for the best, believe me.'

'You keep saying that. You promised that Clair would be no problem. I didn't expect him to be murdered.'

'Who says he was murdered, and what makes you think I had anything to do with his death?'

'Well, you've wanted the old man out of the way since you became Chair.'

'As have you; from the day you arrived.'

Szabo sighed. 'Not like this! Anyway, what did you mysterious caller say?'

Vanessa, Camilla, and Freddie were unable to hear the rest of the conversation. Szabo and Day had moved further down the cloisters and towards the chapel. Until then, Vanessa's room (with the window open) had been the perfect place to listen in to the conversation between the two men. After that, it was only the occasional word that the three students caught: 'opportunity'; 'for the taking'; 'untrustworthy'; 'secret'; 'treasure'. They hardly dared breathe until the discussion had ended and the crescendo and decrescendo of footsteps told Vanessa, Camilla, and Freddie that Szabo and Day were heading back to the administrative offices.

'There is a Board meeting at 14.15 hours. They are already late.' Freddie tapped his watch.

'How do you know that?' Vanessa pouted.

'I study all the noticeboards and memorise everything on them. There's one outside the staff common room that has the redacted minutes from previous meetings on them. It said, "date of next meeting" and gave today's date.'

'What does "redacted" mean, Freddie?'

'It means "to censor or obscure part of a text for legal or security purposes". I looked it up on *Wikipedia*.'

'So why put the minutes on the board for everybody to see if you then take words out?' The twins spoke as one.

'I don't know, but those two have something to hide, don't they? Secret treasure? Here at Templeton Towers!'

'Don't get over excited Freddie. Camilla put her hand on the boy's shoulder.

'You've gone all red! Red Fred! Fred the Red! You're a Viking, that's what! OR a turnip!'

'Stop it, Vanessa. No, I have not!' Freddie May threw a pillow at the teasing twin.

'Oh yes you have!'

'Yes, stop it Vanessa, you're upsetting my boyfriend!'

'Boyfriend! When did this happen? Freddie, Camilla?'

'Stop it, both of you! We have a murder to solve, and we have our first clues!'

'But just because we heard the words "secret" and "treasure" doesn't mean to say that we are talking about "secret treasure". They weren't used in the same sentence for a start!'

Oh, come on, Vanessa, what else could it mean but "secret treasure"?'

'Well, the word "secret" was spoken by one of the men and the word "treasure" by the other; Mr Szabo, I think. The first person could have said: "we must keep our plan secret from all the staff for the time being, and make sure the minutes are redacted", while the Principal replied: "I do treasure our relationship; you are a great support to me". So don't go jumping to silly conclusions, either of you!'

'They are not silly conclusions! It would make sense if Father William was murdered because he knew where the secret treasure was. I've read a book!'

'You're always reading books, Freddie. Which one are you talking about?'

'It's in the library.'

'There are a lot of books in the library.'

'Stop it, Vanessa; you are forever teasing me!'

'I am sure your girlfriend will protect you if I get too harsh.'

'She's not my – my - girlfriend. She's just my friend.'

'Fred the Red!' Vanessa pointed.

'Shut up!'

'Sorry Freddie. I want to hear about your book, even if my stupid sister isn't interested.'

'But I am interested as well. Really. Go on Freddie. I'm sorry; really.'

'Really you're sorry, or really you're interested.'

'Both.'

'Tell us, Fred.' Camilla put her hand back on Commander May's shoulder and kissed him lightly on the cheek.

Freddie looked down at his feet.

'Go on. We are all ears. Isn't that what Dr Foster says when she is waiting for a reply from a student?'

'It's a book about the history of this place – of Templeton Towers. It was written by Sir Templeton – Lord Hartleydale – himself. It talks about his visits to the Templar castles in the Holy Land and the treasure that he brought back. You can see a lot of it in the chapel and the original house – all those glass cases that the tourists come to see. But one thing he brought back is so special he had it hidden somewhere in the castle so nobody would ever try and steal it. It would be safe for all time …

What's the matter you two. You look as though you have seen a ghost!'

Freddie May laughed uncontrollably.

Lisa Watson hated taking minutes of Board meetings. Though they were recorded (with the permission of all attendees, which was invariably given, when requested) she found it tedious in the extreme to have to sit through hour after hour of discussion about the future of the school. Andreas Day was fond of the sound of his own voice and took great delight in regaling everyone with his experience of every subject under the sun. Today (thank the Lord!) was different; Clair's absence had not so much cast a shadow over proceedings as liberated the governors from a constraining albatross. Clement Rankin, DL, the longest-serving member, spoke for the first time in living memory, urging that, now Clair was no more, the school needed to take stock of its future. The four other members (excluding Day and Szabo) nodded vigorously, cheerfully approving the Principal's reordering of the agenda. This brought the item on the sale of land – and the cessation of Clair's precious archaeological dig – up to pride of place on the list of 'items for discussion and decision'.

Lisa could hardly keep up with Day. The Chair made short work of the Minutes, Matters Arising, Principal's Report and Quarterly Accounts. Then the sale of land. Day spoke little; rather he listened to what each of the governors had to say about selling this prime asset. Rankin proposed a motion to accept the Principal's recommendation; it would bring in millions – money that was badly needed to stave off bankruptcy and upgrade the outdated facilities. Melody Grimshaw, international supermodel, local celebrity, and recent addition to the Board, voted, like she always did, for whatever Szabo was proposing. Barbara Halliday, the richest governor by far and another recent appointment, shouted out that it was time to 'bloody get on with it' before the land slumped in value.

Day looked at the remaining two members. 'Do I have your support? According to our constitution, there must be unanimity amongst those present on such a far-reaching decision. A majority vote will not do; nor can you abstain your way out of the proposal. What do you say?'

Harry Riddles spoke first. 'I have been a member of this Board for nearly thirty years, and a friend of William Clair for even longer. I cannot in all conscience go against the Father's wishes. I vote against this proposal. Some other way must – and will – be found.'

'Is that your final answer, Harry?'

'It is, Andreas, especially now that William is dead. Someone must bear the torch for him.'

'And what about you, Mrs Philbey – Pauline?'

Pauline Philbey cleared her throat, pushed her papers to one side and looked round the room. 'Well, I have been sorting out the archives of this place for many years now, but only recently came across some documents of great import – very, very, great import. So much so that I shall have to alert the authorities to what I believe could be a major archaeological find in those woods. Any thought of selling the land must be halted until my investigations are complete and due process has been observed.'

'You don't mean something as ridiculous as secret treasure do you, Pauline?'

'That is exactly what I mean, Mr Szabo. There could well be secret treasure on the school's property. All we need to do is find it!'

4

Fear Abounds

'I'm worried Don. I have been worrying all day, waiting for you to come home.'

'I had to get the investigation under way. I couldn't get home before now. Anyway, you worry too much.'

'Is it safe?'

May nodded as Caz put her head on his shoulder. He ran his hand up and down her arm, then squeezed it gently.

'Yes. It is safe. I assure you. We have taken every precaution. There are uniformed officers at the school 24/7. We have carried out an inch-by-inch search of the place. I doubt the murderer – assuming it is murder – will strike again anytime soon.'

'It might not be murder, then?'

'No, it might not. We won't know for sure until the postmortem.'

'But the circumstances of Clair's death are suspicious?'

May nodded. 'What's more, it reminds me of a murder that took place a long time ago.'

'What, in Hartley?'

May nodded a second time.

'Do you want to talk about it or not?'

Donald May looked down and smiled. 'How do you put up with such a boring man as me for a husband?'

Catherine May kissed her husband's hand. 'I'll cope. You talk – if you want to.' I don't mind.'

'And I don't mind if you don't mind.' The two of them laughed as they remembered Freddie's little game.

'Well, it was twenty years ago. It was just before we met. I was a bobby on the beat in Hartley. I was doing my six months after graduating from UEA. Taylor's mills were still open then, as was St David's Church.'

'St David's?'

'That great cathedral on the hill; the place with the huge spire.'

'I remember. Derelict now, isn't it?'

May nodded. 'Yep, or it soon will be, the rate the vandals are having a go at it. There are plans to put it into the care of the Churches Conservation Trust, but there are all sorts of disputes over ownership; that's the Church of England for you! It's Grade 1 listed; just like Templeton Towers, so it must be preserved as built.'

'It's only bricks and mortar.'

'Well, stone in this case.'

'Anyway, my brave bobby on the beat, what happened all those years ago, before you met the love of your life?'

May snorted. 'I was one of the first on the scene. The caretaker had called into the vicarage to do her cleaning and found the house in disarray, as if there had been burglars. It was a right mess, though nothing had been taken, as far as could be made out. Whoever broke in had been looking for something. The study was turned over good and proper.'

'What do you think they were looking for?'

'Who knows? No idea.'

'Then what, PC May?'

'Oy – watch it! I begin to think you're not taking me seriously.'

'I am! Really! Go on!'

'There was no sign of the vicar. The caretaker said he was a man of habit and would have been at his desk at that time of day.'

'Where was he then?'

'Not in the vicarage. Anyway, the next logical place to look was the church, and that's where we found him. I thought he was just sitting in his stall praying – he was, after a fashion – but then when I got close, it was obvious he was dead.'

'Murdered?'

'It was thought he had died of natural causes, but the medical examiner spotted some odd marks around his neck.'

'Strangulation?'

'Sort of; except that they were the result of pressure applied after death and not before.'

'What did he die of, then?'

'It was never proved, definitively. He had bad asthma. There was a suggestion of breathing difficulties, a panic attack. The 'burglary' at the vicarage was no such thing – someone had tried to make it look like one, or they weren't out to steal.'

'And Clair died - was killed – in the same way?'

'There are similarities, on the face of it. But we will know more once Fizz has delivered.'

'Will you be at the postmortem?'

'After my meeting with the new ACC.'

Catherine May sat up with a start. 'What's wrong?'

'Nothing's wrong!'

'Yes, there is! I can tell. You tensed up when you said, "new ACC"; I felt it!'

'I tell you, Caz, there is NOTHING wrong!'

'What's your new ACC called?'

May disentangled himself from wife and settee, stood up and began to walk towards the kitchen.

'What's their name?'

May stopped in the doorway. Without turning round, he replied. 'Jean Samson.'

'Oh my God! Not her! No!'

Georgie Ellis enjoyed interviewing, especially with Charlie Riggs. As she left Hartley Station on the journey home, she went over that day's encounter with Janos Szabo in every delicious detail.

Ellis thought Szabo attractive; tall, thin, bearded, blue eyes and a natural smile. And articulate with it. He could answer every question;

nothing fazed him. And there was something beguiling about his no-nonsense, educated accent.

'I admit that Father William and I did not get on well. Yes, it is true that we had differences of opinion. But that is inevitable in an educational institution like Templeton Towers. There are traditions to be upheld, and any changes must be made within the context of those traditions. It is only right and proper to work that way.'

'You were never frustrated by Clair's blocking tactics at your meetings?'

Szabo had laughed at Ellis's question. 'To a certain extent, it was inevitable that I – we - were frustrated at what you might call the lack of progress with the plans for the school.'

'Is it true St Saviour's was on the verge of bankruptcy?'

Georgie Ellis remembered asking Szabo that question. She smiled as she recollected how he had reacted. It was the one point where he had lost his cool.

'Of course not! What on earth makes you ask that? And what business is it of yours?'

'Everything is our business, Mr Szabo, especially in connection with a possible murder!'

Ellis had been impressed by Riggs at that point. And afterwards, when the DS drew her attention to Szabo's body language and the rapid movement of his leg. That suggested guilt or deception of some kind. She had never really rated Riggsy, but Ellis had begun to realize he had a dogged cunning that produced results. More to the point, May trusted him. He had told her to listen and learn from the DS. And listen and learn she would; anything and everything that would help get to the top.

The BMW Z4 was purring its way home. Not long now, then once in her beloved flat, she could throw off her work clothes, run a scorching hot bath laced with lots of frothy gel, a bar of Old Jamaica in one hand, and the latest edition of *The Spectator* in the other. Bliss! Absolute bliss! Then a review of the case and Szabo's interview. Would killing Clair benefit the school, or Szabo, or the other trustees? When Andreas Day had been interviewed it might be easier to answer those questions. The boss would be doing that tomorrow afternoon, but first there was the morning's postmortem to attend; not her favourite pastime, though she had never – yet – been sick.

Ellis was home. The car safely parked in its dedicated spot she took the lift to her apartment. As soon as the key was in the door, she knew something was wrong.

'Hello? Who's there? Who are you?'

Ellis was aware of movement in the spare bedroom. She put down her bag and grabbed the walking stick from the antique hat stand.

'Come out, now! Show yourself!'

The bedroom door opened slowly; a figure appeared.

'Oh my God! What the hell are you doing here?'

Charlie Riggs was enjoying being a Detective Sergeant. It had taken him long enough to get there, but now he relished the thought of being in the thick of it as DCI May's NCO. Kate had been less convinced, Riggs knew it. He had apologized for the ever longer hours he was spending at work. She still loved him. He knew that, just as he loved her. Yet again she had raised the question of children; yet again he had said no. Was it wrong of him? After his own childhood and everything he had seen in his job, bringing new life into the world was the last thing he wanted; not now, not ever.

Riggs looked at his watch; another hour before Kate was back from her class. He poured himself a beer and switched on the news. There was little of interest, and only a passing mention of William Clair's death. He channel-hopped for a while: the more programmes there were at his fingertips, the less he could find of interest.

Riggs thought back to his conversation with Ellis after Szabo's interview. There was something not quite right about the man, but he could not put his finger on it. The two of them had agreed to a further investigation into his background, along with those of the other trustees and senior staff.

The mobile had rung several times before Riggs awoke. He must have been asleep for at least twenty minutes – still time to tidy up before Kate got home. He picked up the phone and answered it.

'Hello?'

'Detective Sergeant Riggs?'

'Yes. Who is this?'

'A friend. I have important information about William Clair and his death.'

'His death?'

'Yes, I do. Or rather, his murder.'

An owl hooted and a fox barked. The last train through Holme Hill rattled in the tunnel below. A car sped past down the hill. There was laughter in the distance. A girl shrieked in protest. The visitor looked around: nothing; nobody. Templeton Towers was its usual self: a menacing, ugly, black mass, punctuated by spots and shards of light. A whole role of windows suddenly lost their illumination. That would be the dormitory. Having called for lights out, the duty teachers would be retiring to their apartments on the same floor and, if lucky, would get a good night's sleep before the morning wake-up bell rang at 0600 hours. Then the procession to breakfast in the pseudo-mediaeval Great Hall, often accompanied by the sound of the Grand Organ at the East End of that vast space. How ridiculous: eating porridge to the sound of Clairvoyant crucifying Bach!

The visitor snarled. What a pompous, self-opinionated oaf that man was! And times had not changed, by all accounts!

The Order of St Saviour had much to answer for. The brothers were unredeemable; always had been, always would be. Hell was too good a place for them! Even then, all those years ago, when attitudes were different, what was done was wrong; totally wrong! William Clair was the vilest man ever born!

The narrow path was full of stones, tree roots and a thousand-and-one other hazards. An empty beer can was the visitor's downfall: face first in a pool of dirty water! Despite the shock, the expletives were mouthed quietly.

Time to switch on the torch. Face, hands, coat, trousers: all caked in mud! There was little point in trying to clean up. That would have to be done later, at home. There was something more pressing to be done.

It must be around here somewhere!

The torch was of little use. There was no moon. The great oak trees blocked out any light, natural or otherwise. Was the mission worthwhile? Achievable? After so long, the place would be overgrown. The small cross that marked the spot might be undetectable, assuming it was still there.

No, the goal had to be achieved. The visitor persisted until, at last, a familiar marker came into view, then another, then the third and final one. Five paces west, seven paces north. The directions were still fresh in the visitor's memory. Five minutes later, the quest was complete.

The visitor gasped. A small posy of flowers adorned the cross.

Who had left the blooms? Nobody should know about this grave. And yet, the cross stood upright, the weeds had been removed, the grass was recently cut. The freshness made the visitor sneeze loudly, twice.

Nobody, but nobody, should know about this grave!

The visitor knelt and picked up the posy.

'What the hell!'

The visitor threw the posy into the darkness, then turned back toward the grave.

I will have to return some other time.

Georgie Ellis was angrier than she had been for a long time. Bloody Tiggy! Arriving unannounced, moving herself into the spare room with all her clothes and her products. And now, she announces that Throthgar and Aethelwald are on their way. All because Lucian had left her and there was 'nowhere else to go.'

'When do the boys arrive, then?'

'Just finishing my Clarins order.'

'Pay attention Tiggs! When are the boys arriving? I am really very busy. My first big case as a DC and I want to do well! I can't afford to be distracted and, frankly, I don't want you and all your mess and your kids as well'.

'There. Finished my next order. Good thing I remembered your postcode.'

'You mean your "products" are being delivered here? What the –'

'HE is bringing them tomorrow, darling.'

'I presume by "he" you are talking about your beloved husband.'

'The bastard! The absolute devious, lying bastard! Trading me in for a younger model he met when we were skiing at Verbier last year. AND when I'm pregnant with Ambrosius.' Tiggy snorted.

'What?'

'Unusual name, isn't it? I've had enough of Anglo-Saxon names, thanks to Lucian, so I thought I would go for Romano-British this time.'

'I don't care about his bloody name, Tiggy. Another kid? At your age?'

'Don't be cross, Georgie, darling. We can bring him up together, along with Throth and Aethel. And I can help you solve all those wonderful murder mysteries that you get embroiled in. This is going to be so very exciting.'

Georgie Ellis went over to the cupboard where she kept her secret stash of Old Jamaica. Except when she opened the tea caddy, it was empty.

'Sorry darling. I crave Old Jamaica chocolate all the time, now I am preggers. Hate the stuff otherwise.'

Pauline Philbey woke herself with a large snore. She looked at the cuckoo clock in the corner of the snug. The rest of the house was so cold, even in the summer. This was the only part of 'Holme Hatch' where it was possible to keep warm. She often thought about moving into something smaller. Every time plans were made, she quickly realized that the faff of 'downsizing' would be far too great. No, here she would live out the rest of her days, focusing on the local archive, work she had loved and cherished for so long. There was plenty to be done with the Templeton Taylor Archive now she had access to the 'private and confidential' material: a good ten years' work sorting, cataloguing, digitising and more. And those intriguing maps. It had been as she went to bed the previous evening – supposedly an early night before the Board meeting. The gin had been swigged away; Boris was out through the cat flap in search of squirrels. *One last look at these documents.* And there underneath the pile of papers brought home from Templeton Towers were two maps. She had been right to vote against the proposal to dispose of the land, at least until she had done more research. 100% right!

'I had to say *something!* I couldn't just vote against the proposal without saying why I had done so.'

She remembered the look on Szabo's face; Day was just as bad. If looks really could have killed, then she would have been struck down on the spot.

What sort of treasure could it be? Was it one of Templeton Taylor's mediaeval knight fantasies? Some junk he had brought back from the Holy Land? No doubt he had been ripped off and paid a fortune for some fake Grail or a piece of the true Cross, or that Baphomet thing the Templars were supposed to worship.

'This is getting silly. Time for a nightcap, old girl.'

Philbey looked down at her lap. Boris was sound asleep. He had been for at least the last half hour. She looked at the cuckoo clock again. Why was she so nervous? Would she be attacked for what she had said and done? Would Szabo and Day get rid of her?

The armchair was becoming increasingly uncomfortable, but if she moved, Boris would squawk and claw, and that would be very painful. She decided to endure the discomfort for the sake of her beloved moggy, at least for a little while longer.

The next time she heard the cuckoo clock, it was well after midnight.

'Humph! I must have dozed off.' She looked down at her lap once more. Boris was nowhere to be seen. 'He'll be out on his nightly prowling, no doubt. There will be a mouse on the doormat in the morning.'

Philbey rose creakily from the chair, went over to the sideboard, and poured herself the large gin she had been longing to down. She turned off the standard lamp by her armchair and left the snug. As she walked across the hallway, there was an urgent knocking at the front door.

'What the hell? Who's there? What time do you call this?'

The knocking – more like loud banging now - continued.

Pauline Philbey slipped on the chain, unlocked the door, and opened it slightly.

'You! What on earth do you want? Don't you know it's after midnight?'

'Let me in! We must talk, you and me. You are in great danger; I am in great danger. We both are!'

5

Questions Asked If Not Answered

DONALD MAY FELT LIKE AN ERRANT SCHOOLBOY SITTING OUTSIDE THE ACC's office. He had never been in trouble with anyone – apart from his Dad – and never intended to be, though he had come close in 2019 when his handling of the Holme Hill murders had been criticised. That had been such a complex case, with far-reaching consequences that nobody could ever have envisaged. Was William Clair's murder – if it was a murder – going to be any easier to solve? Those OSS brothers had a shady reputation. May thought back to the rumours of the 1970s. Nothing had ever been proven, and no doubt nothing ever would. Nevertheless, he made a mental note to check back through the files from those days, assuming anything was still available.

The door opened.

'The ACC will see you now, DCI May.'

'Thanks Freda.'

The PA smiled as she beckoned May in through her cubby hole of an office and into the Assistant Chief Constable's vast room. The door closed; May stood waiting for his new boss to greet him. There she was, in her uniform, back firmly to her visitor, gaze steadily fixed on the comings and goings in the courtyard below.

May cleared his throat; once, twice, thrice.

'Morning, Don. How are you? Long time no see!' Samson turned round brusquely.

'I'm well, thanks, Jean – ma'am.'

Samson laughed. 'Call me Jean – at least within these four walls. I don't stand on ceremony, as you well know. Anyway, sit; fill me in.'

They walked over to the conference table at the far end of the room. Samson filled a large mug with strong black coffee.

'Want some?'

May shook his head. 'I drink too much caffeine. Caz is trying to get me to give up completely, but I am not ready to do that yet!'

'Caz? Ah, yes, Catherine. How is she? And you have a boy?'

'She's well, thanks. Freddie – our boy is called Freddie. He's very special.'

'How do you mean, Don?'

'He is very intelligent – off the scale, really. But …'

'Asperger's?'

May nodded. 'It's called ASC these days if you want to be politically correct.'

'And he is at St Saviour's?'

'Yes. He started at the beginning of this term. He's very happy there.'

'Is it wise to let the school continue in operation, given Clair's death?'

'I thought long and hard about that ma'am – Jean – but after discussion with Janos Szabo, the Principal, I deemed it appropriate for them to stay there. It would be difficult to decant to another site without seriously affecting the students' education and wellbeing. The school is separate from the Order's quarters by some distance, apart from some of the student bedrooms, that is.'

'I'll give you that, Don.'

'Are you going to take me off the case?'

May looked at Samson. The uniform suited her; she wore it well – to the manner born. May always knew she would get to the top. That burning, almost fanatical ambition that made her sweep people out of her way when they were in it. Most of the time, they had not been, but in Jean Samson's imagination, everybody was against her; nobody was to be trusted.

'No, Don. I am not. You are the best DCI here by far. I think you should be more than a DCI by now anyway. I'm surprised you are not! Look at me. You need to move on and up!'

Same old Jean. Same snide remarks. Can she never leave well alone? She always did know where to prod people to make them feel pain.

May smiled. 'There's more to life than work, Jean. Bringing Freddie up has been hard, but – in its own way – very rewarding.'

Samson smiled and said nothing.

'What do you want to know about the case, then, ma'am - I mean Jean?'

'I've read your report Don. Early days. Let's see what the PM says.'

'I'm meeting Fizz – Dr Harbord – later this morning. You will be the first to know the results.'

Samson stood up. May did the same.

'Thanks Don.' She walked over to him and held out her hand. 'No hard feelings I trust?'

After a while, he took her hand and squeezed it. 'No, Jean, no hard feelings.'

'That'll be all thanks, DCI May.'

'Donald May nodded and turned to leave the office.

'Just one last thing Don.'

May turned back to hear what the inevitable parting shot. Did she remember their time together at UEA? Probably not. All in the past for Jean Samson.

'What is it, ma'am?'

'I am leaving you in charge as SIO, but I will be keeping a close eye on this case. Always keep me in the loop; regular briefings, please.'

'Yes, ma'am. Of course, ma'am.'

Since Clair's death, the chapel had been out of bounds. Brother Bernard, newly appointed acting Head of the Order of St Saviour, had protested that the brethren should be allowed to say their daily devotions, but May had refused. He had allowed them to use the ante chapel instead.

Thus it was that the remaining members of the Order were sitting in a semi-circle in the 'nave' of the chapel. Candles had been lit for the morning Eucharist and left glowing and flickering after the service. It was a form of comfort to the brothers as they began their 'business' meeting.

'These are difficult times for us, brothers. We must stay strong. Father William would have wanted it. Think of all the times he addressed us in those terms.'

Brother Bernard looked at the other members of the Order. He thought back to the time when there had been 55 of them: the glory days when religion and the monastic, penitent, celibate life had been sanctified and glorified. No more! This secular, greedy, grasping world had no need of spirituality. All was profit! Even when it came to education. What were the remaining brothers to do now their mastermind was dead, murdered? Who would be next?

'I am afraid, Brother – Father – Bernard. I have sinned. We all have!'

'Do not be afraid, Brother Jeffrey. Calm yourself! We have our shield – all of us.'

Father Bernard smiled broadly as he turned to the organ screen that separated the chapel from the ante chapel. He pointed up to the very top of the pipes where a large armorial shield crowned the ornate woodwork. He read out the words. '*In hoc signo vinces*'.

The other brothers said the words, repeatedly. All except one.

Felicity Harbord wondered if it was time to retire. Until recently, she had enjoyed her job; got a buzz from a new death in suspicious circumstances. Ever since walking the coast-to-coast path there had been growing dissatisfaction. What had once been a carefree life now seemed to be a careworn one. No partner, no children, no career path, no hobbies. A nice house, an even nicer car, money to spend on whatever. But nothing more.

Harbord looked down at the corpse. The postmortem was complete. William Clair had been a healthy man, despite his great age; just over 80, according to his record. No major illness. Just death by asphyxiation.

'Asphyxiation, Fizz?'

'Yes, Don. Chemical asphyxiation. Father Clair inhaled something that interfered with his oxygen intake to the point where he ceased having enough in his blood to continue functioning.'

'So not strangulation, then?'

'No. As I said before, those marks relate to postmortem wounds. Perhaps someone was trying to make sure that the old codger was dead, though there was no need. The inhalation of a noxious substance did the job perfectly.'

'What did he inhale, then, Dr Harbord?' George Ellis took out her notebook.

'Interesting that. It was a kind of perfume, judging by the lingering aroma that I found in his mouth, throat, and lungs.'

Charlie Riggs snorted. 'Better check out the local Avon ladies, then!'

May and Ellis looked askance.

'Sorry. Couldn't resist.'

'You need to be looking for someone rather more sophisticated than an Avon lady, team.' Harbord looked meaningfully at each of the three officers in turn.

'What, then, Fizz?'

'Don't laugh when I say this, Don, but Father William was killed by incense.'

'What are we going to do, then Vanilla 1?'

'Stop calling me that, we agreed!'

'Sorry. I can't resist.'

Well, it is now **very** tiresome. Vanessa hates it as much as I do!'

'You always say the same things, you two!'

'What do you expect, May of the Yard? You're supposed to be the detective. We are identical twins. That's how identical twins behave. The clue is in the word "identical"; get it?'

'Alright, alright, you've made your point. So, what are we going to do?'

'Vanessa's here now; ask her!'

'But I shouldn't need to ask her, should I? You should know what she is thinking; what she is going to say, shouldn't you?'

'Oh, get lost, May!'

'What is the matter with you two?' Vanessa closed the bedroom door quietly behind her, checking first that she had not been seen entering. She leapt onto the bed, bouncing up and down gleefully having done so.

'You worried, Freddie?'

Freddie May nodded. 'Perhaps we should call the police.'

'What? Run crying to your Dad?'

'Well, if that's how you want to put it, then "yes".'

'I disagree and disagree violently. What do you say Camilla?'

'Totes agree!'

'Where on earth did you pick up that language, Vanessa?'

Vanessa snorted. 'Off a television programme. I like to use different accents and vocabulary. We both do.'

'Well, we need to take a decision. What are we going to do with what we have found out?'

'Nothing Freddie, nothing at all.' The girls spoke in perfect unison.

'Even if it means stopping a murderer?'

Vanessa and Camilla looked at each other and smiled.

Victoria Perry had a soft spot for Donald May; it had been there ever since A levels at Hartley Grammar School. They had sat in the FE room, the only two studying Latin. You always remember your first kiss; and he had been the one. Then university: she had stayed local; he had gone to Norwich. The next time they met, they were both with others. They saw each other 'in the distance' from time to time but he was a senior police officer; she was a reporter for the *Hartley Gazette and Argus*. But she would never forget that Christmas Party in the upper sixth.

It had come as a surprise when May phoned her. Perry had been shocked at the suggestion they meet for coffee. Intrigued by his invitation and the reasoning behind it, she said yes, and now sat waiting in the *Speckled Teapot*.

'Sorry I'm late Victoria. Just been with my new boss and then a PM to attend; couldn't get away! How are you?'

'I'm well. You?'

May smiled and sat down opposite his guest.

'I couldn't resist the invitation. Meeting up for old times' sake?'

May laughed. 'That was a very long time ago, Vicky!'

Perry laughed in return. 'No one calls me Vicky these days!'

'Sorry, Vic – Victoria.' May beckoned to the waitress at the far end of the café. 'What can I get you? Same again?'

Perry nodded. 'I'll have a latte.'

May looked at the waitress. 'Make that two.'

Once nobody was in earshot, May continued.

'I need a favour.'

Perry laughed. 'Do you now? What could a Detective Chief Inspector want with a lowly crime correspondent on the local rag?'

'Crime correspondent? Since when?'

'Since you arrived about ten minutes ago.'

The ensuing laughter broke the tension. May thought Vicky – Victoria – had aged well. Her figure was as he remembered it; the soft, musical voice still enchanted him; while her eyes …

'You look stressed. Are you OK?'

May pouted. 'I'm fine. Being SIO on a murder case is never easy.'

'I can imagine. William Clair, I presume?'

May nodded.

'A weird lot up there. Those "brothers" give me the creeps; always have done.'

May leaned over the table. 'What makes you say that?'

Perry took a sip of her latte. 'Mmm, that tastes good. They know how to make good coffee at *The Teapot*.'

'Well?'

'Well, it's before our time, but there were all sorts of shenanigans going on in the 1970s at Templeton Towers - allegedly. Don't you have anything in your archives?'

May shook his head. 'Not that we have found so far, but I have put someone on it to see what they can find.'

Perry smiled. 'How about this for starters?' The 'crime correspondent' of the *Hartley Gazette and Argus* reached down into her gargantuan handbag, pulled out a bulging orange folder and slammed it down on the table in front of May. The dust made them both cough.

'What is this, then?'

'It's what I assumed you wanted.'

May smiled. He watched her break into an impish grin as he read the label pasted on the folder. '" The Order of Saint Saviour". How did you know?'

'Come off it, Don. It's obvious! Why else would you want to see me after all this time.'

'But –'

'Don't come the young innocent with me.'

May loosened the tape that bound the documents in order. 'Can I …?'

'Yes, you can take the folder. On one condition.'

'Which is?'

'That I get first scoop on all this.'

'You know I can't do that.'

Perry made to retrieve the folder.

'Alright. I will see what I can do.'

Perry pushed the folder back across the table towards May, nearly knocking the sugar bowl over as she did so.

'And we meet regularly here for coffee.'

May laughed. 'That's two conditions.'

'No, Don. The scoop is business – and that is a condition of working with you; the assignations are for pleasure; pure pleasure.'

Charlie Riggs wondered when he should tell May about the anonymous phone call. The missus had said 'straightaway', when she got home that evening, but for some reason – his gut – he had merely registered the conversation and agreed to meet the informant on the edge of the woods behind Templeton Towers. On the one hand, it went against all the rules of good policing; on the other, Riggs knew full well that if he turned up with a colleague in tow, the mysterious caller would be frightened off. And that would mean a possible early break in the case had evaporated. The call had been untraceable – so far – but Riggs had determined to have IT follow up. Time was of the essence, before the caller changed their mind, as they had threatened to do.

The Taylor Estate: Riggs sat in his car by the high boundary wall. The woman – assuming it was a woman – was late. The voice on the phone was indeterminate in pitch, but Riggs had guessed a youngish woman, with a slight stutter, and a definite Yorkshire accent, but the occasional word that sounded a bit different. The dialect people would have been able to say with more accuracy, but it sounded like someone local, a born-and-bred 'Daler'. Unless they were faking it. There was a tinge of something else; something foreign.

Probably not, thought Riggs. A linguistics expert might be able to put on an accent like that, but would they also be capable of downplaying their vocabulary? Riggs decided he was over-analyzing, like May did. Riggs had the utmost respect for his boss, but there were times when he just wanted to 'gerron wi't job', as his father used to say. Then there was Georgie: he smiled at her Tigger-like enthusiasms. Ellis wasn't so bad, especially now Trubshaw was gone, and he was senior DS.

Riggs looked at his watch. The meet-up was supposed to be midnight. It was 15 minutes after; another 15 minutes and he would leave. Except that he stayed beyond the revised deadline. More than that, he got out of the car and wandered over to the boundary wall. The rusty old gate was open; a light flickered beyond. Riggs switched on the mobile phone's torch and proceeded cautiously.

The light was still flickering. In the far distance, he saw the outline of Templeton Towers, its silhouette set against a watery new moon. The cobbled path turned up towards the main buildings past a small ruin. It must have been a chapel at some point, with its crooked cross atop one end of the roof, or what was left of it. Either side of the building were gravestones, much like Hartley Cemetery. Riggs resolved to visit his parents' grave more often in the future.

The wooden door hung half off its hinges. As he pushed it open, it fell off with a loud crash. Dust went everywhere.

'Get off me! Get off me!' Riggs was assailed by bats as he looked in through the opening.

If there was one thing he hated, it was bats. Freddie May had once given him a lecture on the subject, one of many subjects on which the 'old man's old man' had bored for England. Riggs hated the very thought of the creatures, let alone being attacked late at night in a lonely, strange, place. The origin of the flickering light was inside the chapel, and he determined to investigate. The rendezvous was supposed to be by the boundary wall: perhaps the informant had changed their mind; or was it a trap and Riggs was being lured in, only to be assaulted, kidnapped, or worse?

A few pews faced the front of the chapel. Two large candles provided the flickering light. Something lay on the altar, covered in a large white cloth. Just as he was about to shine his phone down and lift the cloth, a gust of wind blew the candles out. Riggs felt a searing pain in the back of his skull. He reached out his hand and felt the moist warmness of blood dripping through his hair. Riggs fell back on the altar. The last thing he saw was a face. It could have been his father.

The drink had gone dead, assuming it was ever alive. Pauline Philbey got no pleasure out of her gin. Try as she might, there was not a touch of drunkenness about her, despite trying every beverage under the sun to become inebriated. Nothing had worked. Wheat beer had been the worst option. Not only had she remained stone cold sober, it made her break wind uncontrollably.

She sighed, wishing for sleep. That was a forlorn hope; the surprise visit had unsettled her more than she could ever imagine. From the moment Harry Riddles had banged on her door, it had spelt trouble.

Pauline Philbey could see the look of horror on his face even now.

'What on earth is it, Harry?'

'Get me a drink!' Riddles had almost pleaded as he sat down, uninvited, on the sofa. Boris, returning from his nightly hunt to see what all the commotion was about, had taken one look at the surprise visitor, squawked his displeasure and scuttled off upstairs.

'It's this. I received it today.' Riddles handed Philbey a crumpled white envelope. 'I shouldn't be showing it to you. See what will happen to me if I tell anybody else.'

Pauline Philbey opened the correspondence. Inside was a drawing of the recipient – a fair likeness in pencil – with a noose round his neck. At the bottom of the paper were the words *in hoc signo vinces* followed by 'all who get in our way will die. You are next, Riddles. We have seen your death. It is ordained.'

'It's a silly, sick joke, Harry. Someone is trying to scare you.'

'I feel I am being watched everywhere I go. I cannot put my finger on it, I have no evidence, but I am sure I was followed here.' Riddles got up and went over to the window. He pulled the lace curtains apart and looked out.

Pauline Philbey came to join him. She could see nothing; hear nothing; feel nothing. She put a hand on his shoulder. 'If anybody is behind this, it will be Day and Szabo. We voted against them, and they don't like it.'

'Don't be ridiculous, Philbs. You and I have known each other too long to think things like that. Surely, the Chair of the Board and the Principal would not stoop so low as to send dramatic, threatening letters.'

'It's no more ridiculous than your being watched and followed, Harry! Desperate men take desperate measures, and those two are on a mission to make big money out of St Saviour's.'

'Don't give me all that buried treasure malarkey, Philbs.'

Philbey turned around and walked over to the bureau. Opening it, she took out a large document case, unlocked it and handed the contents to Riddles.

'Don't be so sure, Harry. Don't be so sure.'

Outside, the visitor could see the two of them poring over maps and other papers long into the night. At last, lights went out, downstairs, then upstairs. Riddles' murder would have to wait for another day.

6

Impromptu Identity Parades And Parallel Investigations

THE SUN WARMED THE AIR AND LIT THE LAND. BIRDS CONVERSED IN THE woods. The clock chimed eight. Time for Mattins at Templeton Towers.

It was Vanessa's turn to attend. She and Freddie May stood next to each other in the far corner of the ante chapel. Both longed to see the crime scene, but it was still cordoned off. According to Mr Szabo, it would remain inaccessible for some time to come.

Boy and girl watched as the staff filed in. First came the teaching assistants, then the teaching staff proper, in order of seniority, followed by the Principal. Once they were all in place, the brothers appeared from their separate entrance. There was silence as Father Bernard looked around the assembled congregation. Vanessa shivered when it was her turn to be stared at. Freddie squeezed her hand. She felt much better.

After the opening prayers, Father Bernard bade everyone sit down while the choir sang a short anthem. Vanessa noticed how difficult it was for the singers to keep up with the organist, stranded as he was on the wrong side of the chapel screen with no way of seeing the conductor. Why not move the CCTV camera so that old 'Quick-Draw' McGraw could watch the beat from the organ loft?

Vanessa was no musician, but she enjoyed listening to her fellow students' performances. Camilla, on the other hand, hated music, and found it difficult to keep up their deception when it came to lessons with 'Quick-Draw'. There were times when Vanessa thought he was catching on; Camilla kept telling her – and Freddie, now he was in on the act – not to fuss. Their secret was safe.

Having banished the fear of discovery from her mind, Vanessa gazed round the ante chapel. Was Father Clair's murderer here, at this very moment? It was Vanessa's turn to squeeze Freddie's hand as she thought of the possibilities. He gasped; her grip hurt.

'Sorry, Commander', she whispered. 'Just wondering if the murderer is here.'

Vanessa let go of Freddie's hand slowly, then returned to the task of identifying possible suspects. It had to be a member of staff, or one of the brothers, for only they would have access to the 'inner sanctum'. Father William let very few people anywhere near the high altar or the sanctuary. When not in use, the 'sanctum' was alarmed to protect the golden statue of the *Sanctus Salvator,* the Holy Saviour, brought back from the Holy Land by Templeton Taylor. The students were told how it had been the inspiration behind the founding of the Order.

Who knew the keycode for the alarm? Vanessa assumed the brothers would all have it memorised. Did anyone else? Mr Szabo, surely. McGraw? He would need access to the chapel so he could practise on the organ. But then Quick-Draw would have no call to go anywhere near the inner sanctum, except perhaps when arranging chairs and music stands for performances. Any other teachers, like Dr Foster? Would she need to get to the high altar?

Vanessa gently shook her head. No, it had to be one of the brothers, or possibly Szabo. Freddie could find out from his Dad who the code-holders were. The clock struck the half hour; ten more minutes before dismissal and the start of lessons. She determined to study the prime suspects closely for the remainder of the service.

Mr Szabo was a handsome man. Freddie said it was obvious the Principal was Royal Navy, with his full captain's beard, his upright bearing, muscular physique, and immaculate appearance, right down to his shiny shoes. What about his name? It was not English. Freddie said it was Hungarian, though to say he was called 'Janos Szabo', the man had a very British accent. Camilla called it 'upper class'.

Father Bernard sat in stark contrast to Szabo. Whereas the Principal was good looking, physically fit and 'confident in demeanour' (Freddie's words), the new Head of the Order of Saint Saviour looked old and careworn. Szabo must have been at least 6' tall; Father Bernard was short, stocky, balding. Szabo had a commanding tone of voice when he spoke; the reverend father umm-ed and aah-ed all the time. Father William had been much more like Szabo, though they must have been at least thirty years apart in age. Freddie and Camilla had heard McGraw telling Foster he thought Brother Bernard was 'a pale imitation' of Father William and that the OSS 'wouldn't last six months under his leadership.'

What about the other brothers? There they sat in a single row behind Mr Szabo and Father Bernard. Brother Lawrence – 'Lazy Larry' to all the students - was 'away with the fairies' most of the time. It was easy to pull the wool over his eyes. Just get him talking about steam railways and he would go off at a tangent and spend the rest of the science lesson waxing lyrical about Nigel Gresley. Freddie loved it when 'LL' did that, of course. Camilla and she were bored rigid. No, Brother Lawrence was unlikely to have committed murder, unless the National Railway Museum had painted 'Flying Scotsman' the wrong shade of green. If that happened, woe betide the perpetrators of the travesty if LL got hold of them. He had certainly sent angry, threatening letters to the NRM. The students all knew that because Brother Lawrence not only told them, but read the missives – and the studied, cautious, non-committal replies from the National Railway Museum – out in class. LL was no slouch when it came to getting good results in the laboratory, though, and his experiments were always entertaining, especially when the smoke alarm went off, as it frequently did.

Brother Germain ('call me BG', he had said to the students on their first day) was the exact opposite of LL: up at six in the morning, every day, come rain or shine, out for a run round the grounds of Templeton Towers; lessons planned down to the last minute; results always the best in the school. 'BG' was good at his subject, modern foreign languages, priding himself on speaking every single one of them like a native. Could he have murdered Father William? BG had a temper, as the students all knew to their cost: at least once a day there was a tantrum, except when the Head of the Order sat at the back of the class.

LL and BG made an odd pairing, but they were rarely apart in their spare time. Vanessa thought back to the day when she and Camilla had explained to Freddie what the word 'homosexual' meant. Vanessa turned to look at him; he was deep in his own world as he sat there listening to Father Bernard's homily.

Vanessa looked at the clock above the organ case, with its incredible array of gold pipes all over the place. She remembered McGraw telling them how they were just dummies and the 'speaking' pipes were all inside the instrument. Five minutes to assess the last two members of the order. Brother Simon was asleep; not surprising, given his age and the amount he drank. Why had he not been pensioned off? Did he have a hold over Father William? Was he 'untouchable'? It seemed odd that he was still employed within the school even though divinity classes were going to be cancelled and that was all the old duffer could teach. Did he have a grudge against Father William for not defending Divinity? Was he capable of murder? His growing infirmity suggested not, but Vanessa resolved to keep him on the suspect list, after discussion with Freddie and Camilla.

Brother Jeffrey was a brilliant History master. Freddie and Camilla thought so too. He made the subject come alive. The joy with which this fat little man spoke about the archaeological dig in the grounds made Vanessa smile. She had become impassioned, like everybody else, and looked forward to the weekly sessions on site. Had there been a disagreement between Brother Jeffrey and Father William? Brother Jeffrey had asked parents to help fund the dig through gift-aided donations. The project was losing money, 'big time', according to Freddie. Was it going to be shut down and murdering the Head of the Order was the only way of preventing the dig's closure?

Brother Jeffrey was usually the epitome of calm. Vanessa noticed how troubled he looked. His combed-over hair was out of place; it looked as though he had not shaved; his habit was creased; his shoes were covered in mud. Vanessa nudged Freddie, who raised his eyebrows in reply.

'We will now sing hymn number 365: "Let all mortal flesh keep silence".'

Quick-Draw started up the organ and the singing began.

The sun warmed the air and lit the land. Birds conversed in the woods. The clock chimed nine. Grey-green shapes formed across the man's blurred vision. His head throbbed in time to distant music. He shivered. The cold and the damp and the frigid air cut into his soul.

'Must get help!'

The man pushed himself up by his arms. He saw blood on his hand and remembered what had happened.

Or what he thought had happened. Getting up shakily, Detective Sergeant Riggs looked around the ruinated building. He had lain where he was hit. Everything was as he remembered from the dark night before.

The DS felt for his mobile phone and called the station. As he did so, the visitor walked away from their vantage point and back towards Templeton Towers.

'I think it's best if you stay here for now.'

Harry Riddles stared into his mug of coffee. 'Are you sure Philbs? Tongues might wag.'

Philbey laughed. 'Tongues have been wagging about me for years, Harry. One more scandal is not going to make much difference to my reputation in Holme Hill after all this time!'

Riddles shook his head and smiled.

'In any case, Harry, they won't know you are living at my house.'

'What of it?'

'Because, my dear, if this death threat really is serious, then you – and I – need to take it seriously.'

Riddles put his empty mug down on the coffee table and buried his head in his hands. 'You are the only person I felt I could turn to. I knew you would understand.'

Philbey resisted the temptation to go over and sit next to Riddles, even though the gin bottle was on the way.

'Any time, Harry. You and I have known each other since our school days, and that is more years ago than I care to remember.'

Riddles nodded.

'Are you sure you don't want any breakfast?'

Riddles shook his head. 'I would rather get to the bottom of this threatening letter.'

'Let's have one more look at it.'

Philbey held the letter up to the light shining through the dining room window.

'This is expensive paper. You can feel how full it is. And it has a watermark. I am not entirely sure, but it looks like the arms of the Order of St Saviour to me.'

'It's the brothers, egged on by Szabo and Day. You saw how they looked at us when we voted against their proposal at the meeting!'

Philbey pondered for a moment. She tapped the mystery letter on her lips as she thought about Riddles' assertion. 'It's too obvious. Everything points to the brethren – or at least some of them – which I think is what the writer wants you to think.'

'Is it a hoax then, Philbs?'

Philbey shrugged. 'I would like to think that it is, for your sake, Harry. And for mine, come to think of it. I voted against the motion too, remember!

Riddles picked up his empty mug and helped himself to more coffee from the cafetière. 'You make a great brew, Pauline. Just like my Shirley used to!'

'How long it is since she passed, Harry?'

'Too long. Ten years next month. And I still miss her.' Riddles wiped a tear away. 'Why did you never marry, Philbs?'

Pauline Philbey blushed and coughed at the same time. 'Now that is a very interesting question, Harry.'

'And I would be interested in the answer!'

'Well, you will have to wait for it, Harry. We have more important things to be talking about.'

'Such as?'

'Such as who sent this letter and, if the threat is real, who wants you dead! And if whoever it is also murdered Father William Clair because he opposed the sale.'

'Very well. If it isn't Szabo and Day, or the brethren, who could it be?'

'I am not saying it's not them – it could be a double bluff – **but** what about the other members? Don't forget that they, and we, as non-executive directors of the Templeton Trust, stand to gain financially from any land deal.'

'I can't imagine Rankin being behind anything devious. I have known him for years. Old Clement might be a boring old duffer, but he is as straight as a die. And a Deputy Lieutenant, don't forget!'

'Hmmm. And he will move in certain circles, if you know what I mean, Harry.'

Riddles nodded. 'I know exactly what you mean, but they are harmless, I am sure. Just people helping each other out in business and doing good works for the community.'

Philbey snorted. 'If you say so, Harry. I do agree with you, though, that Clement Rankin seems an unlikely person to be threatening murder. Did you see how infirm he looked at the meeting? He might want to kill someone like Clair, but he would be physically incapable of doing it. There would need to be an accomplice.'

'Let's not rule him out entirely. He could be involved in some form.'

'Very well.' Philbey picked up a notepad from the coffee table and began to write. 'But on a scale of one to ten, where one is low or no involvement, I would only give him a three.'

The two of them laughed.

'I agree, Philbs. Three out of ten. What about Halliday and Grimshaw, though? Didn't you know Barbara before she came on the Board?'

'Yes, I did. She was married to Rodney Halliday, the property developer. He was murdered in 2019 by his brother. And – you should probably know this – Ernie Halliday was my fiancé many years ago - briefly.' Pauline Philbey blushed again.

'Is that why you never …'

'Let's not talk about that, Harry. It's all in the past and can have no bearing on the present.'

'But Barbara Halliday and property development?'

Philbey pursed her lips. 'She took over Rodney's business interests, for sure, and I could well imagine Halliday Holdings would be very keen on making a bid for the land when – or rather if – the sale goes through.'

'Shouldn't she have declared a conflict of interest?'

'Her directorships are listed in the register of interests, so the declaration was made when she joined.'

'How did she become a member?'

'Don't you recall the meeting last year at which nominations were received?'

'MEGO at all the paperwork back then!'

'MEGO? What the hell does that mean?'

'My Eyes Glazed Over. I got sick to the back teeth of the mountains of paperwork that Clair use to inundate us with. I didn't read most of the stuff.'

'Well, you **should** have done, Harry!'

'I suppose so. What did it say about Barbara Halliday then?'

'She was chosen by the Nominations Committee, and we agreed to ratify their decision.'

'And the members of the Committee?'

'I looked up the relevant papers after the recent Board meeting.'

'And?'

'Szabo, Day, and Rankin. Melody Grimshaw was appointed at the same time.'

Riddles scratched his chin.

'I know nothing about Grimshaw, except what I have seen of her on television. I tend not to have anything to do with "celebrities". What does she **do**? Where does her money come from?'

'A good question, Harry. She is obviously loaded, judging by the car she drives and the clothes she wears. We need to do some research on both Board members.'

Riddles nodded and smiled. 'In the meantime, tell me more about your buried treasure theory. I would like you to show me those maps and plans again. That old chapel in the grounds; do you really think that's where this "treasure" of yours is buried?'

'Are you sure you are up to this?'

Riggs looked at May and Ellis and nodded.

'Of course I am sure. It was just a little bang to the head. Nothing more.'

'Hmmm. I don't believe you, Riggsy, you took a hell of a blow!'

'I'm fine sir. Absolutely fine!'

'Well, if you start feeling unwell, say so straight away.'

'Wilco, sir.'

'What made you go on your own to Templeton Towers, Charlie?'

'I don't know, George. It was a stupid thing to do, I'll give you that, but the caller said, "come alone".'

'You should have known better, Detective Sergeant! At least you should have informed one or other of us two before you ventured out.'

Riggs nodded.

'What can you remember, Charlie?' Georgie Ellis opened her notepad.

'As I have already said, I got a phone call at home. The caller would not give their name. They said that they had information about William Clair's death – then they changed it to "murder".'

'Man or woman?'

'Woman – or at least I think it was a woman. It could have been a man. It was hard to tell.'

'Why?' Ellis began writing.

'It sounded as though they were outside in a howling gale. Then I thought I heard a train.'

'Carry on, Sergeant.'

'Yes sir. Well, I was supposed to meet them at a side entrance to Templeton Towers. The caller gave me a very precise time and location.'

'Then they never turned up?'

'Not at the side entrance. I waited and waited, and then decided to investigate. I went through the gate and saw a light in the distance. I found this old chapel – I think that's what it was. That's the last thing I remember, until I came round this morning with one hell of a headache. I rang you, sir, and you and George came to pick me up along with some uniforms.'

DCI May coughed. 'Well, the forensic team haven't finished yet, and I have ordered a search of the area around the old chapel. Georgie, when we've finished our meeting, see what you can find out about the ruin. What significance might it have?'

'Yes sir.'

'In the meantime, I want you on desk duty for a day or two, Charlie.'

'But sir …'

'No buts, Detective Sergeant. Anyway, there is an important file here that needs your immediate attention.'

May took a large orange folder from his desk and passed it over to Riggs. 'Courtesy of a friend at the *Hartley Gazette and Argus*. It looks as though we shall have to delve into the past to sort out the present. And this file looks like a good place to start.'

7

People Running Out Of Time

Diana Foster felt good. She looked at her watch: a PB was in sight. The ruinated chapel could be seen in the distance. It was exactly three kilometres from the school. She experienced pleasure when she got to the chapel door, touched it, then sped back a different way to complete her run. What a strange place! Why build a place of worship here? And a round one at that! Or at least the older part – just like the Temple Church in London. Which made sense given Sir Templeton's interests and theories.

She began to think of ideas for a research study using Taylor's book as a starting point. She looped round the ruins and through the nearby cemetery. The idea had legs; what better way of engaging the students than getting them to delve into the planning and building of this estate? Why had it not been done before as part of the archaeology project?

Spots of rain; then drops; then streams; then torrents. Thunder in the distance; each subsequent crack louder than the last. Black sky contrasted with bolt-white lightning. Running became impossible. Foster stopped, caught her breath, wiped her watch face: 40 minutes before the evening shift began. The storm should pass soon; still time to complete the circuit. The ruin was but a minute away, and partly roofed. A train rumbled through the tunnel below, trumpeting its passing as it did so.

Foster was cold and wet, but she had shelter of sorts now at the chapel. Still the storm showed no signs of abating. Another few minutes and she would have to phone Lisa and say someone else would have to take her place: just one problem – she never took her mobile phone; too much bulk in her pockets. Could she get back in this weather? Should she try? Just a few more minutes, then she would have to make a run for it.

She had gone past the chapel every day since arriving at Templeton Towers; sometimes twice – morning and evening – when feeling especially virtuous. This was the first time inside. Unlike the main buildings, this place was plain and bare: no ornate decorations, no grotesque statues, no mottoes; just stone walls, pine pews, canvas lectern, oak altar. No let up. No blue sky. No escape.

More thunder. She looked up. More lightning. More rain. Wetness pervaded her body and her being. Ten minutes to get back to school. She sat down on the priest's chair and buried her head in her hands.

'Shit! Shit! Shit!'

At first, she thought the noise was thunder. Then the creaking of unsafe eaves in the wind. It was neither of those. It was a trapdoor under the altar that groaned as it rose. Once vertical, the door was pushed fully back on its hinges, landing on the altar floor with a crash of dust.

Foster coughed and spluttered as the particles entered her mouth, throat, lungs. A tall, slim figure emerged, turned, and looked at her.

'Oh my God, what the hell are you doing here?'

'Not much progress, from what you are saying in this briefing note of yours.' Jean Samson threw the A4 sheet into her out tray, stood up, walked out from behind her desk, straightened her jacket and half grimaced, half sneered at Donald May.

'Not yet, Ma'am, but it's early days.'

'You always say that. The first 24 hours are the most important and it's been, what, four days at least?'

'Three days, actually, if you don't count the evening of the murder itself.'

'Three days, then, I'll give you that – just about. Anyway, tell me what you have found out.'

May nodded. 'Clair was not much liked by the Principal and the Chair of the Board, especially as he was blocking their plans to sell much of the land to developers.'

'What land is that?'

'Everything to the north of Templeton Towers, right up to the main road from Hartley to Halifax.'

Samson walked over to the framed Ordnance Survey map on the wall. She traced her finger across the boundaries of the Templeton estate. I see that the railway runs under the land there. Any significance?

May shrugged. 'I doubt it. Sir Templeton must have had shares in the railway company and no doubt charged handsomely for permission to burrow under his estate. He made them detour to the edge of his property rather than go straight under his house.'

'Hence the kink in the link, I suppose. And what's this cross?'

'That's the old chapel.'

'You mean the one where DS Riggs got himself mugged?'

'How did you know about that?'

Samson smiled. 'I must keep on top of everything Don. Not good behaviour from one of your team, is it?'

May shook his head. 'I have admonished him. He was following up a lead and got more than he bargained for.'

Samson snorted. 'Well don't let it happen again, Don.'

'What about the anonymous caller?'

'Nothing. We have been unable to trace him – or her. Riggsy couldn't be sure.'

Samson sighed. 'Tell me more about the OSS.'

'It's all in my report, ma'am: Brother Bernard has taken over on a temporary basis. Each has an alibi for the evening of the murder, though they have in effect covered for each other. They say they were having an evening of prayer together. All seem to have led blameless lives. They all admired Clair.'

'Unlike the Board members?'

'Unlike *most* of them, ma'am. The proposal to sell the land did not go through at the Board meeting. Day and Szabo went ahead despite – or even because of – Clair's death, but they needed everybody to be in favour, and two of them voted against – Philbey and Riddles.'

'Have all the Board members been interviewed yet?'

'Day and Szabo have. We will be seeing the others over the next day or so.'

'Any shady pasts, Don?'

May nodded. 'Rankin is straight. Halliday and Philbey have interesting pasts. Grimshaw is an unknown quantity, but you would expect a supermodel to have an interesting back story of some kind. So far, there is nothing obvious that would make any of them suspects. Will that be all ma'am?'

'Almost, Don. What about the murder itself?'

'Well, I have never come across poisoned incense as an MO before, but the marks around the neck reminded me of a cold case from way back. A local vicar – a former member of the OSS – found in his church in similar circumstances. We are following up on that now.'

'And?'

'And what, ma'am?'

'I know there is something you are not telling me, Don.'

'About what?'

'About the Order.'

May stroked his chin. 'There is nothing on file; absolutely nothing.'

'But?'

'But I have got Riggs looking into old newspaper reports from the 1970s about unproven allegations re the school.'

'Child abuse?'

May nodded. 'As I say, nothing was ever proven, and any records there were from that time cannot be located, assuming they existed in the first place. The newspaper files are a start.'

'Let's hope they lead somewhere, for all our sakes.'

'Who did it, and what is going to happen next?'

Freddie May looked at his fellow officers and pondered how to answer.

'Let's eliminate suspects first. That's what Dad does.'

Vanessa and Camilla answered in unison. 'Not one of the brothers. They were all in a meeting when Clairvoyant died.'

Freddie shook his head. 'The incense would have been slow burning and slow acting. One of them could have lit the burner earlier.'

'How much earlier without arousing suspicion and perhaps poisoning someone else by accident? Quick Draw always practises for an hour at night. He might have been gassed by mistake!'

'That's a good point. We need to know more about the effects of the incense. I'll ask next time I see Dad.'

'But will he tell you? He shouldn't really, especially when the case revolves around this place.' Vanessa took the lead this time.

'Who stood most to gain from Clair's death? Szabo and Day! Remember what we overheard the other day before the Board meeting?'

'OK. Let's pursue Szabo and Day as our main leads. 'Isn't it time Dr F was back?'

Freddie looked out of the bedroom window as the clock struck. It was raining heavily, but there was no more thunder and lightning.

'The grave will have got wet, won't it?' He turned to the twins and shook his head.

Georgie Ellis drove the BMW Z4 into the underground car park. Normally she would have got out and zipped up the stairs with glee at the end of another day at the station. Not this evening, or any other evening until further notice. Having Tiggy was bad enough, but the boys were the final straw: so badly behaved! Tiggs just let them do what they want: no discipline, no routine, no manners, nothing! They had wrecked her beautiful flat in under 24 hours!

She touched the steering wheel with her head and started to cry.

'They will have to move out! And soon! Otherwise, I will be the one committing murder!'

She leaned back in the driving seat and shook her head. Tiggy had always expected everything to come to her on a plate; that grand sense of entitlement possessed from birth. Why? She had flunked A levels, finishing school, everything. Then fallen on her feet with Lucian, or so it had seemed, until the recent skiing debacle. Now it was all collapsing for big sister. What could she do but help Tiggy to get sorted?

George Ellis reached for the bar of Old Jamaica that she kept in the glove compartment. As she grabbed it, a plain white envelope fell to the floor. There was no address, nor was it sealed. She opened it and took out a single piece of lined notepaper, roughly torn from an A5 notepad.

'Watch this space, DC Ellis. You will soon learn more about Clair's murder.'

The Detective Constable smiled. It was the best news she had received all day.

Pauline Philbey prided herself on being a good decision maker; but not now. Speeding down the hill in her 4 x 4, she wondered what the hell to do about Harry Riddles and the treasure. It was nearly 7.30: late for choir practice again. St Maurice's car park was full. There was nothing else to be done: she would have to double park behind the organist and choirmaster's Skoda.

Philbey thought that Mozart's *Ave verum* sounded good, at least from outside the church. She opened the porch door quietly and tiptoed down the side aisle in the hope that McGraw would not notice her entrance.

'Good of you to join us.'

The late arrival blushed.

'Sorry'.

The choirmaster pointed to the vacant seat. Philbey picked up her music folder and went to her place. The singing recommenced: Mozart, Brahms, Wesley; psalms, hymns, responses. McGraw told the same old jokes; dutiful laughter ensued. She was in no mood for humour. As she went through the motions of performance, the events of the previous 24 hours came back to her. Riddles had been in shock when he arrived at her house. What could she do but take him in? That was the easy part. How long was he going to stay? What would happen to him if he went home? Should she tell the police about the death threat, or at least persuade Harry to go and see Donald May? Surely that must be the best course of action. But what if it was all a hoax? What if her theories about the treasure were wrong? What if they came to nothing? Harry Riddles believed her; Day and Szabo thought she was a silly old woman and had said so in no uncertain terms. The other Board members: who knows?

Philbey became aware of the utter silence in the choirstalls. Looking up, she caught sight of Quick Draw's sardonic smile. The conductor raised his hand to begin the next piece. There was no option but to watch McGraw more closely from now on. She had followed his beat for long enough, both at St Maurice's and in the choral concerts up at Templeton Towers, but tonight, she saw him in a new light. As she forced herself to pay attention, battling against the mental and emotional turmoil inside, it became obvious that McGraw himself was struggling. His forehead was lined, his short hair whiter than ever. There were bags under his eyes. He had lost weight.

Had Clair's death affected the organist? The two men had never got on; each had cultivated a studied indifference towards the other. Philbey smiled to herself as she remembered the time when McGraw had learned of Clair's indisposition with some ailment or other. 'Nothing trivial, I hope.' Surely that was just a joke. Quick Draw was obviously too wrapped up in his music to harbour dark thoughts about Clair, or at least to do anything serious about them.

Then it dawned on Philbey that McGraw looked unkempt. She had never come across a man as fastidious as Quick Draw. Tonight, he looked like a scruff from top to toe. The shirt was crumpled; the bow badly tied. Buttons were undone and trousers at half-mast. She had never seen his shoes so muddy.

Father Bernard was no archaeologist. Nor was he interested in becoming one. But as the interim Head of the Order of Saint Saviour, he regarded it as his duty to carry on the work of Father William. This was the twentieth year of the dig. The work had begun within weeks of Clair's acclamation as Head back in 2002. There were many more brothers in those days, of course; and some 50 monks had cheered as the announcement had been made. There would be no cheering this time, and as likely as not, no confirmation as Head. Day and Szabo had made it perfectly clear they would do everything to shut down the Order and turn the school into a money-making business. And, if necessary, they would challenge the regulations governing the sale of assets so they could dispose of the land and set up the company that was so dear to their hearts.

The game was nearly up, despite Father William's best efforts and, most recently, the resistance by Philbey and Riddles. Father Bernard smiled to himself: 'Philbey and Riddles' – sounds like a second-rate American cop show!' What was their game? Did they stand to gain from stopping the sale? Neither had ever shown any interest in the dig, even though Philbey was the local archivist. What had she found in the library that was so important? Why were she and Riddles holding out against the inevitable?

Father Bernard got up from his prayer desk, bowed to the crucifix on the wall, opened his cell door, walked along the corridor, down the steps, and out into the school quadrangle. The short cut through the chapel was still barred to him. He resolved to ask DCI May when the police would be finished. It was an inconvenient detour to have to walk past the new buildings. That was a misnomer. You only had to look at the state of the windows and doors to see how old and tired the blocks were.

'Just like me,' Father Bernard whispered to himself. 'If only I could find what Clair was really looking for all these years.'

Hearing the clock strike the hour, he picked up his habit and strode towards the dig site in a vain attempt to arrive on time.

Diana Foster luxuriated in the shower: sheer bliss after the experiences of the last two hours. Thank goodness there had been cover for her shift! At last, she felt warm and even half human again. It was time to get out and get on. The thick towels felt good against the skin. The mug of cocoa tasted heavenly. The bed had never seemed so soft and comforting. She lay down and looked up at the ceiling. The place needed redecorating, for sure.

What a strange encounter at the old chapel! She had been frightened. The storm had been terrifying in its rage. She had been cold and wet and alone. And then – and then – the trapdoor. The sickly feeling returned. It had opened so slowly, then footsteps. Who could it be? And what the hell were they doing there?

'Dr Foster! What the …?'

'I could say the same of you!'

'You look awful. You're shivering. Here, take my waterproof. We must get you back to the school at once. If we don't, you'll start to suffer from hypothermia, and that would never do.'

'I don't think I can move.'

'Yes, you can. Here, let me help.'

'I thought you monks were not supposed to have physical contact with the opposite sex.'

'This is an emergency. I am sure God will forgive.'

Later, as Diana Foster lay snuggled up in bed, she wondered what Brother Germain had been doing at the ruin. His explanation made some sort of sense: he had taken shelter from the heavy rain while out on his run. Fair enough, but the trapdoor and the underground room – was that the truth? Had it really been a priest's hole in the sixteenth century? Anything was possible in this strange place. She determined to do more digging once she had recovered from her ordeal. In the meantime, Diana Foster curled up into the arms of her new lover and fell fast asleep.

8

Suspects And Messages, Past, Present, Future

'Come in, gentlemen. Sorry to keep you waiting. I am not a morning person; only just got up!'

Barbara Halliday ushered May and Riggs into her penthouse. The two men looked around as they entered. Riggs smiled faintly at his boss; May nodded slightly. Never had either man seen such *kitsch*.

'My late husband renovated this whole factory. He took special care over our place.'

Halliday walked over to the Steinway to look at a photograph. She caressed the gold frame.

'He was quite something was my Rod.' She paused for a moment, then turned round suddenly. 'Silly me! I was forgetting myself. Would you like a drink? Tea, coffee, something stronger?'

May cleared his throat. Riggs shook his head.

'No, too early for alcohol – at least for some people.' Halliday looked the two policemen up and down then went to the cocktail cabinet and poured herself a large whisky. 'Do take a pew.' She gestured to the large leather sofa and chairs.

'Do you play Mrs Halliday?' Riggs nodded over to the immaculately polished grand.

'Ha! Not a note! I always wanted to learn, so my Roddy bought me the Joanna. Never had time, though. Too busy doing other things!'

'I imagine you know why we are here.'

'Call me Babs, Inspector, or Barbara if you really must. Sure I can't get you anything, boys?' She sprawled across her armchair. Her tight black skirt rode up. Riggs and May studied the score on the piano. 'We've met before, haven't we, DCI May?'

May nodded. 'In connection with the murders back in 2019, including that of your husband.'

Barbara Halliday pulled out a small lace handkerchief from her sleeve and dabbed her eyes. 'Oh, my poor Roddy. My darling Roddy.'

'Yes, Barbara. That was a very difficult time for you – for everybody in Holme Hill. But that has nothing to do with our visit today.'

'No?'

'No. We need to talk to you about the murder of Father Clair.'

'Clairvoyant! The old duffer! Murder? And you think I'm a suspect?' Barbara Halliday snorted.

'Not at all. We just want to ask you – and all the other members of the Board - a few questions.'

Barbara Halliday nodded. 'Okay. Fire away, Inspector.'

'When did you last see Father William?'

'Hmmm – let's see. Board meeting before last, three months ago. It was only the second one I could get to. And I hardly knew him.'

'You were a new member?'

Barbara Halliday nodded. 'Me and Melody Grimshaw. Have you met her, Inspector?'

'She is next on our list. How did you come to be appointed, Barbara? Did you have any previous connection with the school or the order?'

'You must be joking! I can't be doing with all that religious stuff. No, it was Professor Day who persuaded me to join the Board. He was keen to have me on for my – my "expertise". Mind if I smoke?'

May and Riggs shook their heads. Barbara Halliday took out a cheroot from the silver case on the side table by her chair. They drew breath as she drew a gun from the drawer beneath. Before they could stop her, she pulled the trigger and a flame appeared from the end of the barrel. It took two attempts to light the cheroot.

'Sorry to have startled you gentlemen. It was the sort of trick that my Roddy used to play.'

Charlie Riggs wiped his forehead. 'So why you? What "expertise" are we talking about?'

'Buildings, like this one. Rod and I made a big business out of renovating old properties – and constructing new ones. I may not have much education, gentlemen, but I know my stuff. We were a partnership, my husband and me. And we were good – very good.'

'And how was your expertise going to be useful to the Order of Saint Saviour?'

'Not the brethren, Inspector, but the school. Day and Szabo were keen to get me on the Board so that I could help them with flogging off the land.'

'Tell us more.'

'I still have good contacts in the construction industry. I called in some favours and got valuations and options appraisals and lots more done – FOC – for the school.'

'FOC?'

'Free of Charge, Sergeant. It cost Day and Szabo zilch, nichts, niente. Clair wouldn't spend a penny – if you'll excuse the phrase – on anything like that and he was the only one who could give permission to use the trust funds in that way.'

'And presumably he was not prepared to do that?'

'Nope. No way. He was a stubborn old bugger, the Almighty Father. He looked down his nose at people like me. Used all these Latin phrases to put me off. Thought I wouldn't understand. Well, I did. I went to grammar school and was in the 'L' stream. L for Latin. But I never let on. I pretended to be the dumb blonde with big knockers and short skirts and a pea for a brain.'

'And the results of your friends' appraisals and valuations?'

Barbara Halliday guffawed. 'That land to the north of the school is ripe for development. It's worth millions. A lot of people would kill to get their hands on it. Believe me Inspector May.'

'Give me a drink darling! Throth and Aethel are finally asleep!'

'Get it yourself Tiggs! I've been at work all day. And what have you done?'

'Now, now, Georgie-Porgie. That doesn't sound very sisterly, does it? Gone all Detective Constable Ellis on me, have you? Anyway, why don't you call yourself Ponsonby-Ellis? Are you ashamed of the family name or something?'

'Give it a rest, Tiggy!' Georgie Ellis looked at the opened bottle of red wine. It was just too tempting. She negotiated the toys strewn across her beautiful apartment floor, grabbed a glass from the rack and poured. As an afterthought, a second glass was filled for Tiggy.

'Thanks George. I know I shouldn't, with Ambrosius inside, but one little sipette won't do any harm, will it?'

'Stop calling me George! They do that at work, and I hate it. I am either Georgie or Georgiana and you know that full well!'

'Sorry Georgie. Come and sit next to me and tell me all about your delicious murder mystery!' Tiggy patted the sofa vigorously.

'I'll sit over here, thank you very much, and you know that I can't discuss the case with anybody outside work.'

'But I'm not "anybody". I'm your beloved sister. We used to share everything. Even boyfriends. Remember?'

Georgie Ellis blushed. 'I don't want to talk about our so-called boyfriends. Never, ever, again!'

'Sorry. Come on, can't you say anything about the case? I promise I won't say a word. Anyway, who would I tell? I don't know anyone in this godawful place. Surely you can say **something** about the case, Ellis of the Yard! It's so exciting!'

'Do you really promise, Tiggs? I know you of old. Born with a silver foot in your mouth!'

'And so were you; so were you, Georgiana Lucinda Ponsonby-Ellis. And don't forget that!'

The sisters fell silent. Tiggy scrabbled for the remote and, when located, used it to turn on and channel hop until she found something on Netflix. Georgie drank her wine and thought back to the message she had received, hoping that it would not be long before she was contacted again by her mysterious informant. At least Charlie Riggs had been successful in his search of the orange folder. Someone at the *Gazette and Argus* had kept detailed records of the goings on at Templeton Towers and St David's Church. May had been right to start investigating the former vicar there. The verdict had been suicide. The Reverend Dr Paul Gordon had supposedly killed himself before he was arrested for sexual abuse against minors. The marks around his neck bore a remarkable similarity to those on William Clair. Thirty years separated those two deaths, but were they linked? Gordon was from the Order of Saint Saviour, one of the brethren, and had taught Religious Studies at Templeton Towers. There was nothing in the police files from back then about either the allegations or Gordon's death. The coroner's report was nowhere to be found. Nor was there anything about the school in all the time that Hartley CID had been in existence. It was almost too good to be true. Riggs had been about to take the file away when Georgie had noticed a small slip of paper. On it was the name of the editor of the *Gazette and Argus* and the words, all in capitals: 'They have blood on their hands. They will perish one day.'

Georgie Ellis was wondering what to do next and how to avoid talking to Tiggy when the television was turned off.

'Oh shit, George. I just remembered! This might be important. There was a phone call for you this morning from a young man. He wouldn't give his name. But he said you were to meet him tonight by the side gate to Templeton Towers. He was going to give you some information about a murder.'

'What time was I supposed to meet him?'

'Midnight, I think.'

'That's in 20 minutes!'

Barbara Halliday looked out of the penthouse window. A quarter to midnight. She took out her mobile phone and texted her message:

'It's time. We need to move.'

'More?'

'I couldn't eat another thing, Philbs. My goodness, you make a good supper!'

Pauline Philbey surveyed the scene. Despite serving Harry Riddles with double helpings and matching him for food intake, there was plenty left over. Some of the meal could be saved for later; the rest would either end up in Boris's dish or be thrown into the recycling.

'Coffee?'

'That would go down very nicely.'

'What is it, Harry?' Philbey saw the sudden change in her guest.

'I could swear I saw something – someone – moving in the garden just now.'

'You're imagining things, Harry! That note was designed to scare you – us – nothing more. You're just on edge.'

'There! There it goes again!'

Pauline Philbey turned round and looked out of the dining room window. She could see nothing but black and grey shapes.

'Time to pull the curtains, Harry. What the eye doesn't see, the heart doesn't grieve over, eh?'

Having shut out the outside world, Philbey turned back to continue the conversation with Riddles.

'Harry? Harry? Where are you?'

Pauline Philbey walked into the hallway, then the living room. He was nowhere to be seen.

'Come on Harry. Stop fooling around!'

There was a dull noise in the kitchen, then the sound of glass breaking. Pauline Philbey looked around for a weapon. She grabbed the iron doorstop. It was heavy! She tiptoed towards the door at the end of the hallway: no sound at all. There was nothing for it but to kick the door open.

'Oh my!' The sight that greeted her was not what she had expected. Harry Riddles was quivering anxiously. Behind him stood someone dressed in black, a balaclava over their head. The knife was pointed right at Riddles' throat.

'Where are they? Where are your papers? Get them now, or I will cut this man's throat!'

Philbey could not move; could not speak; could not think.

'Answer me!' The captor flexed his fingers round the knife handle then gripped it hard.

'Do something Philbs! Please!'

Philbey was unable to form words. Her arm ached from carrying the iron door stop. One wrong move and Riddles would be dead; his throat slit; blood all over her new kitchen.

Without warning, Boris appeared through the cat flap. The noise startled the balaclava, who turned to the kitchen door. Riddles seized his moment and broke free. Philbey threw the iron doorstop. It hit home. She followed this up with the frying pan, hastily grabbed from the nearby hob. Having regained his composure, Riddles joined the fray, picking up the knife from the floor and thrusting it threateningly. The assailant was now the assailed. There was no option for them but to make a run for it.

The newly formed team of Philbey and Riddles, tag wrestlers extraordinaire, pursued their erstwhile captor out of the kitchen door, down the back garden and onto the street. Despite their strong motivation to catch them and wreak revenge, fleetness of foot gave the attacker too much of an advantage.

'It's no good Philbs', Riddles gasped.

'I know.' Philbey shook her head. 'And to think I used to run marathons!'

They watched the silhouette fade into the distance. A door slammed; an engine started. Headlights pointed towards Hartley town.

'Come on. Let's go back inside'.

As they set off home, the moon came out from behind the clouds. Riddles looked at Philbey and kissed her gently on the lips.

'Have you ever been kissed by a girl?'

'Oh, that's gross'.

'But you haven't answered the question, Freddie. Have you ever been kissed by a girl?'

Freddie May folded his arms and stamped his feet. 'No, I have not. And I don't want to be either! Ever! It's a drag, all that love stuff!'

Vanessa and Camilla giggled in unison.

'Well, you have no choice, Commander May of the Yard!'

Before Freddie May could escape back to his room, the twins had surrounded him. Grabbing him by the arms, each planted a kiss on his cheeks. The more he struggled to break free, the more the girls tried to kiss him.

'Stop! Stop!'

'No. Why should we?'

'Because I hear footsteps!'

'Did someone hear us? Quick, Vanessa, get under the bed!'

'No. You get under the bed. Why is it always me?'

'Shut up, both of you. We don't want to be caught out, do we?

Freddie looked at the twins. The three of them counted the footsteps as the sound increased in volume.

'Two people!' Freddie mouthed. 'A man and a woman, I think!'

The footsteps came to a halt outside the bedroom. Freddie put a finger to his lips and an ear to the door. Floorboards creaked. Two more ears joined Commander May's.

It was difficult at first, but the three ears quickly attuned to the whispered conversation taking place on the other side of the door.

'That was wonderful.'

'It was.'

'Kiss?'

'Kiss!'

A moment of silence.

'Nobody must ever find out. It would be curtains for both of us!'

'You are silly. "Curtains for both of us". Who talks like that these days?'

'Well, I do for one!'

A second moment of silence. A rustling sound.

'Stop it! Someone might see!'

'I don't care!'

'I do! Do you want to get me fired?'

'I know. I'm sorry. This is so sudden, but I knew from the start. Love at first sight! I can't get enough of you!'

'You **must** go. Now! Someone might hear!'

Freddie looked at the twins. 'What are they doing?' He whispered.

'What do you think, silly boy! Now shush!'

The sound of two sets of footsteps gradually dimmed.

'They are walking in opposite directions. Dr Foster must be going back to her apartment at this time of night', said Freddie.

'What about the other woman?' The twins looked at each other and smirked.

Georgie Ellis had learnt her lesson, and Charlie Riggs's lesson too. Never again would she follow up on a lead without calling for backup. As the BMW Z4 raced towards Templeton Towers, she was busy bringing May and Riggs up to speed, feeling suitably virtuous in the process. It was two minutes to midnight when the three police officers checked in with each other. They had agreed to park some distance away from the supposed rendezvous point with the mysterious informant. Ellis had to run to get to the small, gated opening in the boundary wall. Riggs had told his DC to be especially careful, given his own experience only a few evenings earlier. What was it about this place?

It was cold. Georgie Ellis tightened her coat belt and shoved her hands in her pockets. No sight; no sound; no movement. Nothing. A hoax!

The clock at Templeton Towers struck the first quarter after midnight. Georgie Ellis was about to start walking back to her colleagues when she saw headlights in the distance. She stepped into the shadows. Moments later, a Mercedes drew up at the designated meeting point. Ellis was about to walk over to the vehicle when the driver pushed open the front passenger door. At the same time, the gate opened, and a tall, slim figure emerged and got into the car.

Ellis switched on her torch and strode over to the Mercedes.

'Stop. One moment! Show yourselves!'

Both driver and passenger got out of the car and walked up to Ellis. By now she had been joined by May and Riggs.

'What is the meaning of this?'

Donald May came forward and positioned himself between Ellis and the two strangers.

'I could say the same of you two: sir, madam.'

9

Hoax Or Truth?

'Do you believe them?'

'I am not sure. But given that we have no evidence to the contrary, then we'd better assume they're telling the truth – for now at least.' Donald May looked at the two monitors, switching his gaze from one to the other, wondering what the relationship between them really was.

'Shall I let them go, sir?'

'What? Oh yes, Georgie. But say we'll want to interview them again at some point – and sooner rather than later.'

Ellis left the control room as Charlie Riggs entered it.

'Coffee, boss?'

'Thanks, Charlie. It's been a long night, hasn't it?'

Riggs nodded, looking at his watch and wishing he were in bed instead of at the station at three in the morning.

'And I am not sure we are any further forward. What do you make of it all?' May pointed to the left-hand screen. The two officers watched as Ellis entered interview room one and told Andreas Day he was free to go. Day muttered something under his breath, grabbed his overcoat and stormed out. Ellis looked up at the camera.

'He was the last person I thought we would apprehend after that tip off.'

'Are you sure sir? I would have said the lady in interview room two was the surprise of the evening.' Riggs chuckled sarcastically.

'A real dark horse, that one.' May looked at the right-hand screen as Ellis entered the room where Melody Grimshaw was sitting motionless.

Grimshaw stood up, put on her gloves and hat, and walked out of the room as only a catwalk model could do.

'I wouldn't say this if Georgie were here, sir, but, wow! I could fancy her!'

'Careful Charlie. Keep thoughts like that to yourself.' May laughed. 'I know what you mean, though. I could ...'

The conversation between the two men ended abruptly as Ellis re-entered the control room.

'A quick case conference before we catch up on some sleep.' May motioned to Ellis and Riggs to sit down.

'So, Day says he was there at Melody Grimshaw's request to give her a lift home after a meeting at the school. At midnight?'

'Could have been a long meeting, sir!'

'I have been to some long school governors' meetings, Charlie, but not so long, or finishing so late!'

'This was a one-to-one, though.' Riggs replied.

'True, Georgie. And why shouldn't a member of the Board call in and see senior members of staff? It makes sense for Grimshaw to be meeting Szabo and Foster, especially if she is the link governor for educational psychology.'

'What do we know about Day?'

'We have already interviewed him in connection with Clair's death. He has a cast iron alibi for the time of the murder, though, as is very clear, he stands to gain from a change of leadership of the Order.'

'That's on the assumption the remaining members all vote in favour of selling the land for development. Which they didn't do at the meeting the day after Clair's death. Sorry to interrupt, Charlie. Do continue.'

'That's quite alright, sir. I had just about finished anyway. The rest is all background: ex-vice-chancellor of Hartley University; well-known and respected locally, though he has appeared in *Private Eye* more than once.'

'Oh really?'

'Just the usual. Excessive pay and perks. Including a grace-and-favour house. All while he was getting rid of staff left, right, and centre.'

'Nothing on record?' Georgie Ellis asked.

'Nope. Apart from speeding tickets. And he has received death threats in the past. Nothing came of them. The assumption was that it was disgruntled ex-colleagues.'

'And his links with Templeton Towers?'

'He was once a parent governor; had a child at the school many years ago. He came back on the Board as Chair not long before Szabo was appointed. Day was on the interview panel.'

'And he was just "picking up" Miss Grimshaw?'

'She phoned him; couldn't get a taxi. Melody Grimshaw doesn't drive, and he was the first person she thought of to come and get her.'

May grimaced. 'A maiden in distress and the older, doting man comes running, perhaps?'

Riggs and Ellis shrugged.

'Why didn't one of the staff give her a lift?'

'They couldn't be spared or weren't available at that time of night. Staffing is quite tight up there, according to Day.'

May nodded. 'I can vouch for that, Charlie. They are thinner on the ground than they should be, given what Freddie has told me. Especially when it comes to pastoral care. Perhaps they won't do as well at the next Ofsted.'

'Miss Grimshaw is a recent addition to the Board, apparently, and she was appointed against Father William's wishes. She was everything that Clair detested in a woman.'

'Who says?' Ellis bristled.

'Melody Grimshaw. She told me that Clair made it very clear she was a sinner of the highest order.' Riggs tried to hide a smirk.

'Because of her background?' May added.

'Yes, sir. Immoral earnings from parading around in next-to-nothing.'

'Presumably men like Clair have a very "traditional" view of how women should behave!' Ellis huffed.

May laughed. 'I fear so, Georgie, judging by the time I met him. He was certainly very "polite" and deferential to Caz – in an old-fashioned way – when she visited the school before Freddie started. As well as excluding her from the "real" discussions; they were all meant to be "man-to-man", much to my wife's disgust, as you can imagine!'

Ellis and Riggs stayed silent.

'How did Miss Grimshaw get onto the Board?' May asked.

'Nominated by Day and Szabo.'

May raised his eyebrows. 'Really?'

Riggs nodded. 'Really.'

'Any experience or knowledge of education, especially of gifted and talented children.'

'Very little is known about her past, sir, and she didn't give much away in the interview just now. She is very wealthy, thanks to her modelling career.'

'And why should someone like Melody Grimshaw come to live in Hartleydale?'

Riggs shrugged.

'Find out more about her Charlie.' May pointed at Riggs as he spoke. 'Before we interview her again.'

'Did either of them say why they were meeting at the back entrance to the school?'

'More convenient, according to Day.' Ellis replied.

'Really, Georgie? It would be far easier for him to pick Grimshaw up from the front entrance. Going round the back would be a real detour. Unless one or other did not want to be seen.'

'Indeed, sir. We still have the issue of the anonymous tip-off that Georgie got.' Riggs looked at Ellis. 'Was that a hoax? Was it coincidence that Day and Grimshaw met up just as we were waiting? Was the real informant frightened off because of Day and Grimshaw?'

'Or because they realized that Georgie wasn't on her own?' May added. 'As I said: not much further forward. There is certainly more to Melody Grimshaw than meets the eye.'

Ellis grimaced as Riggs laughed.

'Anyway, colleagues, enough. Let's get some sleep. I must brief Samson later today.'

The three officers got up, walked out of the control room and down the corridor. As they arrived at their base room, the phone rang: the reception desk. Two old people – a woman and a man in a state of some agitation – were waiting to see DCI May about a vicious attack.

'No rest for the wicked.' May sighed. 'Best all stay while we interview these two. Let's hope we get further than we did with Day and Grimshaw.

'We should get some sleep. I'm going back to my room.'
'Are you sure?'
Freddie May nodded at the twins. 'Yes, I'm sure. I doubt there will be any more action this evening.'
'OK.' Vanessa and Camilla nodded in disappointment. 'Do you think our plan is working.'
Freddie May laughed. 'I think so. We have got everybody wondering, anyway, haven't we?'
The twins looked at each other, then smiled and nodded again.
Freddie May got up and took one last look out of the twins' bedroom window. 'O my goodness. Look what's out there!'

Catherine May heard the familiar sound of the Volvo. She could picture the car turning into the drive, then coming to a halt in front of the garage door. She breathed a sigh of relief as Donald May walked into the kitchen, threw his keys down on the breakfast table, sat down and buried his head in his hand.
'A rough night then?'
'Yup. And how!'
'Want to talk about it Don?'
May rubbed his eyes. 'Any chance of something to eat?'
'Bacon and eggs?'
May nodded.
'Feed me first and then I'll fill you in.'
Caz smiled and nodded. As she cooked breakfast he stood in the kitchen doorway and watched.
'What a night! And none of it was what I was expecting.'
'Mushrooms?'

'Why not? Let's go round the house.'

'What were you expecting?' Caz carefully loaded her husband's plate with the contents of the frying pan. Toast popped up; the kettle whistled.

'To apprehend a criminal after a tip off that Georgie received. All we found was a slightly strange encounter between the Chair and one of the governors. We interviewed them back at the station, but there was nothing to report. We let them go. Day was not best pleased. I suspect he will be complaining to Samson.'

'Oh dear. Your favourite policewoman!' Caz snorted.

'Don't. The interfering …'

'Andreas Day was the person you caught? What was he doing at Templeton Towers at that time of night?'

'Picking up Melody Grimshaw.'

'Melody who?'

'The former super model. Except she just went by the name "Melody" in those days.'

'Never heard of her.'

'I have. Melody was a regular on Page Three. Then she graduated to super model status. She was a rival to Kate Moss at one stage. She's still quite something. Gorgeous figure; immaculately dressed.'

'Looks to die for?'

He nodded. 'Looks to die for.'

'Then what?'

He shook his head. 'Not clear. Made her money, I assume. "Retired" back to Hartley. At the tender age of 43.'

'What was she doing at the school?'

'A meeting with Diana Foster.'

'Freddie has a lot of time for her. "Dr Foster from Gloucester". She understands him.'

He nodded. 'She should. She's supposed to be the expert in high-functioning autism!'

'Calm down, Don. More tea?'

'Sorry Caz. Yes please.'

'Why was Day picking her up? Is he her sugar daddy?'

'I wonder. Georgie thinks so. She has quite a nose for these things. Day is a widower. And Melody is very attractive.'

'I get the picture. She obviously made an impression on you! 'What about the tip off?'

'Well, if it's a hoax, it's a hell of a coincidence that at the time and place where Georgie was told to be, Day and Grimshaw meet up. It's as if we were meant to discover them. Perhaps there is more to those two than meets the eye, especially in Melody's case …'

'Stop it, Don!' Caz picked up the *Hartley Gazette and Argus* and hit her husband hard over the head with it.

'Ow. Assaulting a police officer is a serious office!'

'Is that all you have to tell me?'

May shook his head. 'Stop hitting me and I will reveal all.'

'As long as it doesn't involve Miss Melody.'

'No such luck! Pauline Philbey and Harry Riddles. That's who.'

'I know her. She's the local archivist. Writes a column in the local paper and gives talks at the town hall. I've been to them. I even took Freddie once. Very interesting stuff. She knows everything about everything when it comes to the history of this place.'

'She was very helpful on a previous murder case.'

'And is she helping you with your enquiries this time?'

May shook his head. 'No, she's a victim. An attempted burglary gone wrong.'

'And who is Harry Riddles?'

'He's the last of the line.'

Caz poured more tea for them both, then bit off a mouthful of toast. 'The last riddle?'

'Give over. This is serious stuff! His family owned the Riddles factory in Holme Hill. He tried to keep it going. It was hard for old-style textile companies in the 1970s and 1980s. He went bankrupt eventually. Had to sell the family home and everything. Lives in a council house now, apparently.'

'And is Riddles Philbey's boyfriend?'

'I very much doubt it. Though he was staying with her at the time of the attack. And it was a very vicious one. They are lucky to be alive. The robber was looking for documents, according to Philbey.'

'And did the man get them?'

'No, but why do you say it was a man?'

'I just assumed … but no, I shouldn't have done that, should I?'

'Nope. But I'll forgive you, this time!' Donald May laughed.

'So, Riddles is not Philbey's "love interest", but he was living at her house?'

'He had received a death threat. He turned to her; she decided that it would be better if they stuck together. Interestingly, they are both governors at the school; and they were the two who voted against the plan to sell off a large plot of land to the north of Templeton Towers.'

'Why?'

'Pauline thinks that there is buried treasure there, and nothing should be done until her theory has been tested. All to do with Sir Templeton Taylor and his trips to the Holy Land in the nineteenth century, apparently.'

'You'll be telling me that they think the Grail is there next!'

Don snorted. 'Philbey doesn't know what the treasure is. Just that it exists.'

'Her evidence?'

'Documents she unearthed when she was cataloguing and digitising Templeton Taylor's archives; two maps. Here's a photocopy.'

Caz took the two pages from her husband.

As May shook his head in frustration, the house phone rang.

'Don't worry Don. I'll get it. You get some sleep.'

He took his mug of tea into the living room and flopped down on the sofa. He was just about to nod off when his wife returned.

'Don! Wake up Don! It's Mr Szabo on the phone. Freddie's gone missing!'

10

Anticipated Revelations

It was dark. Pitch black. Freddie May reminded himself where the phrase 'pitch black' came from. He closed his eyes and read out the words in front of him: 'Pitch is a black, viscous, and slightly elastic material that is really like tar. Pitch and tar are words that are often used interchangeably, although pitch is more viscous and solid than tar. The phrase "pitch black" may date back to Homer's *Iliad* around 850 BC, if not earlier.' Freddie opened his eyes. He determined to take more of an interest in Classics lessons from now on.

Surely Vanilla 1 and Vanilla 2 would have raised the alarm by now? He smiled to himself knowing how much the twins hated being called Vanilla and a number. He had stopped doing it. Out loud, that is; inside, they were 1 and 2 through and through. After all, they were really a single person, were they not, even though he could now tell which was which? Every time!

'There must be some way out. Surely! What would my father do?'

Freddie saw a chink of light in the distance. Then it faded away. Was his mind – or his eyesight – playing tricks again? He coughed and sneezed. The dust and the decay made him want to retch. The musky smell reminded him of strong vinegar; and sweat.

Freddie kept calm by going over the events of the previous few hours. He and the Vanillas had seen a ghostly apparition in the chapel. It had glided from one window to another: up and down; up and down. Then, just as quickly as the luminescent figure had appeared, it disappeared; vanished into thin air. Vanessa had wanted to go and investigate; Camilla thought it best to report the incident to Mr Szabo and Dr Foster.

'But what will we say, Cam? We won't be taken seriously!'

'Don't be daft Van, of course we will. The teachers know that students like us don't make things up!'

'Yes, we do!'

'No, we don't!'

'Stop it you two. I will go and investigate, then report back!'

Freddie had felt manly as he said it. He never thought Vanessa and Camilla would agree to his audacious proposal. To his surprise, the twins had nodded enthusiastically. There had been nothing for it but to 'put a brave face on it', as Dad was always saying, and investigate.

It was easy enough to creep along the dormitory corridor undetected. He and the twins had done it frequently; this was the first time he had been alone, though. The wind was howling and the rain pouring; not bringing an overcoat had been a mistake. The chapel had soon been reached. The door was unlocked, as always. Father Clair had regularly made a point of telling the students they were welcome in God's house at any time of day or night. Every problem could be brought to the Almighty. He would listen and, if a prayer were directed genuinely and fully, the Lord would answer.

The huge oak door was hard to push open. Freddie had worried the creaks and groans of the hinges would give him away, but nobody came. He had gone right through into the chapel and looked up at the high altar. Should he pray for help, even though he didn't believe any of the Christianity stuff? For a second he had seen William Clair in all his finery, but it had been a fleeting illusion. Father was not there; how could he be?

The police cordon had been removed and the chapel was back to before the murder. Freddie had turned back towards the screen dividing chapel and ante chapel. The gold pipes of the organ had glinted in the candlelight. That's where the figure must have been! It had taken him a while to find how to get up to the organ loft, but he had managed it eventually; and found - nothing. If a presence – ghostly or otherwise – had been on that organ screen – then it was long gone.

Freddie relaxed, relieved not to be overpowered by some dark, malevolent spirit. The clock had struck midnight. It would look bad if he returned to the girls with nothing to report. There must be some evidence to show what had been going on!

All he could find was an open door on the far side of the organ console. He inched across the bench where Quick Draw sat and played and then looked inside. He had gipped as a musty, sweet smell accosted his nostrils. It was like talcum powder, but much, much stronger. Then footsteps close by; the only option had been to hide inside the organ.

And that was where he now was. Big problem! Whoever had come up the organ loft steps locked the door behind which Freddie had been hiding, then proceeded to play the instrument – softly at first, then louder and louder until he thought his ears would burst. Suddenly, the sound of silence. Then more steps into the distance, a door shut, and nothing.

It had to be Quick Draw. But why play the organ – and so loudly – this late at night? Had it been him pacing up and down earlier? And what was the horrid smell?

'There must be some way out, surely!' Freddie banged his fist on the side of the organ case in frustration. As he did so, a panel sprang open to reveal a cubby hole. Inside was the last thing he would have expected.

Harry Riddles was more relaxed than he had been for a whole week. He was so glad to have gone to the police. It was a pity they had not done it sooner. But Pauline had thought better of it, and you didn't argue with her when she had decided! Why had she been so reluctant to talk to DCI May? Was it her previous encounter with the police back in 2019? No matter: everything was now out in the open. And their concerns and fears had been taken seriously. So much so they were now under police protection in a 'safe house' on the far side of Hartley.

'Whoever attacked you, and whatever it is that they want, they will strike again, that is for certain.' Donald May had been adamant they should not return to Philbey's house – or Riddles' - until their safety and security could be guaranteed. As well as moving them, the DCI had ordered regular surveillance of both homes and the safe house.

'Well, Philbs, we're getting a lot more excitement than I bargained for in my retirement; me being 85 and all!'

Pauline Philbey laughed. She drank a coffee and surveyed the small bungalow which now counted as home for her and Harry Riddles. Boris was less convinced of the need to move, especially since he was not to go outdoors for fear of getting lost in a strange part of Hartleydale. As if to reclaim his position in the household, Boris insisted on sitting on Philbey's lap whenever and wherever she sat down. Even Riddles was not spared the treatment.

'That we are Hal! I never expected being a member of the Templeton Board would be this interesting!' Boris purred as Philbey stroked him.

'Is that why we are being targeted? Is it to do with the maps you said you had found? Or is it just plain greed, with Szabo and Day wanting us out of the way so they can make money out of the land sale?'

'I think it's all those things. Those two want the land sold. They need the money for the school and Babs Halliday will help them to get it. My intervention prevents them from parcelling off the estate, at least for now. On the other hand, if my theory is correct, there are riches beyond compare somewhere in those woods to the north of Templeton Towers.'

'Is that why Father William was so keen on that archaeological dig all these years?'

Philbey nodded. 'I believe so. Except he didn't know where to look, or even what he was looking for. The documents I discovered in the archive give a clear indication of location; I know it.'

'You're sure of your facts now, then?'

Philbey nodded. 'All I need to do now is listen to you telling me the truth, the whole truth, and nothing but the truth.'

'Can I get you anything else? We close in 15 minutes.'

Victoria Perry looked at her watch. 'I'll have another latte, thank you.'

The waitress smiled. 'Expecting someone else?'

Perry nodded. 'But it doesn't look like they are going to show up.'

'Don't I know you?'

'Maybe. Why do you say that?'

'I have seen you before! The waitress put her hands on her hips. 'I know. You write for the *Gazette and Argus*. I recognize you from your picture. I've watched you on regional television and I love your radio show.'

Perry smiled and looked at her watch again. 'I am going to need that latte soon if you're closing.'

'Oh, sorry. Yes, of course. I won't be a minute!'

As the waitress scuttled off, Perry looked round the *Speckled Teapot*. Having never been inside the café before, here she was on her second visit within a week. Meeting Donald May had been productive in more ways than one. At the present rate of progress, a coffee with Lisa Watson was unlikely to be as good, assuming it was going to happen at all. The rendezvous had been scheduled – at Watson's request - for 4.00pm. It was now 4.45. There had been an urgency about the phone call that made Perry agree to meet as soon as possible; that and the fact that Watson had promised vital information about the murder at Templeton Towers. Could she be sure it was Lisa Watson anyway? She had never met Janos Szabo's PA. The person had sounded ultra-efficient, no-nonsense, very much in control. Surprising then, that they were late. Someone like Lisa Watson would always be on time.

Victoria Perry looked at her watch again. Five minutes to closing.

The door opened.

'I'm sorry. So sorry. I am never late for anything! But I couldn't get away. I just hope you think what I am going to tell you was worth the wait!'

'Any news?'

Georgie Ellis shook her head.

'It must be awful when your child goes missing. Poor May and his wife!'

'I know, Tiggy. He can't have slept for the last 24 hours.'

'Is that how long Freddie has been missing?'

'Not far off. One of his friends raised the alarm when he was not in his room yesterday morning.'

'A fellow student, presumably?' Tiggy took a large bite out of a shiny red-green apple and chewed it noisily.

'Yes. A girl called Camilla. She is another of the gifted and talented up at Templeton Towers. They are all geniuses. Freddie May certainly is, though he is a bit odd, to say the least.'

'You've met him, then?'

'A few times, yes. He has the most phenomenal memory and an ability to draw conclusions from a vast range of information. Apart from a lack of social skills, he would make a great detective one day!'

'Like his father?'

Georgie Ellis laughed. 'They are very different. Donald is much better with people.'

'How is he with you, Georgie?'

'What do you mean Tiggs?'

'Well, since Detective Sergeant Trubshaw left, I just wondered …'

'How could you say something like that when the poor man is wondering where his son might be or even if he is still alive?'

'I'm sorry Georgie. You're right. I would be worried sick if anything happened to Throth or Aethel. Talking of which, I can feel Amb starting to move. The kick inside, eh?'

'I wouldn't know about that, would I?'

'I always thought you would go for husband and kids after we left Roedean. But becoming a copper, Georgie – what were you thinking?'

'O shut up! It's none of your business. You stick to your life, and I'll stick to mine, Tiggy. I need to get ready for tomorrow.'

'Do you think I would make a good copper, Georgie?'

'You? You're the last person I would have on an investigative team! No disrespect, Tiggs, but what the hell? You in CID?'

'Don't mock me! I think I would be good at it.'

'Huh. It's hard work, Tiggy. *Very* hard work. Lots of blood, sweat, toil and tears.'

'I know. I know. I could do that! And I have ideas.'

'Ideas? About what?'

'About your case?'

'Don't be stupid Tiggs! How could you have "ideas" about Father William's murder?'

'You never take me seriously. Well, I tell you now. You are looking in the wrong places. I know. Just you mark my words!'

'Come on, spit it out Harry. If we are in this together, then we need to be honest with each other.'

'I still don't understand what you mean Philbs.'

'How long have we known each other?'

Philbey watched Riddles put down his coffee cup and look back at her.

'You know full well. We were at school together so, what, 60 years?'

'At least 60 years, Hal. And you should know better than to lie to me.'

'But I haven't been lying to you!'

'Well, you have not told me the whole truth.'

'I have no idea what you are talking about Philbs. Are you barking mad?'

Philbey went over to the window of the safe house. It was getting dark. Would they be secure? Would there be any more attempts on their lives? Before she knew it, Harry had put his arms on her shoulders and turned her around. He tried to kiss her on the lips.

'Stop trying to soft-soap me. I know what you have been up to.' Boris meowed, looking up at the arguing couple.

Riddles sat back down. 'Why do you keep saying things like that?'

'Because you and I are in danger. And we need to come clean, with each other and with the police!'

Riddles looked down at his feet.

'Very well. Alright. I was involved in the property deal. Or at least I was going to be involved.'

'I knew it! I knew you had to be involved somehow. Come on, tell me everything!'

Riddles ran his hand anxiously through his hair, cleared his throat and then finally looked Philbey in the eye.

'It was about a year ago. Father William asked me to stay behind after a Board meeting. He said Day and Szabo were plotting against him; wanting to disturb everything that the Order of Saint Saviour stood for. That they were in league with Barbara Halliday and were planning a major property development that would make them all very rich – and save the school from bankruptcy in the process.'

'Nothing you say surprises me – so far. What else?'

'Well, William – Father Clair – asked me to make a counter bid.'

'What does that mean Harry?'

'I know you are cross with me when you call me Harry and not Hal.'

'Should I be cross with you Harry?'

'I wish you'd go back to calling me Hal.'

'I'll call you what I like. Now tell me the rest of the story!'

'A counter bid is where I put together a financial package to buy the land so that Day and Halliday and Szabo can't develop it.'

'So, the land would have lain fallow?'

Riddles nodded.

'And the three property developers would not be able to do anything about it?'

Riddles shook his head.

'And where were you going to get this money from?'

Riddles put his head in his hands.

'Harry – I'm waiting.'

Riddles looked up at the ceiling.

'From the treasure of Templeton Towers, that's where.'

John Sebastian McGraw surveyed the scene and smiled. The streetlights were on; houses and shops and factories and hospitals were illuminated across Hartleydale. The 20.04 Northern Fail train into Hartley Central from Holme Hill was late. Two minutes late. McGraw tut-tutted to himself. It would not do. It would not do at all. He flicked through the dog-eared pages of the timetable. Why was the EMU not on time? The other trains were, so why not that one?

McGraw looked at his pocket watch. He was already late for the lesson. Would another five minutes matter while he re-ran the last part of the new timetable? No, that would not do either. The whole thing would have to be re-run. And that would take 90 minutes. There was nothing more to be done but switch off the model railway and hurry towards the chapel. McGraw took one last look at his layout. He could not put his finger on it, but something was out of place. Everything would need to be checked.

The problems with the timetable were still in McGraw's mind as he ascended the organ loft stairs. A note had been pinned to the door.

'Sorry. Couldn't wait. Till next time. M.'

McGraw screwed up the paper and put the ball into his pocket. No organ lesson for her tonight. And he was rather looking forward to it. She was such a quick learner, and so musical! Should he go back and play with the model railway some more or, now that he was in the chapel, was it best to stay – for a little while at least – and practise for his upcoming recital?

He unlocked the loft door and entered. The music was all over the place. Why did students leave it in such a mess? Who had been playing most recently? The scores had all been neatly arranged when McGraw himself had last been there. He had seen to that. Alphabetical by composer then by title of composition.

He switched on the instrument and waited for the bellows to fill with wind. Drawing the requisite stops for a 'full organ' effect, he played a grand chord of C major. Except there was nothing grand about the sound; nothing at all. He changed the stops and tried again. The noise was just as ugly as before. What on earth?

McGraw slid off the bench and unlocked the door to the inside of the instrument. He switched on his torch and surveyed the scene. No wonder the organ sounded so horrible. The bellows were not rising as they should. How could they when a body was lying on top of them?

'Are you sure you want to stay? Wouldn't you be better at home?'

Freddie May shook his head vigorously.

Donald May looked at his wife.

Caz put her arm around her son. 'It's alright Freddie. I believe you.'

'So do I Freddie. There must be an explanation for what happened.'

The boy looked at his parents in turn. 'So, you don't think I'm lying when I said there was a golden head in that cubby hole in the organ?'

Donald May shook his head. 'No, I don't. But someone must have moved it while you were asleep on the bellows. It's a good job that Dr McGraw here thought to look inside the organ when he did. We were so worried about you!'

'I'm fine! You've no need to hug me. You know I don't like being touched!'

'Leave him be, Caz. He'll be OK, I'm sure. Dr Foster will keep an eye on him and that girl he talks about is bound to look after him.' May winked at his wife.

'I hope so, Don. I really do!'

They watched as Freddie stomped down the organ loft stairs and out of the chapel. Diana Foster nodded and went after him. Catherine May followed.

That left just Georgie Ellis, Donald May, and McGraw.

'Do you mind if we ask you some more questions, Mr McGraw?'

'Dr McGraw, please. I have a Mus Doc from Hartley University. Honorary, of course, but valid nonetheless.'

'Of course. Sorry, Dr McGraw.' Ellis beckoned the organist to sit down on the choir pews in the loft. May remained standing.

'Who has access to this organ loft?'

'A good question! Far too many people for my liking. It is only supposed to be me and the Head of the Order. Others must sign for a key at the reception if they wish to have access to practise; and only those that have my or the Reverend Father's permission will be allowed to take it.'

'So, three keys, in theory?'

'In theory. But I am sure other keys have been made. There are too many occasions when I have got up here and things have been disturbed. Music not in its proper place. Stops left out when they should have been pushed in. That sort of thing. Like this evening, for instance.' McGraw pointed towards the organ console and the mess of music surrounding it.

May joined in the questioning. 'And what about access to the inside of the organ?'

McGraw grunted. 'There is only one key and that is kept in a secret place known only to me and the organ builder who maintains the instrument.'

'And where is that sir?'

McGraw reddened almost imperceptibly, feigned a cough, then turned to the organ console. He pulled out the lowest positioned stop on the right-hand side of the keyboards. As he did so, a drawer clicked open. Inside was a small bottle of whisky and a key. McGraw pointed. 'There you have it, Inspector. But the mechanism only works if you turn it in a particular way. Nobody else is supposed to know how to operate it.'

'Freddie says that someone came and played the organ while he was hiding inside. Then they locked the door when they went off. Was that you, sir?'

McGraw laughed. 'It was not, I can assure you. I was busy with my timetable, Inspector.'

'Timetable, sir?' Ellis looked quizzically at McGraw.

'I run a detailed, comprehensive, historically accurate timetable on my model railway, Constable. Nothing, and nobody, disturbs me once I have started.'

'Of course, Dr McGraw. Who else could it be, then?'

'I haven't the faintest idea.' McGraw drew out his pocket watch and tutted. 'I really must be going. Are there any more questions for me?'

'Just one, sir. What about the cubby hole that Freddie opened by accident?'

'I never knew it existed. And I have no idea what it could be for.'

'And the golden head?'

McGraw broke into hysterical laughter. 'Forgive me, Inspector, I know Freddie is your son – and a very talented lad he is – but I am sure that the vision of a golden head is a figment of an overactive imagination fuelled by hunger, cold and fear.'

May nodded. 'Thank you for your co-operation, Dr McGraw.'

'I am going now. If I am late for my evening duty again, Father Bernard will kill me.'

Victoria Perry had warmed to Lisa Watson, especially after their conversation in the *Speckled Teapot*. Szabo's PA had been unusually forthcoming about life and work at Templeton Towers and the heated debates in the Board meetings. Watson had put together a dossier of recent discussions about selling - or not selling – land. What was so important about the woods to the north of the school? And why was the archaeological dig so precious to Father Clair and, according to Lisa, his successor, Father Bernard?

Why had Lisa Watson confided in her, a humble country bumpkin reporter, rather than go to the police? Watson had said she wanted no fuss and couldn't be certain that anything illegal was happening. She just wasn't happy with all the plotting and planning over the land. Perry had said she understood and promised absolute anonymity and secrecy, just as May had promised first refusal on any breaks or leads in the case. But Don had yet to give her anything, and Watson's information – while helpful – was already public domain stuff, though neatly summarized in the dossier. The PA was worth cultivating nevertheless, and a further coffee at the *Speckled Teapot* had been organised for the following week.

Perry put Watson's documents away then pulled out her copy of the *Gazette and Argus* folder she had given to Donald May. It was a different world in the 1970s. So much had changed. What had happened - or might have happened – would not be tolerated now. If the perpetrators of any historic sex abuse crimes were still alive, they would have a case to answer, and prosecution was much more likely. Or had someone taken the law into their own hands and done away with Clair because he had got away with it all these years? If so, why now? What had motivated the murderer to seek revenge on a man well into his 80s with presumably not many more years to live? Except nothing had ever been proven. Could there be smoke without fire? Would she have done the same if her child had been sexually molested? What would Don say? He had a son, after all. And at the same school.

Perry went through the dossier one more time: pictures, notes, cuttings. All pointed to misdemeanours at the school involving staff and students – all boys in those days – but nothing ever proven. She made a note of the names that kept coming up in the documents. One stood out time and again.

Nicholas le Grand.

Georgie Ellis had taken an instant dislike to Melody Grimshaw; right from the moment when the former super model had got out of Andreas Day's Mercedes. And now she was meeting her again, for a follow-up interview. What a pity that Donald May was not in charge on this occasion rather than Riggs. What was it about men and curvaceous blondes like Grimshaw? Why did Charlie have to drool over her so?

Melody's house was just as Ellis had expected it to be, right down to the miniature poodle with diamante collar. Everything was 'so boutique', as Tiggy would say. Clothes by Catherine Walker; décor by – who knew or cared?

The interviewee had eyes only for Riggs. Ellis contented herself with listening and taking notes.

'It's very good of you to see us again so soon, Miss Grimshaw.'

'Oh please, Sergeant, do call me Melody. All my friends do.'

Riggs blushed every time Grimshaw looked at him, or so it seemed to Ellis.

'You have been a member of the Board at Templeton Towers for how long, Miss – Melody?'

'Less than a year, Sergeant. Hartley is my home now, and I want to play my part in the community. What better way to do that than to support the education of gifted and talented young people?'

Ellis almost believed the sentiment behind the eye fluttering.

'And why Templeton Towers in particular?'

'Why not, Sergeant? It is a very special place. Andreas didn't have to do much to persuade me to join the Board.'

'Professor Day and you know each other well?'

'We do.' The super model laughed. 'I got an honorary degree from Hartley University last year. I deserved it, of course.'

Ellis's pencil nearly broke.

'And just to confirm what you said to us at the station, Melody. You were visiting Mr Szabo and Dr Foster, you couldn't get a taxi home, nobody from the school was available to give you a lift, so you phoned Professor Day. Is that correct?'

Melody nodded. 'And if you wondered why it was so late, it was the only time I had spare and Mr Szabo and Dr Foster were free. Every minute of the day is accounted for at that school. I couldn't work like that.'

'And your reason for visiting?'

'Was to discuss the scholarship that I want to endow.'

'That's a wonderful thing to do Melody. Why?'

'It's in memory of my grandfather. I never knew him. He died in his early 20s in the Second World War. He was a fighter pilot. I just wanted to commemorate his bravery. I am the last of the line now.'

'But – forgive me for saying so, Melody – you could have children of your own.'

For the first time, Ellis had sympathy for the super model. The façade dropped, the expression was genuine, and the tears were real.

'Good of you to say so, Sergeant Riggs, but no, I cannot have children. There is no possibility of that. My children are the ones studying at Templeton Towers.'

11

Can Anybody Be Trusted?

'Are you sure you're alright, Freddie?'

'Stop fussing, you two! I'm fine, now I have had a good night's sleep. And get your hands off me!'

'We were worried about you, weren't we, Cam?'

'Yup. You bet, Van!'

'Do you have to talk like that?'

'We like putting on different voices and ways of speaking.'

'Well stop it. Just act normal!'

'You mean normally.'

'Alright. Alright. Don't you want to know what happened?'

'Sorry, Fred. Of course.'

'I found a golden head in a cubby hole inside the organ.'

Vanessa and Camilla looked at each other.

'Would I lie to you?'

'Is that the "Baphomet" thing you told us about?'

Freddie May nodded. 'I think that's it. And they keep it there ready for when they have their dark rituals!'

'Who is "they", Fred?'

'The brothers, of course. I think they are the centre of a secret society – nothing to do with Christianity – but certainly linked with the Templars and their rites.'

Vanessa and Camilla looked at each other.

'Are you serious?'

'I am. What better place to keep it. Convenient, wouldn't you say?'

'You mean the ceremonies go on in the chapel?'

Freddie nodded.

'I think that's what all these ghostly apparitions are about. Late night ceremonies in the chapel.'

'And where does McGraw fit in?' Was it him who came up and played the organ, then locked you inside?'

'No, I doubt it.'

'Why?'

'Because whoever played the organ while I was inside the instrument was nothing like as good a performer as McGraw. I should know. I have listened to him carefully since he started teaching me. He never makes mistakes, whereas this person was all over the place – wrong notes and everything.'

'Perhaps McGraw was pretending to play badly so that people would think it was someone else.'

'Who was he trying to fool? No, I think it was the other way round, and this other person was attempting to be McGraw.'

'That makes sense.' Vanessa and Camilla nodded in tandem.

'There is one sure way of finding out what goes on in that organ loft, especially when I was up there.'

'How's that Fred?' Vanessa made to touch Freddie May on the arm, but he quickly recoiled.

'That camera that Quick Draw uses to see the choir and everything else that is going on in the chapel.'

'What about it?' Camilla asked.

'It is recording all the time. I worked that out while I was in the loft. The cabling from it goes down into the organ case and into the school's network. Somebody can observe what is happening in the chapel whenever they wish.'

Freddie, Vanessa, and Camilla looked at each other.

'And we need to find out who it is.'

***

Melody Grimshaw was tired. There was a mountain of fan mail to deal with and she could not face replying to all the letters; it would take the whole morning to sort. She needed a good PA to sort it all out. Perhaps Lisa Watson could help. It was time she befriended the school secretary anyway. Secretaries were always the power behind the throne.

Melody lit a cheroot, her favourite brand. How thoughtful of her lover to buy them! She would have to return the compliment. What did they most like in this world? They would go on a long holiday together – Melody's treat – once all this business at Templeton Towers was over and done with.

She switched on her laptop, logged on to the school's intranet, and fast forwarded through the last few days' CCTV footage before pressing the delete button, then opened her desk drawer, and took out a piece of paper, looked at the names on the list and circled the next one to be dealt with.

'Do you believe him, sir?'

'I do, Charlie. Freddie would never lie.'

'Sir?'

'He has autism or– to be more politically correct – he is neuro-diverse. One of the features of that is telling the truth. He has this very strong sense of right and wrong and would never keep something to himself. My son is the proverbial "open book". What he said he saw, he will have seen, and remembered accurately. That is another thing about being on the spectrum – having an incredible memory.'

'I'll vouch for that, sir. I have only met your son a couple of times, but he remembered all sorts of things about me, including from when I was in uniform.' Georgie Ellis reddened slightly as she spoke.

'Could Freddie – your son – have hallucinated? He was in there for a long time, no food or water. He must have been frightened.'

May laughed. 'I don't think so, Charlie. He doesn't seem to suffer from anxiety, and he has incredible powers of concentration and endurance.'

'What about Quick Draw?'

'Excuse me?' May laughed.

'Quick Draw McGraw. An American cartoon character.' Ellis replied. 'That's what all the students call him.'

'He's an odd ball. With his fascination with model railways and his secret compartment on the organ.'

'Don't knock it, Charlie. My son is – or was – an avid model railway enthusiast.'

'Sorry, sir. But I think McGraw knows a lot more than he is letting on. That organ loft is an excellent vantage point. And a place where the poisoned incense could have been let loose perhaps?'

'Good point, Charlie. Have forensics been up there?'

Ellis nodded. 'Nothing so far sir.'

'What do we know about McGraw?'

Ellis opened her notepad and began to read from it. 'A brilliant musician. Been at the school since the early 2000s. A loner. No partner. Devoted to his music. Also plays at the local church and conducts the choral society there.'

'Freddie speaks highly of him, despite the man's eccentricities. But then just about everybody at Templeton Towers is eccentric. That's why it's so special – and so good at getting results out of children with high-functioning autism. The place has already done wonders for Fred. McGraw is even teaching him the organ!'

'I didn't know your son was a musician, sir.'

'He wasn't, really, Georgie, until McGraw got hold of him during August when they had the transition school. He discovered that Freddie had perfect pitch amongst other things!'

'Impressive, I'm sure! We should try and find out more about key holders to the organ loft, sir.'

'Good idea Charlie; add it to the 'to do' list when you are back at Templeton Towers.'

'Could it have been McGraw who put the golden head in the cubby hole, and then removed it for some reason while Freddie was asleep on the bellows? Is it used for some ritual or other, to do with the Templars?'

'He's the obvious person, Georgie, perhaps too obvious. Get forensics to do a full sweep.'

'Yes, sir. 'Ellis got up from the conference table, went to the murder wall, added a few notes about the recent incident then returned to her seat. She waved to a WPC in the general office to bring coffee.

May, Riggs, and Ellis looked at the wall.

'Why do we think William Clair was murdered? Georgie?'

'We have several possibilities. The obvious one relates to the land. Clair was in the way. He would never agree to the disposal of so much of the estate – all those acres to the north of Templeton Towers. Szabo, Day, Grimshaw, Halliday – all the directors – stood to gain from the sale. And, as I already discovered, the school's finances were not in good shape.'

May nodded. 'It's the obvious reason for getting rid of Father William. Because Philbey and Riddles voted against it, the decision to sell still hasn't gone through. And – what's happened - they have both since been intimidated and attacked.'

May paced round the room before continuing. 'Pauline Philbey voted against it because of her "discovery" of new information in the archives. The archaeological dig was dear to Clair's heart and that would not have continued if Halliday Holdings had built their luxury housing complex, would it?'

'Why all the digging?'

'All to do with Sir Templeton, Charlie. Clair was convinced there was some incredible treasure that the old man had buried in the grounds somewhere near the Templar chapel.'

'What made him think that, Georgie?'

'The book that Taylor wrote. He talks of how he brought "untold riches" back from the Holy Land. Most ended up in the chapel, but the most precious thing had to be hidden. He wrote that it was buried for all eternity. And Philbey found some document or other that seems to indicate where it is located.'

'So why did Clair want to find it, if Taylor did not want it to be found?'

'I don't know, Charlie. Unless there was some religious significance to it – like all the other stuff. The *Sanctus Salvator* by the high altar is worth a million or more, apparently.'

'What?'

'Yes, Charlie. It is solid gold. And very old.' May smiled at his unintentional rhyming. Ellis and Riggs looked at each other but managed to avoid smirking.

'Georgie – the head that Freddie saw. Could that have been the "buried treasure"? Somebody found it and was hiding it away until they could sell it and cash in?'

'It could well be, Charlie. There is nothing on the inventory that Sir Templeton compiled that shows a head. Everything in that list is accounted for.'

'But it is a possibility.' May went up to the murder wall and wrote "Golden Head" in large letters, with an arrow to another new bubble "Templar Treasure?"

'Sir?'

'Well, there are lots of crackpots about who think there is some great mystery surrounding the Templars. You know, *The Holy Blood and The Holy Grail*, Dan Brown's *Da Vinci Code* and all that. Could there be superstitious elements to all this? What if there is some dark society underpinning the Order of Saint Saviour? Perhaps they worship the Golden Head. As you were suggesting earlier – some secret rite or other.'

'I like the idea sir, if only for a film.'

'And the other possibilities, Georgie?'

Ellis looked at Riggs. 'Revenge. That's the other obvious alternative motive. Revenge for what went on at the school in the 1970s.'

'But what went on at the school? That folder is all innuendo. Something may or may not have happened. It was a different world back then. Nothing was ever proven.' Riggs pointed to the documents he had pored over endlessly.

'That's not to say it didn't happen, though, is it?'

'OK, you two. We need to delve further. Have we interviewed all the brothers yet?'

Riggs and Ellis shook their heads in unison. 'Only Brother – now Father – Bernard in detail, sir. We got uniform to take statements from the others, but we have yet to follow up on that.'

'Then that's your next job, you two. On the double!'

The three officers downed their morning coffee and prepared to start the day. As Riggs and Ellis were about to leave May's office, there was a knock at the door. May beckoned the visitor in.

'Sorry to disturb you, but you need to know this now; a body has been found in the railway tunnel near Templeton Towers.'

MOVEMENT II

Lento

12

Underground And Overground

'The trains have been suspended in both directions until further notice, sir. We have possession of the line.'

May shivered as he and Georgie Ellis walked into the tunnel under the Templeton Estate.

'Who discovered the body?'

'The driver of the 12.17 from Holme Hill to Hartley, Halifax and Wakefield.'

'What time did the train enter the tunnel?'

'It was ten minutes late – as usual for Northern Fail – so it was about 12.28. What are you laughing at sir?'

'Just thinking of Freddie. He would be able to tell you exactly, based on time of departure from Holme Hill and likely speed from there to the tunnel mouth. Perhaps I will ask him later!'

'Or old Quick Draw?'

'How so?'

'I bet he could do the same.'

'No other driver saw anything?'

'Not that we are aware of so far.'

'Would they have missed it?'

'I think that drivers of trains coming the other way would not have seen the body. It was propped up against the supporting arches facing towards Holme Hill. With the headlamps on, any train going in the direction of Hartley should have been able to see it.'

'Interesting, Georgie. When was the previous train in that direction, then?

'The 11.17. The trains are once an hour in the middle of the day.'

'The body arrived sometime between the times the two trains entered the tunnel then?'

Georgie Ellis nodded. 'That's my assumption, though I guess we need to get the rail experts to advise.'

The SOCOs had already set up powerful spotlights to ensure the crime scene was well illuminated.

'Here we are again Fizz.'

'We can't go on meeting like this, Detective Chief Inspector May. Afternoon Detective Constable Ellis; settling in? Enjoying the new role?'

Ellis nodded and smiled.

'Good. And I suppose you want to know what I have got for you Don.'

'That's the general idea, Dr Harbord.'

'Well, I won't know much more until I get our victim back to the lab and do the postmortem but, I believe the victim was murdered elsewhere and the body deposited here.'

'Time of Death?'

'I'd say within the last 24 hours. Some form of asphyxia. And look at the marks on the neck, Don.'

'They're similar to those on Clair's body!'

'They are.'

'And the asphyxiation?'

'Could be that special incense. I will let you know as soon as I have anything. Do you recognize him?'

May and Ellis advanced towards the cadaver, still propped up against the tunnel archway. It was the naked body of an older man; short, skin slightly wizened, no body hair, apart from the pubes, and even that was thinning. Ellis shone her torch on the face at May's request.

'Well. I didn't expect that!'

'No sir, neither did I!'

'Are you sure you don't want me to ask the other Board members to attend, Professor Day?'

Day shook his head. 'No thanks, Lisa. This is – shall we say – an 'unofficial' meeting of the Property Sub-Committee.'

'But there isn't a Property Sub-Committee.'

'There is now, Lisa. Professor Day and I thought it would be a good idea in the light of Father Clair's "departure" that we streamline things to aid speedier decision making.'

'And do you wish me to take minutes, Mr Szabo?'

'That won't be necessary Lisa. I will just write up a short file note in due course.'

'Very good, Mr Szabo.'

'Thank you and – Lisa – make sure we are not disturbed for the next hour, please.'

Lisa Watson smiled vaguely, picked up her laptop and left the Board Room.

Andreas Day surveyed his fellow Board members. Chalk and cheese, those two women sitting next to each other: Halliday, blousy, busty, bloated, loud, common; Grimshaw, regal, elegant, tall, slim, radiant, the perfect woman. Halliday had made him an offer, but there was no way 'Babs' would ever entice a man of his power and influence into bed. Melody Grimshaw was a completely different ball game. Oh, to get off with a super model! Day had fallen in love with her from the first; or was it fallen in lust?

Melody had eyes only for Szabo. Day liked the Principal. Janos was his kind of man: strong, decisive, knew his own mind, didn't take prisoners. They could go places, especially now Clair was out of the way. What did Szabo feel about Melody? It was difficult to tell. He seemed immune to the super model's charms, preferring to spend his time with Diana Foster. She was the school's educational psychologist, no arguing with that, but did Szabo need to be so attentive? What was it about Foster that was so alluring? It was obvious that Melody Grimshaw was Szabo's for the taking, so why didn't he do something about it? Foster was an opinionated, falafel-eating geek. He had seen too many of those at the University. It must have been her mind that turned Szabo on.

'Come on, Andy. What are you waiting for?'

'Sorry, Babs.' Day looked at his watch. 'But we are one short. I don't want to start until the final member of our group is here.'

'Are we? Who's that then?'

'The weirdo! He's probably still playing with his trains.' Barbara Halliday inspected her nails.

'I thought we'd agreed: McGraw shouldn't be involved! We don't know whose side he is on, do we?' Melody Grimshaw spoke softly but firmly. Andreas Day smiled at her, blushing slightly as he did so.

The group fell silent. The Tompion struck the quarter past. The door burst open. 'My apologies. Trains were suspended between Holme Hill and Hartley. I was stuck for hours. I had to get a taxi in the end.'

'Stop fretting about your bloody trains, McGraw. It's only a model, for God's sake.'

'No, no, no. I don't mean my railway. I mean the real thing. A body was found in the tunnel that runs under the estate. And I know who it is'.

'What do we do next?'

Freddie May looked at the two girls. He felt funny inside. He had never felt this way before. But what was he feeling? Was this what they called 'love'? For Vanessa? Or could it be Camilla? They were so very different, and yet the same!

'Come on Fred, what do we do next?'

'I don't know. I'm thinking. Don't you two have any ideas?'

Freddie looked at the two girls again. What was it about them? He felt slightly sick. But he was excited at the same time. He thought back to when they tried to kiss him and touch him on the arm. Would they do it again? Maybe he should be the one to do the kissing next time.

'Fred! What are we going to do? You're in charge!'

'That's a first! I was under the impression you two did the bossing around here!'

Vanessa and Camilla burst out laughing.

'What's so funny?'

'You are a comic, Fred. That was very good. We didn't think you had a sense of humour!'

Freddie grunted. 'Well, little did you know!'

'Ooh, get him!'

'And I have a plan! This is what we are going to do. We are going to set a trap for the murderer. Just you wait and see!'

The leaves were falling fast. The visitor shivered. More flowers had been put on the grave. They had been lovingly arranged and placed on the earth right where the boy's head would be. The visitor wondered what the corpse would look like after all these years. 'Ashes to ashes; dust to dust.' That's what would be down there, along with a few bones. How could a living, breathing, person end up like that. What a lovely boy he was! What would he have become? Prime Minister? Concert pianist? Professor of History at Cambridge? He had the world before him. And look what happened!

The visitor knelt in front of the wooden cross, touching it.

'My dearest Nicholas. I am so, so, very sorry. If I could have my time again, I would not have let it happen. I swear. But I will make it up to you, both in this world and the next. I promise. On my word and my life.'

'Ooh, Georgie! Who would have guessed? Tell me more, please, please! Throth and Aethel are really excited about it all!'

'What! What have you told them?'

'Er – nothing. Well, nothing, really.'

'Tiggy? What aren't you saying. Have you told the boys about the case?'

'No, honest!'

'Are you sure?'

Tiggy broke a huge chunk off the Old Jamaica bar and threw it into her wide-open mouth. 'Sorry can't talk with my mouth full!'

'Oh yes you can. Now give me the rest of **my** chocolate and start talking!'

Georgie Ellis watched as Tiggy gulped the Old Jamaica down, belched and looked back sheepishly. 'Sorry George. It's the baby. Plays havoc with my digestive system, this pregnancy lark.'

'Stop calling me George. You know I don't like it, even from you! No, I don't mean that: especially from you!'

Tiggy heaved herself out of the armchair, waddled over to the Chesterfield and sat down next to her sister. Tiggy put her arm out and gently encouraged Georgie to lay her head on the ever-growing stomach.

'Listen and feel, Georgie. Isn't it wonderful? New life being formed in there. You should try it sometime.'

Georgie remained silent. There was nothing to say. She had set herself against motherhood for all time. Her career was far more important than babies. Always would be. And yet, as she lay there feeling the bump and catching a sense of the developing human inside, she had an image of her, and a partner, each holding the hand of a child. Their child. The partner was real; someone she knew already. And the thought shocked and excited her in equal measure.

'What's the matter Georgie? Cat got your tongue?'

'I don't like cats, and you know it. Not much in favour of dogs, either.'

Georgie Ellis did not resist when Tiggy began to stroke her hair. It felt good. 'Just relax. You can tell me. I promise I wouldn't break a confidence. I swear I haven't said anything to the boys, apart from the fact that you are working on a complex murder case. That's no secret. They can read about it in the local rag – online, of course! A woman called Victoria Perry is writing a lot. Interesting to know where she is getting her information from. It seems to me that she has a hotline to Hartley CID or the school, or both.'

'Don't be daft, Tiggs. It's the other way round if anything. She has shared some old documents with us about what might have gone on at Templeton Towers in the 1970s.'

'Abuse?'

'Who knows? Nothing was ever proved. It looks to us as if there was a massive cover-up at the time. But there could be a link to do with a cold case from back then.'

'You mean the murder of that vicar?'

'We don't know if he was murdered.'

'But it looks as though he might have been killed now you look at the case in the light of William Clair's death, doesn't it?'

Georgie nodded. Soothing, stroking, and intelligent conversation were so welcome after a harrowing day. 'Yes. We have just received permission to exhume the body. We will have a better idea in a week or two.'

'And what about the latest murder? Another cleric bites the dust. No wonder the Church of England is short of clergy!'

Georgie laughed. She had forgotten Tiggy had a great sense of humour when she was on good form.

'It was a surprise, in more ways than one.'

'Yes, beloved sister?'

'O stop it, Tiggs.'

'You can say anything to me, Georgie. I know you think I am vain and shallow and all those other things that you don't want to be and aren't, but I do care about you – very much – and I would always be on your side, especially in a crisis!'

Georgie looked up. 'I know Tiggs. I know. It's hard sometimes. Fitting in.'

'And you want – need – to fit in?'

'Some and some, Tiggy. It's still a man's world in the police.'

'The bastards!'

'May is good, and Charlie is alright in his own way.'

'And the rest?'

'Well, the ACC is a woman! First one at Hartley. Not sure I like her much though. Something of a Queen Bee.'

'What does that mean?'

'It means that ACC Samson has a down on women in her workforce.'

'Come off it! "In this day and age"?'

'Yup. She's crawled and fawned her way to the top and is now determined to make sure that no other woman gets there.'

'People like her should be encouraging other women to do the same.'

'If only. There's only one Queen Bee. I'll give you a book to read. It talks all about the Syndrome. And Samson is a classic QB, believe me.'

'And the book?'

Eve on Top.

'Sounds more like porno to me! Who's it by?'

'Some crusty academic. Anyway, it's good. All about women's experience of getting into senior positions.'

'Just as you will do one day, Commander Ellis of the Yard!'

'Stop it Tiggs! That's what Freddie calls himself. "May of the Yard".'

'How is your SIO, anyway?'

'Stressed, I'd say.'

'I'll bet, with two bodies on his hands!'

'It all has to do with something that has gone on or **is** going on at Templeton Towers.'

'Surely not now. Aren't we beyond all that after Jimmy Savile? I'd commit murder if anybody tried to interfere with Throth or Aethel.'

'You'd think so, though there are skeletons galore in the Church of England's cupboard still being exposed.'

'We must be talking about historic sex abuse and those monks are paying the price for past sins.'

'Easy, Tiggs. We don't know that – yet.'

'It's obvious, isn't it. Clair gets murdered; you find a link back to a former member of the OSS, now thought to have been murder rather than suicide – using the same MO – and then a second brother gets taken out just over a week after the first.'

'I agree. It's stacking up. But where do Szabo and Day and their cronies on the Board fit in? They have just as much motive to get rid of Clair as someone out out for revenge.'

Tiggy belched, moved position, and settled back on the Chesterfield.

'That's better. Sorry about that. Amber is very restless tonight.'

'Do you want me to move?'

'No. You're fine, Georgie. I'm enjoying this. I haven't felt this close to anyone for a long time. It got very lonely, living with Lucian.'

'I'm sorry, Tiggs.'

'So am I. It's hard when you feel lonely inside a relationship.'

'I believe I understand that. I think Donald May feels much the same.'

'Ooh, tell me more!'

Georgie Ellis blushed. 'There's nothing to tell.'

'You always did go for older men. I remember when you were in the sixth form.'

'Stop it! Stop it at once!'

'Don't get your knickers in a twist, George. What was his name? You know. The Director of Music. Brilliant organist if I remember rightly. Bet he's still around. You should ask Quick Draw if he knows your former paramour'.

Tristan Bishop was **not** my paramour. Never, ever, ever!'

'But you fancied him, didn't you, Georgie?'

'Oh, alright then. Yes, I did. Well, just a bit. I certainly had a crush on him. Why else do you think I joined the choir? I didn't exactly enjoy the music!'

'You should ask Bishop about McGraw. You never know what he might reveal about his fellow organist!'

'Actually Tiggs, that's not a bad idea. We haven't found much out so far, but old Trissy might know more about someone like McGraw than meets the eye – or the ear!'

'See, Georgiana Ellis. I told you I could be useful to you!'

'Sorry Tiggy. I should have believed and trusted in you more.'

'Are we friends again?'

Georgie Ellis nodded. 'We are!'

'Great! Now tell me all about your new paramour!'

'Who the hell is that?'

'DCI May, of course.'

Georgie Ellis jumped up and turned to point at the beached whale lookalike on the Chesterfield. 'Don't be ridiculous! And don't you say anything like that again. Don has eyes only for Jean Samson!'

✦

'So, what now, Don?'

'A pattern is emerging, ma'am.'

'Same MO?'

'Same MO. Brother – Father – Bernard was killed by incense inhalation.'

May shivered. It was cold in the courtyard. All so that ACC Samson could smoke. What would the others think of their meeting there, innocent though it was?

'So, it all links back to Templeton Towers and the OSS. Any suspects?'

'It must be an inside job. It would be difficult for an outsider to have committed the murder and got the body down into the railway tunnel.'

'How the hell did they do that? Are we looking at more than one perpetrator?'

'We must be. Quite how the body ended up there we don't know. He wasn't murdered there, Fizz – Dr Harbord can confirm that, alongside the incense poisoning and the postmortem bruising around the neck. Pauline Philbey has a theory about the railway tunnel.'

'Philbey: the batty old woman who does all that archive stuff?'

May snorted. 'Don't underestimate her. She's very bright and has a lot of knowledge about that place and the locality in general; at least when she's sober.'

Samson threw her cigarette on the floor and stubbed it out with her immaculately polished shoe. She began to take out a second cigarette from the pack then thought better of it.

'Go on then, Don. Enlighten me.'

'A network of underground passages leading from the Towers to the old Templar church and then added to when the railway was bored through the hills underneath the estate. Sir Templeton was heavily involved in the project.'

'Didn't tunnels loom large in the Holme Hill murders?'

May nodded.

'A long forgotten nuclear bunker underneath tunnels that Ernest Riddles, the local mill owner had dug.'

'And this was his rival's equivalent?'

'Could be, ma'am.'

'Bonkers, Don. But get it all checked out, JIC.'

'Ma'am.'

Samson nodded. 'Can we meet off duty? A drink this evening perhaps. There's something I need to talk through with you off the record.'

May smiled. 'If you say so, Jean. To do with Father Bernard's murder?'

No, Don. To do with us.'

Pauline Philbey was fed up: to the back teeth and beyond. She looked across at Hal, snoring behind his newspaper. Being in the safe house was boring; stultifying; depressing; mind-numbingly dull. Ditch water was more interesting. Even Boris was bored. Philbey could tell by the way the cat mewled at her.

The snoring was getting louder. The stress of Templeton Towers was taking its toll on him. Sad thing that he was, with his sleep apnoea! The noise was appalling. The silly duffer was no spring chicken. Mind you, neither was she. It was no fun getting old.

Hartley Grammar School, 1957. He had been in the sixth form; she was in the fourth. Her first date with a boy. They had agreed to meet on the six o'clock bus from Holme Hill to Hartley. But it had to be a secret; nobody could know the Head Boy was going out with such a young girl, and especially one from the wrong side of the valley. She was to sit at the front; he at the back. Pauline was nervously early; Harry nearly missed the bus. *Gunfight at the OK Corral.*

'What are you laughing at, Philbs?'

'Sleepy head! Finally awake, are we?'

'Sorry. I must have dozed off.'

'Dozed off? You've been asleep for nearly two hours!'

'Sorry. It's all getting too much for me.'

'But we haven't been doing anything!'

'*You* haven't. **I** have!'

'What have you been doing, then, Philbs?'

'Thinking, Hal. That's what I've been doing.'

'And?'

'And what?'

'What have you thought?'

'I have thought about you.'

Riddles snorted. 'And I have often thought about you – Pauline.'

'Don't be stupid, Harry. I have thought about you and the treasure.'

'Oh, I see what you mean.'

'And you really don't know where the treasure is?'

Riddles shook his head. 'Father William was going to tell me the night he was murdered.'

'What?'

Riddles nodded. 'He telephoned me and asked me to meet him in the chapel.'

'But why didn't you say this before? Why didn't you tell the police?'

Riddles shook his head. 'I know. What was I thinking?'

'You should have told me, at least! Don't you trust me?'

'It's not that, Philbs.'

'So, what is it?'

'Well, it wouldn't have looked good, would it?'

Philbey snorted. 'It certainly won't look good when I tell Donald May what you've just told me!'

'Pauline!'

'Don't you Pauline me!'

'Alright, alright. Keep your hair on.'

'So, tell me everything.'

'Clair rang that afternoon. I had arranged for the necessary documentation to be put together. It just needed proof that the resources existed so the bank would stop pressurising us to sell.'

'It's bad, isn't it?'

Riddles nodded. 'Whatever else we think of Szabo and Day, they are right to sell the land if that's the only way of staving off bankruptcy. And the school is almost flat broke. I believed Father William had found where the treasure was and could demonstrate there was no need to sell all those acres.'

'Right. He phoned you?'

'Yes. I was to meet him in the Chapel at 7.30 pm after he had finished his devotions. He said that he would "reveal the treasure" to me. Its value would be more than enough to solve the Order's problems.'

'And you went?'

'I did.'

'What happened?'

'Nothing. Absolutely nothing.'

'Did you see Clair?'

'No. I couldn't get in.'

'Why not?'

'The door was locked.'

'It's never locked. That building is open 24/7. William Clair has always insisted on it. "God listens any time of day or night", he used to say.'

'Well God was out that night.' Riddles guffawed.

'Did you not try the other entrance?'

'What? From the monks' quarters?'

'Well, why not?'

'There's no way I could have got in from their accommodation.'

Philbey shrugged. 'No, I suppose not.'

'What did you do?'

'I wandered around for a while, then I tried the door again.'

'Still locked?'

Riddles nodded. 'I was getting cold – very cold – so I left.'

'That's it?'

'Yup. That's it.'

'Your face says something different Hal!'

'Well, I could be wrong, but I thought I saw someone.'

'Where?'

'A light came on. Only briefly, but I am sure of it.'

'Where, Harry?'

'In the organ loft.'

'Right! I have had enough of this! I can't sit here any longer. It's time for action.'

Philbey stood up, throwing Boris off her lap as she did so, walked out to the hallway, and donned her hat and coat. She looked at Riddles as she put on her gloves.

'Well?'

'Well, what, Philbs?'

'Well, are you coming or not?'

'Is this wise? What if we are attacked again?'

'Huh! I would rather go on the attack. Come on Harry – Hal. Last chance.'

Riddles cleared his throat, then looked down at his feet. 'You're on Philbs. Where are we off to?'

'To get that treasure. That's what!'

'Are you sure this is a good idea?'

'Darling – it's the very best. Trust me. I have a hunch – and I am good at these things – that Trissy will be able to help us.'

Georgie Ellis looked at her sister sitting there in the front passenger seat of the BMW Z4. There she was, effortlessly elegant in her Catherine Walker outfit. Even pregnant, Tiggy was beautiful. The boys were remarkably well behaved, squashed in the back of the car, glued to their i-pads. Not a peep out of those two since they left Hartley on the long journey to see Tristan Bishop. Was this the best way of spending an afternoon off work?

What if it was a wild goose chase? Would it be a wasted journey? The phone call to Bishop suggested otherwise. Georgie's former music teacher had laughed eerily when the name of John McGraw had been mentioned. He had refused to discuss the subject over the phone. What had to be said was to be relayed in person. Bishop's voice was as sexy as ever. Georgie had trembled slightly as she listened to him. There was something about that sound; it wasn't the timbre or the depth, but the way in which her whole body – her very being – was enveloped in Tristan Bishop.

Bishop had been – what – mid thirties and Georgie Ellis was fifteen or sixteen. She had loved him like she never loved. So had Tiggy, in her own Tiggy-like way. Bishop had eyes only for his wife. And now she was dead. That was the one piece of information Bishop had imparted over the phone. 'Cancer. Two years ago.'

'What do you think he will look like now, George? I wonder if he is still as fanciable as he was when – well, you know.'

'Stop it, Tiggs. That was a long time ago and I was young and foolish.'

Tiggy began to whistle "Down by the Sally gardens". Georgie joined in.

Satnav rudely interrupted their performance. 'Turn left into the destination street.'

Tristan Bishop was waiting at the gate of his immaculately tended garden. He waved as the BMW came to a halt in the gravel drive.

'Georgie! Tiggy! How lovely to see you both. And who are these two young men?'

'Aethel! Throth! Enough of those i-pads! Say hello to the best music teacher in the world!'

As the boys got out of the car, a large Labrador bounded out of the house and enthusiastically greeted them, plastering their faces with sloppy kisses then madly running round the front garden.

'Mummy. Can we play with him?'

'Of course, my darlings. But be careful!'

Bishop looked at Georgie and Tiggy. 'Don't worry, Baxter will take care of them. He is a very wise old dog. Anyway, come here you two and let me give you a hug, and then get you some tea and cake. I'll get the boys some squash and biscuits. And you must all stay for dinner. I insist.'

Georgie thought Trissy had aged since they had last seen him. Ten years was a long time, especially if you had spent the last three of them caring for a wife with terminal cancer. Bishop smiled as they were ushered into the music room, complete with grand piano, harpsichord and, at the far end, in pride of place, an ornately cased pipe organ. A pot of tea, cups and cake were already laid out.

'What a wonderful room this is! And that gorgeous organ.' The sisters went up to the instrument to inspect the carving in more detail.

'Mahogany, I presume?'

Bishop nodded. 'Yes Georgie. And look at the motto over the top of the central pipes.'

Georgie Ellis stood on tiptoe to read the words. '" In hoc signo vanquo". But that is the motto of the Templars!'

'Is it?'

'Yes. Where did the instrument come from?'

'Funny you should ask that, Georgie. John McGraw arranged for me to have it. And he's the real reason you're here, of course.'

'Yes. We wondered if you could give us any inside information on the man.'

'What a dreadful business at his school. Templeton Towers, I think you said? Dreadful. But then, I am not surprised something like that might happen, with old Quick Draw in charge of the music there.'

'No, not me, please! I beg you. Let this cup pass from me. I am not the one.'

'But you are. God has spoken. He has chosen you!'

'But what will happen to me if I say yes? You know, don't you!'

'It is God's will Brother Jeffrey. It is God's will.'

The three brothers fell into silence. The candles flickered wildly as a gust of air passed through the chantry chapel where they were meeting.

'Please. Brother Germain – you are the obvious candidate – take it. Take the chain of office.'

'God has chosen you, Brother Jeffrey. You must obey.'

'Because I drew the short straw in your silly little game? No, I won't! I won't. I won't!'

'It is your time, Brother Jeffrey.'

'O fuck off, Simon. What would you know about it? You're drunk or asleep most of the time. You're as good as dead anyway. No, it will be me they are after if I become Head of the Order. And I won't. I won't. I won't. I want to live!'

13

Three Partnerships Take Shape

THE *SPECKLED TEAPOT* STAYED OPEN LATE ON FRIDAYS AND SATURDAYS, turning from a café into a bistro. Business was slow that evening; too many people going home from work to start the weekend and not yet ready to celebrate the fact with a meal out. As a result, Donald May found himself the only person in the restaurant, sitting in a quiet corner at a table reserved for two. He declined the waitress's offer of a drink while he was waiting for his guest; instead, he watched the world outside: people going about whatever they were going about; coming and going, some with more purpose than others.

He looked at his watch again, a Christmas present from Caz and Freddie together. No sign of the woman. Was this the old Jean Samson, given to last minute changes of heart and abrupt U-turns, both in her professional and her private life? Or had she just been held up at one of those high-level policy meetings that an ACC would have to attend? May went through the steps and stages he would have to take and make if he were to become an Assistant Chief Constable. It had been his ambition once upon a time, but now it seemed like too much hard work. More to the point, he would stop being a detective, a real policeman of any sort. And whatever else he had been, now was, and ever wanted to be in the future, it was not a paper-pusher.

Unlike Jean Samson. She seemed to relish it all, right from the top management programme at the College of Policing to the MBA and then the DBA. All possible if you were single, no kids, no attachments. May tried to convince himself there were no regrets about marrying

Caz and not Jean – he and Samson would probably have been divorced within about six months – nor could he ever think of a life without Freddie.

Dear, sweet, strange, brilliant, unique Freddie. How had they produced a genius like him?

Samson was now 15 minutes late. May looked out of the window and down the High Street. Shops and cafes closed; lights went out; workers locked up and went home. Nothing unusual going on here. Apart from a well-wrapped-up Victoria Perry heading towards the *Speckled Teapot*, that is. May wracked his brain: was he supposed to be meeting VP here tonight? Oh shit! Not a double booking?

Perry was walking towards the café; nowhere else. May decided to look the other way and hope she had not seen him. The last person he wanted her to see him with was – well - was Jean Samson.

May peeped out from behind the menu. Perry was standing there, as if waiting for someone. Perhaps he was not her dinner date after all. It had started to rain. She got out a small umbrella and managed to open it up, despite the strong wind. It was bucketing down now. May wondered if he should beckon her in and offer her a coffee, given Samson's continued absence. Just as he was about to stand and wave, another woman, wisely sporting an opened umbrella, walked down the High Street, and greeted Perry. The two of them talked for a few moments. The unknown woman then gave Perry a large brown envelope. They nodded and parted, each going back the way they had come. Once Perry was out of sight, May went over to the café door to get a better view of the other woman. It was difficult. The umbrella was in the way, but there was one moment – just a few seconds – that gave May a good line of sight as she passed by the café on the far side of the road.

It was Lisa Watson.

'Well, I never. That's a turn up for the books!'

'And which books are those, Don?'

'Jean! You crept up on me!'

Samson laughed. 'I was always good at doing that to you!'

May blushed. She looked a completely different person out of uniform. Slinky black jeans, ribbed Henley top, hair down, make up on; ten years younger.

'You look – well – you look great!'

'Thanks Don. It's good to get out of that uniform. I spend too much time wearing it. Goes with the territory, I suppose. Anyway, are you going to invite me to sit down? I'll have a gin and tonic, please.'

May went over to the counter and ordered two drinks.

'What are you having Don?'

'Tonic without the gin. Slimline at that. I need to lose weight. Not enough exercise now my son doesn't want to go cycling with me.'

'How is Freddie? None the worse for his ordeal, I hope!'

May shook his head and laughed. 'He seems to be better for it. He doesn't stop talking about his "adventure".'

'And you believe his story?'

May nodded. 'I do. I said to Riggs and Ellis that Freddie would never lie.'

Samson pursed her lip. They stopped talking until their drinks had been served. The waitress asked if they wanted food.

'Give us a few more minutes, will you?' Samson took the lead, like she always did. 'I think just nibbles, don't you Don? Some of this tapas-type stuff, perhaps. I'm not very hungry. But a glass of dry white wine will go down very nicely alongside something to munch.'

'Gin and then wine? You're not driving?'

'I only live round the corner. Got myself a rather nice flat in that converted mill you can just see. It's only five minutes away. You live in Holme Hill, don't you, Don?'

May nodded. 'Born and bred.'

'Anyway, what was all that about just now?'

'Victoria Perry, the reporter on the local newspaper was walking up the High Street. I know her. I thought she was coming in here, but then she met Lisa Watson just over there. Watson gave Perry a brown envelope, the two parted company and each went back the way they had come.'

'Lisa Watson? Have we interviewed her?'

'Uniform took a statement the morning after Clair's death. The focus was on finding out if anything was missing from his study or the Order's offices.'

'And was it?'

'Nope. Nothing. According to Watson, everything was as it should be.'

'Perhaps we should interview her again. One of your people, this time.'

'I'll get Riggs or Ellis to do it.'

Samson nodded, approvingly. 'How are those two shaping up in their new roles?'

May clasped his hands firmly. 'Well. Charlie is relishing his promotion at last and Ellis – well - Ellis is Ellis. Very ambitious, very enthusiastic, very clever, a bit naïve. Good at 'left field' thinking if you know what I mean.'

Samson nodded. 'You used to be good at that Don.'

May snorted. 'I know. Perhaps it's something you are better at when you're young.'

'I can think of other things where that happens.'

May blushed. 'Don't be so sure, Jean. Practice makes perfect. Experience counts for a lot. And that takes time. Wine matures with age; best not drunk too soon.'

It was Samson's turn to blush. 'I presume you are talking about detective work now Don.'

'What else, Jean?'

The two of them laughed, then fell into silence.

The food arrived. Samson raised her glass and May reciprocated.

'What's the toast, Don?'

'What do you want it to be, Jean?'

'It's up to you to say.'

'You are my commanding officer though. You should decide.'

'Then, DCI May, I order you to make a toast.'

May swirled his drink round in its glass, then slowly sipped some of the liquid. Eventually, after a few moments that seemed like eternity, he spoke.

'Here's to good relations – personal as much as professional – and a speedy solving of these murders.'

Samson raised her G&T, clinked glasses, downed the rest of the drink and looked at May.

'We have a lot to talk about. Let's eat first and then I will fill you in.'

The M62 was its usual gridlocked self. Half a mile in half an hour.

'Can't you put your blue light on or something?'

'No, I can't, Tiggy. That would be a misuse of my position.'

'It would be fun, though. And we would get home a lot sooner.'

Georgie Ellis looked in the mirror. Fortunately, Throthgar and Aethelwald were both asleep. But for how much longer? It was surprising they did not need a wee. She certainly did.

'We'll go off at the next exit. I know a back way to Hartley. It's down a lot of country roads and very winding, but at least we'll be moving reasonably quickly. There's another advantage of going that way, of course.'

'What's that George?'

'We drive past Templeton Towers.'

'Gosh! You mean where the actual murders have been taking place?'

Georgie Ellis nodded. 'The very same.'

'Oh fabullissima, dearest sister o' mine. Perhaps we can solve the case while we're there!'

Ellis laughed. 'I think it will take more than just your intuitive powers.'

'But what a start, darling!'

'We'll see Tiggs. Here's the turnoff now.'

'Anyway Georgie, what do you make of Trissy's revelations?'

'Interesting; very interesting. I thought McGraw was a dark horse. I never expected him to be an ex-member of the brotherhood, though. And to have been asked to leave his last job before he moved to Hartley. I have texted Don – DCI May – to tell him what we have learned, at least in outline and that Quick Draw is rising up the suspect list all the time.'

'Oh, texting Don, now, are we?'
'Shut up Tiggy. He is devoted to his wife, or something like that.'
'Don't be so sure.'
'Give over, Tiggy. You've never met him.'
'I don't need to, Georgie Porgie. I know all I need to know to pass judgement.'
'How come?'
'From everything that you have told me.'
'Pass judgement? Just what does that mean?'
'How you feel about him. Like you used to feel about Trissy.'

Diana Foster had never smoked a cheroot before. It was not something she wished to do again, either, but her lover liked them, so she was giving it a try. The taste was bitter, and she felt slightly sick. After a couple of puffs, she gave it back.

'Sorry, Mel. It's not for me.'

'No worries, my love. It's bad for you, anyway.'

'And it's bad for you too. You should stop.'

Melody Grimshaw laughed. 'Oh, my dearest Di. You are such a sweetie. And I love you so!'

'Me, too, Mel. Me too. But …'

'But what?'

'But it all happened so fast. I never thought to be in a relationship again – at least not so soon!'

'If it's meant to be, it's meant to be. I am a fatalist that way. And you and I were meant to be, Diana Foster. From the very first moment I saw you, you were mine. I wanted you; I will always want you.'

'But why, Mel? What on earth do you see in me?'

'You are beautiful, Dr Foster.'

'No, I'm not. I am alright, at best. But nothing like you. That gorgeous, stupendous, magnificent body of yours!'

Melody Grimshaw flung back the duvet. 'Ta-da! You mean this, I believe!'

'Oh Mel, I do. I go weak at the knees every time I see you like that.'

Melody took Diana's head in her hands and looked straight into her eyes. 'You could be just like this. I swear. I will show you. I have a plan for us. We are going to take this place by storm. I promise you. You haven't seen the half of it yet!'

Harry Riddles was frightened. Why exchange the warmth and security of the safe house for this crazy escapade, all because Pauline thought she could solve the murders at Templeton Towers in one fell swoop? Riddles looked out of the car window. Once they were off the main road from Hartley to Holme Hill there was little traffic. Why would there be at midnight, especially when the temperature had fallen below zero on the car's dial? Classic FM played quietly in the background. Christmas carols! How he hated them, especially since his wife had died. He took exception to all that saccharine stuff by John Rutter. *Messiah* was the only thing worth listening to at this time of year. John McGraw conducted an especially fine performance in Hartley Town Hall. Not that there would be one this time. Why had McGraw suddenly resigned as Musical Director of the Choral Society? And all his other local roles to boot? Was Quick Draw on Pauline's list of suspects?

Pauline! The gin must finally have got to her. What made her think that the answer was at the old chapel on the Templeton Estate? Yes, the maps she had shown him suggested there were old mine workings underneath there, but why were they important? He looked across at his chauffeuse (he shouldn't really call her that, she was his chauffeur, of course) and wondered if she was on the right track. Philbs probably was, for there had to be a link between those workings and the railway tunnel. That would fit with the deposit of Father Bernard's body. How else could it have got down there? Unless it was someone from Northern Fail who planted it there. Riddles laughed at the thought.

Harry had never liked Father Bernard: a waspish man, petulant in the extreme. How could the brothers have voted him into the role after Clair? Brother Germain was the obvious choice. There was a man you could work with! Someone who knew how to do business! He had been an MD before receiving the call. At least Bernard had been better than Joker Jeffrey or somnolent Simon!

Occasionally, Riddles felt the car veer slightly.

'Black ice, Pauline. Take care!'

'You're being very formal, Hal. What's wrong with you?'

'Nothing, just, well, just – scared - to be honest.'

'Trust me, Hal. I know what I'm doing. And before you say it, I'm stone-cold sober. I haven't had a drop in hours, so I am perfectly fit to drive!'

Riddles snorted. 'Sorry. Are we friends again?'

'Well, I'm calling you Hal, aren't I?'

Riddles nodded and relaxed back into the passenger seat. Over and down to the right of the country road, he could see a green light. That must be the railway line. Sure enough, it was. A train's blurred lights flashed past and into the tunnel. The last one to Hartley from Holme Hill. Late again! It wasn't as easy to memorise the timetables as it had been in British Rail days, but Harry Riddles still knew all the local times without any reference manual, virtual or otherwise.

To the left was Templeton Towers. A small number of lights at the front of the building still shone. The rest of the place was in darkness. It was way past bedtime, at least for the students if not the staff. Was anyone still awake up there?

'You really are glorious!'

'Why thank you, kind sir!'

'That was wonderful.'

'My pleasure. Anything to be of assistance. After all, I am a member of the Board, and it is my duty to support the Principal in any way that I can.' Melody Grimshaw stretched out and rolled over onto her front. 'Now stroke me, my great big Commander. I need some TLC too.'

'You can't stay much longer! You can't be seen here, and you know it!'

Melody Grimshaw rolled over onto her back.

'Can't be seen. Like this, you mean?' She leapt up from the bed and skipped over to the window. As she struggled with the sash, Szabo caught up with her and stopped her from releasing the catch.

'Stop it, Mel. 'You'll get me into trouble.'

'You are already in trouble, Principal Szabo. Big, big trouble – with me! And unless you do everything that I say, I will tell everybody – absolutely everybody – what a naughty boy you have been.'

Melody Grimshaw flopped onto the bed, face down. Szabo sat on the edge and began to stroke her.

'You are the most beautiful woman I have ever seen.'

'Of course! And what a beautiful couple we will be. I have great plans. Great big plans, for you and me!'

Szabo laughed. Grimshaw giggled.

'Szeretlek', they said in unison.

'Ooh – how exciting! A real murder hunt. And George and Tiggs will solve the case.'

'Don't be silly, Tiggs. This just happens to be the quickest way home if you're not going to use the M62 all the way to Hartley.'

'Oh darling, we must stop and look. Survey the scene, eh?'

'No, we must not! It would be against the rules. And very stupid. Anyway, what about the boys?'

Tiggy looked to the back of the BMW Z4. Her babies were still fast asleep; except they weren't babies any more, 10 and 8! God! Where had all the years gone? And now Lucian had traded her in for a newer model. Would he want the boys; would *she* want them, or would they be sidelined in favour of the second litter Lucian would have with his young love?

'They'll be fine George. They aren't babies anymore. Look at them – out for the count.'

Georgie looked in the mirror.

'See what I mean? Now keep your eyes on the road, Detective Constable. It looks slippy out there! Isn't that Templeton Towers?'

Georgie nodded. Sooner or later, she would agree to slow down and stop so that big sister could see the scene of the crime. They passed the main entrance, complete with large sign announcing Templeton Towers, the Order of Saint Saviour, and lastly, the School for Gifted Children.

'Aren't we going to stop, George? At least briefly. Please, George!'

Georgie Ellis shook her head. 'No, not here. Round by the side entrance.'

'The one where you were the other night? The one where Charlie Riggs was supposed to meet an informant and where you apprehended that glamour model with her sugar daddy?'

'That's the one.' Georgie Ellis nodded. 'But why should Melody Grimshaw need a sugar daddy? She's loaded.'

'You sure she hasn't fallen on hard times?'

'Not as far as we can tell from our background checks.'

'Well, mark my words, she'll have Day twisted around her little finger, and all the men she takes a fancy to. I should know. I have done much the same in my time. Anyway, are we there yet?'

'Nearly.' Georgie snorted.

'Bloody hell, George! What's that? Stop!'

Georgie Ellis managed to stop the BMW Z4 without sliding on the black ice. The boys woke up as the car jolted to a halt.

'Stay here you three. Don't you dare leave the car.'

Ellis grabbed her torch from the glove compartment and headed down the road to the side entrance. She reached the gate. There at the side of the road was a lifeless body. Standing over it, long knife in hand, was a woman, weeping.

'Who the hell are these two?'

'Tiggy, I told you to stay in the car!'

'Well, I didn't. So, who are they?'

'The woman is called Pauline Philbey. I am not sure who the man is, but it looks like one of those monks. Now phone for police and ambulance. Quickly!'

MOVEMENT III

Fuoco E Furioso

14

Freddie Deduces; Philbey Descends

'Isn't it time you went to your own room and got some sleep?'

'I'm not sleepy.' Freddie shook his head.

'Well, we are. Can't you take a hint?'

'We need to work out who's going to be murdered next.'

'It's obvious, Commander May. Haven't you twigged yet?'

'Twigged?'

'Cottoned on, realised, deduced, you know!'

'Oh, right. Yes, I see. Well, who is it then?'

'Father William, Brother – Father – Bernard. It must be the new Head of the Order!'

'I had decided that. I wanted to try and work out what will then happen to Brother Simon and Brother Germain and Brother Lawrence. Assuming Brother – Father – Jeffrey is next for the chop.'

'So why didn't you say so earlier, instead of keeping us awake all this time?' Camilla and Vanessa yawned simultaneously.

'I wanted to be sure of my reasoning.'

'And that is?' Camilla leaned her head against her sister's shoulder and closed her eyes.

'It's about revenge, money, or both. That's my conclusion!'

'That's not very insightful, Freddie. I thought you would have come up with something more earth-shattering than that by now!'

'Don't rush to judgement on me!'

'Well, get on with it then.'

'My Dad told me there were rumours about this place in the 1970s.'

'Bad things happening to students?' Vanessa rubbed her eyes.

Freddie nodded. 'Nothing was ever proven. And there is little evidence to suggest that anything did happen. At least that's what Dad said.'

'So?' Camilla stretched her arms.

'What if something did happen? The brothers would have been responsible for it. They were in charge then, as they are now, and even if they didn't commit the abuse, they were culpable.'

'What does that mean?'

'They are the ones to blame.'

'And if they are, then someone is settling old scores.'

'Settling old scores? That's an odd phrase to use, Freddie. Like Quick Draw. He's always researching those dusty music manuscripts in the choir library.' The twins looked at each other.

'Quick Draw is harmless. Just an eccentric organist. He would never hurt anybody.'

'Who would then?'

'Someone who wanted William, Bernard, and Jeffrey dead. Those three were at Templeton Towers in the 1970s.'

'Not Simon, Lawrence, and Germain, then?'

Freddie May shook his head. 'No Camilla. They didn't arrive until the 1980s or the 1990s or even more recently. Brother Simon is not as old as he looks, though he acts like an ancient. I thought he was the same age as William, Bernard, and Jeffrey. Simon was a teacher in the south of England before becoming a monk. Brother Germain was in the armed forces before joining the Order. I bet that's why he is so fit. All those long morning and evening. runs I'm not sure about Lazy Larry.'

'Wasn't Mr Szabo in the Navy?'

'Yes, he was. If Germain was as well, there may be a connection.'

'But Brother G must be at least 25 years older than Mr Szabo.'

'That doesn't matter. They could have been senior and junior officers together. Anyway,' continued Freddie,' they are not the focus of my – I mean our – investigations.'

'I think it's all to do with the little grave we found in the woods.'

Vanessa burst into tears. Camilla put her arm round her and looked at Freddie.

'She gets like this sometimes. Vanessa gets so sad.'

'Buried all alone. With nobody to care for them.'

Freddie looked at the two girls as they sat entwined in each other's arms.

'At least until we came along. They have someone to care about them now. Here: blow your nose.' Freddie took a tissue from Camilla's desk and gave it to Vanessa.

'Thanks Freddie. Sorry. I am just so frightened of death. About not being here anymore. I can't bear to think of what happened to the person in that grave.'

'What if they were murdered? Back in the 1970s. And someone is seeking revenge.'

'And the brothers are paying the price now.'

'It makes sense. But who is the avenger, Fred?'

'Someone who joined the school recently. It must be. There were no problems until Szabo and Foster arrived.'

'It's one of them, then?'

'Or both, Vanessa. They seem very close. I have been observing late night comings and goings both to Szabo's rooms, and to Dr Foster's. I think they are having an affair.'

'You mean all that love stuff? With sex and everything?'

Freddie and Camilla burst out laughing.

'Shhh! We don't want to be discovered, do we? I know that people do it. But goodness knows why!'

Camilla smiled at Vanessa. 'Keep talking Freddie! I thought you said that there was another possible reason for the murders – that's assuming Father Jeffrey is the next – if not the last – on the murderer's list.'

'That's the theory that my Dad is working on. That it's all to do with money and the sale of the land to the north of the school. That would fit with the conversation we heard between Mr Szabo and Professor Day. Remember?'

The girls nodded.

'And with the old guard out of the way, those two could get approval for all sorts of things to happen.'

'What about that other theory you were telling us about?'

The one about buried treasure. That's the batty old archivist's idea. I don't think so, somehow.'

'You do not have to say anything. But it may harm your defence if you do not mention when questioned something which you later rely on in court. Anything you do say may be given in evidence.'

'I didn't do it! I swear!'

'The knife that killed him was in your hand when Detective Constable Ellis apprehended you.'

'But – but – but, I had picked it up from the side of the road.'

'Why?'

'I already told you. I don't know why! It was a stupid thing to do. I admit that. I panicked. I know it looks bad.'

'It does. Yours are the only fingerprints on the handle, Pauline.'

'Obviously the killer wore gloves!'

'And you just happened to pick up the knife afterwards?'

Pauline Philbey fell silent. She looked across at her interrogators. Charlie Riggs turned wearily to Georgie Ellis then announced a break from questioning. 'Interview terminated at 05.00 hours.' Ellis switched off the tape, closed the file and stood up first. Riggs looked across at Philbey for a moment as if weighing up the woman's innocence – or guilt – then pushed his chair back, got up and left the room, quickly followed by Ellis.

Alone with a uniformed constable standing guard, Pauline Philbey buried her head in her hands. What a stupid thing to do! Harry was right! We should never have come out!

No! Pull yourself together! Think!

She began to go through the events of the previous few hours, trying to make some small sense of her predicament. Hal had tried to persuade her to stay in the safe house, but to no avail. The chivalrous soul had then agreed to go with her, despite his misgivings.

The roads were empty. They got to the school in half the usual time. How different it was from daytime driving: the traffic jam on the road up to the school had made her late for the last Board meeting. Hal had questioned why they were driving right past the main entrance, especially since, unusually for that time of night, the gates were open: not good, given the need for security and safety in a boarding school, and a house and chapel full of valuable artefacts.

'That's not where we need to be, Hal. It's the old chapel. I know how Father Bernard's body got to the railway tunnel.'

Riddles had been silent throughout the journey. He knew better than to counter Philbey on a mission. Once parked by the side entrance to the Templeton Estate, he had dutifully followed her into the grounds and towards the old chapel. For all her bravado, Philbey had welcomed his presence, even though she knew Riddles doubted her reasons if not her sanity.

What was she looking for? What would give credence to her belief? It was one thing to look at a plan of the chapel; quite another to see the place on the ground.

Two torches focused on the sanctuary area. That had to be the point of access. But whereabouts? On her command, Riddles took one end of the stone altar and Philbey the other. It was the handprint on the edge that gave the game away. Riddles spotted it first, but it was Philbey who worked out the significance of those finger shapes preserved in the dust of ages.

'Look, Hal. Someone gripped the altar at this point so they could steady themselves as they went underneath the table.'

Riddles had laughed as Philbey had placed her hand over the print and then lowered herself down beneath the altar.

'Give me your torch, Hal!'

With twice the light, Philbey believed she had a chance of finding the access point to the tunnels that she so believed – or wanted to believe – were below the chapel. As if to confirm her conviction, she could feel the vibrations of a train passing below.

'It must be a goods train, Philbs. All the passenger ones have stopped now. Sounds like a heavy freight diesel engine – possibly two.'

'Not now Hal. We haven't got time for trainspotting!'

As Philbey turned round to respond, she noticed the monogram on the altar pillar. It seemed an odd place to put something like that where nobody (except God, of course) would be able to see it.

DAVID BAKER

'That's it, Hal! I've found it!'

Sure enough, pressing the ornately carved stone activated a catch and a trapdoor beneath the altar clicked open.

'I knew it! I just knew it! Come on Hal, this is our chance.'

'Are you sure, Philbs. Why don't we just call the police?'

'Without proof? They already think me a silly old bat not to be believed about anything. They will only listen if I have irrefutable evidence. So, stop dawdling and join me!'

Philbey and Riddles managed to lift the heavy trapdoor to reveal a stone spiral staircase.

'Ladies first,' Riddles joked.

She had led the way, determined to prove her theory correct…

Philbey snapped out of her reminiscence as Riggs and Ellis re-entered the interview room.

'Are you ready to continue, Pauline? You were telling us what happened when you and Mr Riddles descended into the chamber of horrors, as I think you called it.'

'That's right, Sergeant. And is there any sign of Harry – Mr Riddles – yet?'

Philbey looked at the two officers as they shook their heads in tandem.

'Nothing whatsoever. Almost as though he had never been there.'

Georgie Ellis longed for sleep. It was now more than 30 hours since she had last slumbered. But there was work to be done, and detective constables needed to be alert, especially in the ongoing interrogation of a suspect in a murder enquiry. Was it murder or murders? Three of them! Could this white-haired old woman be responsible for all those deaths? Ellis had learnt the hard way that appearances could be deceptive. Being in the police taught you that.

She thought back to the previous day's meeting with Trissy. Now *he* was a *good* example of deceptive appearances. Tall, slim, handsome, relaxed, at ease with himself. Yet beneath that laid-back exterior, Tristan Bishop was the most passionate man she had ever met – and probably ever would meet. It was obvious when you knew where – or rather how – to look. The music gave the game away.

McGraw was so different: the typical, eccentric, bachelor musician. And yet, the music master at Templeton Towers had supposedly led a blameless life. The school would never have employed him otherwise, given the tightness of their safeguarding policy, surely. Appearances could be deceptive, though. McGraw had a shady past and a previous life in the OSS.

Ellis would have to follow up on the leads from the meeting with Trissy. But for now it was time to refocus on interviewing Pauline Philbey, still vigorously protesting her innocence.

'Interview recommenced at 0551 hours. Ms Pauline Philbey, Detective Sergeant Charles Riggs, Detective Constable Georgiana Ellis in the interview room.'

'It's Mrs, not Ms!'

'Sorry. Mrs Pauline Philbey.'

'You were telling us how you discovered the secret passageway underneath the altar, Pauline.'

'More to the point, Detective Constable, have you found it?'

Ellis looked at Riggs and then at Philbey. 'We have, Pauline. That part of your story checks out.'

'And what about the rest? I was right about underground tunnels that led down to the railway line, wasn't I?'

'Yes, you were. We give you that, Pauline.' Riggs cleared his throat.

'I – we – Harry and I, that is - went right down to the tunnel below. It's such an interesting archaeological find! Dates from Sir Templeton's days.'

'Then what did you do?'

'Started to explore the chambers between the chapel and the railway line. There are two, but we only had chance to look round the first. Just some old furniture in it. I expect you are looking round them now, as we speak.'

'We have a SOCO team on their way.' Georgie Ellis smiled.

Then my torch went on the blink. Hal – Harry – Mr Riddles – said we should get out while we could. But we lost each other on the way up the stairs. I thought he was behind me and then, when I reached the trapdoor beneath the altar, I looked back and he wasn't there.'

'And you didn't go back to look for him?'

'I did, briefly, but my torch went out. I was going to call the police at that point, but there was no charge in my mobile.'

'That was very unfortunate, Pauline.'

'Are you accusing me of lying, Detective Sergeant?'

Riggs shook his head. 'Of course not, Pauline. Just a lot of bad luck. Like being found with a knife in your hand.'

'I already told you. I just picked it up from the side of the road.'

'And how did you arrive there, Pauline?'

'I heard voices!'

'Voices?'

'Yes, voices. Two people arguing.'

'Did you recognize either of the people?'

Pauline Philbey shook her head at the two police officers. 'No. They were too far away. Then I heard footsteps. Running. Running away. I decided to follow them. I could see two monks heading to the garden gate. I tried my hardest, but by the time I got there, there was only the body on the ground, face down.'

'And that's when you picked up the knife?'

Pauline Philbey nodded. 'Yes, idiot that I was.'

'And you saw nothing of the other monk?'

'No sign. No sign whatsoever.'

Ellis and Riggs looked at each other. 'And did you know the deceased, Pauline?'

'I don't know, do I? Detective Constable Ellis here whisked me away before I could see. Who was it then?'

'You don't know, Pauline?'

'No, I don't! Who do you think I am?'

'Well, you could be the murderer.'

'What do you think?'

Donald May tensed his shoulders. 'I find it difficult to believe that old Philbey is a murderer. She's had various scrapes with the law in the past, but I doubt she could kill someone – at least not in cold blood.'

'A crime of passion then?' Jean Samson looked through the one-way mirror and into the interview room. 'Ellis is doing well. You think a lot of her, don't you, Don?'

May nodded. 'She did save my life, Jean, back in 2019. And she has the makings of a great copper. I've already told you that: lots of drive, initiative, imagination, thinking outside the box.'

'And a disdain for authority and an unwillingness to follow orders.'

'Well, there is that. But I can live with that if she – and we – get results.'

'And how are we doing on the results front, Don? Could be better, couldn't it?'

'We have made some progress. Thanks to Pauline Philbey we know how Brother Bernard's body got onto the railway track. And we may find more evidence in those chambers.'

'Anything so far?'

'Not yet. But it's early days.'

'You always say that. Early days? And three murders on our hands. Do we have enough to charge Philbey?'

May did not reply. He looked closely at the mirror, observing Philbey's every movement. He took a particular interest in the way she held her coffee cup. Eventually, he turned to Samson.

'No, we do not, because she didn't kill the latest victim. And I doubt she killed the others.'

***

Victoria Perry heard the Town Hall clock strike six in the morning. The latest documents from Lisa Watson made interesting reading. *Very interesting reading.* The new members of the board – appointments pushed through without due process or diligence checks. Inquorate meetings without the key opponents of the land sale – including Clair - present. Perry felt sorry for Lisa – doing her best as Clerk to the Board when some of its members were undermining the authority of the Head of the Order of Saint Saviour at every turn. Was this what a school governing body was supposed to be like? Surely the students – and the staff, for that matter – deserved better?

Perry left the most important file to the end. The red folder was labelled 'Finances and Resources Committee'. At first sight, not something to get the investigative juices flowing, but Lisa had stressed the highly confidential nature of the information inside. She had even stuck post-its to the relevant pieces of paper to help Perry follow the audit trail.

And follow it she did. Right to the core.

'You are free to go, Pauline.'

'What?'

'You are free to go. Thank you for helping us with our enquiries.'

'You don't think I killed the monk?'

Donald May shook his head. 'We have strong evidence that now suggests you were not the killer.'

'Thank God for that! I had just about decided that I was going to oversee the prison archive at Wakefield, serving my time for murder!'

'That would have been an interesting sight, Pauline. Wakefield is a men's prison!'

Philbey laughed. 'I know, Don. Just my little way of trying to lighten the proceedings, especially now I am deemed to be innocent.'

'Don't stray too far from Hartleydale, though, will you?'

'I have no intention of going anywhere. Too much excitement for this old dear already, I can tell you! Anyway, why don't you think it's me?'

'It came to me while I was watching you being interviewed last night. You're left-handed, aren't you. I saw you drinking your cup of tea.'

'Yes, I am. Why do you ask?'

'Because the way in which the victim was murdered clearly shows the killer was right-handed.'

'Phew. I always thought being left-handed was an inconvenience - until now, that is.'

Philbey got up from the seat she had been occupying for far too long. Her back ached. May held her stick while she put her overcoat on. Suddenly, she leapt into life.

'Harry! What are we going to do about Harry! He's in danger! I am sure of it!'

15

Death; Liberation; Danger

'He looks far more relaxed in death than he ever did in life.'

'You confirm that this is the body of John Sebastian McGraw?'

'I do.' Janos Szabo looked at May, then Riggs. 'A sad business. After the other deaths at Templeton. We are in the national newspapers and some parents are threatening to take their children away. If it weren't for the generous bursaries that we offer, we would have run out of students by now.'

'Indeed, sir. I think the time has come to move the school's operations elsewhere. We must protect the staff and the students.'

Szabo nodded. 'I understand that Inspector. I know your own son has been affected by all this, but I would ask you to reconsider. It will do more harm than good, moving him, and the others now. You will know only too well how unsettled neuro-diverse children are by change. And we have done our very best to protect them from what has happened over the last few weeks.'

May laughed. 'Freddie wouldn't tell me or his mother if he was affected. He's turned into the typical uncommunicative teenager!'

'I don't think anybody would ever describe Freddie as typical! He is a brilliant boy in every subject that interests him.' Szabo said.

'Very well. I take your point. I will think about it. But for now, is there anything more you can tell us about Mr McGraw?'

'I don't think so, Sergeant. You have it all in my statement. He was a brilliant if eccentric musician; one of the greatest organists in the country. McGraw was somewhat unorthodox in his teaching and his choir training, but he got results, and everybody respected him and feared him in about equal measure!'

'Did he have any special friends among the staff or in the locality?'

'Not that I am aware of. He was very much the loner. Devoted to his music and little else – apart from …'

'Yes?'

'Apart from his model railway. It was his pride and joy. It was a special privilege for the students who were allowed to see it – though they never got to play with it ever. He ran it with a detailed timetable, like a real train service.'

'Better than Northern Fail, I hope, sir!'

'McGraw was always complaining about the local trains. Though he still went trainspotting down at Hartley Central.'

'Thank you. And you last saw him at the morning service, playing the organ?'

Szabo nodded. 'He taught his classes as timetabled, and then did his dormitory duty until lights out.'

'And that would have been?'

'10 pm for the older students – like Freddie, for example.'

'And then he would have – what? Retired to bed?'

'I imagine so. He would have had an early start the following morning. Choral rehearsal at 07.45 before breakfast.'

'Can you think of any reason why McGraw was wearing a monk's habit when his body was found?'

'None whatsoever. The brothers are very particular about who wears the habit – unless you are a member of the Order of Saint Saviour, it is strictly forbidden.'

'Thank you. We will be in touch again tomorrow. I presume that someone can cover his duties until a decision is taken about what to do with the students.'

Szabo nodded. 'A stroke of luck, really. An old colleague of McGraw's is going to be in the area visiting his sister. He was scheduled to give a recital in the Chapel next week, so I have asked him if he would take over for a while.'

'That is very lucky! I am sure Freddie will be pleased. He enjoys his music. He loves learning the organ. What's the name of the stand-in?'

'Bishop. Tristan Bishop. He will be staying with his sister Jo in Holme Hill until we can get some accommodation sorted out.'

Brother Jeffrey was a different man; completely different. Gone was the nervous, apologetic ditherer. *Father* Jeffrey was confident, authoritative, charming, to the point, efficient, and a thousand more attributes nobody would ever believe the old monk could ever possess. The new Head of the Order of Saint Saviour was so good that, at the end of the emergency Board meeting, Andreas Day led the members in a round of applause.

'I never knew you had it in you, lad! That's the best meeting we've had in a long time!' Day looked at Lisa Watson to make sure he could be so complimentary about an *ex officio* member of the Board. 'Now all we need is to agree on this land deal and we are set fair.'

'Well, Professor Day, there is the small matter of the murders – and especially of Mr McGraw. I would like you and Mr Szabo to say what you are going to do to counter all the negative publicity. As an aide to our discussion, I have prepared this little document. It has the potential to be a new marketing strategy for the school – and the order. Given that the official meeting is over, we can discuss my thoughts informally. We will not need you to take notes, Lisa. I am sure you have other things to be getting on with. That's assuming you agree with that, Professor Day.'

Day nodded. Watson grimaced as she gathered her papers together, got up, and started to leave. 'I will start writing up the minutes straight away, Professor Day.'

Szabo held the door open for his Executive Secretary. He smiled apologetically as she left the Board Room.

Day looked round the room at his fellow Board members. 'Now let's get down to business. You're among friends, Jeff. And none of the naysayers are here to stop us getting our way. What have you got in mind?'

Harry Riddles wondered how much longer he could survive. It was the strangest feeling he had ever had in his long life. The pain came and went as he slipped into and out of consciousness. He tried to piece together the events of the last few hours. How long had he been down here? Riddles touched his head and felt moistness. There was enough light for him to see the redness on his fingers. There was a vague recollection of being hit from behind as he was following Philbs back up the spiral staircase, but the rest was a complete blank.

Try and work out where you are! Think! It's a chamber; brick. Looks like something from the days of the railway. Can I hear a train? Rumbling, certainly. God, I hurt!

Riddles got to his knees then tried to stand. That was the point at which he realized his right ankle was shackled to the wall. He heard footsteps coming towards him.

When Charlie Riggs was eleven, his Dad bought him a Hornby train set. There were big dreams of the loft being converted so the layout could have a permanent home. Redundancy and the move to a smaller house put paid to that. The box containing track, engine and some of the carriages was in the garage – somewhere. For an instant, Riggs wondered about rekindling the one-time interest, but however many plans he drew up, however hard he tried, however long he laboured, he would never have a model railway like the one that took up most of John Sebastian McGraw's flat at Templeton Towers.

'Have you ever seen anything like this, Charlie?'

Riggs laughed. 'Nope. It's a schoolboy's dream!'

The train set ran all the way round the room, with a void in the middle where the controls were. Riggs lifted a section of the baseboard to allow the two of them access.

'How did you know how to do that, Riggsy?'

'Standard practice. I'll bet I could get this thing going in no time.'

'Huh! Boys with their toys!'

'What's wrong with that?'

Georgie leaned over one side of the layout to get a better look at the scene depicted. Riggs did the same on the other side of the room.

'It's incredible, Charlie. The amount of detail in these figures and buildings and vehicles and animals. Everything!' Ellis leaned over some more. 'Whoa! What's that?'

Trains, cars, buses started moving.

'What have you done, Charlie?'

Riggs laughed. 'Set a sequence in motion. There's even organ music coming out of the church!'

'How the hell did you do that?'

'A mere press of a button, Georgie. It's all controlled by computer. McGraw must have programmed this. It's unbelievable. It must have taken hours to build!'

'And cost a fortune! Where does a music master get the money for something like this?'

'No other outgoings! No partner. No kids. No rent on this flat. Easy!'

'Spoken with feeling, by the sound of it, Charlie. Anyway, much as I want to stay and play trains, we need to get on, don't we?'

'Hmmm. I guess so. What's going to happen to the layout, I wonder?'

Riggs powered down the program. The various modes of transport stopped as suddenly as they had started. He and Ellis checked the layout to make sure nothing was left running. Then it dawned on them.

'You realize what this is, don't you Georgie?'

Ellis nodded. 'I do. And it's creepy.'

'It's more than creepy, George. Look.' Riggs walked over to the immaculately detailed scale model of Templeton Towers. He went over to the ruinated chapel in the estate grounds, lifted the building from the surrounding scenery, then pointed to the miniature underground chambers that linked to the railway tunnel below.

'Weird. Really weird. Look at Father Bernard's body by the track.'

'Was McGraw the murderer?'

'If so, who killed him, then?'

'You let Philbey go then?'

'No choice, ma'am. She may have been implicated on discovery with the knife, but it's very unlikely that the old dear killed McGraw, given that the murderer was right-handed and Philbey is left-handed.'

May watched as Samson fiddled with her pen. She wanted a cigarette. He had always hated her smoking. Surprising that someone with such discipline couldn't give up the awful habit.

'If Philbey didn't do it, then who did? Any clues so far?'

'The murder weapon was an old dagger from Sir Templeton's collection. Brought back from the Holy Land, like all the other stuff.'

'What about the habit that McGraw was wearing?'

'It's the type worn by the brothers. It looks old. Forensics are going over it.'

'And McGraw?'

'John Sebastian McGraw is not who he seems. DC Ellis has found out that McGraw was once – if only briefly – a member of the order.'

'That's news. How did she find out?'

'Used her initiative and got in touch with her old music teacher, who happened to know McGraw and – would you believe – was a student at Templeton Towers in the late 70s. He told her; and said there was some trouble at McGraw's last school. We are following up on both leads as a matter of urgency.'

'Thanks. It's a bit different from the other murders, eh, Don?'

'Definitely: different MO, and McGraw was not part of the inner cabinet that runs the school, even if he used to be a brother. I had determined that if there were any more murders, it would be the new head of the order.'

'Brother Jeffrey?'

'Brother Jeffrey.'

'Tell me about him.'

'Long-serving member of the Order of Saint Saviour. Brilliant History teacher. Heavily involved in the ongoing archaeological dig. Something of a joker. Rarely taken seriously by the rest of the organisation.'

'The dig: you said that lots of money was spent on that? Despite the school's tight finances? What is it about that project?'

'It's been a school tradition for years. Since the founding of the place. It was Sir Templeton who instigated it.'

'And they are looking for what, precisely?'

'Something relating to the Templars. Taylor had a theory that the medieval knights who built the church had buried treasure there.'

'I thought Sir Templeton had done that himself.'

May nodded. 'Carrying on the tradition. He saw himself as a Templar.'

'Have you searched their records?'

'We are on the case. Pauline Philbey was helping us on that.'

'Do you trust her? You've only just released her from interrogation for murder.'

'I trust her as much as I trust anybody involved with Templeton Towers!'

Samson rubbed her eyes and looked at her watch. 'I am going to have to go soon. Reception at the Town Hall. All part of the job.'

'Networking? Winning friends and influencing people? Rather you than me. Jean.'

'Sure I can't interest you in that promotion, Don?'

'I'm still thinking about your offer, I promise. Let's see what life looks like when this case is over. I'm not in the right frame of mind now, for all sorts of reasons.'

'It would make it easier for us. Not being in the same command. You would be good in a different role.'

'Let's talk later.'

The two of them nodded. Samson drained her coffee mug.

So, the least managerially able brother is now *Father* Jeffrey. It makes no sense. Why not one of the others, with more leadership experience?'

May laughed. 'This is a religious organisation. It doesn't have to make sense. Except in the eyes of God, perhaps!'

'Crazy. A recipe for incompetence.'

'Jeffrey was next in line in terms of order of service, so he got the job.'

'Germain seemed highly competent. With a life before the OSS. He would have made a good Head. Or could it be that he is pulling the strings and will only make his move when the others are out of the way? Find out more about Germain, Don.'

'Already on the case. He was in the Royal Navy. Commander. Like Szabo.'

'You never know.'

Yes, ma'am. And what about McGraw. Where does he fit in?'

'Keep following up! Anything more from the sweep of those underground chambers?'

Absolutely nothing. More to the point, no sign of Harry Riddles, either.'

'That's worrying. Unless Philbey was dreaming?'

'Well, he's nowhere to be found. Not at the safe house, certainly.'

'Where's Philbey now?'

'Back at the safe house, along with Boris, her cat.'

Samson snorted. 'No more threats from masked men?'

'None, ma'am, though you can't be too careful.'

'Hmmm. Perhaps it's time we started taking risks. Don. I have an idea…'

'I don't want to go home!'

'Neither do I!'

'Neither do I!'

'What are we going to do?'

Vanessa and Camilla threw their hands up in horror. 'You will have to sort it Frederick Dawson May.'

'Me? How can I do that?'

'You'll think of something.'

Freddie May grunted. 'I can't think what!'

'Talk to your Dad. Persuade him to keep the school open.'

'But he's the one who wants to close Templeton Towers down. It's Mr Szabo who is trying to talk him out of it.'

'We'll never find the murderer if they shut the school down!'

Freddie looked at the two girls. He would miss them – terribly – if they were split up. He had come to rely on them, to enjoy their time together, being and working with other people, even – especially – of the opposite sex. A strategy began to form in his mind.

16

New Sounds, New Hopes, Expectations Fulfilled

Freddie knew something was different as soon as they all filed into the chapel the following morning. It was the sound of the organ! Quick Draw's playing was – well – so much more exciting. The instrument had come alive. He was a different person. The piece was one that Freddie had heard before, but never like this.

Freddie managed to whisper to Vanessa. 'Quick Draw's on good form.'

'I agree. Wow!'

The prelude came to a triumphant conclusion as Principal Szabo and Father Jeffrey took their respective places on the stage.

'Please be seated.' Szabo turned to Father Jeffrey, who nodded slightly to the Principal in response. 'I have some very sad news for you all – staff *and* students. I regret to announce that – that Dr John McGraw, our esteemed Organist and Director of Music, is dead. He died last night.'

Freddie felt the collective sharp intake of breath across the whole of the chapel. He had not experienced such a situation before and said so to Vanessa. She responded by squeezing his hand hard and smiling sweetly at him.

'But it can't be! It should have been Brother Jeffrey!'

'Shush Freddie! Keep quiet.'

'I know that you will all be shocked to hear such news. I have already been in discussion with the police about temporarily closing the school.'

Another congregational gasp. Freddie winked at Vanessa.

'But in the light of recent communications and following further advice from the police, it has been decided that the school will remain open. Business as usual, in fact.'

It seemed odd to Freddie that applause should burst out at that point, but Vanessa later said it was probably something to do with a 'release of tension'.

'Which means I can now introduce Mr Tristan Bishop, MA, Mus Bac, FRCO, as our interim Director of Music. It was fortunate that Mr Bishop was in the area for a short holiday. We have managed to persuade his employer to let us have him until the end of term so that our excellent music making can continue without interruption. Mr Bishop – come and join us.'

There was a third gasp when a tall, slim, handsome grey-haired man in his late forties or early fifties(Freddie and Vanessa surmised), skipped jauntily down the organ loft stairs and onto the podium.

'A round of applause for Mr Bishop, please.'

The new Director of Music bowed and smiled. Even Freddie could see why the female students would find this man attractive.

Szabo cleared his throat and continued. 'Now, while Mr Bishop returns to the organ loft, Father Jeffrey will lead us in prayer. Then, as you file out at the end of this service, please do so in silence and listen to Bach's *St Anne Fugue in E flat*, Dr McGraw's favourite composition.'

Freddie, Vanessa, and Camilla (when they reported back to her afterwards) could not work out how a person could change as Brother Jeffrey had changed. Had his jittery whimsicality (Freddie liked that word a lot) been an act; or was the new, confident, ebullient Father Jeffery (Freddie liked that word even more) the real thing?

'Perhaps they are both acts. Perhaps the new Head of the Order of St Saviour is a devilish, devious, devouring murderer. Who knows what a person is really like inside?' Freddie looked at the girls, who shrugged in response.

'We are nearly there. Not long now, my darling.'
'Not long at all, sweetie.'
'What's wrong, darling?'
'How do you mean?'
'Well, you've gone all sad on me! Why?'
'It's nothing.'
'It is! It's something I said, isn't it?'
'No, of course not, sweetie. It's just – well – after my wife died, I never thought I would be happy again. It didn't occur to me that I might love again. And here I am with you. This is the most wonderful thing that has ever happened to me. I shouldn't say it, but I will – I love you like I never loved. You are my life, Melody.'
'Don't be so silly. I bet you've had lots of other women!'
'None like you, I swear it.'
Melody Grimshaw got out of bed and wandered over to the window.
'Careful Mel! People might see!'
'What if they do see? You will be the envy of every man in Hartley when they find out you have bedded a super model.'
Melody waggled her naked rear as she opened the window.
'Melody!'
'Only teasing, my darling.'
'Don't do that to an old man. My heart won't stand too much excitement, especially after what we have just done!'
Melody Grimshaw clambered onto the bed and crawled on all fours back to where she had been lying.
'And what we are about to do again, my darling. We have just enough time before you meet Szabo.'
'We'll have to be quick, though.' Andreas Day looked at his watch and giggled.

Harry Riddles tried to work out how long he had been incarcerated. It was well nigh impossible. The only calculation he could make was based on the rumble of the trains. Knowing the Northern Fail timetables (and particularly the one for the trains that linked Hartley and Holme Hill) so well, he determined it had been two days – 48 hours – since Philbs had driven them to the side gate at the Towers and their sleuthing had begun. Why hadn't she listened to him? Why had he listened to her? She had always been telling him what to do, right from when they were at school together. What would she be saying now? What *was* she saying now? Surely, Philbs would have alerted the police and they would be out searching for him. What was taking so long?

Why was he being held here? He had seen and heard nothing. He was not a witness to any of the murders, though he was party to the discovery of the trapdoor and the secret passages down to the railway tunnel. There had been nothing in the chambers, as far as they could discover, other than old furniture. It was dark, and Philbs had been keen to report her discovery to the police, for once.

Then it dawned on him. If he had been out of circulation for two days, then that meant he would miss any special board meeting that Day convened. Still, Philbs would have been there and held her own, voting against the plans, good and proper. Once such a meeting was over, there would be no need to keep him prisoner. It was only a matter of time before he was free. Riddles began to relax for the first time since his imprisonment. He felt cold air on his face. This was it! They would blindfold him so he could not identify anyone and then take him somewhere and leave him to be found. Yes. There was no need to worry. He was going to be fine. Not long before he was back in Pauline Philbey's arms.

Barbara Halliday was pleased with herself. She put pen to paper (no Excel spreadsheets for her) and began to work out how much money she was going to make from the sale of the Templeton land and the completion of those luscious, expensive executive properties on the gated complex that would look down and across the whole of the upper Hartley valley. Even the smaller properties were to be priced at £1.5m. The bigger ones? TBC; POA.

She took out a cheroot from the case on the Steinway and lit it. 'Perhaps I will live in one myself when this is all over.' She laughed to herself. 'Everybody underestimates me. Always have done, always will. But one day soon, they will pay. They will all pay for ignoring me.'

The intercom phone rang. She answered it.

'It's me. It's time to cash in Babs.'

'I wondered when you would come calling. Come up. I've unlocked the front door. I will put the kettle on. Or would you like something stronger to celebrate your – our – victory? Palinka, perhaps?'

'Well, this has been a real surprise. The last thing I expected!'

'A pleasant one, I trust?'

'Hmmm. Not sure, Trissy. I wish the flat wasn't such a mess. Couldn't you stay at Templeton Towers until I've finished the redecorating? I'll be done in a week.'

'Sorry, I expect it will only be for a few days.'

'Are you sure? What about your full-time post? How can you take the time off?'

'Janos Szabo, the Principal, was desperate to fill the job. He got the Chair of Governors at Templeton to phone my Head to let me stand in. No doubt they are part of the same old boy network, so not a problem.'

'What about your own students?'

'They will be very well looked after. I have an excellent deputy, unlike Templeton. McGraw seems to have done it all.'

'And do you really want to do it?'

Tristan Bishop smiled ruefully. 'Sort of. I was a student at Templeton, remember? And I had a soft spot for old John Sebastian.'

'John Sebastian?' Jo Bishop laughed uncontrollably.

'Don't laugh. He's named after the great Johann Sebastian Bach. McGraw had to be an organist with a name like that.'

'And you knew him?'

Tristan Bishop nodded. 'Yes. We trained together for a while at the Academy. A brilliant player, but an eccentric man.'

'Aren't all you musicians a bit odd?'

'Watch it! We need to be odd to be brilliant. You – and I - wouldn't have it any other way. He was into trains in a big way. And he got me my little pipe organ.'

'What pipe organ?'

'It was a cast off from Templeton Towers, of all places. Not needed any more. He just rang me up one day and asked if I wanted it. Free to good home. Of course, I said yes. The school even paid for the dismantling and transport.'

Jo Bishop looked at her brother. 'Well, let's have a coffee and you can fill me in on what you've been up to since – well – you know.'

'Haven't I seen you since then?'

'No, you haven't!'

Jo Bishop was glad her brother had come. He was as tall and as handsome as ever. There was no middle age spread – he obviously still ran - and the grey-white hair just made him look distinguished. She could understand why women found him so attractive. Those eyes!

'I'm sorry. It just didn't – well, you know.'

'I know.'

Jo Bishop went over to the settee where her brother was sitting. She put her arm round him. He leaned into her and began to cry.

'Sorry. I should have got over it by now.'

'Don't be silly. No, you shouldn't. You saw her waste away to nothing. You'll never fully get over that. It will just become more bearable. And who knows? Someone else might come into your life to fill the void.'

'You wanna bet?' Tristan Bishop snorted.

'They will, eventually, when the time is right. I promise. Everything comes to him who waits.'

The visitor now knew who put flowers on the grave. Two students at Templeton Towers! But why did the boy and the girl do it? What did they know? Nothing, presumably. Just a little game they played, having discovered the grave. Surely that was all it was. They couldn't know who was buried there, or why. And they would not be aware of a visitor. Or would they? Were they? These two children were clever – gifted and talented, high-functioning neuro-divergent students. Just like it had always been. The visitor would need to know what they knew, what they had found out.

What was done back then was wrong. So very wrong. But these things happened. People thought nothing of it. Harmless fun. Until somebody got hurt. Like Nicholas had got hurt. Hurt so badly he had died. And nobody – absolutely nobody – had done anything.

What if Nicholas had survived? He would have been a grown man, perhaps a great success, with a wife and family. Music would have been part of his life, certainly. He had been the best treble in the chapel choir; pure top notes, soaring above the other choristers in some great anthem.

If the boy and the girl knew about the grave, did others know as well? It was well hidden. You had to know exactly what you were looking for. Only three old monks were supposed to have the location. And two of them were already dead.

Harry Riddles said the words out loud, even though nobody – except perhaps his god – could hear him.

'Please, God, get me out of here!'

At least another day had gone past – according to his reading of the rumbling trains. But he had grown weak and confused so the counting was not as good. The goods trains had again motored through the tunnel all night, to be followed by the early morning commuter trains into Hartley and beyond.

Riddles was almost certain it was 6 o'clock in the morning when he heard footsteps. There had only been one passenger train so far since the overnight schedules had been completed. He had not been brought food as early as this before. Assuming it was food. His heart sank at the thought of what might now happen.

The door was unbolted and in walked a tall, slim figure in hat and coat, with a scarf covering nose and mouth.

'Quickly! This way! We don't have much time!'

'Who the hell are you?'

'Never mind who I am. A friend. That's all you need to know. Now come on. We don't have any time to lose.'

Riddles groaned as he attempted to move his body. His rescuer took pity on him and held out his hand.

'Can I trust you? Is this a trick?'

'Stop asking questions. Now come on!'

Riddles and his surprise visitor edged out of the room and down a dark corridor.

'You seem to know your way around these tunnels.'

'Shush! We don't know who is down here!'

Riddles decided not to say more. The visitor walked so quickly that he had to run to keep up. That was the advantage of being tall, and slim, and, by the looks of it, fit.

Riddles felt cold, fresh, air on his face.

'You'll be alright now. Ahead is an exit that will take you to the side entrance to Templeton Towers. Wait there and I will phone the police. They will pick you up from there, I am sure.'

'But who are you? Who captured me? Why was I kept down there?'

'Don't ask me all these questions! And be grateful that somebody was on your side!'

'I never thought I would get out of there. I thought I was a gonner.'

The visitor laughed. 'Everything comes to him who waits.'

'Is that grave we found linked to the murders, then?'

Freddie May nodded. 'Yes, I think so. It's all about revenge for something that happened a long time ago. I'm sure of it. We need to find out who is buried in that grave, and what their link to Templeton Towers was. If we can do that, then we can check out the school's records.'

'And who was teaching here at the time. Father William has certainly been here forever. But there must be other brothers.' Vanessa banged her fist on her bed.

'Careful, Van. We don't know any of this. Freddie could be wrong. We have no proof. And we must find the person who is linked to the body in the grave. How do we do that?'

Freddie scratched his head. He realised that Dad did the same thing when he was puzzled.

'I think the time has come for us to spill the beans.'

'How do you mean?'

17

Spilt Beans And Plentiful Surprises

'Does your father know what you have been up to?'

Freddie and Camilla stood there in silence. They looked at each other and then at Georgie Ellis.

'No. We came to you first for – well – for some advice.'

Ellis snorted. 'I don't know where to start. You know that it is a serious offence to withhold information from the police.'

'We weren't withholding it – we just hadn't got round to telling you.' Camilla stamped her feet in serious irritation.

'Hmmm. Well, that's a moot point. DCI May will not be at all pleased. But let's see what we can do first. I assume you think that I will smooth the path when it comes to letting your Dad know about your antics.'

'They're not antics. They were lines of enquiry that we chose to pursue on our own before concluding that we had sufficient evidence to put a case to the police.'

Georgie Ellis raised an eyebrow as she looked at the two sheepish yet defiant students sitting in front of Janos Szabo's immaculately tidy mahogany desk.

There was a knock at the Principal's door.

'Yes. Who is it?'

In walked Lisa Watson. 'I just wondered if people would like drinks.'

Charlie Riggs smacked his lips as if to confirm his thirst. Ellis looked at Szabo then Freddie and Camilla.

'Yes please, Lisa. Tea for me and the police officers, I think. What about you two?'

Freddie and Camilla nodded. 'Tea for us as well, please,' they replied quietly.

Szabo smiled knowingly at his Executive PA who nodded and left the office. He then turned to Riggs and Ellis. 'I am happy for this little "chat" to take place in my presence. But it is not to be recorded in any shape or form, and what Freddie and Camilla say is said within these four walls only. Is that understood?'

Charlie Riggs nodded.

'Freddie and Camilla. You are not in trouble, I promise you. These police officers simply want to hear from you and learn what you have found out. Are you clear about that.'

'Yes Mr Szabo. But don't blame Camilla, sir. It is all my fault.'

'It's nobody's fault Freddie. No-one is to blame. Now just tell your story. Both of you. But take your time.'

The door opened just as Freddie May was about to speak.

'Tea. And cake.' Lisa Watson could hardly carry the massive tray, on which was a large teapot, cups, saucers, plates, and a huge vanilla sponge. Riggs helped her to lay everything out on the conference table while Szabo looked at the Tompion. The grandfather clock struck the hour.

When all was arranged and the five of them were seated round the refreshments, Szabo nodded to Freddie and Camilla to start their narrative.

'We never thought it would come to this. All these murders. If we had only known …'

'Just tell your story, Freddie. And you, Camilla, when you want to add something.' Georgie Ellis smiled as kindly as she could.

Freddie took a deep breath.

'I – we – had only been at the school for a week. We were doing the cross country run and – well – I hate running.'

'And I do too. It shouldn't be compulsory at our age!' Camilla stamped her foot gently to reinforce her indignation.

Szabo coughed as a way of covering his irritation. Riggs and Ellis looked away.

'Go on Freddie. You hated running.'

'Yes, Mr Szabo. We took a short cut, Camilla and I. We were going to hide until the other runners returned and then join in at the back. But we got bored and decided to investigate while we were waiting. We knew we had about twenty minutes, didn't we, Camilla?'

Camilla nodded. 'Yes. Just away from the cross-country path was a ravine, I suppose you would call it, so we clambered down there and looked around for interesting plants. There was a little sort of cutting and when we went through that we found a grave.'

'A grave?'

'Yes. There was a little wooden cross at one end, a bit like you get in cemeteries, but it had fallen over. Somebody had left flowers a long time ago. They were all rotten.'

'Anyway, we tried to find out whose grave it was, but there were no clues as to who was buried there. We assumed it was a young person, not fully grown. The grave wasn't very long, was it Camilla?'

'No. We searched the area, but we found nothing. We were late getting back to the school because of looking around.'

'And why didn't you say anything to me or one of the other members of staff?'

'I – we – wanted to know more about the grave before we reported it. After all, sir, it might have been nothing. A favourite pet or a shrine or something else.'

Szabo looked at Riggs and Ellis. The two officers nodded as a way of encouraging the Principal.

'Do continue. There is no need to be afraid of any repercussions. I can assure you of that. Both of you.'

'Thank you, sir. Well, after that, we decided to tidy up the grave and find out who was buried there.'

'Yes sir, we did.'

'Which? Tidy the grave or find out who was buried there?'

'Both, Mr Szabo. Every leisure period we went there and cleared all the weeds and other stuff away. The thing was …'

'Yes, Camilla. What's wrong?'

'Well …'

'What Camilla wants to say, Mr Szabo, is that we were digging the weeds and stuff, and we found the body – well the skeleton. It can't have been very deep – only a few inches. I think that's what they call a "shallow grave", isn't it, sir?'

Szabo nodded slowly. Riggs intervened. 'And then what did you do? Freddie? Camilla?'

'We just tidied it all up, covered the skeleton again and made it look nice. We go as often as we can and put fresh flowers in a vase.'

'And that's it? You didn't think to report any of this to Mr Szabo?' Charlie Riggs tut-tutted. Georgie Ellis shook her head as a way of restraining him from saying more.

'Don't worry. As I said earlier, you two. You are not in any trouble. I promise.'

'Is there anything more you want to say before you show us the grave?'

Freddie and Camilla remained silent as Georgie Ellis looked at them. The Tompion struck the quarter past.

'Well, there is something more. We know the identity of the person buried there.'

'Yes?'

'Yes, Mr Szabo. When we were tidying the grave, we found a name tag. He was a pupil at the school in the 1970s.'

'How do you know, Freddie?'

The yearbooks in the library; we looked him up. There is even a photograph of him in there.'

'That's all we found out about him,' Camilla added. 'But we have some more information for you.'

'Yes. We have been observing someone visit the grave; every day since Father William died.'

⁂

Pauline Philbey was surprised how lonely she felt in the safe house without Hal. She curled up with Boris and a large gin and small tonic to comfort herself. She looked out of the lounge window before drawing the curtains. It would soon be the shortest day. Already it was dark.

She was reassured by the police patrol car at the bottom of the road, but the visits were increasingly infrequent. Cutbacks, no doubt. And other priorities.

She sat back in the armchair, turned on the television and began to watch *Pointless*. The next time she looked at the screen, it was the regional news. Where had all the time gone? She turned to find the control. As she did so a hand gripped hers.

'Oh my God! It's you!'

Andreas Day had never felt like it. Never, ever. Not in his teens, when love had first struck. Not at university when he must have slept with a dozen or more women. Not in all the years he was married. Not until now.

He loved and hated how he felt. The gut-wrenching ache of a desire so base it made him high and low at the same time.

It had happened so very suddenly. One minute he was still mourning the long-drawn-out death of his wife; the next he was totally besotted with this creature who had walked into his life and turned it upside down. Every crevice of his body, mind, spirit, and soul had been taken over. What mattered once mattered no more. There was only one thing in Andreas Day's life now: Melody Grimshaw.

'Where did you get that name? Grimshaw. It's not exactly romantic. Reminds me of an old Lancashire mill town on a bad day.'

'I only ever called – call - myself Melody professionally. But Grimshaw is my real surname – well, part of it, anyway.'

'What's the other part, then? Something exotic, I hope.'

'Not telling you.'

She had licked her lips with her tongue and shaken her head in mock refusal as he pressed her for an answer. He had not asked further; Melody's sudden near-nakedness had made him forget everything and anything.

Day burrowed his head in the pillows. He could still smell her musk. Some classy perfume, no doubt. He resolved to give Melody the most expensive cologne that money could buy. And he would certainly have plenty of it once the deed was done. All was possible now those interfering brethren were out of the way.

He sat up in bed. There was just one problem: the mystery caller. Was it a hoax? Nothing more had come of it. Nobody had turned up at the rendezvous. There had never been any further contact. After discussion with Szabo, the two of them had dismissed the threat of exposure. And yet, could they be so sure their secret would not be revealed? There was only one thing for it. Day jumped out of bed and looked for his mobile phone.

'Szabo? I've been thinking. I know we said we'd lie low for a while, but I'm still worried about that phone call. What if it wasn't a hoax? What if the stranger goes to the police?'

Day looked at his naked body in the mirror. Not bad; not bad at all. Older men had their advantages; Melody thought so, anyway.

'You agree? No? Let's get on with it, man! I'm going to come over, now!'

Diana Foster stared at her laptop. The email was ready to send. Should she? The end of her career – short and sweet – at Templeton Towers. The students – for all their problems and eccentricities – were wonderful. Such an opportunity to research neurodiversity up close! Freddie and Camilla were especially interesting. Though there was something odd about the girl; almost as if she was two personalities. She would miss them. Unlike most of the staff and the brothers. Clair? Good riddance. Brother Bernard? Good riddance. Quick Draw? Brilliant musician, but … Brother Simon was worse than useless, even if he could teach. Lazy Larry – well, the nickname said it all! And what kind of future did the place have with Brother Jeffrey as Head of the Order? Were they for the chop as well? Germain was the only one who approached normality. She and he had struck up a kind of relationship ever since that day in the pouring rain. Things might have been different if he had taken over. He was an attractive man. There might have been something between them if he had not been celibate and she had not …

Diana Foster laughed out loud. She pressed 'save'. 'Act in haste, repent at leisure'. That's what mother had said. Perhaps she would stay a little longer. What would happen to her and Melody if she resigned from the school? It happened so quickly! Melody had been so 'persuasive'. Think of it! Diana Foster in love! Gut-wrenching, stomach-aching, mind-bending love. There had never been anything like it before – and there never would be anything else like it ever again. She knew that. Nothing could be so perfect – in every way.

They would run away together. That's what they would do. Melody had said that her work in Hartley was nearly finished. She would ask her the next time – when, oh when, would that be – that they would be together. On their own. In each other's arms.

Foster looked out of the window. There she was, in all her wonderful, glorious, glamorous beauty, walking towards the main entrance to Templeton Towers. Melody looked up and waved.

Yes. They would run away together. Once Melody had completed her work in Hartley. And she, Diana Foster, would do anything to help the love of her life get on with the job.

Janos Szabo smiled as Melody Grimshaw walked up the steps and through the grand entrance to Templeton Towers. He imagined her striding elegantly through the Great Hall, then up the main staircase past all the portraits and memorabilia and along the corridor that led to his rooms. There would soon be a gentle knock on the door, and she would be in his arms.

Melody was like the most powerful possible drug a man could take. He was addicted. He could not control his desire for her. Here he was, a man priding himself on his cold, calculating, emotionless approach to life gone mad with love. He could not bear to be away from her. When he was, he just trod time.

Soon, it would all be over. The project would be complete, provided Day's impatience didn't get in the way. They should have waited. What was the rush, now the two brothers and interfering old Quick Draw were out of the way? Jeffrey would do everything necessary to complete the arrangements and then Barbara could get started.

How different life was going to be! Szabo thought back to his first days at the school and what he had intended to achieve. But now he knew the secret of the treasure, as revealed by Melody, he had no intention of staying as a schoolmaster. None whatsoever. There was just the little matter of Freddie and Camilla and their little 'discovery'. That was unfortunate. Very unfortunate. Even more reason for telling Day to slow down ever so slightly. 'Everything comes to him who waits', Szabo had said to Day.

He thought about the grave and the investigations that would now have to take place.

There was a gentle knock at the door.

'Come in.' Szabo quivered in anticipation; his throat went dry.

He turned round slowly.

'Oh, it's you. I was expecting … well, someone else.'

***

'Do you think we got away with it?'

'Don't know Freddie. We aren't under arrest, are we? We are still here, allowed to continue with our studies.'

'What do you think, Camilla?'

'How should I know, Freddie, I wasn't there, was I?'

'But you two do thought transference, being identical twins and all that.'

'We're not that good! Though I did have some bad feelings about Mr Szabo, especially now he knows about the grave.'

'What happened to that little boy happened years ago. Szabo would have been a boy himself then.'

'Perhaps he knew the victim.' Freddie ruffled his hair.

'Your Dad has just the same mannerism. I've seen him do it.'

Freddie took his hand away from his head. 'I'd better stop doing it, then.'

'It's a thought, though, isn't it?' Camilla looked at the other two, then continued. 'Did you know that Szabo is a Hungarian word?'

'Is it? What of it? Mr Szabo sounds very English to me.'

'Yes, you two, but Hungarian ancestry. I looked him up on the school website. His grandfather was from Hungary. Fled from the Nazis.'

'I still don't understand what you are getting at, Camilla.'

'I did some more searching. Did you know that Szabo means Taylor in English? As in Templeton Taylor?'

'That's just coincidence, Camilla. Honest. Anyway, we have far more important things to be worrying about. Thank goodness we weren't asked about the phone calls. We really would be in trouble if anybody found out about those.'

***

'I'm so glad it was you, Hal.' Pauline Philbey rubbed Riddles' forearm and beamed a smile at him. I thought you were dead!'

'So did I, Philbs! It didn't look good at all.' Riddles and Philbey looked across from their vantage point on the settee. Ellis took notes; May ruffled his hair.

'You have no idea who your captor was, Mr Riddles?'

'Call me Harry, Detective Constable. Everyone does. Unless you are a close friend, in which case it's Hal.'

Riddles put his hand on Philbey's arm. She let him keep it there.

'Captors, I think. I heard two distinct voices in the distance.'

'Men or women?'

'One of each, Inspector. The woman had a strong accent.'

'Tell me more, sir.'

'Call me Harry, Detective Constable!'

'Sorry, Harry.' Ellis reddened slightly as she looked at her boss.

'Quite a hard sound.'

'German?'

'I thought so at first, but it wasn't guttural enough. And I speak a bit of German and I decided it was more Eastern European.'

'They weren't speaking in English?'

Riddles shook his head. 'Not all the time. Sometimes the conversations got heated. That's when they spoke in this other language.'

'Russian?'

'No, I don't think so.'

'Something like Russian? Polish? Bulgarian?'

'I am sorry, Inspector. I don't know.'

'Don't you think Harry has had enough for one day, Donald? It's been a real ordeal for him.'

'I know Pauline. Forgive us. Just a few more questions, and then DC Ellis and I will be on our way.'

Philbey looked across at Riddles, squeezed his hand and smiled. 'You sure you want to do this, Hal?'

'I'm fine, Philbs. We need to get to the bottom of all this.'

Philbey looked at May and nodded.

'Thank you. We'll leave it at Eastern European for now. But if anything occurs to you, then do let us know. Anything more about the two people?'

'The woman had a northern accent when she was speaking in English.'

'Anything about her - or his - appearance?'

'They were both tall and slim. I remember that. They were of similar height. She had incredibly long legs.'

Philbey looked askance at Riddles.

'And what about your rescuer, Harry?'

'Male, with a posh English accent.'

'What did he say to you?'

'Very little DC Ellis. They communicated mostly by pointing and taking me by the arm.'

'What did they look like?'

Riddles shook his head. I have no idea, Inspector. The man wore a balaclava. In any case it was very dark, and not just in the place where I was locked up.'

'Why do you think you were kept there?'

'I wish I knew. I'll tell you what, though – with me and Philbs – Pauline – out of the way, Day, Szabo, and their cronies could get the proposal through – and they did. It's all going ahead!'

'By that, I assume you mean the sale of the land.'

'Yes, Donald, they will make a mint out of it between them.'

'But I thought you all had to be present, and the vote must be unanimous.'

Pauline Philbey shook her head and laughed. 'Not so simple, Donald. The vote must be unanimous *among those present*. If people are absent without having sent prior apologies, and the meeting remains quorate, as long as all those in the meeting vote in favour, then a proposal to dispose of major assets will easily succeed. Which it has done in this case, especially since Father William and Father Bernard are out of the way and Father Jeffrey is a spineless pushover.'

'That's your motive, Inspector. Money. People have killed for much less than the Templeton Estate is worth.'

It was the first time that Georgie Ellis had driven Donald May's car. Having left the safe house where Philbey and Riddles were now holed up once more, the DCI pleaded tiredness. As they approached the Volvo, Ellis had been thrown the keys and told to get on with it.

'Where to, sir?'

'Templeton Towers, Georgie. I want to look round the estate, including that old chapel and the underground chambers. Then there's the burial site. And the archaeological dig. Anyway, I need some fresh air.'

'Very well, sir.'

The Volvo was a much heavier, clunkier vehicle to drive than the BMW Z4. Much to her surprise, it was automatic transmission. Georgie Ellis had always assumed May would want to 'feel the gears', just like Dad did. She thought back to when he had taught her to drive. He had been a strict but brilliant teacher; she passed first time after very few lessons. Wearing her school uniform might have had something to do with it as well. The examiner had certainly been more attentive than expected.

By the time they were on the open road out of Hartley and past Holme Hill, Ellis had relaxed. The sun was as high in the sky as it would get on a December day in Yorkshire. She had come to love the rolling hills and narrow, steep-sided valleys of Hartleydale, though the locals still bemused her. Goodness knows what Tiggy made of them. Templeton Towers hove into view.

'You alright, Georgie?'

'Yes sir, of course. Why on earth do you ask?'

'No real reason, except you seem to have been a bit edgy of late. Under pressure? It's nothing to worry about on a big case like this. Especially when it's your first in plain clothes.'

Ellis smiled. 'It's not that, sir.' She turned to May. What a strong, rugged face he had.

'What is it, then? I don't want you to be worrying about anything while you are on this investigation. You – I – we – must stay focused. Come on, Detective Constable.'

Ellis sighed. 'Well, sir, if the truth be told, I am worried about you.'

May laughed. 'Me? Why me?'

'Because you aren't your normal self. You haven't been for some time.'

'Haven't I? Really?'

'No sir. Not since DS Trubshaw left and ACC Samson arrived.'

May fell silent. Ellis blushed, then cleared her throat.

'Sorry sir. I didn't mean – well, I didn't mean to pry. I was just – well, I am worried about you.'

May shook his head. 'Well, I did tell you to spill the beans. I just didn't expect such a spicy variety!'

They laughed. May continued.

'I am flattered that you are worried about me, Georgie, but there is no need, I can assure you.'

Ellis drove the Volvo right up to the main entrance to Templeton Towers and switched off the engine.

'Are you sure, sir?'

'Well, I have had some – personal – problems of late. I admit that. Caz – Catherine – and I have had our difficulties and disagreements. Freddie is not an easy child at the best of times. We are both very proud of him – he's a genius – God knows where he gets it from!'

'From you, sir, undoubtedly!'

'Flattery will get you everywhere, Georgie.'

'It's true, sir. I have learnt so much from you since I arrived in Hartley, and especially since I became a DC – thanks to you!'

'I like to support and encourage good people. And you could go to the very top if you chose, Georgie.'

'You sure? Anyway, what about you, sir? Couldn't – shouldn't - you do the same?'

'Hmmm. I'm not so sure anymore, Georgie. Do I want the hassle of senior management?'

'You mean like ACC Samson?'

Donald May blushed.

'Something like that, Georgie. But that's another story. We need to see what's going on at the grave site first.'

May and Ellis got out of the Volvo and began to walk up the steps to Templeton Towers.

'Georgie?'

'Yes, sir?'

'When we are on our own together, just call me Don.'

'Yes, sir. I mean Don.'

Ellis was about to say something else when Charlie Riggs appeared.

'You look excited Charlie. What's up?'

'Better come quick, you two. An interesting discovery at the grave site. It could explain a lot.'

18

Revelation And Consternation

'We should have done this sooner.'

'Yes, we should.'

'Has it been worth the wait?'

Pauline Philbey looked at Harry Riddles and nodded. 'Yes, Hal. It was.'

Riddles laughed. 'I have wanted to be with you since we were at school together! How sad and silly is that?'

'It's not silly at all! Why shouldn't love blossom at our age? Except you took your time to get going. 60 years or more!'

'That's unfair! I was spoken for. Whatever my feelings for you, I am not an adulterer!'

'But we are both free now, aren't we? What kept you?'

'I don't know, Philbs. I thought I was past it. I had given up hope of finding somebody after I was widowed. I kind of got used to being on my own. Then you came back into my life. I wanted to talk to you so many times after the Board meetings up at Templeton Towers, but it never seemed right, somehow. Until we were thrown together with all this hoo-hah. It's the only good thing to come out of this mess.'

Pauline Philbey nodded. 'I agree with you.' She paused. 'But if we are going to make this work, Hal, we have to be completely honest with each other, haven't we?'

'I know, Philbs. It was wrong of me not to tell you about the rival bid for the Templeton Estate. That's all academic now, though, isn't it?'

'I fear so, Hal. I fear so. I investigated the rules and regulations governing the Templeton Trust. We would have a hell of a fight to get the decision overturned.'

'Barbara Halliday gets her way! She will have luxury houses up there before you can say 'Saint Saviour.' What a travesty!'

'Your alternative bid was never going to succeed, though, was it, Hal?'

'What do you mean?'

'Where were you going to get the funding from? No disrespect, my love, but your credit isn't exactly hunky-dory, is it? Since the firm went bust.'

'Hunky-dory? Who says that nowadays?' Riddles laughed.

'Don't avoid the question. How were you going to put together a serious rival bid to Halliday and her crew?'

Riddles looked away.

'Come on Harry! Tell me!'

'Oh dear. You're calling me Harry again! I told you. It was the Templeton treasure that William Clair said he had found!'

'Ha! I don't believe you! And I am going to be very angry with you if you don't tell me everything.'

Harry Riddles got out of bed, put on his bathrobe, and went over to the sofa on the far side of the room.

'Do you mind if I smoke?'

'Yes, I do, Harry Riddles. Now put that cigar away and get on with it. I'm all ears!' Philbey sat up, covering herself with the bedclothes as she did so.

Riddles buried his head in his hands.

'Come on, Harry, I'm waiting!'

'Very well'. Riddles clasped his knees with his hands, then began his story.

'You're right. It was nothing to do with Templeton Taylor's treasure. I was going to see Clair that night to tell him I had found the funding for a rival bid.'

'Funding? Where from?'

'I tried very, very hard to keep Riddles going. You know that don't you, Philbs?'

'I remember the factories across Hartleydale that closed in the 1970s and 1980s. You did well to keep Riddles's open as long as you did.'

'I sold my soul for that place. And I mean that!'

'Your soul?'

'I couldn't get any more money from the banks, so I turned to organised crime.'

'What?'

Riddles nodded. 'It's true. I got in with a bad lot. A very bad lot.'

'Who?'

Riddles shook his head. 'That's the strange thing – and you probably won't believe me – but I don't know. After all these years I still don't know.'

'Come on, Harry! You must know!'

'It's all done remotely – over the internet; has been since the very early days of the worldwide web. Occasionally there is a phone call, but I have never been able to find out who it is.'

'And what do they ask you to do, these criminals?'

'I launder money for them. Big money.'

'So that's how you can afford to run that Mercedes even though you live in a council house.'

'Yes. The council house is a cover. I own a place in the south of France. And a villa in Spain. And a boat. I want us to go and live abroad, Philbs. You and me. Just the two of us.'

'I will do no such thing! At least not until you are straight with me. How could you lie to me?'

'I didn't lie, Philbs.'

'Yes, you did!'

'No. Well, I just didn't tell you everything that there was to tell.'

Pauline Philbey got out of bed and put on her dressing gown. 'Oh Harry. What have you done? And things were going so well between us!'

'They still can be good between us, can't they?'

Philbey walked over to the bedroom window. It was raining heavily outside. The unmarked police car was still on the far side of the road. She turned to face Riddles.

'Is that the real reason I – we – were attacked in my house. Is that why we are now here in this "safe house"?'

Harry Riddles said nothing.

'It's true, isn't it Harry?'

'Yes. It's true. I promised them I would be able to persuade Father William to let me buy the land. They would have been able to launder millions that way. They needed to do it quickly, and I was their best option – their only option in the time available. But when Clair was murdered, that scuppered their plans and I was "for it", if you see what I mean.'

'I see exactly what you mean. And you thought fit to come to my house and endanger me as well?'

'I didn't mean to, Philbs. I swear. It never occurred to me that they would go for you as well as me. I had nobody else to turn to.'

'And what were they looking for when they broke in?'

'I don't know. I honestly don't know.'

Pauline Philbey rubbed her forehead and turned back to the bedroom window. The streetlight flickered apologetically then went out. The rain was beating down heavily; she could hardly hear herself think. Who would be out in such weather? She looked around before pulling the curtains. They were nearly closed when she saw – or thought she saw – a figure standing at the garden gate. Was it shadows, her imagination, or a real person?

Tristan Bishop was pleased with himself. He had long wanted to play the great organ at Templeton Towers. It was world renowned. And now it was his, at least temporarily. He looked up and down the four keyboards and the rows and rows of stops. He pulled out the ones that would make the most noise and began to play a Bach Toccata – from memory, of course. His favourite – the F major. With that glorious pedal part.

As the final chord on full organ died away, Bishop heard a slow clap from down below in the chapel. He swivelled around the organ bench, stood up and went to the edge of the organ gallery.

'Welcome to the school, Tristan. It's good to have you here. Your playing is wonderful. More, please. Then we need to talk. McGraw left such a mess. And I am relying on you to clean it up, once and for all.'

Bishop smiled. 'Of course. That's why I came, isn't it. I wouldn't miss it for anything. Happy to help in any way I can.'

'That was quite something, wasn't it?'

'If you like that sort of thing. What do you think Camilla?'

'Well, I do. I think it's great. I want to learn the organ. Especially now that we have Mr Bishop as our music master.'

'What do you mean?'

'Well, Freddie, he is quite something, isn't he? And I don't just mean his playing.'

'I think there's something strange about him. I saw him and Mr Szabo talking. Like they were good friends. How and why did Bishop turn up so quickly – within days, remember - after Quick Draw was killed. It was as if he was ready and waiting to fill the vacancy.'

Vanessa looked at Freddie and Camilla and shook her head. 'I think we will have to keep a close eye on Tristan Bishop.'

The *Speckled Teapot* was busier than ever. Its location on platform one of Holme Hill Railway Station made it a haven for fed up travellers as they experienced Northern Fail's woeful attempts to provide a train service. Cable theft had meant services were 'delayed' yet again – the third time in a month. As if that were not enough, the police investigations in the tunnel between Holme Hill and Hartley had meant a week-long suspension of services.

Jo Bishop had difficulty finding a table. There was just one left in the far corner. The area must have been part of the original waiting room. It was good that the owners of the *Teapot* had preserved or restored as many original features of the Victorian station as possible. To add greater authenticity, the walls were covered with sepia prints of scenes from Hartleydale in the 19th century. Bishop studied the series depicting the building of Templeton Towers. She marvelled at the ingenuity of the original builders and the hydro-electric power system, the first of its kind in the world. But how grotesque the architecture! It reminded her of Rosslyn Chapel in Scotland and *The Holy Blood and the Holy Grail*. All that stuff about Jesus and Mary Magdalene being married and having children. That and Templars. Templeton Towers: what a joke!

The waitress arrived.

'I'll have Earl Grey tea, with lemon, not milk. And a piece of Victoria sponge. My friend will be here shortly, I'm sure. She's late, but then she's always late.'

The waitress noted down the order then disappeared into the main part of the Teapot.

Templeton Towers. It had served her brother well, though. Tristan had flourished at the school. His talent for music had been spotted and nourished to the point where he had won a scholarship to Cambridge, gained a double first and a blue in cricket to boot. Perhaps she would have done well there too, except it was boys only in those days. Very boys only if the rumours of the time were to be believed. Jo Bishop had never been jealous of her handsome, witty, charming, erudite, hugely talented brother. No, she loved him too much for that. But she wished for some of his success. It all seemed so easy. While he did no work and got A★ in everything, she trudged along studying hour after hour to get C+ at best.

Jo Bishop suddenly felt guilty. How could she compare her woes to those of a man who had watched his wife die of the most awful cancer? Trissy had borne it all so bravely, but she knew that he was hurt badly inside. Nothing could be worse than losing a loved one like he had. Perhaps the temporary move back to Templeton would become permanent. Then they could start a new and much better chapter in their relationship. It would be good to have her brother back in her life.

'Sorry I'm late, Jo. I made the mistake of catching the train rather than driving. It was meant to save me from the rush hour, but I would have done the journey in half the time if I had come by car!'

Victoria Perry sat down so enthusiastically that the table vibrated, and the crockery rattled.

'Better late than never, Vicky!'

'I know, Jo. You don't need to tell me off. I'll never be organised like you. That's not how it works in the world of journalism.'

The waitress returned with tea and cake.

I'll have the same. That sponge looks delicious. I know I shouldn't, but, hey, the diet starts tomorrow, like it always does!'

The waitress noted down Perry's order then left.

'What have you been up to, Jo? How's the PhD?'

'Not much, Vicky. Same old, you know. I have nearly finished the dissertation, though, thank God!'

'That's taken you a while, hasn't it?'

Bishop nodded. 'I had to intercalate. I – well, I fell out with my supervisor. I got somebody else in the end. It all worked out OK. I'm back on track now.'

'What's the topic again, Jo?'

'Hartleydale during the Second World War.'

'Sounds interesting.'

'It was until I had to write up all my research! What do they say? "If you want to kill your interest in a subject, do a PhD on it". That's how I feel.'

'Oh, come on Jo! You love your historical studies. It's just a blip. You'll be great. Just keep at it.'

'Like you are doing with your unfinished novel?'

'Ouch! That was below the belt, Josephine Bishop!'

'Sorry. You are right though. But I will get it finished one day. I have just so many other things on the go, especially now. Murders up at Templeton Towers, mainly. And, strictly confidentially, doing some off the record detective work assisting the police with their enquiries.'

'Explain.'

'It all dates to the 1970s. Strange goings-on at the school. Nothing ever proven, of course, but there were rumours of molestations and worse. I don't trust monks: never have done, never will. And it looks as though the stories were true, given the latest discovery.'

'What latest discovery? Is it to do with the murders of those priests?'

'The body of a young boy. That's what. A hidden grave in the grounds. Found by two of the students. My theory is that the lad was murdered by the three senior monks all those years ago and their deaths are revenge for the child's death. Someone is out to get them for what they did back then. You alright, Jo? You look as though you've seen a ghost. You've gone very pale. Is the sponge off?'

Jo Bishop laughed nervously. 'No, I'm OK. It's just that – well – my brother Tristan – he was a student at the school in the late 1970s and early 1980s. He might have known this child. But he never said anything about anybody going missing. And there was no talk – not ever – about mistreatment of any sort. He really enjoyed his time at Templeton. I was quite jealous of him. They didn't take girls back then, and I would have loved to have gone – if only to try and beat him at something.'

'Sibling rivalry strikes again!'

'He's always been better than me. But when I have my doctorate, I will have one up on him, at long last! The funny thing is, he's back in Hartleydale, and at the school.'

'Really?'

'Yes, really. He is standing in until the end of term after the death of McGraw, the Director of Music.'

'Interesting. Can I interview him?'

'Possibly. He'll be very busy sorting things out. Incidentally, McGraw wasn't there in the 1970s, was he?'

'Hmmm. Perhaps McGraw had discovered the truth about the brothers and was going to let the cat out of the bag.'

'But that would mean he was killed by someone other than the man – or woman – who was seeking revenge on those who murdered the little boy.'

'Ah well, I will have to go back to the drawing board on that one.'

'I'll tell you what though. I discovered something interesting in the archives about Templeton Towers. It was Pauline Philbey, the local historian who put me on to it.'

'Do tell, Jo!'

'Right at the end of World War II, a plane reputed to be carrying Nazi gold crashed on the Templeton estate. Though it was all hushed up at the time, apparently. And to this day, nobody knows what happened to either plane or treasure.'

'God! That might explain a lot, Jo. Where did you find this out?'

'I'll show you, but ...'

Jo Bishop looked out of the window. A train had just pulled into the platform outside. As the doors opened, she saw a tall, grey-white-haired, extremely handsome man get off, to be greeted by the most gorgeous creature she had ever laid eyes on. It was her brother, no doubt of it; the woman looked familiar, too.

19

Old Problems, New Leads

DONALD MAY HAD ATTENDED MORE POSTMORTEMS THAN HE CARED TO remember. This one was different. The boy had been dead for at least forty years; possibly more. The remains were well preserved, and there were even shreds of clothing attached to the skeleton. Fizz Harbord showed May and Ellis the pieces of what she took to be a school blazer.

'I haven't finished trying to join up all the bits yet, Don, but it's my guess that the victim was a student at Templeton Towers. The grey fibres look the same sort as the present school uniform. Worth checking what it looked like back then.'

'Back when? Early 1980s?'

Felicity Harbord nodded. 'Sometime around then, judging by the rate of decomposition.'

'How old was the boy when he died?'

'I'd say about ten or eleven, given the stage of development. He would just be entering puberty.'

May thought back to when Freddie was eleven. What a handful he had already become. Autism had kicked in. That and the growth spurts. The voice had broken long ago, and the facial hair grew fast enough to need a daily shave. The attempts at mainstream schooling had quickly broken down, despite the excellent reputation of Hartley Multi-Academy Trust and their continued efforts to meet Freddie's very special needs. It had not worked; nobody's fault, just one of those things. Home schooling had been the only option. Caz had given up her job to do the tutoring as best she could, with Dad taking over at the evenings and weekends. Grandparents had helped until they became too infirm – both physically and mentally. Somehow, between them, they had survived Freddie's transition to teenager.

Unlike the boy on the slab. May noticed a tear running down Georgie Ellis's nose. He had not seen her display such emotion before; too career orientated to be interested in children, or a relationship – presumably with a man. May had heard something of her sister and the two boys, with their ridiculous names, but they seemed a hindrance rather than something to nurture and treasure.

'What did he die of Fizz?'

'Interesting, that, Don. At this distance, I'm not sure. There are no broken bones or other signs of attack. He may even have died of natural causes, though the boy was healthy enough, by the looks of it – excellent teeth, good nutrition.'

May looked at Harbord. 'Nothing more, then, Fizz?'

Harbord shook her head.

'OK. Come on, then, Georgie. Let's go and have a drink. Riggsy will be here shortly. There's a machine just down the corridor. My treat.'

They sat in the corridor sipping their cups of coffee.

'Still enjoying the job, Georgie?'

'Very much so, sir. It's what I always wanted.'

'No regrets?'

'Absolutely none. Why?'

'Just wanted to be sure that you are on board with this work and my approach.'

'Your approach, sir?'

'Well, we haven't made much headway yet, have we? The ACC doesn't think so, anyway. She is snapping at my heels again. Always wants everything done yesterday, that woman.'

'Again, sir?'

May grimaced as he tried to drink the undrinkable. 'Not very good, is it, Georgie?'

'You mean the ACC snapping at your heels or the awful coffee?'

May laughed. 'Both are equally sour.'

'Sorry to hear that, sir. My tea is OK. Lots of milk and sugar helped.'

'I wish I could sweeten Samson as easily.'

'You knew her before, didn't you, sir?'

'Who told you that?' May threw his plastic cup into the bin.

'Well.'

'Go on.'

'A couple of people back at the station. They got in touch with colleagues at the ACC's previous HQ in Norwich. And it all came out.'

'Hmmm.'

'Don't be cross, sir.'

'Cross?'

'It's a natural thing to do. To find out about a new boss. How were we – I mean they – to know that you and she were – well – you know?'

May laughed. 'Yes, I do know. And, yes, it is natural – sort of – that you would want to find out about your boss's ex.'

'You mean the other people in the office?'

'Do I?'

Georgie Ellis blushed. 'Was she really your ex, sir? It must be odd – her being your commanding officer.'

May breathed in deeply. 'It was a long time ago, Georgie, before I met my wife. Jean and I were very different people then. It was young love – first love, even. Nothing more. Jean Samson is an excellent copper and a great boss in her own way. You would do well to have her as a role model. A better one than I could ever be.'

'Really, sir?'

'She's a woman, Georgie. She's come up through the ranks in a way that I never had to. We should be making more progress, though. The ACC is right!'

'But we are! Cases like this will never be easy. She should be patient and leave it to the experts.'

May laughed. 'Jean Samson has never been patient. And she is an expert! Anyway, Charlie should be here. What's keeping him?'

'We never did find the anonymous caller, did we? And there have been no more, have they? Not to him, and not to me.'

'I know, Georgie. Prank calls; wasting police time. Except why focus on the old chapel? Charlie was asked to meet there; and so were you. It was as if someone was pointing us towards that place. A member of staff from Templeton Towers, perhaps?'

'Definitely. Quick Draw McGraw; must be!'

May snorted. 'How can you be so sure, Georgie?'

'His model railway?'

'A-ha. Charlie didn't believe me when we checked out McGraw's rooms. But it's a scale model of Templeton Towers – or at least the bit of the estate with the old chapel on it. And the railway tunnel, of course. The interesting thing was - it was set out with our police cars as they were when we caught Professor Day and Miss Grimshaw.'

'Why didn't you say something sooner?'

'Charlie pooh-poohed it all. I didn't think any more about it. I agreed with him that it might have been coincidence.'

'Georgie – I don't believe – we shouldn't believe – in coincidences. Never. Charlie should know better than to even suggest that! We need to take a closer look at that railway layout. A pity that Freddie can't join us!'

'How's that, sir?'

'Have you forgotten his fascination with model railways?'

'Of course. I remember him telling me when I visited your house once. He's grown up a lot since then, though, hasn't he?'

'Tell me about it! He is still very young in some ways, but I think there are the first stirrings of romance, or at least interest in the opposite sex. Poor thing!'

Ellis laughed. 'I know the feeling, sir!'

She blushed as May looked at her quizzically.

'I was about the same age when I had a mad crush on my music teacher at school. The very handsome older man. Old enough to be my father. I was fifteen and he was in his early forties.'

'And what happened?'

'Nothing, sir. Absolutely nothing. Except – except my older sister had a crush on him as well. She never let on to me, but I suspect it went further than just flirting in the corridor.'

'Is there something you're not telling me, Georgie?'

'Well, sir, he's here, in Hartley. Working at Templeton Towers.'

'Really?'

'He's called Tristan Bishop. He was my – our – music master. Father Jeffrey has hired him as a temporary replacement for Quick Draw. Until the end of this term if not longer.'

'And who told you this, Georgie?'

'Tristan Bishop. I met him recently. He remembered me straight away. Well, there's more to it. You need to know. Tiggy and I went to see him recently. We wondered if he might be able to shed some light on McGraw and the music scene. It turned out that he knew Quick Draw well. Bishop even had a cast-off pipe organ from Templeton. *And* he was a student at the school in the early 1980s when our boy was around by the looks of it.'

'You should have mentioned all this sooner, Georgie. It could be important. Another reason to get back up to Templeton Towers.' May nodded past Ellis. 'And here comes Detective Sergeant Riggs, in some distress, by the looks of it.'

'What's wrong Charlie. You look as though you have seen a ghost.'

'Not quite sir. Another death. You'd better come quick!'

MOVEMENT IV

Allegro Marziale

20

Puzzles And Possible Solutions

'What's happening Fred?'

'Stop calling me Fred! It's either Freddie or Frederick. You know that!'

'Well, now you know how we feel when *you* call us Vanilla 1 and Vanilla 2'.

'I haven't done that in ages, Camilla, and you know it!'

'Just reminding you, Fred ... Eric. Making sure you know not to!'

'Stop it, you two. Don't we have more important things to worry about than some silliness about names?'

'Sorry, Vanessa.' Freddie and Camilla apologised in tandem.

'How do we find out what's going on?'

Freddie sighed. He went over to the bedroom window and looked at the scene below. Every light in the main building was on. Blue lights flashed: police cars and an ambulance. Then he recognized another car as it drew up to the main entrance to Templeton Towers. Out got three people: Riggs, Dad, and the new Detective Constable. Freddie had met Ellis before, when she was in uniform. He had blushed when she addressed him, surprised that the woman knew his name. He remembered her sad brown eyes, and how beautiful she was. It had felt odd, talking to her back then; he could recall his emotions, just like he had sometimes when he was with Vanessa and Camilla, only more so.

Ellis looked up. She smiled and waved at Freddie. He started to wave back, then thought better of it.

'What are you doing? Who's she?'
'It's Georgie Ellis, Dad's new DC.'
'DC?'
'Detective Constable.' Freddie turned back to the girls, confident in the knowledge he was the one with the special link to the police. 'I think it's another murder', he continued. 'Why would there be all these cars here, and an ambulance, and the SOCOs? And Dad and his inner cabinet, of course.'

Vanessa and Camilla groaned in tandem.

'Oh yes, sorry – Scenes of Crime Officers – SOCOs.'

'Go on, then, Commander May, who is it?'

Freddie said nothing for a while. He put his hands in his pockets and wandered up and down the room. Then he went back to the window. 'Come over here, you two.'

Once the girls were either side of him, Freddie pointed across the quadrangle.

'Look at the first-floor windows. Dad and Riggs and Ellis have just gone in there – can you see? You know whose office that is, don't you? I didn't think they were going to be the next victim.'

Vanessa and Camilla looked at each other and then at Freddie. 'Neither did we.'

Freddie shook his head. 'Perhaps we need to review our theory about these murders.'

'Did you expect this sir?'

'Nope. Not at all, Georgie. This is the last person I expected to find dead.'

'At least it looks like suicide this time.'

The three officers heard Felicity Harbord snort from the far side of the office. 'Don't be so sure, team. I think we are dealing with a suspicious death.'

'So, she didn't just hang herself?'

'No Don. I think Dr Foster was already dead when she was strung up.' Harbord shook her head.

'And that is because?'

'The bruising round the neck, Sergeant Riggs. I think it's postmortem. I'll know more when I get this young lady back to the lab.' Harbord stood up and made to leave the scene.

'What about this, sir? Suicide note?'

Ellis pointed to the computer screen.

'Read it out Georgie.'

'Very good, sir.' Ellis cleared her throat and began.

> *I am sorry for everything. I killed them all. I did it on my own. Nobody else was involved.*
>
> *It was revenge. They murdered my brother. And now they have their comeuppance. They got what they deserved.*
>
> *I have no more reason to live. My work is done.*
>
> *Goodbye.*
> *Diana Foster.*

'Anybody could have written that, Don. It's not as if it's in her handwriting or has her signature, is it?' Harbord motioned to the computer screen.

May shook his head. He had only met Diana Foster once, after the murder of Father William. He had interviewed her, as he had done all the senior staff at Templeton Towers. Freddie had spoken warmly of 'his' educational psychologist. The daily sessions with Foster had been wholly beneficial. May even wondered if his son had a teenage crush on 'Dr D', as she was known in the school. She was certainly a good-looking woman: tall, slim, long black hair, immaculate dress sense (or so Georgie Ellis had judged). And now May was looking at her lifeless body.

'Who found her?'

'I did, Inspector.'

Janos Szabo had appeared in the doorway.

'Stay where you are, sir. This is a crime scene.'

'I tried to save her, Don – Inspector – I gave her CPR, after I cut her down, but it was too late. She was already dead. I did what I could.'

May walked towards Szabo. 'Let's talk in your office, Janos, not here. Riggs, Ellis – you know what to do.' Sergeant and Constable smiled and nodded.

'And I'll see you at the post-mortem Fizz.'

The two men were soon in the Principal's Office.

'Drink?'

'Not while I'm on duty, sir. And I'm supposed to be tee-total. My Methodist upbringing.'

'Mind if I do?'

May laughed. 'You're already halfway through a whisky anyway, by the looks of it.'

'It's something far more interesting than whisky. It's palinka. Hungarian. That's part of my ancestry, that is.' Szabo held the drink up to the light, closed one eye as he looked through the glass as if sizing up a diamond, then downed the spirit in one go.

'Tell me about Diana Foster.'

'Not that much to tell. She was very good. The students all loved her. Your Freddie in particular. He's made great strides since he came here, you know.'

'I do indeed.' May nodded. 'He is transformed already.'

'Oxbridge material, definitely.'

'We were talking about Diana Foster, Janos.'

'Sorry – we were.'

'Came with excellent references. Stellar career in academe. I knew about her before I started here. The work on high-functioning autistic teenagers was world beating.'

'And yet she chose to come and work at Templeton Towers?'

'Once we saw her application there was no point in considering anybody else. She said she wanted a change from the lecture theatre. Back into practice: and what better place to do that than here? Somewhere that has always specialised in children and young adults that are the focus of her academic interests.'

May nodded. 'I'll need to see her personnel file, and we'll be wanting to see her apartment. I'll have Ellis sort that in the morning.'

Szabo sat down and crumpled over. 'God! What a term! This is like a nightmare. Thank God it's over!'

May looked at the picture on the wall. Row after row of navy officers in uniform. He thought he could see Szabo on the front row; behind was the other familiar face. 'Time we took a closer look at Brother Germain', he thought to himself.

Midnight. Hartley Town Hall clock confirmed the hour with its dull chime. It had been raining since teatime the previous day. The heating had gone off in the safe house. To keep warm, Pauline Philbey flicked on an electric heater in the bedroom which had now become her base room. She liked a special place where she could carry out her investigations. It was exciting to be doing detective work. And this was no ordinary enquiry. Boris decided to join her, managing to sit on the most important papers on the desk in the process.

'I'm glad you're doing this rather than me. I've never been any good with computers!' Harry Riddles put his hand on Philbey's shoulder.

'Not now, Hal. I need to find out about these friends of yours!' Boris hissed in Philbey's support.

'I'm sorry I didn't confide in you sooner. I didn't want you to think ill of me. I know I'm in above my head. I'd understand if you dumped me!'

Philbey laughed. 'No, I won't be doing that any time soon. You're stuck with me a bit longer. I'm not ready for a pipe and slippers nonentity just yet!'

Riddles squeezed Philbey's arm and kissed her on the forehead.

'Give over, Hal. No time for that now! We need to get to the bottom of all this before anybody else gets hurt – and especially you and me!'

'I think it's wonderful the way you can find out so much on the internet!'

Philbey laughed. 'Especially if you go on the dark web.'

'What's that, Philbs?'

'That's a very interesting question. It's where bad people do evil things. And I bet that goes for your mafia. Now make me a drink while I get us where we need to be.'

'What do you want?'

'What do you think, Hal? And make it a double!'

Riddles needed no further incentive. He left her to get on with her cunning plan. He had seen a whole new side to Hartley's renowned archivist. There was obviously much more to the role than met the eye. When he returned from the kitchen, she was staring intently at the computer screen.

'How are you getting on Philbs? Here's your gin. I didn't know what to do about the tonic.'

'Leave it out. I need to take my drink neat just now.'

Philbey scrolled through screen after screen. Riddles was in awe.

'Got it! Look at this. These are your mafia friends. I have managed to trace your link to them.'

'How the hell did you do that?'

Philbey laughed. 'Years of practice. I have my own secrets.'

'You?'

'Yes, me, Hal. You don't know the half of it. I'm not just the local archivist, you know. And I do more than digitise old photographs!'

'You are a dark horse!'

'Well, this dark horse has discovered where your mafia friends are based.'

'Romania? Bulgaria? Hungary?'

'Nowhere so exotic, I'm afraid.'

Riddles watching his lady friend scrutinising the moving screens. 'It's all gobbledygook to me.'

Philbey hit various keys to stop the automatic scrolling through the data. 'There! Just look there!'

'What am I looking for? I can't see anything.'

Pauline Philbey traced her finger over the screen. 'It's obvious, when you know what to look for, Hal. There! Just there!'

Riddles leaned over his paramour. As he read the lines, the truth gradually dawned on him. 'By Jove, I see what you mean, Philbs. So, these are the people I've been dealing with all this time: the bastards who have been putting me through hell, using me, taunting me, making me sick with worry every single day of my life for the past – well, for the past ten years and more.'

Pauline Philbey swivelled round on her seat and looked Harry Riddles in the eye.

'And they have been operating under your nose - our noses – all the while.'

21

A Ruse Or Two In Time

THE *SPECKLED TEAPOT* OPENED AT 10 O'CLOCK, MONDAY TO SATURDAY. That Thursday morning there were two people waiting on the doorstep for the café to welcome customers. Once the place was unlocked, the couple rushed in out of the rain and headed for the furthest table away from the counter.

Victoria Perry couldn't wait to open the white A4 envelope that Lisa Watson lay down on the table.

'I thought you would be interested in these papers, Vicky.'

'Too right, I am!'

'I shouldn't really be showing you all this stuff, but I am not happy with what's going on up at Templeton Towers. It's not been the same since Mr Szabo started.'

'You look upset, Lisa.'

'It's awful. All those murders. Especially Dr Foster. I liked her.' Lisa Watson pulled out a handkerchief and blew her nose loudly.

'Tell me about her.'

Watson was about to begin her narrative when a waitress came over to take their order.

Perry ordered two coffees, no food.

'She was popular with the students. They really liked her. The improvements she made in such a short space of time. The rumour is that she killed herself.'

'Suicide? Really?'

'Well. That's one rumour. The other is that she was murdered, like the others.'

'Did she make any enemies amongst the staff?'

Watson shook her head. 'Quite the opposite. Everybody adored her. Even the monks!'

Victoria Perry laughed. 'The dirty old so-and-so's!'

'They weren't all old. Brother Germain is quite something, for starters!'

'I didn't know about him!'

'Ooh – tall, dark, handsome. I used to see him and Diana running together in the grounds.'

'And what about the others? Who do you think murdered them?'

Lisa Watson took the papers back from Victoria Perry. She pointed at the signature at the bottom of the final document.

'That's the killer, if you want my opinion.'

'I do. Very much.'

'The suicide note says *they murdered my brother*.' Donald May paced up and down his office, his hands in his pockets. 'Father William, Brother Bernard, and – somehow - McGraw were responsible for the murder of a child. Our body in the woods near the old chapel, presumably.'

'It would seem so, sir. Just one problem.'

'Yes, Georgie?'

'Diana Foster was an only child. I have been in touch with her parents – they are coming to identify her body tomorrow morning. They deny all knowledge of another child. It's a mystery to them as to why their daughter should say that.'

'Except it wasn't Diana Foster who wrote that, was it?'

The three police officers looked at each other and shook their heads.

'It's too "off pat". Solves the first three murders and makes out that the fourth is a suicide. It even ties up the loose end of the boy from the 1970s. If Diana Foster is the murderer, everybody else is in the clear.

'If she is the murderer, well …'

May laughed. 'I know what you mean, Charlie. Either the real murderer was being naïve and amateurish, or very clever.'

'How do you mean, sir?'

'Well, perhaps it was meant to be obvious. Perhaps the real message from that "suicide note" is that those three murdered the boy and they – and Foster – were killed by his real brother or sister.'

'That's an interesting thought sir.' Georgie Ellis wrote it down on the murder wall, with arrows across to the four victims. 'But how do we move the case forward from there, sir?'

'ACC Samson has had an idea.'

'Really, sir?'

'Really. And we had better take it seriously, so pay attention you two!'

Riggs and Ellis looked at each other, then at May. This was not what they had expected from the morning briefing.

'What does ma'am propose then?'

'To flush out the murderer once and for all.'

'That sounds very dramatic, sir.'

'Those were her exact words, Georgie.'

Ellis and Riggs raised eyebrows simultaneously. May looked away towards the murder wall.

'Don't knock it, you two. Her plan has merit.'

'What is it then, sir?'

'We are to let it be known that having searched the grounds of the Templeton Estate, we have located the secret treasure that Father Clair has been searching for all these years.'

May nodded.

'And that will reveal the murderer?'

'It might well do, Georgie.'

'Well, I think it is far-fetched, to say the least.' Ellis crossed her legs and folded her arms as if to confirm her indignant scepticism.

'It might give us the break we need though.' Riggs scratched the back of his neck.

'How do we do it, sir? What is the treasure supposed to be?'

'We don't know, but we don't say we don't know; we don't need to. Samson feels the murders all revolve around the treasure on the estate. That's what the archaeological digs were about; that's what prompted the attack on Philbey; that's why there have been three – now four - murders.'

Ellis shook her head. 'I don't agree with that, sir. The first two murders at least were surely about the *sale* of land. If you sell the estate, then you lose access to the treasure, assuming it exists.'

'And what about McGraw and Foster? Were they in on the act, whatever that was?' Riggs scratched the back of his head in frustration.

'I still think that those two got too close to the truth, whatever that was.'

Ellis flipped through her notebook. 'There are – were – rumours that Foster was having an affair with one of the other members of staff, possibly Szabo.'

May and Riggs looked at each other.

'Who said that, Georgie?'

'Lisa Watson, Szabo's PA. She thought that Foster was having a liaison with someone else at Templeton.'

'And why did she think it was the Principal?'

'Because she said Szabo and Foster were often together in his office. And –'

'And?'

Ellis cleared her throat. 'And because Szabo was the only man at the school worth going after – apart from brother Germain, and he's taken a vow of celibacy, so he's off the agenda, presumably.'

'Some women might take that as a challenge, Georgie.'

'Now, now, Charlie.' May snorted.

'Just a possibility, sir. I know I couldn't be celibate.'

It was May and Ellis's turn to raise eyebrows.

'Szabo certainly must be one of our main suspects. He has good access to every part of the school and the monastic buildings. I saw a photograph in his office when I spoke to him last. Some sort of graduation ceremony or passing out parade from when he was in the navy by the looks of it.'

'What of it sir?'

'The interesting thing, Georgie, is that I recognized someone else on that picture.'

'Sir?'

'Brother Germain was on the row immediately behind Szabo.'

'What?'

May nodded. 'And neither of them has said anything about a previous connection.'

'Should we interview them both again, sir?'

'Not just yet, Charlie. Let's see how things go with the ACC's plan.'

'Very good. Anyway, how are we going to "make it known", sir?'

'That's easy, Charlie. We get in touch with the local newspaper. I have a good contact there.'

'Tell us, then!'

'Yes, tell us. We have a right to know.'

Vanessa and Camilla gripped Freddie by the shoulders, one in front of him, the other to the rear.

'Alright, alright.'

'We've been waiting.' Camilla took Freddie's hand and squeezed it.

'We don't think you have an idea, anyway.' Vanessa nudged him in the back.

'Yes, I do. I do!'

'Oh no you don't!'

'Oh yes …'

Freddie pushed the girls away and got up. He moved the hair out of his face and turned to look at them.

'It's taken a while for me to work it out, but I know what we must do now if we are going to flush the real murderer out.'

'Real murderer?'

'Well, it wasn't Dr D, was it? It's too obvious for her to be the murderer and then to commit suicide having avenged the little boy's killing.'

'Very true, Commander.' Vanessa looked at Freddie, then Camilla.

'Come on then, Freddie, tell us all.'

'We told Mr Szabo about the grave.'

'But I thought that was to keep us at the school rather than to be closed down.'

'Maybe. And maybe it was because I had a word with Dad.'

'Oooh – get him. The high and mighty son of the Detective Chief Inspector!'

'Give up! Give up if you want me to tell you the plan!'

'Sorry!'

'Yes, sorry, Freddie.'

'But it's interesting that Diana Foster turned up dead after we told Mr Szabo about the grave. And she was in the interview with us.'

'She was killed because of knowing what we said to the Principal?'

'It's a thought.'

'I don't get your reasoning there, Commander May.'

'Perhaps it's coincidence, Freddie.'

'There's no such thing as coincidence in police work, you two!'

'We know. Anyway, come on – the plan?'

'We must find the treasure. That's what the murderer is looking for. It's got nothing to do with the sale of land or the little boy's death. It's all about Nazi gold. That's what has been the reason for the archaeological dig all this time.'

'Nazi gold? Don't be ridiculous?'

'I am deadly serious. At the end of the Second World War, a plane flew out of Budapest carrying vast amounts of Nazi gold. I think it landed on the Templeton Estate and was hidden here.'

'And how do you know all this?'

'Research in the local archives for my history project. Someone else has been doing the same.'

'The murderer?'

'Well, she is one of the governors here at the school. I saw her name in the log of people checking into the local studies library. But I don't think she has discovered what I have found out.'

'How so?'

'Because the document that shows where the Nazi gold is – as opposed to the so-called Templar treasure - really is, was misfiled. I discovered it quite by accident the other day.'

'So, we really will be able to find it and let it be known that we have found it?'

'Yes. But we will be in danger when we do tell.'

'Are you sure you want to do this?'

Philbey nodded.

'I'm sure, Hal.' She leaned over and kissed him on the cheek.

Riddles put his hand on hers and squeezed it. They smiled.

Philbey switched off the engine, got out of the car and nodded to Riddles to follow her. She shivered in the December cold. It would snow before the evening was finished.

The two of them linked arms as they walked to their destination.

'Shouldn't we have told the police?'

'And incriminate you in the process, Hal? You know that would never do.'

'I know. I don't want to spend the last few years of my life inside. I would rather spend them with …'

Philbey turned to Riddles and put her finger to his lips. 'Save it for later, Hal. If we get through all this, then who knows where fate might take us?'

Riddles smiled and nodded.

Rankin Hall looked as imposing as ever. It was only the second time Philbey had been. Riddles had never visited. Little did they realise what lay behind the imposing black front door.

22

The Game Is On!

'Well, this is a pleasant surprise. Somewhat late in the evening, but very good to see you both, nevertheless. I assume it's to do with the recent Board meeting. But do come in. It's cold out there, and don't I know it, especially at my age!'

Rankin Hall had been hard to find. Hartley Moor was full of winding, unlit, unsigned, single-track roads. All looked the same; none seemed right; satnav was useless. The only way to get there was to keep remembering the stately home bordered the very north-western tip of the Templeton Estate.

And now they had reached their destination. Philbey and Riddles looked at each other in response to Rankin's invitation. Riddles nodded and beckoned Philbey to lead the way.

'Come through into the drawing room. The fire is still in. You'll soon warm up in there.'

The hallway was almost as grand as Templeton's; portraits hung all the way round the vast space.

Rankin beckoned the two visitors into the drawing room. Philbey thought it was the least homely place she had ever been in. There was no wife to sit alongside, no family photographs on the mantelpiece. The room was notable only for its bareness, apart from the intricate scale models of steam locomotives.

Philbey and Riddles sat down either side of the fireplace.

'Tea? Coffee? Something stronger?'

'No thank you.' Philbey took the lead in replying. Riddles simply nodded in agreement.

'So. What's all this about?'

'We know your little secret, Clement.'

Rankin laughed. 'Little secret? I have lots of little secrets. Which one were you thinking of?'

'Your racket, Clem. And I have been your dupe in it all as well!'

'You? My dupe? Pull the other one, Riddles.'

Philbey got up, walked over to Rankin, took out her mobile, pressed a few buttons and then showed him the phone. 'Money laundering, Clement. I have found all the information I need to have you arrested. I know my way around the dark web, and *you* could go away for a seriously long time. In fact, you would never see the light of day again.'

Rankin scratched the back of his neck, clearing his throat as he did so. 'Nonsense. I have never heard such rubbish in all my life.'

Philbey laughed. 'You were the last person I thought would be a master criminal! But why?'

Rankin shook his head and rubbed his eyes. 'I think it's time you two left. I'm very tired, and I want to go to bed.'

Riddles stood up and made to join Philbey. As he did so, the drawing room door creaked open.

Rankin smiled and beckoned the visitor inside. 'Come in. I need your assistance with these two people. I thought them innocent friends, but now I realise they are a serious threat to our operation. See to them for me, will you.'

At which point the visitor took out a revolver and pointed it at Philbey and Riddles.

'Follow me please.'

'It's good to see you again, Don. I was beginning to think you had forgotten me.'

May blushed slightly as Victoria Perry made eyes at him over their cups of latte at the *Speckled Teapot*. He looked out of the window into the early evening darkness. It was beginning to snow. People hurried past on their way home.

'No chance of that Vicky, especially when you are such a key element in our ongoing investigations.'

'Ooh. Tell me more, Detective Chief Inspector! I'm all ears.'

'Stop it! You – we - need to be serious.'

'I'll be serious when you keep your side of the bargain, Don.'

'How do you mean?'

Victoria Perry declined to reply as the waitress arrived with tea and cake.

'Mmm. Delicious! Only the *Speckled Teapot* produces cakes like these! Can I try a bit of yours, Don? And you can have some of mine. Share and share alike, just like the old days.'

'Vicky!'

'OK. OK!'

'What did you mean "keeping my side of the bargain"?'

'I said I would share what I knew if you kept me informed of developments.'

'Yes, I did, and I will.'

'But you haven't, have you?'

'There is a limit to what I can tell you. You know that really, don't you?'

'Hmmm. You could have told me more than you have done.'

'Such as?'

'Such as why you exhumed the body of that priest; and whether Diana Foster's death was suicide or murder, and what you did with that folder I gave you. And that's just for starters.'

'There's more?'

Victoria Perry laughed so loudly she nearly choked on her chocolate cake.

'There is much, much, more, Donald May, and I am not letting you go until you tell me all.'

May looked down at his untouched *pastel de nata* and then out of the tearoom window. A Northern Fail train was disgorging its disgruntled passengers. He looked at his watch. Freddie would know the exact time of arrival and departure and how many minutes – and seconds – the train was behind schedule.

'If I swear you to absolute secrecy, do you promise not to tell a soul, at least until the case is finished?'

'Cross my heart and hope to die, Don.' Perry made the sign across her chest then squeezed his forearm.

May looked around. Their end of the café was empty, and the waitresses were engaged in hearty conversation behind the counter.

'That Vicar was murdered all those years ago. It wasn't suicide. Fizz – Felicity Harbord - the pathologist, examined the remains. There were traces of poison.'

'Same as killed Clair?'

May nodded. 'There's a strong chance that it was the same MO.'

'Hmmm. Linked to the Templeton murders then.'

'Don't speak with your mouth full Vicky.'

'But this cake is so very, very, delicious.'

May looked down at his food and pushed it away. 'Have this as well, then.'

'Really?'

'Really.'

'And it was murder.'

'What was?'

Diana Foster's death. She was strung up after she had been killed.'

'Ooo-er. The Templeton Terror strikes again!'

'And that's why I need your help.'

'As always Don, as always.'

'Good. Which is why you are going to print an exclusive front-page story in the weekend issue. All about a major police discovery on the Templeton Estate.'

'I knew you would come good, Don!'

May looked at her and smiled.

'Are you sure this will work, Cam?'

'Of course, Van. I trust Freddie, for all his faults!'

'Isn't it a bit risky, after all we've done so far?'
'Remember what Dad always used to say?'
'No, what's that?'
'Might as well be hung for stealing a sheep as a lamb.'
'Not funny!'
'Sorry. But it's true.'

'Is it? I thought those phone calls that Freddie made were bad enough, then telling Szabo about the grave and everything. We haven't heard the last of that one. And now this!'

'I know Van. But we've got to do something if we are going to catch the killer. Or killers. Haven't we?'

'Do you agree with Freddie that more than one murderer is involved?
'I'm not sure, Van. There's a lot of killing for one person to handle.'

'Not if they were angry enough. I would if I thought my sister had been murdered by the brotherhood, just like the little boy.'

Camilla hugged her sister. 'I don't know what I'd do without you.'
'Me neither!'

'Anyway, it's too late. Freddie's done it now, so we'll have to wait and see what happens next. And we must support your boyfriend!'

'He is not my boyfriend. That love stuff is a drag!'
'Oh yes he is.'

At which point, Vanessa smacked her twin sister harder than she intended.

'Sorry!'
'I'll give you sorry when this is all over!'

MOVEMENT V

Variazione E Fuga: Lento E Piacevole; Furioso; Allegro Maestoso

23

Sunday Surprises

ANDREAS DAY RELISHED SUNDAY MORNINGS. IT WAS THE ONE DAY OF the week when he had a lie in. No business meetings; no trips to London via Northern Fail; nothing. The perfect opportunity to do absolutely bugger all. He could smell bacon, and sausage, and beans, and more. Ashley was a good lad; always breakfast in bed for Dad, without fail. It had been a meal for two not long ago. It wasn't the same without a woman next to you. The last years had been hard. But things were on the up!

Day got out of bed, went over to the dressing table, and unwrapped a pack of cigarettes. He was about to light one when he remembered that she didn't like him to smoke. There were far better ways of enjoying yourself! Looking round the room he remembered what they had been doing just a couple of days ago. It had never, ever, been this good. For all he loved his wife – body and soul – this was different: beyond belief, earth shattering, out of this world.

He looked in the mirror: not bad, not bad at all. There was room for improvement, though, definitely room for improvement. That cross trainer in the games room still worked; and then he would take up cycling! He and Mel would bike round Hartleydale! Wonderful summer afternoons; OS maps, picnic, shaded spot, lying on the grass looking up at the blue sky with its wisps of white cloud.

'I must do this. I only have one life and she is – well – she is –'

The bedroom door opened. Day put the photograph of his wife back down on the dressing table.

'Thanks, son. I really appreciate it.'

Ashley Day motioned to his father to get back into bed and eat his breakfast.

'And don't make a mess!'

'Would I do that?'

'Too bloody right you would! And I'm not clearing up after you!'

'Oy! Don't speak to your father like that!'

'I'll – never mind. I'm off out now anyway. Won't be back till late.'

'Where are you going?'

'None of your business!'

'A girl?'

'None of your business!'

'Just be careful. That's all. Remember what happened last time!'

'How could I forget, Dad, with you reminding me all the time. Leave it, will you! Just eat your breakfast.'

Andreas Day began to form a sentence on his lips, then thought better of it. Ashley was out of the room before his father uttered the words 'have a good day, love you!'

Breakfast was its usual tasty treat. Ash might be a dropout and a druggy, but he sure knew how to cook. Marjorie had taught him well. Poached eggs, bacon, sausage, mushrooms, tomato (tinned), and – the *pièce de resistance* – black pudding. Day savoured every single mouthful. An enormous belch at the end of the meal signalled his approval of the *cuisine*.

'Oops! Good job I am not chairing a Board meeting now!'

Day moved the tray onto the dressing table, unfolded the weekend edition of the *Hartley Gazette and Argus* and took it back to bed with him.

It took a few minutes for the front-page story to register.

'Bloody hell. Bloody hell! No! Not now! Not after all this time!'

Sunday morning was the best day of the week by far. A day of worshipping God in all his glory. Alleluia and thrice Alleluia! What better way of spending one's time than in the service of the Lord! It had always been hard, this monastic life, but now, as *de facto* Head of the

Order of Saint Saviour, Father Jeffrey had a whole new Vale of Misery to go through. Or was it a Slough of Despond? Both!

The chapel clock struck twelve. There was time for a brief respite before the traditional communal lunch. He relaxed in Clair's favourite old leather armchair. How many times had he sat opposite the old man, listening to him pontificate about some theological point or other? It was boring beyond belief. These were supposed to be Sunday evening debates but there had never been any real discourse; just Clairvoyant telling everybody what he thought and therefore what everyone else had to think.

And now, here he was, himself, *Father* Jeffrey, OSS. At last! For much of the journey, it had been better to travel hopefully than to arrive. But now, the hour was nigh. In the end, in the final analysis, as William Clair was wont to say, the appointment as Father had come much quicker than anyone, not least 'hapless old Brother Jeffrey', had ever envisaged. The one point of doubt, the single fly in the ointment, the only apple that might upset the cart, was Tristan. Yes, he had agreed to Szabo inviting Bishop to take over the music temporarily after Quick Draw's unexpected demise. What choice had there been, given Templeton's reputation as an outstanding music provider? No, there had been no alternative.

Enough! The crossword in the weekend *Gazette and Argus* beckoned. A quick look at the headlines on the front page, then the cricket scores, then the cryptic.

Father Jeffrey, OSS, never found out if Holme Hill First Team had beaten Hartley CC. The crossword was never started, let alone finished.

'Effing hell! Bugger! Bugger! Bugger! Why now? Why bloody now! When everything was going to plan! What have I done to deserve this?'

Ashley Day had never been in *The Speckled Teapot* before. Not his kind of place at all. Too middle class. Too comfortable. Too remote from real life. Everyone must be looking at him. Even the waitress who had taken his order for a latte. But this is where she had told him to meet her. And he couldn't say no to her; not now, not ever.

DAVID BAKER

She was late. She was always late. She would always be late. But he didn't care. One look with those eyes and he was transformed. She was the drug that he had been longing for; he felt whole, healed, alive, able to do anything. The way her hair fell across her shoulder.

Melody Grimshaw was breathless.

'Sorry, darling boy. Forgive me! Just had to get a copy of the weekend's *Hartley Gazette and Argus*.'

Day junior smiled.

'Bloody road works! Anyway, I'm all yours now. Promise!'

'Have you ordered? I'll have a cappuccino.'

Day beckoned the waitress over to their table as Melody Grimshaw started to read the *Gazette*.

'A cappuccino; and I'll have another latte. What's the matter, Mel? You look as though you have just had the shock of your life!'

'Sorry, darling, can't stop. Must dash!'

As the door slammed shut, Ashley Day picked up the abandoned newspaper and began to read the front-page headline.

'Well, I never. That's a surprise! But what's it to Mel?'

'What a way to celebrate your birthday!'

'Your birthday? I never knew it was your birthday! Why didn't you say something?'

Philbey snorted. 'Is that some kind of joke, Harry Riddles? I – and you, for that matter – have been rather tied up, of late!'

'Sorry Philbs. I didn't think!'

Philbey and Riddles looked at each other as best they could – not an easy task when they were tied hand and foot, back-to-back.

'Well, birthdays are not something to celebrate at my age.'

'Steady on, old girl!'

'My point exactly – an old girl – a very old girl, in fact!'

'But I don't feel old! Not with all this excitement going on!'

Philbey burst out laughing. 'I don't think I can take much more of this excitement. After all – I am eighty today!'

Riddles fell silent for a moment, but only for a moment.

'I always did have a penchant for older women …'

'If I could hit you now Harry Riddles, I would give you the biggest smack in the mouth you have ever had!'

'Yes please, Philbs! I love it when you talk dirty!'

'O give over! We must do something! Who knows when Rankin and his henchman will be back to finish us off? They meant business, as far as I could see!'

'Don't be so sure, Philbs. Clement Rankin always was good at the talk; not so good at the action!'

'Hmmm. I don't agree with you, Hal. Rankin knows exactly what he is doing and has done so for a very long time, it seems to me. And he has had you – and a lot of other people – over a barrel. Who would have thought a doddery old codger like him would turn out to be a criminal mastermind, with links to the Hungarian mafia?'

'Why hasn't he already killed us, now we know the truth about him?'

Pauline Philbey shook her head. 'I wondered that. Perhaps we should have called the police.'

Philbs – you know we couldn't have done that. Rankin would have taken me to jail with him. I feel sick thinking about it.'

'What, going to jail with your – and my – school buddy?'

Riddles shook his head. 'No, the fact that he sat there in silence at all those Board meetings knowing what I ended up doing, leading me into this horrible life of crime.'

'I always did have a penchant for bad boys …'

'It's not funny Philbs.'

'I know, Hal. I know.'

'What did you make of the other one?'

'Very good looking!'

'Is that all you can think of at a time like this?'

'Well, he was handsome in the extreme. If only I were – what, twenty years younger? Or thirty for preference…'

'I can't make you out sometimes! He had a gun in his hand and was prepared to use it. "Handsome is as handsome does", as my mother used to say!'

'Ha! You're only jealous, Harry Riddles.'

'Who do you think he was? Rankin clearly rated him. I could tell from the way Clement tensed up when the other man came in.'

'I hadn't noticed.'

'Hmmm. I wonder why. What a strange language they used!'

'Hungarian. It was Hungarian, to be sure. I remember meeting some of the emigres after the 1956 uprising. What an awful time We welcomed them at a special tea at Holme Hill Methodist Church. I was fourteen or fifteen. There was a boy there who taught me a few words and I taught him English.'

'You never told me any of this. All the time we were at school together?'

'Not all the time, Hal. Just for a few months and then the family were moved away somewhere. I never saw him again.'

'So, what were Rankin and your Mr Handsome talking about?'

'It was odd; really, really, odd. It was something about an article in the *Gazette and Argus*. That's all I could make out. That and what they were going to do with us.'

'And what are they going to do to us?'

Philbey looked around the room. Oh, for a large gin and (not much) tonic! There were no obvious ways of getting out; a door locked and bolted from the outside; windows boarded up; no furniture. Just an old model railway that must have occupied at least a third of the available floor space. Despite her depression and despair, Philbey began to take notice of the layout.

'What do you make of the trains, Hal?'

'Nothing. It's just a train set.'

'It's a very interesting layout, though. Can't you see what it's depicting?'

Riddles strained to get a good view of the scenes depicted.

'Well, I never. I see what you mean. It's Hartleydale!'

'And a very specific part of it too! That's Templeton Towers, and, over there, that's the tunnel, right underneath the old chapel.'

Riddles nodded. 'Pauline?'

'That sounds ominous!'

'Didn't McGraw have a train set like that?'

'I don't know. I never saw his flat.'

'I did – just the once – and he took great pride in showing me his layout. He even had a timetable that he had to follow right to the end once he started the trains going. I don't understand why there is an aeroplane over there by the lake.'

'Say that again!'

'An aeroplane, over there by the lake. It looks like a World War II bomber. As if it's crash landed.'

'That's it! That's just it! It all makes sense now! If only we could get out and tell the police!

Victoria Perry was looking forward to meeting Donald May again, and so soon after their last encounter. She was not normally up so soon on a Sunday morning. She was proud of what she had done and excited that he had trusted her to play a part in the ongoing investigation. The request to put a story about an aeroplane crash after the war in the newspaper had seemed odd, but she had complied, with the knowledge that DCI May would keep his promise to give her an exclusive when the murderer was caught.

Perry motioned to the waitress for another latte. As the drink was being delivered, May walked in. He was not alone. A tall, slim, short-haired woman with the straightest, most rigid posture ever, followed him, smiling at the waitress as she brushed aside the offer of a table. May rolled his eyes at Perry in the meantime.

'Sorry we're late Vicky. Urgent business back at the station. I'd like you to meet ACC Samson.'

'Call me Jean.' The ACC held out a long, thin, hand. Perry was struck both by the coldness of the palm and the strength of the grip.

'I could murder a cuppa. What are you having, Don?'

'A latte, please.'

Samson raised a hand and asked for two lattes. A woman used to being obeyed, thought Perry.

'I – we – just wanted to touch base with you on the case – and to thank you for all your help, Victoria. If you don't mind me calling you Victoria?'

Perry reddened slightly as she looked at May, then Samson. 'It's OK. Everybody calls me Vicky.'

'Thanks, Vicky. And, as I say, we are appreciative of what you have done.'

'It was nothing. I just put an article in the paper, like you told me to.'

'And gave us all that information about Templeton Towers in the 1970s.'

Perry looked at May again. 'What ...'

'Don't worry Vicky, your secret is safe with me. Very useful, that folder, especially since there was so little in the official files. And, while I am not yet at liberty to say any more, some of the information it contained has helped us move the case forward.'

'I am pleased to hear it.' Perry took a large swig of her coffee then looked across at the two police officers. 'What news, then, in the light of the article?'

Perry could see May forming an answer on his lips, but Samson got there first. 'Early days, Vicky. Things are stirring. Which is why I have a question for you.'

'A question? Go ahead!'

'Well, two questions, actually. Firstly, could we trouble you to put a second article in the paper?'

Perry raised her eyebrows and looked at May.

May nodded.

'Well, I don't see why not. If you give me some idea what I am writing and there is at least some semblance of truth in what you are giving me!'

'Oh, there will be truth alright!'

'Very well. And the second question?'

'Has anybody been in touch with the *Gazette and Argus* since the article came out?'

Victoria Perry snorted. 'I'll say. Loads of phone calls and emails since it came out last night.'

'Anything that we should know?'

'We log everything so take a look. It's all on this memory stick. I thought you – well, Don here - might ask. But nothing of relevance as far as I can tell.'

'No?'

'Well, not really. Except one strange phone call. It was really garbled. Claiming all sorts of strange goings on at Templeton Towers. But what's new up there? Said they knew who the murderers were.'

'Murderers?'

Perry nodded.

'Is it working?'

'Early days.'

'What does that mean.'

'It means that it is too soon to tell!'

'O I hate you when you are like that, Frederick Dawson May!'

'Hey! Go easy on him, Camilla!'

'I begin to think he doesn't know what he is doing. Just making it all up as he goes along!'

'I know exactly what I am doing! I do! I do! I do!' Freddie May stamped his feet and shouted and screamed almost to the point of apoplexy.

'Careful. Shush! You don't want anybody to hear us. Calm down! Both of you.'

After a period of silence, Vanessa restarted the conversation. 'Now then. Is there nothing to report? No progress at all?'

Freddie and Camilla looked at each other, then at Vanessa.

'You go first Freddie.'

'You sure, Camilla?'

Camilla nodded.

'Well, I think I know who the murderers are.'

'Murderers?' gasped Vanessa.

'Yes. Murderers.' Camilla shook her head in disbelief.

24

Revelations Galore

'GO ON GEORGE, TELL ME! COME ON. YOU KNOW YOU CAN TRUST ME! Who can you confide in apart from me?'

Ellis looked at her sister. It was true. Who else could she confide in outside work? Could she confide in anybody inside work? Charlie was becoming a good mate but wasn't that interested in her theories. Donald May? Possibly, but she was hesitant to say too much too soon, and would it ever be possible to tell him what she really thought about ACC Samson and the case?

'Well?'

'Well, what?'

'Well, are you going to tell me what you think is going on? If you can't talk to your big sister, who are you going to explain your theory to?'

Georgie looked on with a mixture of horror and resignation as Tiggy devoured a whole bar of Old Jamaica chocolate.

'Sorry. Anyway, come on, I'm waiting!'

Georgie Ellis sipped some red wine. It smelt and tasted good. She looked down at the liquid as she swirled the glass.

'Okay. Here goes. But if I get even the slightest whiff of treachery, you will wish you had never been born, Tiggy! I swear.'

'I swear on the family motto.'

'I bet you can't even remember what it is!'

'I can!'

'Go on then! What is it?'

Tiggy stopped munching for a moment.

'Told you! You don't know it, do you?'

'Yes, I do, it's – it's – it's *AB IPSO FERRO*. Yes, that's what it is!'

'And what does it mean?'

'Why aren't you satisfied with my answer? It means "from the same iron", that's what it means, so there!'

Ellis was disappointed that Tiggy had – much to her surprise – passed the test. There was no option but to share her worries now.

'I have told you about ACC Samson, haven't I?'

'You mean your rival for DCI May's affections?'

'Say that one more time and I will thump you!'

Tiggy smiled sheepishly. 'Sorry.'

'I don't think Jean Samson is what or who she seems.'

'Really? But she's a senior police officer!'

'Well, she may be, but there is something I don't like about her.'

'What?'

'She has been doing a lot of interfering in this case.'

'But it's an important one. It's in the national newspapers: a serial killer at loose in Hartleydale. The ACC is bound to be taking a particular interest.'

'She reads all the papers. Never a day goes by when she is not calling DCI May into the office to ask what is going on.'

'So?'

'Then she suggested our latest tactic.'

'What's that?'

'We flush out the murderer – or murderers – by putting some information in the local media that will tempt them to reveal their hand.'

'Oooh – sounds interesting! But what's wrong with that? Why shouldn't she suggest something like that? What was it, anyway?'

'Well, our ACC has apparently discovered some history to do with Templeton Towers that nobody else has, apart that is - according to Samson – the murderer, or murderers. Some kind of tip off that only she has received.'

'Why do you keep saying "murderer, or murderers"? Are you teasing me? Is more than one person involved?'

'It would make sense, given the number of people killed. But that's just a theory.'

'And Samson's discovery?'

'You know the archaeological dig that has been going on at Templeton Towers all these years?'

'The one to do with the Templar treasure that Taylor hid in the grounds of his estate back in the 19th century?'

George Ellis nodded.

'Well, Father William was not digging for some historical artefact or the Holy Grail, he was digging for Nazi gold!'

'What?'

'That's what Samson would have you believe.'

'Isn't this all a bit far-fetched?'

Georgie laughed. 'No more so that the communion cup of Jesus!'

'I suppose so. But how did Nazi gold get onto the Templeton Estate?'

'At the end of World War II, an aircraft crashed into the woods on the north side of the grounds. Samson has been told about a document that suggest it was carrying bullion – millions – billions – of it.'

'And what happened to this gold? Why was it on an aircraft flying over Hartleydale?'

'Captured by Hungarian partisans as the Nazis were leaving of the country and flown out of the country before the Allies could get their hands on it.'

'And why fly to Britain?'

'Because the partisans had friends here.'

'Friends?'

'Members of the Order of Saint Saviour.'

'What? The monks who run Templeton Towers?'

Georgie nodded; Tiggy shook her head.

'I know. Fantastical, isn't it?'

'You could say that!' Tiggy looked over at the kitchen cupboard where the Old Jamaica was kept.

'No, you don't! No more chocolate!'

'Sorry, George! Go on, this is intriguing. I'm hooked.'

'And how come the OSS had links with Hungarian partisans?'

'That's where Templeton Taylor comes in. He often holidayed in the old Austro-Hungarian Empire – a place called Pecs, known for its wines. He founded a school there to train priests. It became a sister college to Templeton Towers. After his death, the two places kept in touch. During the Second World War, the Pecs college was taken over by the Nazis and used to store their ill-gotten gains. As the war went against the Germans, they arranged for the gold and other treasures to be stored there, but the partisans had other ideas as to what would happen to it all.'

'So where is it, then?'

'That's the problem. Nobody knows. Which is the real reason William Clair kept organizing his digs.'

'But wasn't the treasure destroyed when the plane crashed?'

'Not according to Samson's sources.'

Tiggy's incredulous look made Georgie chuckle.

'What are you laughing at?'

'Nothing. Just the way you were looking at me in disbelief.'

'Well, it is a pretty incredible story, isn't it?'

'I know. It fits in with what Pauline Philbey has been trying to tell us all this time.'

'That old archivist woman?'

'That's the one. We rather ignored her testimony, but it looks as though she was onto something, hence the attack in her home.'

'What was that about?'

'Someone trying to find out what she had discovered – namely where the treasure was. Only she – and we – thought it was to do with the story of Templeton Taylor hiding something he had brought back from the Holy Land. And it was nothing of the sort.'

'Perhaps that was the golden head that young Freddie discovered.'

'I wondered that, though we have never found anything to corroborate his story.'

'Was he making it up, then?'

'I very much doubt Freddie May would make anything up.'

The two sisters laughed.

'Georgie?'

'What?'

'Why hasn't Samson shared it with you all before now?'

'Good question! Don – DCI May – said that's how she works. Keeps things to herself until the last moment and then demonstrates her superiority by giving you the information fully packaged!'

'Ouch! That doesn't sound like the basis for a good working relationship! Hero narcissism. That's what I call it!'

'I'll say. But there's more to it than lording it over her ex-lover. I just can't work out what it is.'

'Is it working then?'

'It's working.'

'Are you sure?'

'I'm sure.' Freddie May looked at Vanessa and Camilla and smiled. His plan was coming to fruition. It would not be long before the murders would be solved, and he, Frederick Dawson May of the Yard would be recognized for his superior skills of detection.

Or would he? Was his theory the correct one? There was just this nagging doubt at the back of his mind as to the real reason for the murders. But truth will out, surely.

'Is it working, sir?'

'Too early to tell, Georgie. Let's see what Charlie has to say.'

DCI May nodded to the door as Riggs walked through it.'

'Any news?' Georgie Ellis bit her lip in anticipation.

Riggs shook his head. 'Nothing. None of our suspects has made a move; everything seems normal. Except …'

'Yes?'

'Well, sir, Pauline Philbey and Harry Riddles have disappeared.' Charlie Riggs sighed and looked at his two colleagues.

'What?'

'I know, George, they were told to stay put. After their last adventure, I would have thought they had learnt their lesson.'

'Ha! You don't know Philbey as well as I do. She's a stubborn old so-and-so. She'll never take no for an answer!'

'What about the bobby outside? Didn't he see anything?'

Riggs shook his head again.

'By the time he realised the safe house was empty, they were long gone.'

'Did they leave voluntarily, or do you think someone forced them?'

'There were no signs of any struggle. Everything was in order. They had even left extra food out for Boris – the cat.'

'Where the hell are they, then?' May scratched his head and looked at the other two members of his inner cabinet. 'Best alert all units to be on the lookout for them. In the meantime, …

May never finished the sentence. ACC Samson opened the door so violently it shook on its hinges.

'They're on the move! Things are happening. You need to act, now!'

'Will we ever get out of here? I'm beginning to give up hope!'

'That's not like you, Philbs!'

'I know, Hal, but how will we?' Rankin has us just where he wants us! There's no escape.'

'We'll be rescued, I know it. The police will have discovered we are not at the safe house, and then they'll come looking, I am certain.'

'How will they find us? Who would think of looking here? Rankin is the last person the police would suspect of any involvement in these murders. Think about it – we never thought of old Clement as a criminal mastermind, did we?'

Riddles snorted. 'Never liked him, even when we were at school together. Kept himself to himself. A bit odd really.'

'You've never said that before, Hal. I always thought you and Clem were good friends.'

'Haven't I? Well, it's true. I had to deal with him because of business, but I never really took to him. And now I know why. I wish I had never met him.'

The two prisoners fell silent. Before long, Philbey could hear gentle snoring. She smiled and shook her head.'

Poor Hal! I'm going to have to be the strong one! That's men for you!

Philbey decided it must be late morning or early afternoon. Sunday by the sound of church bells earlier. It was difficult to tell, in this windowless room, with its ever burning, shadeless light. Thank God it was only a low wattage, and they were in a darkened corner. Otherwise, they would both have gone mad by now. Unlike Hal, she was not at all sleepy. The ropes tying them both to their chairs were as tight as ever. The knots had been expertly tied – by a mariner, perhaps? She looked around the room for the hundredth time for some crumb of comfort; an escape route, a means of raising the alarm, something that gave them hope that all was not lost.

Philbey thought back to the fateful day when she had revealed her discovery in the Templeton archives. What if the treasure map had not been found? Would she and Hal be here now? She thought about waking him to share her thoughts. As she tapped on his arm and tried to squeeze his hand, she heard a clicking sound. The door opened slowly.

'O no. This is it! Hal! Wake up. They've come for us! We've had it now!'

'Shhh! Keep your mouth shut! Both of you! We don't have much time.'

With that instruction, the surprise visitor untied the two captives, helped them to their feet and beckoned them to follow. Riddles looked at Philbey, who pointed at the shadowy figure in front of them.

'Quickly!' came the barked order.

Philbey assumed that they were going back to the main house, but that was not to be. Whoever the rescuer was, they knew their way around Rankin's place. Was it a trick? Was it a dead end? Before the two captives knew where they were, they could feel cold, fresh air on their faces. It was light; a sunny morning over Hartleydale.

'This way!'

Riddles was wheezing. Philbey caught up with her companion and put an arm round him, willing him on through the undergrowth that had greeted them as they went through an exit hatch. The bushes were moist from previous rain. What now?

25

Getting Near The Truth

'I THOUGHT YOU SAID IT WAS WORKING.'

'Well, it is!'

'You call this "working"?'

'I knew – I just knew – we should never talked to Mr Szabo like that. It's all your bloody fault, Frederick Dawson May of the Yard. The back yard more like!'

Freddie May had never heard Vanessa swear before. He hated swearing to the point where he would put his hands over his ears and shout and scream stop! That would do no good now though. In any case, he had grown up; he had accepted that he was neuro-divergent; he knew how to cope with it. And shouting at people who swore was one thing he knew not to do. He looked at Camilla in the hope that she might support him, or at least say a kind word or two, but she looked just as glum as Vanessa.

Freddie's reputation as a super sleuth lay in tatters. The plan had worked – too well in some ways – but now the three of them had paid the price, not only for knowing too much, but also for provoking the evil forces behind the murders at Templeton Towers into action. Telling Szabo about the grave; then making it known they had discovered where the 'treasure was'. Very clever; and even more dangerous. Here they were, incarcerated in the Principal's executive suite, unsure of what their future was to be – if they had any kind of future at all, that is.

'They won't kill us, will they, Fred?'

'You know I don't like being called Fred!'

'Well tough shit! That's the least of your worries, matey!'

'Stop it, Vanessa! He didn't mean any harm!'

'Well, look where his harmlessness has got us now! I knew we should never have told Szabo anything!'

'How do you know telling Szabo made them come after us? Are you sure he's involved in all this?'

'Who else knew about the grave? We didn't tell anybody, apart from him. Did we? Unless you told your Dad. Did you?'

Freddie May felt himself reddening.

'You did, didn't you?'

'No, I didn't. I swear.'

'You little liar. I bet you did! And then making it worse by finding references to buried treasure when you were researching in the archives. Why the hell did you do that?'

'Because – because – because I wanted to solve the case so that I could impress you!'

'Oh, piss off, May!'

'Stop it, you two! You never know who is listening in. I wouldn't be surprised if they haven't got this room bugged.'

'You're right. What better way of finding out what we know that leaving us together until we talk.' Freddie May whispered, then looked around the room. There was nothing obvious, but his Dad had told him all about listening devices. They could be anywhere. He motioned to Vanessa and Camilla to look round the room. The girls and he took a third of the total area each. They studied the furniture – desk, chairs, sofa – the portraits and the mirror on the wall – the lampshades and the other light fittings.

Nothing.

Freddie shrugged. The girls shrugged back.

'Let's whisper, just to be on the safe side.'

Vanessa and Camilla nodded.

'We're still angry with you, though, even though we are talking quietly! Just so you know, Frederick Dawson May!'

'I'm sorry; very, very sorry! Does that make you feel better? I'm not good at apologizing. I don't like being wrong, I admit it. You should take it as a compliment that I have said sorry. So there!'

The girls looked at each other. Vanessa was the first to speak.

'You're not wrong. And you have stirred things up. The criminals have made a move. We're just angry because – because ...'

'Because we are frightened.' Camilla spoke out, then immediately thought better of it, repeating the words *sotto voce*.

'They won't kill young people. It's one thing to kill a grown up, but young teenagers like us! They would have to be heartless bastards to do that!'

Freddie could see the reaction on the girls' faces. He had said the word, and enjoyed saying it, too. But he would have to stop. Someone had to take charge and there was no other option – it had to be him. Then he had an idea.

'I know. Let's take stock.'

'Going over it all is just going to depress us! We know we can't get out of here!'

'Well, at least it will keep us occupied until – well, until further notice.'

'If you want', the girls said in unison, without conviction.

'But there's more to it than that. If we work out the motives behind the murders, then we might be able to sell a story to our captors that will keep us alive. We must find a way of convincing them that we have more value to them if we are living and breathing. We need an insurance policy.'

Freddie beckoned Vanessa and Camilla to sit next to him on the large leather sofa. Despite its age and poor condition, it proved to be comfortable. For the first time since their detention, the three of them began to relax. The food left for them on the coffee table looked increasingly tempting. Vanessa was the first to scoff a sandwich. Then Camilla. Then Freddie.

'These sandwiches are just like the ones we get for tea.'

'Even better, I'd say!'

'Come on, you two. Let's talk about the case.'

'Yes sir!' The twins saluted.

Freddie started to sulk, then thought better of it.

'Have either of you seen the people who captured us before?'

Vanessa and Camilla shook their heads.

'Me neither.'

'But I bet they were acting on Mr Szabo's orders.'

'We don't know that, Camilla.' Vanessa elbowed her sister.

Camilla took no notice and continued. 'Remember when we overheard Mr Szabo with that man – you know – the Chair of Governors.'

'Yes.'

'Well, I haven't told you this before, but I have seen them together since, many times. With Brother – Father - Jeffrey.'

'So what? The Principal and the Head of the Order and the Chair of Governors together? You'd expect them to meet up. Between them, they run Templeton Towers.'

'But would they be talking about murder?'

'Camilla – we've been here before. Of course, they would be talking about murder. There have been four murders to talk about.'

'Who is it, then? Who's the murderer?'

Freddie stood up and pointed to the door. As it opened, he turned to the girls and whispered.

'That's who it is.'

'I don't trust him one bit. I really don't!'

'He freed us, didn't he?'

'I know. But I think it's a trap!'

Riddles nodded. After all the adventures of the last few weeks, it was clear that Pauline Philbey was a shrewd old bird; and one with an interesting backstory. The penny had dropped when he saw how easily she got into the dark web. No local archivist could do that, however digitally minded. At first, Riddles had not believed her when she talked about working for MI5 and MI6. He had listened incredulously to the tale of her recruitment into the service after school thanks to her mastery of mathematics and a recommendation from the head teacher at secondary school. She had begun as a code breaker then graduated to more active service, both at home and abroad, including behind the Iron Curtain. That was supposedly in the past, but once a special agent, always a special agent. Philbs had realised the significance of the documentation in the Templeton archives as soon as she had discovered it. Except she had not given him the full story then; only just now when they had thought their lives were about to end. But here they were, still alive, rescued by the last person they would have expected.

'We have to trust him. At least for now. Let's face it: we don't have many others on our side just now!'

'What's going on between you two?'

Brother Germain reappeared with two mugs of coffee.

'Here we are. I could add something stronger if you like. You've been through a lot. You're safe now. We will take care of it.'

'We? Who is "we"?'

Germain laughed as he sat down in his battered old leather armchair.

'Why, your old mob, Pauline. MI5! Once a special agent, always a special agent, eh? *Regnum defende*. Remember what that means, Pauline?'

Riddles looked at Brother Germain and then at Philbey. He watched as she laughed.

'Of course I do. "Defend the realm." Now who are you? Who are you really?'

Riddles had never seen Philbey look like this before; never ever, in all his life.

'I told you who I am. Who I was; who I am; and who – or is it what – I always will be.'

Riddles looked across at the man he had once greeted as a new member of the Order of Saint Saviour; the most brilliant languages teacher Templeton Towers had ever seen or ever would see. He watched as the two former agents stared each other down. Philbey was the first to break the silence.

'Very well. So why are you here, now, at Templeton Towers?'

'Because I saw the light.'

'Saw the light? What does that mean?'

Germain smiled. Riddles could not help but notice the absolute calm of the man. He really had seen the light – the Light of the World.'

'I got up one morning, and I heard a voice. And that voice told me what to do.'

'And what was that Germain?'

'The voice just said, "Follow Me". Matthew 19, verse 21.'

'Where?'

Germain laughed again. 'Why here, of course, Pauline!'

'It's a far cry from MI5 to Templeton Towers to teach MFL.'

'Strange but true, I swear.'

'So how is it that you ended up rescuing us from Clement Rankin's basement?'

Riddles noticed how Germain's face fell; the beatific smile had gone, to be replaced by a sad grimace so mournful it pervaded the monk's study.

'My past caught up with me, that's what. I told you – you should agree with me here Pauline – once a secret agent, always a secret agent.' Germain snorted. 'Perhaps it was meant to be; perhaps it was God's will that I came here. The first years were wonderful. Then one day, I got back from my run to find two people here in my study.' Germain looked at Philbey and Riddles. 'They were from MI5. They needed me to go back into the service. It must have been too good to be true. Here I was on site, a short walk from where the head of one of the biggest international crime rings of the decade lived.'

'I – we – presume you mean Clement Rankin.' Philbey glanced at Riddles as if to make sure he agreed with her deduction. Riddles nodded slightly, more interested in what Brother Germain was going to say next.

'I do. What a surprise – for me as much as you, I imagine! The last person any of us would expect to be a criminal. But it's true, as you now know. What could I do but agree to go under cover? I was already here. My situation was perfect. Who would ever think that I was anything but a monk teaching languages to gifted students?'

'What did MI5 ask you to do?' Riddles saw Philbey's jaw flex as she spoke.

'Nothing much at first. Just keep an eye on things. Observe Rankin's movements, keep him as close as I could.'

'But how could you do that, up here at Templeton Towers where you are to meditate and study when you are not teaching? You are supposed to be leading a simple monkish life?'

Riddles wondered how Germain would get out of that one.

'That was easy,' came the laughed response. 'Rankin has a real penchant for languages. He was looking for someone to teach him

Hungarian, and there aren't that many teachers around. It's one of my specialities, so he welcomed me with open arms. That was when I began to think that this was God's will "Take up thy cross and follow me" (Matthew 6 verses 24-5) – to come to Templeton Towers and help the service rid the world of this evil man and his associates. You have discovered that, haven't you.'

Philbey nodded.

'I fed back to MI5 periodically. We were about to act when you discovered the documents about the Nazi gold. I don't think you realised what you had stumbled on. That's when things started to happen.'

'And the murders began?'

'Something like that.'

'Wait a minute, you two. Father William was murdered before Philbs – Pauline, I mean – made it known that she had uncovered something in the archives. That's right, isn't it?'

Philbey reddened slightly. 'That's right. Well, more or less right.'

'What is it Pauline? We need to know everything.' Brother Germain looked at Riddles then Philbey.

'Now I come to think of it, there was someone who knew about my discovery before the Board meeting. I felt it was only right to tell them.'

'And that was?'

'It was the Chair of the Board. Andreas Day.'

Samson entered May's office and sat down at the conference table.

'Proceed, Detective Inspector. What's the latest on our four murders?'

'Of course, ma'am. Charlie, will you summarise our conclusions so far, please?'

Riggs nodded. 'Three of the murders were committed the same way, ma'am. Inhalation of a poisonous substance mixed with incense. The victims had also suffered strangulation postmortem. The same MO was used many years ago on the then Vicar of St David's Church in Hartley. He was a former member of the Order of Saint Saviour. It was originally thought he had died of a heart attack, despite the ligature marks around his neck, possibly a failed attempt at suicide according to the ME. Once the body had been exhumed and examined by Dr Harbord, it became clear that here was another murder.' Riggs looked at ACC Samson.

'Please do continue, Detective Sergeant.'

Yes, ma'am. Of course. Dr McGraw, on the other hand, was murdered with a knife. We initially thought that the local archivist, Pauline Philbey, had killed him. DC Ellis discovered her bending over the body with the murder weapon in her hand. But we later cleared her because she was left-handed, and Dr Harbord is convinced the murderer was right-handed.'

'And why was McGraw wearing a habit?'

'He had been a member of the OSS briefly as a young man. We think he may have been involved in some initiation ceremony. Perhaps he was rejoining the Order, though the monks deny any involvement.'

'What else have you got? What about Riddles' imprisonment?'

May spoke for the first time. 'As I mentioned in our last briefing, ma'am, we think it had something to do with keeping Riddles from voting at the Board meeting. Because he and Philbey were absent, the proposal to sell the land went through without a hitch.'

'We questioned Day, Szabo, and the rest. Not only did they deny all knowledge of the event, but they also have cast-iron alibis for the time of Riddles' imprisonment.'

'What about Barbara Halliday? She has form, does she not?'

May nodded. 'She does indeed. A shady character. Almost as shady as her late husband. "Babs" stands to gain if the land deal goes through.

'And then we have the earlier attempt on Philbey and Riddles. That fits with the land and the property deal being the key to all this.' Ellis cleared her throat as she spoke.

Samson nodded slightly in reply. 'It seems that way. But what of the young boy? Another murder?'

'It seems that he died of natural causes, as far as Dr Harbord can tell.'

'Have we traced any relatives?'

The three detectives shook their heads in concert.

'Nicholas LeGrand appears to have been an orphan. There is nothing in the school records about him that gives any next of kin. And the only people who would have known him back then are both dead, with one exception, Brother Jeffrey.' Ellis grew in confidence as she spoke this time.

'Have we asked him about the boy?'

'We have, ma'am, but he denies all knowledge.'

'We wondered if these murders are revenge killings. It fits with all but Dr Foster, though it could be that she discovered what was going on and had to be silenced.'

'Was there any indication that was the case?'

'None, ma'am. I wondered if she was the person who made the calls and left the notes for me and Charlie. Perhaps she was trying to tell us something.'

'Well, somebody was. The fact that the tips have stopped fits with her demise.'

'It does indeed, DC Ellis. How is our leaking of the story about the World War II plane coming on?'

'We have noticed increased activity – phone calls, emails and now meetings -between Szabo and all the Board members – apart from Philbey, Riddles, and Melody Grimshaw that is – those three seem to have disappeared.'

'Well, thank you for the update, colleagues.'

Ellis and Riggs nodded in reply to the ACC.

May poured himself more coffee and nibbled on a digestive. 'But that's not why you're here, is it, ma'am?'

'What do you mean, Don?'

'I mean that you are going to tell us all about MI5's involvement in this case and next stage actions.'

'I'm not going to hurt you. I promise'.

Freddie May shook his head and stamped his feet. 'I – we – don't believe you! You are evil.'

'Yes. We know what you did. You killed those four innocent people!' Vanessa pointed to the woman sitting opposite them.

'Shhh. No. I am just here for the gold. I don't want to see anybody get hurt. Especially you two. Now just tell me where it is, and, once I have it, you can go. I would never harm little children.'

'We're not little children. We're young adults!'

The woman laughed. 'Well, if you're young adults, you will know what is best for you. Believe me, it is in your interest to talk. Just answer my questions openly and honestly, and I will leave you alone.'

'No, you won't. We have seen your face and know who you are. You will have to kill us once we tell you.'

'In any case, my Dad will have people looking for us. It won't be long before he finds us, then you'll be in trouble!'

The woman laughed. 'But your father doesn't know you are missing. Nobody does! Mr Szabo has seen to that. As far as everybody else is concerned, you are safe at school. The fact you are both quarantined because of a bout of COVID is merely a minor inconvenience. Your father sends you his love, by the way, Commander May of the Yard.'

Tiggy looked at her watch and wondered when Georgie would be home. She was glad that Throth and Aethel had made friends with the next door neighbour's kids, though it was so lonely in the flat now they had gone to a sleepover with them. But they would be back in the morning.

She looked around for more Old Jamaica, but none was to be found. Every secret stash had been pillaged and every hiding place ransacked.

Tiggy wandered into Georgie's makeshift study and began to sift through the papers on her desk. She smiled as she read the neat writing. At first, none of it made sense. She sat down and turned the pages of the notebooks and cross-referenced the summaries in the ring binders on the shelves above.

They're missing something. They're missing the blindingly obvious! Why haven't they worked out who is behind all this? I just have!

Tiggy tried to phone Georgie, but the phone went to voicemail.

Nothing for it! I will have to get on the case myself! How exciting! My little sister will be so proud of me!

26

The Plot Thickens In All Directions

'Why are you here?'

'I told you, Jo. I am helping Templeton Towers out until the end of the year. They are desperate to keep the music going, especially given what else has been going on here over the last few months. And I couldn't turn down the offer. Especially as an old boy of the place.'

Jo Bishop looked at her brother. She almost believed him. But then he only had to look at her – at any woman, for that matter – and the truth became an irrelevance. And now he was back in her life. She had enjoyed his companionship when he stayed at her flat and was saddened when he moved into his apartment at Templeton Towers. It was a grand place: living room, kitchen, study, two bedrooms, bathroom, Steinway grand in the bay window that looked out over the main quadrangle with the chapel on the far side. Trissy had seemed perturbed by her arrival. Was he not pleased to see her here in his new home?

'More tea? Cake?'

'Yes please, at least to a drink. I'd better not have anything more to eat, even though it's heavenly. Did you make it Trissy?'

Tristan Bishop laughed. 'You must be joking. I'm hopeless, remember? No, this is from the school kitchen.'

'So why are you here? Really? There's more to it than just helping your old school out. They could have got someone from Hartley to hold the fort. Why go all the way to hire you?'

Tristan shook his head; Jo put her cup and saucer down on the coffee table and looked her brother in the eye.

'I won't go until you tell me!'

'Why is it so important to you, Josephine Bishop? Why does it matter?'

'Why? Because I'm worried about you. Parachuting yourself into this place. There have been four murders in a matter of weeks, one of them your predecessor as music master. Nobody has been caught and you rock up out of the blue from the south when there were good people – not as good as you, I accept – locally who could have looked after things till January. No Trissy. I just don't buy it. So come on. Fill me in. I promise I won't tell anybody. You can tell me – everything!'

Tristan Bishop got up, walked over to the bay window, strummed a few notes on the piano, turned back to look at his sister and began to speak.

'What you are about to hear must never be spoken of again. I am breaking the Official Secrets Act by telling you who I am and what I know. But I am going to do it for you, now, just in case something happens to me over the next few days.'

'What?'

'Keep calm, Jo! You wanted to know why I am here, so I am going to tell you. Do you promise never to tell a soul what you will hear today?'

Jo Bishop nodded.

'Don't just nod. Say it out loud. Say you promise!'

'I promise, Trissy. I promise never to tell anybody what you are going to tell me.'

Tristan Bishop went over to his drinks cabinet and poured himself a whisky.

'Want one?'

Jo Bishop shook her head.

'When I was at Cambridge, I was recruited by MI5. I have worked for them ever since. Well, at least until – well, you know. Then I resigned.'

'What! All this time? And you never told me?'

'Of course I never told you. You are damn lucky that I am telling you now. I wouldn't breathe a word normally.'

What have you been doing for them? Are you a spy?'

Tristan Bishop laughed. 'It's not as glamorous as you think, Jo, but yes, I have been spying for MI5. My main task has been to keep tabs on the children of rich Chinese and Russian oligarchs in the schools where I have taught, but I have also been on away missions.'

'When you went on your concert tours?'

'Yep. That's right.'

'Of course. I remember those organ recitals you gave behind the Iron Curtain in the 1980s; and then afterwards when you went to help the Hungarians set up their music schools.'

'I thought I had finished with it all. Then the oddest thing happened. McGraw offered me a chamber organ. It was a curious instrument. It combined pipes and a keyboard with ornate bookcases. I had never seen anything like it. I fell in love with the organ at first sight, and I decided it would be a good project to restore it as a way of taking my mind off things.'

'You always were practical, Trissy, unlike me – and Dad!'

The two of them laughed for the first time since the kettle had boiled.

Tristan Bishop moved back to his armchair. He downed the rest of his whisky in one gulp.

'Sure I can't tempt you?"

Jo Bishop shook her head. 'I've given up. I'm more interested in your story, anyway.'

McGraw had the chamber organ delivered to my house. It had been partly dismantled. The instrument needed work, but I was happy to take the project on. I even got some students from the sixth form to help. The mechanism had to be stripped down and completely rebuilt. That's when I discovered the document.'

'Document?'

'It was inside what we call the windchest. It gave details about a large cache of Nazi gold, flown out of Hungary at the end of World War II. The plane crash landed on the Templeton Estate and the gold disappeared. I informed my former bosses at MI5. I thought nothing of it until I heard that McGraw had been murdered.'

'All because of some old bullion?'

'Well, there were millions in that shipment. But there was something more than just money.'

'And that was?'

'Plans for an atomic bomb that would be ten times more powerful than anything we have ever seen in this world. Hitler's *Wunderwaffen*.'

'Wonder weapons! I remember studying that for my history degree!'

'Not only much more powerful, but easy to build and carry around! It had to be investigated and I was the obvious choice. I was instructed to volunteer to take over from McGraw when he was murdered. I phoned Szabo, the Principal, and he accepted my offer like a shot.'

'So now you know everything.'

'Not quite, Trissy. Who murdered those four unfortunate people?'

'Well, that's an interesting question. We're closing in on the killer, but we haven't yet got the evidence, and more to the point, the plans – and the bullion – have yet to be located. But my fellow agent is on the case.'

Tristan Bishop looked at his watch. 'In fact, I need to catch up with him. There have been some developments over the last few hours. Stay here if you want. I'll be back soon.'

'It's OK. I had better go anyway. But do take care! Now you are back in my life I want to keep it that way.'

'I'll be careful. I promise.'

'Do you really think you can get me in?'

Lisa Watson nodded. 'Yes, if you are very careful. I have keys to just about everything and I know most of what is going on.'

'Most? Not all?' Victoria Perry looked around the *Speckled Teapot* to make sure nobody was listening and then leaned over to Watson. 'Let's do it this evening then. I want to find out what's so special about that place and who the murderer is. My dossier and your files add up to a pretty interesting picture!'

'I will be waiting at the side entrance to the hall tonight at 6.30. It will be dark by then. Don't tell anybody else, will you? Make sure you come alone.'

Victoria Perry gulped. 'Of course. I promise.'

'Is there no sign of them?'

'None. We must act now. There is no alternative.'

Clement Rankin got up from his leather armchair. Had it not been for his walking stick, he would have fallen over, but he managed to steady himself. He looked over at his companion. She really was the most beautiful creature he had ever seen.

'What about those three brats? Have they talked yet?'

'En. Semmi. Nothing!'

'What are we going to do with them?'

'I will deal with those three before we leave. They know too much about us. They are at Templeton Towers for now. I have left Janos in charge.'

'Is that wise?'

The woman laughed. 'He will do anything for me! Right now, he is entertaining that fool Day. He will have to be dealt with as well. And that stupid bimbo Halliday. I will take great pleasure in getting rid of her *personally*.'

Tiggy tipped the taxi driver and watched the cab drive away towards Hartley. She could see the vehicle's lights for an age. Eventually the red dots disappeared into the darkness. It was cold; pregnancy had made her body's thermostat behave erratically.

Templeton Towers, that a great sprawling, ugly, gothic monstrosity; lights glared across the front of the building from all floors. There was occasional movement behind some of the windows.

Why had she come? What did she expect to achieve? Tiggy felt a kick inside. She smiled and rubbed her stomach. As she started to regret her recklessness, a hand closed over her mouth. She felt a gun barrel in her lower back.

'What about that? MI5!' Charlie Riggs laughed. 'That's the last thing I would have expected from old sourpuss!'

'Eh?'

'You know! Samson. She's a mournful so-and-so.'

'Well, she must be good at her job to be an ACC.'

'When May is still only a DCI!'

'Come off it Charlie!'

'That's what you were thinking though, isn't it, Georgie? I think you have a soft spot for the boss.'

Ellis blushed. 'Of course, I don't. Just focus on the job ahead! We've got to meet two MI5 agents, remember?'

'Humph! And they will take over this case and we won't get a look in after that!'

'That's not what Samson said. They are assisting us; not the other way round!'

'Well, that's to be seen! I'm not convinced.'

Ellis put her foot on the BMW Z4's accelerator. Riggs jolted forward as the car pushed rapidly up the steep incline towards Templeton Towers.

Once parked in front of the main entrance, the two detectives headed towards Brother Germain's quarters.

'I suppose you and your lot take places like this in your stride, don't you?'

'What do you mean "me and my lot", Charlie?'

'You know! Blue blood. Aristocracy. Double-barreled names.'

Ellis burst out laughing. 'I wish! We're not really aristocracy, you know. And I hate the double barrel, so stop going on about it!'

'But you know all about places like this, don't you? I bet your ancestral home is even bigger!'

Ellis watched as Riggs looked up at the high-ceilinged reception rooms and the grand central staircase with its magnificent pipe organ in the far gallery. She shook her head.

'Come on Charlie. Stop it! Let's crack on with this case. I want to meet these agents!'

Riggs grimaced at Ellis. The two detectives stopped talking, increased their walking pace and entered the monks' accommodation block. Germain was easy enough to find. Each door had the name of the brother written in elaborate gothic script over the lintel, along with the OSS motto.

Ellis tapped lightly on the door. She could hear voices. Riggs motioned to her to move back to one side while he took the other.

'You must be Riggs and Ellis. I have heard a lot about you. But come in; we do not have much time.'

Brother Germain appeared.

'What? Who?'

'Meet the others. Come in, please.'

Germain pushed the door open and ushered the detectives into his rooms.

'What the hell are you doing here?' Riggs pointed at Germain's visitors and then at Ellis.

'Meet my associates. I think you already know Pauline Philbey and Harry Riddles. But let me introduce you to my fellow agent, Tristan Bishop.'

Philbey and Riddles nodded their acknowledgement of the police officers. Bishop, on the other hand, stood up and walked towards Ellis.

'Good to see you again, Georgie. I am sorry I could not say more when we met the other week. Believe me, I would have told you more.'

'What's all this Georgie?'

'Charlie – meet my former music master. I knew Trissy – Mr Bishop – when I was at school. We hadn't seen each other since, until we visited him last week. You know the rest.'

'And you are the second MI5 agent?' Riggs scratched his head.

Germain laughed. 'We're retired agents, Detective Sergeant. But we have been forced out of retirement because of the present emergency. Has your ACC briefed you on the situation?'

Ellis and Riggs nodded.

'And where's your SIO. Where's May?'

'He's checking on Rankin, along with Samson.'

'Right. I hope he has taken other officers with him.'

'Don't worry, he has, I can assure you.'

'Good.'

Riggs turned to Philbey and Riddles. 'And what about you two? Why are you here? Don't tell me you're from MI5 as well!'

'Well, as it happens, I am Sergeant. Or at least I was. Harry here is the young innocent.'

Riddles snorted. 'Well, innocent, maybe. But we owe our lives to Tristan here. We were imprisoned by Clement Rankin. We had confronted him about his criminal activities. It was a foolish thing to do in retrospect.'

'Very foolish!' Bishop clenched his fists. 'It meant that MI5 had to move sooner than was wise. But never mind, we are where we are. We need to act quickly, before any more harm is done.'

'Who is in charge then?'

'A good question, Georgie. I suppose we will have to take orders from one or other of you two!'

Brother Germain and Tristan Bishop smiled at each other. Germain cleared his throat. 'Over to you, Trissy. You outrank me. You always did!'

'Coffee?'
'No thanks.'
'Sure?'
'Sure.'

It was cold lying in wait for Rankin. May had questioned the wisdom of staking out the house when, in his view, everything pointed to Templeton Towers as being the place where they should be focusing. But Samson had insisted. So, while Riggs and Ellis had gone to the school, May was sitting in his car next to the ACC. He tried to stifle a yawn but failed.

'Tired Don?'

'No, I'm OK. Long hours go with the territory, don't they?'

Samson nodded.

'This case has taken its toll on you, though, hasn't it?'

May tensed up. 'No more than any complex case like this.'

'Coming on top of the Holme Hill murders though …'

'What are you implying Jean?'

'Nothing, Don. Absolutely nothing. Just worried about you, that's all.'

For a moment, Samson put her hand on May's arm. As he recoiled, she disengaged contact.

'Why didn't you tell me about MI5? Didn't you trust me?'

'Oh Don. It was nothing like that!'

'What was it then?'

'I didn't know. I genuinely didn't know. I found out an hour before I told you. I swear! It was as much a surprise to me as it was to you. I wasn't aware that Germain and Bishop were MI5 sleepers. Believe me!'

'OK. I believe you. Very convenient that Germain just happened to be on site, though. And just a coincidence that Bishop found the key to the "missing gold" story?'

'I thought that. But it could be the truth. We had already checked out Germain, remember? Though we didn't know about MI5, at least some of his past seems credible. He really does seem to have "got Jesus". Brother Germain has been a diligent Christian and a highly respected member of the OSS since he joined.'

May nodded. 'But we need to know more about Bishop.'

'I have already made phone calls, Don. Don't worry!'

'The one we need to worry about is Szabo. He has more of a past than we realize and he isn't letting on.'

'I agree with you. Look there.'

27

Plans Go Awry

VICTORIA PERRY HAD NEVER BEEN AS NERVOUS OR AS EXCITED IN HER life. This was the big moment; the opportunity to make a name for herself in investigative reporting. A contract with one of the nationals? An opportunity to work for Channel 4. Everything beckoned. Just one small problem: getting into Templeton Towers.

The main gates were locked. The walls were too formidable to climb. What other ways are there of getting into this place? Think! Remember the open day! The interview with Janos Szabo; the tour of the school; the walk round the grounds.

The walk round the grounds! Of course! The side entrance!

Victoria Perry pulled her cap down tightly over her head and strode alongside the stone boundary wall. Occasionally a car went past. Once a bus drove towards the school. She could hear students singing. Perhaps she should sneak in as the gates opened to let the vehicle in. No, that would be too obvious. Keep going towards that side gate. It led to the old chapel. And beyond is where that boy's body was found.

Perry felt guilty that she had not shared everything with May, whether it be the link between the Vicar of St David's and Nicholas, or what she had found in the files that Lisa Watson had let her 'borrow'. But if she had shown them to Don, he would have taken over, stolen her thunder, and despite his promises to the contrary, would not have given her the big scoop she so desperately craved.

Yet, as she stood at the side gate, the cold wind blowing up the dale all the way from Hartley, Perry questioned the wisdom of her go-it-alone strategy. What if nothing happened? What if her theory was wrong? The murders could be revenge for the lad's death all those years ago. She was certain that Paul Gordon had died because he was responsible for Nicholas LeGrand's demise. But the recent deaths – even the first two – were to do with something else. She was sure of it. When Don challenged her theory, she decided not to pursue it further, but in her mind, Perry was convinced that only two murders – Father William and Brother Bernard – were ever planned. Yes, they had the same MO as Gordon's, but that was a copycat scenario designed to put the police off the scent. The real killer had not been out for revenge, but reward. Gold bullion beyond a thief's wildest dreams.

What then of McGraw and Foster? How did their deaths fit in with the Perry theory? Two individuals who had got caught up in the murders; been told or found out too much and then killed to stop them from talking. As simple as that. What did Don call it? Collateral damage it!

Perry opened the gate. There was just time to get to the meeting point where Lisa would have left the door unlocked. Eventually she came to the place Watson had described to her. Victoria Perry recognized it immediately.

'Good old Lisa!'

Perry tried the door, but it was locked. Had she missed the time? Was she in the wrong place?

'I'll give it five minutes. Come on, Lisa!'

Nothing. Victoria Perry's nose starting running. As she rummaged in her pockets for a tissue, she heard the noise of bolts being slid back.

'Great!'

She looked round to make sure that nobody was watching. As she turned round to greet her ally, she was met with a searing pain that seemed to crack her head open.

Perry fell to the ground, motionless. Two people emerged from the building. One took Perry's legs, the other her arms. They carried her inside and down the corridor. One of them unlocked the door, then the other dragged the body inside. After a few moments, the two of them reemerged, locked the door, and headed to the main house.

'Mennünk kell', said one to the other.

'What the hell's going on, Szabo? What's all this nonsense about a plane and bullion? It will ruin our plans if we have to delay building the complex! You know that, and I know that. Babs is incandescent! She has sunk her whole fortune into this project. And so have I! Do something!'

'Calm down Andreas. It's just a temporary setback, I promise. I will sort it.'

'The hell you will! *We* will sort it. You answer to me. I am Chair of the Board.'

Day paced up and down the Board Room. He puffed on a Gurkha. Szabo looked at his watch.

'Waiting for somebody, Janos?'

Szabo shook his head. 'No. Of course not. Just wondering what time it is.'

'Let's go into your office. I need a drink, and a strong one!'

'I will bring your drink here.'

'No. Your office. I don't feel comfortable here. It's too open. Let's go.'

'It's very untidy in there.'

'That doesn't bother me. Is there something I am not supposed to see in there?'

Szabo shook his head. He opened the door that linked the Board Room with the Principal's Office and motioned for Day to go in.

'Now let's get this sorted. We must get everything secured as soon as – what the hell? You? What are you doing here? I thought we agreed I would take care of everything. And yet I find you in Janos's office. What are you two up to?'

Szabo followed Day into the room, locking the door behind him.

'I – we - are sorry you had to find out about us like this. Truly sorry, Andreas.'

Donald May had forgotten how much Jean Samson enjoyed driving. The long country drives in north Norfolk; she had insisted on taking the wheel. He had let her. That first weekend away in an out-of-season

B & B; salty sea air and vinegared chips on Cromer pier. Idylls never last, though, do they?

Twenty years later, sitting next to each other in a car, driving at speed down country lanes: Norfolk with hills. Who would have expected this back then? May had kept his counsel when Samson suggested they go alone to Rankin's house. Why two such senior officers? And without backup? Was it so top secret? May shut the questions out of his mind and tried to enjoy the chase.

Was Clement Rankin aware that he was being followed? Not if Samson had anything to do with it. She could teach Hartley's CID a thing or two about shadowing a suspect. May noticed the shape and then the lights of Templeton Towers in the distance. Just the final stretch up the long, steep, winding road and they would be at the school.

'Who is Rankin going to see, Don?'

'Has to be Szabo. He's our man. Have you had any news from your MI5 contacts?'

Samson shook her head. 'No, apart from the fact that they have Philbey and Riddles with them, but you already knew that. What about your people? Riggs and that DC of yours?'

'She reminds me of you, Jean, at times!'

'What!'

May laughed. 'Don't be surprised, and don't take offence. You should think of it as a compliment.'

'Compliment?'

'Of course! Determined, ambitious, single-minded, ruthless.'

'Enough Don. I get the picture.' Samson turned momentarily to May. 'I know. She'll get to the top. Just like I did. And you will help her. That's an order!'

'Of course, ma'am.'

May took out his mobile and checked for messages. 'They have arrived at the Towers. They are in the main building now.'

Samson looked ahead and nodded. 'Here we are.'

Rankin had driven to the side entrance to Templeton Towers, parked his car next to the adjacent boundary wall, got out, opened his umbrella, and headed through the gate, having checked that nobody was watching him.

May and Samson gave Rankin twenty seconds, then moved their car next to his, got out of theirs and quickly followed him through the side entrance.

'Best get reinforcements, Don.'

'Already requested. I texted Georgie to have the place surrounded. We should have officers in place within the next 30 minutes.'

Samson smiled. 'That's more like it, Don!'

For a moment – just a moment – May felt he was back in Cromer.

Samson pointed ahead. Rankin could be seen pressing a doorbell and waiting. No reply. Rankin had then knocked on the door, softly at first, then increasingly loudly as his call was not answered. Eventually, the door was opened brusquely; Rankin was ushered in. May and Samson caught sight of Rankin's host.

'Did you expect that, Don?'

'I have had my suspicions. Are they on MI5's list?'

'Not the last time I looked; but they should be, if they are mixed up with Rankin.'

'Who the hell are you?'

'I might say the same of you!'

'I came to Templeton Towers to find some answers.'

'So did I!'

The two women looked at each other, then at their surroundings.

Victoria Perry had always loved books and libraries. She had never seen so many leather-bound volumes in one location. The smell of knowledge was intoxicating.

The room reminded Tiggy of school, Tristan Bishop, and a certain wonderful evening after the Christmas Carol Concert in her last year.

'Go on then. Who are you?'

'Why should I say? You go first if you are so keen to share secrets!'

'Stop it! Stop playing tit-for-tat.'

Perry went to the door and tried the knob one more time.

'It's still locked. They aren't going to let us out in a hurry, are they? Something murky is going on here, and we've stumbled on it. Let's share information. I'm Tiggy. You probably know my younger sister, Georgiana Ellis. She's a Detective Constable with Hartley CID.'

Perry smiled and took the proffered hand, shaking it firmly. 'Ah right. Yes, I know Georgie, she works for Don – DCI May! I'm Victoria Perry. I am a reporter with the *Hartley Gazette and Argus*, and I have been helping the police with a cold case that's probably related to the recent murders at Templeton. But why are you here, and in your state? Shouldn't you be leaving it all to the professionals?'

'What state? Just because I'm pregnant doesn't mean to say I can't function.' Tiggy looked around to see if there was anything to eat. 'I could say the same of you. You're a reporter, not a police officer, for God's sake!'

'Well, I've more right to be here than you have!'

'No, you don't!'

Before Tiggy could say another word, Perry had shushed her.

'Quiet. I hear footsteps.'

The two women hid either side of the door, listened, and waited.

'What are we going to do with them?'

'What do you think. Have you still got your revolver?'

'Yes, but …'

'But nothing. Go get it – now!'

'And what about the children?'

'They're next.'

28

Life, Death, Regrets, Discovery, Honeymoon

FREDDIE AND HIS FATHER HAD TALKED ABOUT DEATH MORE THAN ONCE. The topic came up in conversation naturally each time. How he wished he and Dad were on a bike ride now! If he ever got out of this mess, he would go every time he had the opportunity. He would stop being the sullen teenager.

The first conversation had been at the old railway bridge leading into Holme Hill from Hartley.

'I'm going to die.'

'What on earth makes you say that, Freddie?'

'I've just realised what death is. I'm going to die. We all are.'

'Well yes, but not for a very long time yet, son.'

'You and Mum will die first. And grandpa is nearly dead already.'

'Let's not talk about that now, Commander May.'

That was the end of the conversation. The next time was almost a year later. As always, Freddie could remember the day, the date, the time, and the place when and where they had spoken about dying.

'It comes to us all, son. It's the natural way of things. Grandpa was a good age, and he was ready to go. He was so pleased to see how you were growing up; so proud of you! So am I, Freddie. You will go on to great things! Oxford or Cambridge. You'll end up as a professor somewhere!'

'What will it be like not to be alive Dad? Not to be able to feel anything?'

'We don't know what the future holds. None of us. Just enjoy life and make the most of every opportunity you are given.'

They had not talked about death again. But it came up in classes at Templeton. The monks gave him a new perspective, and he had felt better about it all.

Until now.

Freddie looked at Vanessa and Camilla. The bravado was all gone. They sat on the sofa in Mr Szabo's office holding each other close, looking down at their feet and not speaking.

It was surprising the three of them were still alive. He had lied to the girls when he said that they wouldn't kill children. Of course they would. They had to. Especially now Freddie knew who the murderer was. Or at least he was 90% sure who the culprit was. And Mr Szabo! Their theories about him and Andreas Day had been correct! They had got rid of the two monks because they stood in their way, stopping them selling the land and making big money. Quick Draw must have found out what they were up to and been silenced as a result. Just like Dr Foster. She had been silenced as well as a result.

And now Freddie, Vanessa, and Camilla were going to be silenced. Some words from the morning's Bible reading came to him. He always listened intently to the chapel services, even though he did not believe any of it. Yet he could not stop his inner voice (as Dad called it) from talking to him.

"When I was a child, I spake as a child, I understood as a child, I thought as a child: but when I became a man, I put away childish things."

Freddie stood up and went over to the two girls. He knelt in front of them and took their hands in his.

'We are going to get out of this. I promise you. And this is what we are going to do. Listen carefully and do exactly as I say. But quickly, I hear footsteps!'

Despite all the anxieties, stresses, and traumas of the last few weeks, Philbey was enjoying herself. She was not at all tired. Quite the opposite. She was alert, energised, ready for action. And here she was, back in MI5, sworn in by Tristan Bishop and Brother Germain. She looked across at Hal. Poor, sweet Harry Riddles! What must he be thinking now he knows the truth about me? But then, Hal was a dark horse as well! She should have known there was more to that man than met the eye. His business "dealings" made sense now. She was no longer angry; just sad that a good man like him had got mixed up with the Hungarian mafia, and fronted by Clement Rankin, of all people!

'It's time. May and Samson are here, and the place will be surrounded within the next fifteen minutes.'

Philbey looked across at Bishop. Despite him being the younger of the two operatives, he was clearly in command. Brother Germain went over to his desk, unlocked the top right-hand drawer, and took out two revolvers. One he gave to Bishop, the other he offered to Pauline Philbey.

'Really? I am very rusty.'

Germain smiled. 'Somehow, I think you will get back into the groove pretty quickly, Pauline.'

Philbey took the proffered weapon, checked it, then put it in her jacket pocket and smiled.

'Very well. On His Majesty's Secret Service! But what about Hal – I mean Harry?'

'You're the bait Harry.'

'What?' Philbey and Riddles exclaimed in unison.

'Don't worry, we'll be right behind you. Clement Rankin has arrived at the school. I presume he's meeting up with Szabo and Day now. You are to go to meet them and offer a deal.'

'What deal? It would be madness to go and see them now!'

'No Philbs! It's the least I can do. I need to atone for what I have done. It will be alright, I promise you. Then we will be off to Sorrento on honeymoon.'

'What!'

'Honeymoon – Sorrento – you and me!'

'But …'

'Pauline Philbey – will you marry me?'

'What a fool I have been! What an absolute, utter, complete fool!'

Andreas Day pulled at the handcuffs binding him to the bookcase. How many times had he been in that room? But never like this! What would people think of him? There was no fool like an old fool! And Professor Andreas Day was the biggest of them all!

How could he have been taken in? Easy! Vulnerable, arrogant, sex starved. What better prey? And he had been filleted good and proper.

He had expected better of Szabo. Ex-Navy Commander; top references; a breath of fresh air at Templeton Towers. Where they might have gone together if Janos hadn't been seduced into this ridiculous scheme! Building a multi-million-pound estate was one thing; what Szabo was planning now was quite another.

Father Jeffrey looked up at the San Salvator. The terrible foreboding would not leave him, however deeply he tried to pray. He had attempted to say Compline, but he had broken off the service three times already.

He got up and walked to the high altar, then turned round and gazed at the grand organ. Above its central tower, he observed the crown of thorns, that cruel, awful centrepiece of Christ's passion. Beneath, the words *in hoc signo vanquo*: 'conquer in that sign'.

Father Jeffrey turned back to the altar. For the first time since he joined the Order of Saint Saviour, he noticed the way the thorns carefully pointed down towards specific organ pipes. Walking towards the organ loft door to test out his theory, he smelt a faint scent of incense.

Freddie May had a perfect memory: total recall. Well, almost. He knew every inch of the school, even the parts that he had never visited.

Why? Because he had studied the plans of Templeton Towers, from when it had been built and then subsequently altered, first as a monastery, then as a school for gifted and talented children. Some of the older documents had been framed and hung on the administrative corridor; others he had found and analyzed in the extensive archives. Two of the architect's largest, and earliest, drawings were now in the conference room, where Freddie, Vanessa, and Camilla, were imprisoned.

'What the hell are you doing, Freddie. This is no time to be gazing at the wall!'

'No, it isn't! We're about to die and all you can do is look at those bloody drawings!'

'I can understand your disquiet, both of you, but this is our salvation; here is the escape route.' Freddie traced a line across the glass of one of the pictures. The girls were decidedly unimpressed.

'Oh, get lost, May. You and your fancy ideas!'

'That's it. I'm done. Are you ready?'

'Ready for what?'

'Ready to escape! I have worked out how we get out of here! It's dead simple. Beyond belief, basically. I just hope you are not afraid of heights. Are you?'

Vanessa and Camilla looked at each other, then shrugged back at Freddie.

'Don't think so – why?'

'Because this is how we get out!' Freddie pointed to the window. 'Now Dad told me how the original building needed a lot of renovation, so it shouldn't be too difficult to pick this latch and push up the sash. But I will need your help – both of you. OK?'

The girls said nothing.

'OK? Just do as I say, and we will get out of this alive – I promise you.'

'Do we have to do what he tells us?'

'Yes, Vanessa, unless you have any better ideas. At least Freddie has a plan – at long last!'

'Right! Each of you – both hands on the lower frame and when I say "push" – then push up as hard as you can! One-two-three!'

As Freddie attempted to free the latch that locked the two halves of the sash window together, nothing budged.

'It's useless. The lock has rusted, and the lower window is painted in!'

'Don't be so negative, Vanessa! Freddie knows what he is doing, don't you?'

'Of course! Once again – harder – one-two-three – push!'

Still nothing. Freddie looked around the conference room. At the far end was an old roll-top desk. He ran to it and pushed it open as quietly as he could. It was almost empty, apart from an ornate paper knife neatly arranged in the centre of the leather desk.

'This will do!' He ran back to the window and began to chip away at the rust on the latch and the paint on the window grooves.

'Try now!'

The three of them pushed again. A crack! Then another; and another!

'It's moving! It's really moving!'

'Shush! They might come back at any time!'

'Yes commander!' Camilla gave a mock salute.

'Can you squeeze through there?'

'Yes, but it's a sheer drop on the other side! We're not going through that window!'

Freddie gritted his teeth. 'Look! Do you want Mr Szabo to kill you - us - when he gets back? Or do you want to live?' We know far too much to be left to tell our story – and theirs, or at least what we know of it. So just do as you're told and follow me! I'll go first!'

The girls said not another word. Freddie went feet first through the half open window. He was just thin enough – as were the girls - to get through.

'Be very careful, you two. There is a thin ledge below the window. Just very gently move along until we get to the balustrade at the end of this wall. From there, we will be able to reach the chapel tower and then down into the north side of the organ loft. We have lots of escape routes from there. Come on; nice slow steps, and whatever you do, don't look down, look straight ahead!'

Freddie inched away from the window.

'Come on girls. It's easy! Just relax. If I can do it, you can!'

Vanessa decided that she would go first. 'It'll be fine Camilla. Just you see.'

She stepped up to the window and put her legs out. Where was the ledge?

'Put your feet down! Trust me. I will guide you.' Freddie tried to whisper. What if Mr Szabo heard them?

Vanessa did what she was told. There was a ledge. Once both feet were on it, she straightened up, her back flat to the window, her arms outstretched. She inched along the minuscule ledge, listening to Freddie's soft words of encouragement. She heard Camilla grunting. Her sister must be doing the same manoeuvre. But why did it have to involve so much noise?

Freddie was waiting for Vanessa on the balustrade. He lifted her over to relative safety at the mid-level of the chapel. She did not stop him when he kissed her full on the mouth. They embraced. She hugged him and hugged him and hugged him.

'What about Camilla? Was she not behind you?'

'I thought so Freddie. I heard her grunting as she came out through the window.'

The two of them looked back. The window was shut. Behind it, Camilla was screaming for her life.

The screams could be heard all the way along the corridor and down the main staircase at Templeton Towers.

'You'll have to hold on! You can't give birth now!'

'How am I supposed to bloody stop it? Haven't you had kids?'

Victoria Perry shook her head. 'No. Never had the opportunity. Not sure I wanted them anyway. It's too late now though.'

'Ever seen a baby born.'

'Good God no! I faint at the sight of blood!'

'Well, you'll have to get a grip. I don't think there's long to go!'

Perry went to the library door and banged and shouted. Then banged again some more.

'Help! A baby's about to be born here! Help! Please!'

For a moment, Tiggy's screams subsided to a long, low moan. The next wail was ear-shatteringly loud. Expletive after expletive, mingled with snorts and coughs.

'Please! Help! Someone! Anyone!'

Perry heard footsteps. Then the sound of a key being turned in the door.

'You! What are you doing here? You're the last person I expected to see!'

29

New Life, New Suspect

ELLIS HAD NEVER CARRIED A FIREARM BEFORE. CHARLIE RIGGS KEPT saying how it got easier with practice: 'like golf', he winked. She had ignored the innuendo. Why do men always fixate on sex? Riggsy seemed to think about nothing else, assuming he thought at all!

Tiggy would be at home now, stroking her bump, stuffing ever more Old Jamaica into her mouth, while Aethelred and Throthgar played games on their i-Pads. Ellis could not be like her elder sister; never, ever: dear, sweet, gormless, scatty, disorganised, absent-minded Tiggy! Georgie Ellis was even growing to like the boys and the stupid games she ended up playing with them. It certainly took her mind off work!

'Why is it so quiet round here? Where is everybody?' Ellis whispered to Riggs as the two of them crept through the empty corridors that led to the administrative wing and on to the chapel.

'Have the students been sent away or something?'

'Dunno,' Riggs shrugged.

'It would be convenient if they were out of the way at the moment.' Ellis grimaced.

'Yup.' Riggs motioned Ellis to stop. 'Do you hear that?'

Ellis shook her head. 'What?'

'That. It's like a low moan.'

'Ah, I see what you mean. I hear it now.'

Both officers were taken aback as the moan turned into a shriek, then another, and another. Each more piercing that the last.

'What the hell? It sounds like someone is being tortured!'

'It sounds like a woman! Come on!'

Without thinking, Ellis took the lead. She tiptoed quickly down the oak-panelled corridor past the staring portraits to left and right. Riggs followed, periodically looking round to make sure nobody was behind them.

'It's coming from in here.' Ellis looked up to see the words ψγxhσ Iatpeion over the door.

'What the hell does that mean? It's all Greek to me!' Riggs laughed.

'Charlie! It means 'the house of healing for the soul! It's a library.'

The shrieking had subsided to a low moan once more. Riggs and Ellis positioned themselves either side of the door, pistols locked and loaded. Riggs gently tried the door: locked. The two of them looked at each other and nodded.

After a moment to draw breath, Riggs and Ellis turned and tried to shoulder the door open: no movement.

'Again!'

A second shoulder charge and Riggs and Ellis felt the door shudder.

'You kick and I'll charge,' Riggs barked, Ellis nodded.

The third attempt was successful to the point where the lock creaked and the door opened.

'Tiggy! What the hell are you doing here?'

The moan was now dialling up to a shriek once more.

'What do you think I'm doing? I'm having a baby, for God's sake!'

At which point, seeing blood, Detective Sergeant Charles Edward Riggs fainted.

Ellis sighed. 'Bloody men!"

'You can say that again, George. Now help me, will you?'

'Why are you here, Tiggy?'

'I was bored. I thought I could help. But – ooh – ooh!'

'Bored? Help? You idiot! You might have ruined the whole operation!'

'I'm sorry, George. I meant no harm.'

'You never mean any harm. But then …'

Ellis thought better of continuing the conversation. Instead, she helped Tiggy lie down on the old Chesterfield that was placed centrally in the library, next to some glass display cases.

'How far do you think you have gone?'

'Too far – ooh – ooh. There's no time to get me to hospital. The head will be out shortly, I can feel it!'

Getting her sister to hospital was the last thing on Georgie Ellis's mind. There was no way she was going to let a little distraction like this stop her from being in at the kill at Templeton Towers.

Any minute now and the baby – what was his name? – would emerge into the world. Ellis tried to remember her first aid training. It was coming back to her. The chord! Remember the chord!

Georgie Ellis was shocked at the sounds now emanating from her sister. She had seen films of children being born but that was nothing compared to the real thing. Without thinking, she shouted: 'push with the contraction!' Push! Relax if it's gone. Then push, and pant!'

In the next instant, Ellis became an aunt again. She cradled Ambrosius in her arms. The sight of a newborn was something else. The perfection of hands, feet, eyes, mouth – everything. It changed her then and there.

'Why isn't he crying? What's wrong?'

'I don't know.'

'Well do something sis. Please! Now!'

Ellis thought back to the training again. It can't be the chord. So, what is it? She was about to take what she thought was the necessary action when someone entered the library.

'Stop. I'll take over!'

'Trissy!'

'Not quite the ideal follow-up to our last meeting! Give him to me. We need to get the boy breathing!'

Bishop gently took Ambrosius from Ellis and rubbed him front and back, then blew air into the baby's mouth. The tiny body remained limp and motionless.

'What's wrong, Trissy? What's wrong with my baby?'

'He'll be fine, Tiggy. I promise.'

Bishop repeated the movements – front, back, mouth-to-mouth. For what seemed an eternity, nothing happened, then Ellis saw a leg twitch. Then an arm, then a sharp intake of breath and a shriek almost as loud as Tiggy's.

'Congratulations! You have a baby boy, and a healthy, lusty one at that. Treble C sharp if I am not mistaken!'

Tiggy beamed as Bishop handed a squalling Ambrosius back to her. 'Now what the hell are you doing here?'

Ellis put her hand on Bishop's arm. 'It's a long story, Tristan, and my sister has a lot of explaining to do but let her have her moment of joy!'

'Yes please! But you need to get your Sergeant sorted. And then you have to find Victoria Perry.'

'What? Why her?'

'I don't know, but she and I were locked up in here. Victoria must have been on the same quest as I was. I know it was totally stupid of me. Hormones and boredom in equal measure, I think!'

'You can say that again, sister dearest!'

'Hurry up. I am fine. Leave me here. I think Victoria is in danger. She was taken away by the murderer – I am sure it's her!'

'Who?'

'That PA woman. Vicky – Victoria told me about her. What's her name? Ah yes – Lisa Watson.'

Harry Riddles thought himself mad. Madder than he had ever been. 'You bloody fool', he said out loud as he walked down the corridor from Brother Germain's cell to Szabo's office. Now that he had something to live for, he expected he would end up dying. 'By close of play this evening, most likely,' he grumbled to himself.

It was Philbs who had persuaded him. He had never liked Brother Germain: too holier than thou for his own good. Even the man's walk was saintly. It was as if he was on castors; either that or the monk hovered above the ground rather than walked on it. 'It's your duty, Harry. You must do this,' Germain had said. 'No, I don't,' Riddles had replied.

It was Philbey who had persuaded him to be the bait with Szabo, Rankin and – it was assumed – Day as the trio of miscreants. It all made sense now. It wasn't the sale of the land; it was what they wanted to find on it before Barbara Halliday and the bulldozers moved in. The proceeds from the estate would go to the school for the most part; the

Nazi bullion would be theirs, and theirs alone. But was that enough to involve MI5? Riddles had asked the question. Germain and Bishop had refused to answer until Philbey had pointed out that if her fiancé was to put his life at risk then he needed to know the truth – the whole truth, and nothing but the truth!

And that was how the real secret of Templeton Towers had come out. The bullion was part of the plot, certainly, but something else had been on that plane out of Hungary that was worth far more than a ton of gold: secret plans for a *Wunderwaffe* – a wonder weapon – that the Germans had invented just before capitulation. No wonder people would kill for a weapon such as this: something infinitely more powerful than an atomic bomb. And that was why Harry Riddles said yes and said yes gladly. In the wrong hands, well, it was too horrific to contemplate.

And now he was standing outside Szabo's office door. He could not remember how he had got there, but it was now or never. The Tompion clock struck the hour. Riddles took a deep breath, said a little prayer, put his hand firmly on the knob, turned it, pushed the door open, and walked in, trying to think of a long holiday in Sorrento with the love of his life as he did so.

'Uniform have the place surrounded, ma'am. The residences are cordoned off. The students should all be safe there.'

Samson looked at May as the two of them surveyed the scene.

'OK. Jean. But Riggs and Ellis have encountered a "situation".'

'What "situation"?'

'You're not going to believe this, ma'am, but somehow, Georgie's sister has got involved in the case and ended up giving birth in the school library!'

'What?'

May nodded. 'I don't know whether to laugh or cry. Apparently, she was bored and decided she would do some detecting herself. Crazy! I can only think that hormones drove her to do it. But she was captured by a person or persons unknown and ended up being locked in the library. When Riggs and Ellis arrived, she was about to give birth. Ellis and Tristan Bishop did the rest.'

'What are you laughing at, Don?'

'Sorry. I shouldn't. He won't live this down though. Charlie fainted at the first sight of blood!'

Samson joined in the laughter.

'Enough! What of the rest?'

'Guess who Ellis's sister was holed up with?'

'No room for guesswork in policing Don. Just tell me!'

'Victoria Perry! Another amateur detective!'

'God give me strength! Why can't these people leave it to the professionals?'

'I know. But they meant well. Vicky did, anyway.'

'Meant well? Vicky? What's all this about Vicky? You're blushing, Don.'

'We were at school together. That's all. Anyway, guess who – sorry – Vicky – Victoria was taken away by?'

'Lisa Watson, of course!'

'What? How did you …'

'It had to be her. She has access to everything, Don. Never underestimate personal assistants. I was one for a while after I graduated, remember? I knew everything about my employer and what he was up to within about three months of starting there.'

May's mobile buzzed.

'Yes? OK.'

May put the phone down and turned to Samson.

'Riddles is in Szabo's office.'

'Then we move once we get the admission of guilt. Is the signal coming in clearly?'

'According to the teccies. Shall we go and listen?'

'Yes.'

May and Samson got out of the car and walked towards the unmarked vehicle by the gatehouse. They were about to get inside when Samson tugged May's arm.

'What the hell is that?' She pointed up to the chapel roof.

'Oh my God! No!'

'We should be rescuing Camilla, Freddie. She's in danger! She must be!'

'First things first Vanessa. There is someone in even greater danger. I can smell it right now!'

'Smell what?'

'The incense! The poisoned incense. It's coming from the chapel. Follow me!'

Vanessa grimaced as she looked back to see if she could see Camilla: no sign. Freddie was busy clambering through the skylight window that let him into the chapel tower. He must have a hell of a nose if he can detect poisoned incense at this distance. But then Frederick Dawson May was something special. Why was it that, despite all the threats, and the risks, at this moment, all she could feel, as she looked at him, was a strange fluttering feeling in her stomach? Would he love her as much as he did Camilla?

'Come on! We don't have much time. That incense is lethal!'

The spiral staircase was narrow. Vanessa felt sick more than once. Where were they going? Who knows. But then Freddie would.

Eventually, the staircase came to a long narrow landing.

'The organ loft door is there. Quickly!'

Freddie took Vanessa by the hand and pulled her along. Her heart raced. The door was unlocked, unusually.

'Start looking!'

'What for, Freddie?'

'For the source of the incense. We'll be overpowered soon if we don't stop it.'

'Look! Down there! It's Father Jeffrey! He's dead.'

As she tried to point to the body lying on the chapel floor below, Vanessa began to feel faint.

'Oh my, I feel so odd…'

30

Rescue And Revelation

'Thank God you're alright!'
　'Of course, I'm alright. What's the fuss all about?'
　'We thought you were in danger, along with your girlfriend here.'
　'I am NOT his girlfriend. Ugh!'
　Vanessa looked at Freddie; the two of them burst out laughing.
　'It's not funny. Why shouldn't I be your boyfriend?'
　'No! At least not while Camilla is in danger.'
　May looked at his son and then the girl.
　'Who is Camilla?'
　'She is my sister: my identical twin.'
　'Don't say any more Vanessa!'
　'It's alright Freddie. It was going to come out sooner or later. Because we are identical twins, and to save money, we have been pretending to be one person.'
　Samson tut-tutted and shook her head.
　'We will have to investigate this later. Tell us what happened, and then we will find your sister, we will find Camilla.'
　'It was all Freddie's doing. We were locked up; the three of us. Mr Szabo and his secretary asked us what we knew about the old plane and the gold and the plans. Then somebody phoned him. He looked shocked and he said to Mrs Watson that they would have to go. He told us that he would deal with us later. Freddie managed to free the window and he and I escaped and then got in through the chapel tower.'
　'And your sister?'

'She was starting to get out onto the balu – balu – balustrade when somebody came back and stopped her from escaping. She is in terrible danger. Please do something!'

'Don't worry, we will. What happened then?'

'I smelt the incense. I had smelt it before, and I knew that it was poisonous. Then I saw Father Jeffrey lying on the chapel floor below. I thought he was dead; I had to do something. The door down into the chapel was locked, so I managed to grab hold of the Saint Salvator hanging from the ceiling and swung down on it.'

'You were very foolhardy Freddie. You could have been killed!'

'Not so Dad. I have seen how the chain extends and knew it could carry my weight.'

'Foolhardy but brave!'

'Thanks Dad. But how is Father Jeffrey?'

'He will live, thanks to your quick action. How did you know what to do?'

'First aid training. Brother Germain has taught us all. It's part of his fitness regime. And Freddie saved me, didn't you? The incense knocked me out as well. I don't know how you managed to get me down those stairs!'

'Easy. When I knew Father Jeffrey was breathing again, I came to get you. I knew where a key to the loft was hidden, so resuscitated you and then carried you down the stairs.'

'So, you saved my life?'

Freddie shrugged in answer to Vanessa's question.

'Who set the incense alight? Who was trying to poison Father Jeffrey? Did you see anybody?' ACC Samson asked impatiently.

Freddie and Vanessa looked at each other then smiled. 'No, we didn't see anybody, but we know who killed Father William and who tried to kill Father Jeffrey. And we bet they killed the others two. Mr McGraw must have discovered the recording that showed who Father William's murderer was, so he had to go. We are not sure about Dr Foster yet, though.'

'Enough Freddie! Shouldn't we be trying to save Camilla now? I feel that something is very wrong. She and I can communicate with each other, and I just know that she is in great danger.'

'I know you.'

'And I know you!'

'Where have I seen you before?'

'Don't you remember?' Victoria Perry laughed out loud as she looked at Andreas Day, sitting opposite her on the other side of Szabo's desk.

'Of course! You're that bloody interfering reporter who tried to stitch me up over pass rates at the university. How dare you?'

'Just honest investigative reporting. That's what, and why!'

'Bloody rubbish. You cost me my job! I had to take early retirement because of your scandalous articles!'

'Every word was true, and you know it!'

'It was not!'

'Anyway, Professor Day, don't you think we have more important things to do than argue about the veracity of reports in the *Gazette and Argus* about your dodgy dealings?'

Perry raised her handcuffed hand. Day looked down at the chain on his leg.

'I suppose you are right.'

'We need to raise the alarm somehow. What are Szabo and his lady friend going to do with that young girl and the old man?'

Day shook his head. 'You mean Harry Riddles? The girl is a student here. Camilla is her name if I remember rightly. She and Donald May's son discovered a corpse in the grounds.'

'Freddie?'

Day nodded. 'Janos Szabo is not the person I thought he was.'

'Who is he then?'

'Your guess is as good as mine. He came with first-rate credentials. Commander in the Royal Navy. Head of the Training College. I thought he was just what we needed, a breath of fresh air, a new broom, set to get rid of all the fusty monastic stuff and make this college the vibrant place that it could be, given half a chance. We saw eye to eye on so much, and especially the land sale. We could have made millions for the school – and a bit on the side for us two – and all the Board members - as well.'

'What went wrong then?'

'*Cherchez la femme* Victoria.'

'What? You mean Lisa Watson?'

'Who else? It makes sense, doesn't it? Sitting there taking the minutes all these years; filing papers, having access to the most secret documents. The ideal person to know everything about anything, and everybody. Pauline Philbey wasn't the first to discover that secret document about the "treasure"!' I reckon it was Watson. And she enlisted Szabo in her plans.'

'How?'

Day burst out laughing. 'How do you think? I knew that Janos was having a relationship with someone, but it was only when the two of them cornered and cuffed me that I realised it was her.'

'What happens now, then?'

The Tompion struck the hour.

'Who knows? I'll tell you one thing; Clement Rankin will be involved somehow.'

'What makes you say that?'

'Because Lisa Watson is his daughter.'

Pauline Philbey was an impatient woman: always had been, always would be. She looked at the large clock on the wall. The library of Templeton Towers was a magnificent room, full of that heavy opulence so characteristic of late 19th century furnishings. The ceiling was modelled on the Great Hall at Hampton Court Palace; the Templar insignia draped everywhere, including a jewel encrusted skull brought back from the Holy Land along with all the other paraphernalia so obviously beloved of their owner. The numerous portraits hanging on the library walls were a curious assembly of local worthies, some of whom, at least, were related to Sir Templeton Taylor, later Lord Hartleydale. He was the last of his line: no male heirs after the death of his beloved David; no wonder he had left everything so that he could found the school and the Order of Saint Saviour.

At the far end of the library was the hidden entrance to the archive room, a classic *trompe l'oeuil* door that guarded the documents and papers at the heart of all the intrigues of the last few weeks. Still, the deed was done, and some good had come out of the discovery. Harry Riddles was the shining light in all of this. He might have turned out to be a bad boy, but he was *her* bad boy, and she loved him for it.

Her train of thought was broken by a baby's bawling. She looked across at Tiggy (what a ridiculous name!) and her newborn son, Ambrosius (an even more ridiculous name, though 'Amber' had a distinctive ring to it). Philbey was suddenly struck by the attention that Tristan Bishop was giving both mother and child. More to the point, the interest was being reciprocated. What was their back story?

Philbey cleared her throat.

'Isn't it time we did something Tristan? It's over thirty minutes since Hal - Harry - went as bait and we haven't seen hide nor hair of Brother Germain since then either.'

Bishop looked at Philbey.

'You're right. Of course, you're right. But we can't leave mother and baby here on their own, can we?'

Philbey wanted to say of course they could but thought better of it.

'No, I suppose not.'

'You'd better stay here, then Pauline, and I will go and see what's happened.'

'You will do no such thing Bishop. I refuse to stay here as wet nurse! You stay - you obviously want to, by the looks of it - and **I** will investigate. I am not afraid. In any case, 'she added without thinking, 'I am concerned about Hal and have nothing to lose. If he has been harmed, then … well, you don't need to know the rest.'

Bishop nodded his head slowly, gazing down at Tiggy as she fed Amber, who gurgled appreciatively.

'I understand that, Pauline. I understand that only too well.'

The two of them smiled and nodded at each other.

'Lock the door behind me when I leave.'

'I will, Pauline.'

Philbey laughed. 'Of course!'

'Freddie and Vanessa are safe. More than that Charlie, they saved Father Jeffrey from certain death – by incense!'

'Another bloody murder!'

'Attempted murder, Charlie. Anyway, the boss and Godzilla are with them now.'

'Godzilla? Who's that?'

'Take a guess, Charlie!'

Riggs burst out laughing.

'Sshh!'

'I get it. ACC Samson! Who else could it be?'

'That's right. The supreme commander!'

Riggs smirked. 'If I didn't know better, Detective Constable Ellis, I would say you were jealous of her, cozying up to the DCI like that …'

Ellis blushed. 'Stop it! What rubbish! I'll tell you this, though, there is something I don't like about her. I've said that before and I will say it again!'

'Nah! She's fine, at least with the men on the force …'

Riggs never finished his sentence.

'There! Look!'

Ellis pointed. From their vantage point in the West Gallery of the Great Hall, they could see out over the grounds of Templeton Estate. In the distance were six figures: three men, two women, and a young girl, all hurrying towards the old chapel. They had emerged from the Greek temple folly at the edge of the formal gardens.

'WTF? We had the place surrounded and they have got past the cordon!'

'Too right, Charlie. This place is riddled – if you'll excuse the pun – with secret chambers and passageways. Think of that rabbit warren under the old chapel for starters.

As Ellis and Riggs watched the group disappear into the woods, they could see two others in pursuit: a tall, fit man in a monk's habit striding along, followed by a bustling older woman trying to keep up with him.

'I know the woman George – that's Philbey, the old busybody. Remember?'

'How could I forget? We thought she was the murderer at one point!'

Riggs chuckled. 'That was a red herring if ever there was one. Who's the Reverend?'

'He's a monk, not a vicar, Charlie. That's Brother Germain. He's one of us. Or rather, one of them.'

'What do you mean?'

'MI5. Been a sleeper for years. Keeping an eye on this place.'

'How come you know that, and I don't? Who told you?'

Ellis averted her gaze. 'The boss. Need to know basis, Charlie, need to know.'

'So, you work for MI5?'

'Sort of. I used to. But once an agent, always an agent. I was reactivated a few weeks ago. Just about the time you and Georgie came to see me.'

'Mmm. I remember that well. It was so good to see you again after all this time.' Tiggy smiled, making sure that Amber had good access to the milk bar. 'You know I always had a thing about you when I was at school.'

'Of course, I know! I haven't forgotten that evening at your leaving do!'

Tiggy looked away. 'That was very naughty. You a married man, and me a teenager. Georgie was very jealous.'

Bishop leaned over and kissed Tiggy's forehead.

'You look so lovely, lying there, with Amber cuddled up to you. Just like a Madonna!'

'Some Madonna! Anyway, shouldn't you be chasing the criminals, whoever they are?'

'Not until a WPC arrives to look after you. Then I'll go. Someone is on their way according to DCI May.'

'How did you get involved in all this, anyway?'

'The chamber organ.'

'What chamber organ?'

'Remember when you came to see me? I had just taken delivery of an old organ from Templeton Towers. John McGraw let me have it. It was surplus to requirements. What he didn't know was that inside the mechanism was a piece of paper that revealed the true story of the Nazi gold – and more – but I can't talk about that; classified and all that. I alerted MI5 as soon as I found out, and the rest, as they say …'

'Do you think that's why McGraw was murdered?'

'Almost certainly. There's an evil brain behind all this; they must be caught! Now!'

'I agree. I know exactly what and who you mean!'

31

Hunting For Killers

IT WAS THE LAST THING HE LOOKED AT AS HE LEFT HIS OFFICE. SZABO stared hard at the photograph in his desk drawer and thought of what might have been. There he was on the front row, along with all the other officers from the training college. Everyone was smiling; except one. The man on the back row glowered, his eyes glared evil. Brother Germain warned me about him. If only I had never met the evil bastard! I could have had a good life here! Hartleydale has its attractions and, who knows what might have been? Nagy[1] had put paid to that.

Why did Nagy's father have to come to the training college? Why did he have to reveal the family's terrible secret? How could the Szabos be Nazi sympathizers? His father had never said anything, and grandfather was just that lovely, lonely, white-haired old man who came to tea twice a week and told his fantastical stories of flying and fighting during the war, until he died of old age when Janos was seven. What make believe it had seemed! Except it had all been true, especially the one part of the story that Grandpa Sandor had never told: the piloting of the plane full of gold and plans for the most destructive wonder weapon ever conceived.

Nagy senior had told him all about the flight, and the crash into the Templeton Estate. By the time the undercover agents on the German side had got to the scene, gold and plans had disappeared. Nothing had ever been located. Now was the time to find the documents and the

---
[1] Pronounced 'nudge'.

bullion would finance the building of the weapon; once the land was sold, the chance of riches and much, much, more would drain away like wet cement. Janos Szabo owed it to his country to help.

'But England is my country. It always has been, and always will be. Nothing you can say about my family's past or do to me now will make me betray my homeland.'

Nagy senior had laughed: Hanna and the children back in Hungary would be killed if Szabo did not cooperate. How could he not save his sister? At least those two lovely nieces had been protected, until now, that is. If only he could have got to know them better! To tell them who he really was!

But Vanessa and Camilla had to be protected. They must never know that he was their uncle, and their mother was his sister. So, he had gone along with it. The whole sordid show. It had been easy enough to become Principal at Templeton Towers. Szabo had prided himself on being the obvious candidate for the job and he had accepted the role without regret at leaving the Royal Navy. At first, he thought that he could control Nagy, but then things had got out of hand, as first Father William, then Bernard, then the others had to die because they were too close to the truth. He had pleaded for Diana Foster's life, but to no avail. And in the middle of all this, he, Commander Janos Szabo, RN, had fallen in love. All sense of right or reason had flown out of the window. He was smitten from the moment he first saw her; and he would love her till the end of time.

Ironically, it was Clair who had shown him the secret passageway from the Principal's study to the Greek folly in the grounds. It had been one of Templeton Taylor's many foibles, in this case tunnels that allowed him to pass unnoticed out of the grand mansion to meet his latest beau for one of his many illicit liaisons. Szabo thought how odd it was that Taylor's scandalous secret life would have meant nothing nowadays.

Rankin had been persuaded not to kill Day and Perry, but merely to tie them up. Lisa, dear, sweet, efficient, loyal Lisa had done that without question: ever the perfect personal assistant, doing anything and everything that Szabo asked of her. Szabo regretted taking advantage of Lisa's unswerving loyalty and even worse, her undying love for him. It was a relief to Szabo that Rankin had insisted the others be kept alive as an insurance policy. So it was that Riddles and Camilla were herded along the dank, dark exit from Templeton Towers.

Szabo was the first to emerge into the Greek temple. He nearly retched as he came up for air.

Rankin followed. 'I'm too old for this. Let's get on with it! The helicopter arrives in 30 minutes!'

Szabo looked back down the tunnel entrance as Camilla emerged, holding hands with Lisa Watson. In a different world they could have been mother and daughter, except the handcuffing together told a different story.

Then came Melody Grimshaw. Even now Szabo's heart melted when he saw her. Perhaps they would have an idyllic life together once they had retrieved the plans and the gold and escaped to Russia and new identities. They would be better there than in a defenceless western world threatened by a terrible weapon worse than anything previously conceived.

'Stop! Stop at once! Drop your weapons and hands up!'

'Please Dad. I beg you! We know what the criminals are going to do. And we don't have long to catch them!'

'Freddie. It is far too dangerous for you and Vanessa to have anything more to do with this case.'

'But you won't solve it without us! I know where all the tunnels lead. I have memorised all the plans for this place.'

'That's true, DCI May. I have seen you son in action earlier this evening. He is the only one who knows what is where. And you *must* save my sister!'

'You have a sister? Where?'

'Here, Dad. They are identical twins. They double up for lessons and stuff. This is Vanessa, and her sister is called Camilla. She didn't escape like we did. They got her. And we are frightened what they are going to do with her.'

'The fact that she and I are totally alike might help to trick them.'

'Come on Dad. Hurry. I know the quick way out of this place. How do you think they managed to escape the police cordon that you've put around the place?'

May looked at Samson, Riggs, and Ellis. Samson bowed her head slightly. Riggs shrugged; Ellis remained motionless.

'Very well. But DS Riggs and DC Ellis will always be right next to you!'

'Excellent, Dad. "The game's afoot!"'

★★★

Pauline Philbey had surprised herself. Brother Germain was fit; she wasn't. He was tall and slim; she was – well - not so tall and slim. Their differing physical attributes had not stopped her from keeping up. Was it the excitement of the chase, the urge to see justice done, the need to save Hal? All three, probably, but now Riddles had become such an important part of her life, she was determined he was going to live. Hal's brief, brave, attempt to entrap the criminals had fallen apart at the first hurdle. There was no interest in discussion on the part of Szabo and the others, who wanted only to escape. And they had the advantage, for the tunnel from the central quadrangle to the Greek temple had provided not only the most effective way of eluding the police cordon now in evidence around Templeton Towers, but also the quickest path to the old chapel.

Did Szabo and Rankin have the exact location for 'the treasure'? They must have. Why would they be striding so purposefully away from the most obvious escape route out of the grounds? Unless, of course, they were to be picked up on the other side of the estate boundary wall. She wondered about sharing this thought with Brother Germain, but decided against it, given his reluctance so far to engage in any meaningful conversation with her. Did he resent her presence? Was she an encumbrance? Germain had never been one for many words, even when he had been asked to present his ideas for curriculum change to the Board Room.

Not that any of Germain's proposals ever got through. Clair had seen to that. And it was obvious now why Rankin had been so eager to support the *status quo*. It had suited Clement to keep the Order of Saint

Saviour just where he wanted them, while he sought out the riches he so obviously still craved, despite his vast ill-gotten gains.

Philbey and Brother Germain had slowed as they reached the Georgian temple. Voices could be heard. Szabo was talking, then Rankin. Lisa Watson intervened, asking, nay pleading, for the hostages to be freed. Philbey had swollen with pride as she heard Hal telling the criminals to let the girl go. 'She is just a teenager; she has her whole life in front of her. Whereas I, well ...'

Philbey could stand it no more. Despite Germain trying to hold her back, she took out her revolver and strode through the temple entrance.

'Stop! Stop at once! Drop your weapons and hands up!'

Both captors and captives were shocked and surprised. Pauline Philbey was the last person anyone expected to see. Harry Riddles' face turned into a warm smile. He winked at her. She nodded.

'Put that damn thing down, Pauline! You might hurt somebody!'

'I sincerely hope so, Rankin, starting with you!'

'You'll ruin everything that I've worked for if you're not careful!'

'You should be in jail! How dare you play with people's lives like this!'

Philbey looked at the others. The little girl stood there, remarkably unmoved, despite having been abducted. Lisa Watson held on to Janos Szabo's arm. Her face made the proverbial white sheet look colourful.

'I didn't mean to do it, Mrs Philbey. I ...'

'You fell in love, didn't you, Lisa? Anything for Janos Szabo, eh? And look where it has got you!'

Watson laughed. 'With Janos?' No. You must be joking!'

'I don't think she is, Lisa, my darling. But who cares anyway?'

Philbey recognized the voice but could not put a face to it. Then, from the dark recesses of the temple, a figure emerged.

'Now be sensible, old lady. Someone might get hurt. And if everybody does as I tell them, there is no need for anyone to die anytime soon. We just want to be allowed to leave this place with what is ours. I have worked for this moment for so many years, and nothing will stop me, even if it means killing you all, especially you and your boyfriend, Pauline.'

'You! It was you all along! Melody Grimshaw!'

The supermodel laughed. 'That is only part of my name. I am Melody Grimshaw-Nagy. My mother was from Lancashire; my father is Hungarian.'

'And why all this? Why the interest in this damn treasure? You are rich already! Why are you, Rankin, and Szabo so fixated on it?'

'Because, dear old lady, it is not the gold, it is the plans for a super weapon beyond anyone's wildest imagination.'

'And you will sell the secret to the highest bidder?'

Melody shook her head. 'No. We will give it to Mother Russia. My family have been communists for generations. It is time the decadent West was taught a lesson to end all lessons. The Americans and their allies have humiliated us for long enough.'

'World domination, I suppose.'

'Something like that, Pauline. Now give me the gun.'

Philbey shook her head. Instead, she pointed the revolver straight towards Grimshaw.

Melody laughed, then nodded at something or someone.

'I wouldn't do that, if I were you, Pauline.'

Philbey suddenly felt the barrel of a gun being pushed into her back.

'Now be a good old dear and do as Melody says. Give her the gun. Gently does it now.'

'Germain. How could you? I thought you were on our side!'

'That's what you are all supposed to think. I have been a double agent for years. Melody's father recruited me, just like he blackmailed Janos here into going along with our plans.

Szabo looked down at his feet. Melody Grimshaw-Nagy held out her hand, ready to accept the revolver.

Pauline Philbey looked at Hal, as she tried to determine what to do. He raised his eyebrows and nodded.

'Very well. But whatever you do, spare the girl,' Pauline Philbey pleaded, as she handed over her gun to the supermodel.

'Yes, Melody. Spare my niece.' Szabo was in tears as he spoke.

'Enough. We must get to the old chapel, now!'

One thing first, Melody. Why did Father William and Father Bernard have to die?'

'Why? Because of what they and Paul Gordon did to my uncle, Nicholas LeGrand. Or should I say Miklós Nagy. My father's brother. The boy in the grave. He was a student at the school. Nobody knew his real identity. It was better that way. Miklós was smuggled out of Hungary in the late 1970s by the brothers in Pecs and brought to Templeton Towers. Once the government knew who his father and brother were, he couldn't stay there. But he was caught up in Paul Gordon's abuse. William and Bernard – and Jeffery – covered it all up.'

'So that is why they had to die?'

Melody nodded.

'And the strangulation marks?'

'Poetic justice. That's what Gordon used to do. Deprive Miklós of oxygen as part of his depraved practices.'

Philbey nodded. 'And McGraw and Foster?'

Melody laughed. 'They were useful to me – just like Day and all the others. Got me to where and when I needed to be, and what I wanted to do. It was so easy.'

Pauline Philbey looked at the supermodel. Yes, all that was eminently believable.

'Are you sure this is where they will be?'

'Yes, Dad, I am convinced.'

May looked at Samson.

Ellis looked at Riggs, then turned to her commanding officer.

'What shall we do sir?'

'Get uniform to carry out an extensive search of the grounds. Roadblocks on any and every route out of the Templeton Estate and beyond.'

'Don't forget the railway tunnel, Mr May!' Vanessa squeezed Freddie's hand as she spoke.

'Good point. Charlie – alert Northern Fail – I mean Northern Rail – to what is happening. Get officers guarding both entrances to the tunnel, immediately.'

'Sir!'

As Riggs and Ellis carried out their orders, a helicopter could be heard in the distance.'

'One of ours, Don?'

'No, ma'am. One of theirs.'

Camilla wondered what Freddie would do now. Were he and Vanessa safe? Perhaps they were. Perhaps they had raised the alarm. She tried to sense what her sister was feeling, but, unusually, nothing came. It must be the fact that they were underground. Freddie had talked about the labyrinth beneath the old chapel often enough. If he were here now, he would know exactly where they were and how they might escape, whether down to the railway, or back up to the house via yet another secret passageway. Freddie had explained that this was why Quick Draw had to die. His detailed modelling of the Templeton Tunnel, based on plans and examinations of the real underground passageways, had led him to discover the hidden rooms – rooms where the secret documents were stored.

She had seen Szabo and Grimshaw-Nagy remove them from the back of the old wardrobe. She had watched as Brother Germain vouched for their authenticity. She had heard them wonder what had happened to the bullion and been surprised when the three criminals had agreed that what they now had in their hands was far more valuable than a thousand tons of gold. All that needed to happen now was for the rescue helicopter to arrive. She had heard Melody on the radio to her father, directing him to land as near as possible to the old chapel.

Camilla decided to think for herself, instead of wondering what Freddie would do, unlike her love-stricken sister, always hanging on Commander Frederick Dawson May's every word. She looked over at Pauline Philbey and Harry Riddles. They looked like a homely, white-haired pair. What threat could old dears like those two be to Szabo, Watson, Rankin, and Grimshaw-Nagy?

Watson looked scared, as if she wanted to be anywhere else but here. Perhaps she was the one they should work on. She looked at Philbey and

Riddles and then nodded gently in the personal secretary's direction. The old couple smiled back in agreement.

Riddles was the first to speak.

'I never expected you to be involved in anything like this, Lisa."

'Shut up Riddles! Don't listen to him Lisa!'

Watson looked at Szabo who turned to Melody Grimshaw-Nagy.

'And you, Szabo. Where are your high ideals now? I – we – expected so much better of you. Is this what they teach you in the Royal Navy? How to betray your country? You should be ashamed of yourself. What has that woman got on you?'

'Don't listen to her, Janos!' Brother Germain waved his gun at Philbey and Riddles. 'Shut up you two, or I will shut you up for good!'

'The police are already in the tunnels. I can feel it.'

'What do you mean little girl?' Melody came up to Camilla and stared right into her soul, or so it seemed.

'I can feel my sister's presence. We are identical twins, remember? And we know all about what you have been up to!'

'Shut up! Shut up, you stupid little girl!'

'Don't talk to her like that!' Szabo turned his gun on Grimshaw-Nagy.

'Jan! What are you doing?'

'Just don't talk to her like that.'

'I'll talk to her however I like!'

'Stop it, you two! Don't ruin everything now! We are minutes away from completing our mission. We can't afford for anything to get in the way!'

Germain turned to Philbey, Riddles, and Camilla, his gun pointed at them.

'I am sorry. There is no other way.'

Germain took aim, ready to kill the three captives.

The gunfire echoed round the small room. Lisa Watson gripped Janos Szabo by the arm. The two of them watched as Brother Germain fell to the floor, a look of complete surprise on his face.

'What have you done? You stupid man! What have you bloody-well done?'

'This has gone far enough! You are not killing my niece, and I am no longer prepared to betray my country. I have seen through you,

Melody. You don't love me; you have no principles; you only love yourself.'

'Kill him, Melody! Kill them all!' Rankin stamped his walking stick on the floor impatiently. The sound was enough to distract the supermodel long enough for Pauline Philbey to leap on Grimshaw-Nagy. At the same time, Harry Riddles landed the biggest punch on Rankin.

'I've wanted to thump you for years, Clement! What a pleasure I finally get to do it!'

Riddles' glee was short lived. He heard a gunshot. He turned to see his beloved Pauline on the floor underneath Melody Grimshaw-Nagy.

'Oh no! Philbs! My dearest!'

The two bodies were still. There was not the slightest movement. Then, a lifeless Melody rolled off a very-much-alive Philbey.

'Don't worry Hal. I know how to use one of these things. I might be a sleeper in MI5, but I am still wide awake!'

The lovebirds chuckled. Riddles helped Philbey up.

'Are you alright Camilla?'

Camilla nodded as she watched Philbey point the gun at Szabo and Watson.

'Are you going to put up a fight, you two?'

Szabo shook his head, tears in his eyes. He turned to Watson and kissed her gently on the forehead, then went over to Camilla and hugged her tightly.

'I am so sorry Camilla – and Vanessa. I couldn't tell you the truth about who I was. Your mother Hanna – my long-lost sister - was being blackmailed by Rankin and Melody Grimshaw's father, and I had to find a way of keeping you safe. So, I arranged for you to come to the school where I could keep an eye on you.'

'I know. We all three know.'

'Yes. Me, Vanessa, and Freddie. We worked it out ages ago. That's why we tried to keep tipping off the police with anonymous phone calls, and then told you about the grave we had discovered. The dead boy was Melody Grimshaw's father's little brother, wasn't he? Part of all this was about revenge, wasn't it?

Szabo, Watson, Riddles, and Philbey stared in amazement.

'Anyway, if I am not much mistaken, the police will be arriving shortly. In the meantime, Mr Szabo, Miss Watson, Mr Rankin, Mrs Philbey and I are going to make a citizens' arrest. Mr Riddles – will you take Mr Szabo's gun off him?'

Samson, May, Riggs, Ellis, Freddie, and Vanessa watched as the helicopter circled round the old chapel. Samson gave uniformed officers the order to fire but before any decent shots could be landed, the craft had begun to head east, the pilot having realised his intended passengers were never going to appear.

'Don't worry, Don. We will catch them by the time they reach the coast. Army, Navy, and Air Force have all been informed.'

May had eyes only for his son and the girl, holding hands. At one point the two of them kissed. Freddie and Vanessa then pointed to the altar in the centre of the ruined chapel. The trapdoor underneath the stone table opened. The first thing that they all saw was a white-haired lady emerge.

'Don't worry everybody. We have won the day! This nightmare is over, once and for all!'

Postlude

NOTHING MORE WAS EVER HEARD OF THE SUPER BOMB PLANS. High-ranking officials from the Ministry of Defence and MI5 saw to it that all evidence of the wonder weapon 'disappeared'. Where was the gold bullion? Freddie May held the answer to that question. As he abseiled down the chain on which the St Saviour Cross hung, he noticed the ornamental arrow pointing to the organ. The dummy front pipes turned out to be made of pure gold. Every single one of them.

Janos Szabo and Lisa Watson were arrested on suspicion of treason, conspiracy, and aiding and abetting murder. All charges were later dropped. It was rumoured that the two of them had been given immunity from prosecution in the wake of their testimonies, because of which, key arrests were made all over Europe, including Nagy senior.

Father Jeffrey oversaw an amazing resurgence of the Order of Saint Saviour, investing the OSS's share of the bullion (after the government had taken its cut) in a series of schemes for religious education. The William Clair International Summer School became renowned, and very profitable. Jeffrey entered a business partnership with Barbara Halliday that saw the construction of Templeton Court, the cheapest houses selling for £1.5 million; the most expensive – POA.

Day was also granted immunity from prosecution in return for giving the authorities valuable information about Rankin and Grimshaw-Nagy's circle of evil. Thanks to a brilliant PR campaign by Victoria Perry aimed at restoring his reputation within the valley, Day not only kept his position as Chair of the Board at Templeton, but became 'Mr Hartleydale,' feted by all around. He and Perry could often be seen *tête-à-tête* in the *Speckled Teapot*.

Tristan Bishop became Principal of Templeton Towers. Freddie May was elected Head Boy; Vanessa and Camilla were both Head Girls. Freed from the clutches of the Nagy family, Hanna moved to England to be near her daughters. Already qualified as an educational psychologist, she later joined the staff at Templeton.

Aelthred and Throthgar became students at Templeton Towers, excelling at every sport offered. Tristan Bishop and Tiggy were married in the School Chapel in a double wedding with Harry Riddles and Pauline Philbey. Jo Bishop and Georgie Ellis were the bridesmaids; Barbara Halliday was Matron of Honour to Pauline Philbey (who insisted on keeping her surname). Father Jeffrey officiated, while the school choir sang Templeton Taylor's favourite anthem, 'Seek ye the Lord', by the eminent Victorian composer, John Varley Roberts. Given McGraw's death and Tristan's unavailability, a renowned organist was drafted in from St Michael's, Mytholmroyd, in the next valley. His playing was so impressive that Bishop offered him the post of Director of Music at Templeton, which he accepted on the spot.

Jean Samson left Hartleydale soon after the Templeton murders case had concluded. Having taken credit for leading the successful investigation, she was appointed Chief Constable of Wakefieldshire. Donald May was promoted to Detective Chief Superintendent and appointed to lead a specialist cold case squad for the whole of Yorkshire. Newly promoted Detective Sergeant Georgiana Lucinda Ponsonby-Ellis joined the team, along with Detective Inspector Charles Richard Riggs. Their success rate to date has been almost 100%. Dr Felicity ('Fizz') Harbord retired from active service, setting up a private consultancy based in Hartley.

Clement Rankin died awaiting trial. The priest and the undertaker were the only people at his funeral. Brother Germain eventually returned to Russia in a spy exchange with the British and US governments. Melody Grimshaw-Nagy was buried in the grounds of Templeton Towers, next to the reinterred remains of Nicholas LeGrand, alias Miklós Nagy.

Pauline Philbey was awarded the DBE in the following year's birthday honours list. The citation read 'for service to King and country'. Rumours abound across the valley that before long she will be elevated to the House of Lords as Baroness Philbey of Hartleydale. After a long honeymoon in Sorrento, she and Harry Riddles retired back to a quiet life at 'Holme Hatch', along with Boris, whose role in all these adventures remains top secret for at least 50 years ...

Milton Keynes UK
Ingram Content Group UK Ltd.
UKHW010651170124
436175UK00001B/43